"Witty and imaginative ... The story is strong throughout and the writing is simple yet captivating. It is always a challenge to start a novel with two separate and very different worlds then smoothly bring them together. But this writer was not about to present a been-there, done-that fantasy tale. The writer has certainly crafted an entertaining work that reaches out to young readers."
- J.M. Northern Media.

"Non-stop action adventure ... fun and unusual."
- ForeWord Clarion Magazine.

"I would recommend this book to people who like action, adventure, and fantasy. I think that kids age nine to fourteen or so would especially like this book. "Defenders of the Scroll" by Shiraz was an awesome book and I think that most every one that reads it will like it."
- ReaderViews Kids.

Winner
in the
Fantasy and *Best Editing Fiction*
categories of the 2009 National Indie Excellence Awards

Finalist
in the
Action-Adventure and *Young Adult Fiction*
categories of the 2009 National Indie Excellence Awards

Finalist
in the
Multicultural Fiction
Best Overall Design Fiction
and
Best E-Book Fiction
categories of the 2009 Next Generation Indie Book Awards

Honorable Mention
in the
Science Fiction
category of the 2009 New York Book Festival

Honorable Mention
in the
Science Fiction and *Teenage*
category of the 2009 Beach Book Festival

Honorable Mention
in the
Teenage
category of the 2009 Hollywood Book Festival

Honorable Mention
in the
Wild Card
category of the 2009 San Francisco Book Festival

History, *Legend and Lore*

Created by *B. Singh Khanna and Rupinder Malhotra*

Written by *Shiraz*

Art by *Steve Criado*

iUniverse, Inc.
New York   Bloomington

Defenders of the Scroll
History, *Legend and Lore*

iUniverse books may be ordered through booksellers or by contacting:

iUniverse
1663 Liberty Drive
Bloomington, IN 47403
www.iuniverse.com
1-800-Authors (1-800-288-4677)

ISBN: 978-1-4401-4477-6 (pbk)
ISBN: 978-1-4401-4480-6 (dj)

Library of Congress Control Number: 2009935557

Printed in the United States of America

www.defendersofthescroll.com

For those who refuse to settle

Acknowledgements

Thanks to Norina, Furrukh, Bill, and Nolan for enduring the pain of reading an unedited, evolving story (sometimes repeatedly) and still giving me the feedback I needed to make this what it is.

Thanks to Johanna for going above and beyond in getting this book to print, to Cathy for being as much a coach as an editorial consultant (and making her son a fan), and to Mandy for becoming my personal consultant at iUniverse through all this.

Special thanks to Sheryl for the editing and insight, and to Brad for the art that inspired all of us.

Defenders of the Scroll

History, *Legend and Lore*

Prologue

In a different time, in a different place, Mornak ruled the realm of Mythos from the city of Aspiria. Besides being a king, Mornak was also the world's most powerful wizard, but you wouldn't have known it by looking at him. Barely forty, he had a young, kind face framed with thick black hair, which started as a widow's peak in front and ended in a ponytail just below his shoulders. His eyes were deep brown with specks of gold, his nose slim, and he chose not to wear a beard or mustache—the custom of most men. Neither skinny nor fat, but somewhere in between, he did not stand out in a crowd even in the way he dressed.

As the realm's ruler, Mornak's servants pushed him to wear kingly attire. However, while he would listen to them on special occasions, he preferred to wear his baggy brown pants well suited for walking; his tanned shirt that kept him cool in the sun; his many-pocketed vest that matched his pants and held all sorts of useful items; and his wooden sandals, which, though practical outside, made his footsteps echo through the palace halls. Mornak liked his outfit so much that he had several sets made and just switched from one to another. This lack of variety in wardrobe caused many people to wonder just how often he changed his clothes, since he always seemed to be wearing the same attire.

Today marked a special day in the realm. From his bedroom balcony in the great whitestone palace, Mornak looked out over Aspiria as the morning sun lit the city. Surrounded by an outer wall six storeys high, most of the buildings in the sprawling city consisted of one- or two-storey sandstone houses. Warehouses, inns, and other large buildings separated the clusters of homes into distinct neighbourhoods. In the center of the city, large white canopies hid the marketplace from view and protected shoppers from the summer sun. The main roads were laid with cobblestones while the smaller streets were of soft dirt or sand. The green of huge parks scattered across the landscape broke up the whites and grays of rock and sand; trees planted up the middle of major roads brought the feel of nature to this stony environment. The smell of freshly cut grass from the park, along with the warmth of the morning sun and the touch of a gentle breeze on his face, brought memories of picnics with his wife back to Mornak, making him smile as he looked out over the buildings across the city.

The most prominent structure in Aspiria was the one building Mornak could not see—because he was standing in it. The ten-storey circular whitestone palace contained dozens of bedrooms, bathrooms, and several other large halls such as the ballroom, the library, and the audience chamber. Five shorter circular towers surrounded the main structure by connecting hallways, three storeys off the ground. All the buildings had bulb-shaped roofs and wide windows that let in plenty of sunlight. Marble walls and floors ran through the palace; granite balconies and friezes adorned the outside. Over two hundred people worked in the wonder that was the palace or its gardens behind it, but only twenty resided there.

The palace awed every citizen with its splendor—both outside and inside—but it never had an effect on Mornak. It was simply home to him. What did awe him was his view this morning, and he smiled at what he saw: thousands of happy, prosperous people in his city engaged in festivity on this day. Mythos had known peace for nine years now, and like every other city in the realm, Aspiria celebrated. The melody of roving musicians made its way up to him, and Mornak tapped his foot to the drummer's beat without realizing it. He was focused on the smell of freshly baked bread and pies already being served somewhere below him. He leaned over the marble railing to find the source but, instead, spotted some children running through the main street, waving colourful flags and laughing. He sighed at the joy of it all, still remembering clearly the day peace had come.

Just over nine years ago, neighbouring cities warred with each other. Thieves and bandits robbed the countryside. Leaders ruled unjustly. Monsters raided villages for the sheer pleasure of it. The realm became ever more dangerous, evil spread, and Mornak knew something had to be done quickly. So, he created the Hall. He sent word out that the Hall would serve as a prison for the evil in the realm and that if the people wanted to live a good life, they should use the Hall to remove all evil. Within weeks, things changed. The wars stopped, the bandits stopped their raids, and only good, just leaders remained in power. The evil creatures, though still present, retreated back to their lairs—frightened by the goodly realm knights, by the way people now looked out for each other, and, of course, by the thought of being sent to the Hall.

It came to be known as the Hall of Shadows; it was built deep in the forest of Darkwood, which was only a day's march from the palace. People began to refer to Darkwood as Shadow Wood (sometimes just "the Wood") until, eventually, the name stuck. No one ventured into Shadow Wood anymore. Although Mornak assured everyone that nothing could escape the Hall, almost no one was willing to make sure. Some even feared that if they got too close, they'd be swallowed up by the Hall and trapped inside with all the evil from the realm. The Hall and its forest became a place of bedtime stories and parental threat. "You will do as you're told, or I'll make you spend a night in Shadow Wood!" some parents would warn. The threat always made children behave.

Shadow Wood did have its periodic visitors. Mornak himself ventured into it to check on the Hall and, at times, to reinforce it with his magic. His elite guard, the Axemen, accompanied him; the Axemen were comprised of fifty of the most skilled knights in the realm, who all used an axe as their chosen weapon. It was said that the Axemen could chop down any enemy, and it was true, not simply because of their skill but also because Mornak had enchanted the weapons of this elite guard. Each man's axe increased his best ability, be it strength, speed, accuracy, or even cunning. Since most of the men had different skills, as a team with all those skills working together, they were as yet unbeatable.

In this world of peace, some people thought the Axemen existed just for show, but every now and then, some evil creatures—ogres mostly, and sometimes trolls—would come out of hiding to see what trouble they could cause. The Axemen dealt with them swiftly and efficiently, keeping the peace in the realm.

Nine years of peace, and in that time Mornak had raised a daughter alone—a beautiful chubby-cheeked girl named Dara. Dara, who was an inquisitive little ten-year-old scamp, kept a smile on her father's face with her antics. She had hair like Mornak's—black and thick—although her long bangs hid her widow's peak and her ponytail hung down to the back of her knees. She had big brown eyes and a tiny nose—both features she had inherited from her mother—except that her eyes had her father's same gold flecks. She was so cute that when she pouted, you couldn't refuse her—a trait she sometimes took advantage of. Inheriting her mother's petite size, she didn't quite reach her father's chest when she stood up straight. While she had a slightly chubby build, it didn't hamper her motions in the least. Quick and agile, she loved to get dirty, which seemed to contradict her fondness of wearing floral dresses. After a day of play, it was impossible to make out a single flower on her clothes.

"What are you looking at, Papa?" she asked as she grabbed his leg.

Mornak jumped. He had been so lost in thought that he hadn't heard her walk up. She giggled when she realized she had scared him.

"I'm just enjoying the view, Little Rose," he answered, picking her up. She smelled like her nickname: a little rose.

Dara looked out to see what her father saw: the decorated buildings, the fancily dressed people.

"It *is* pretty," she agreed. "Look how people have decorated their houses in coloured streamers. And the parade is this afternoon. Don't forget, Papa."

"How can I forget?" he laughed. "I'm in it!" He hugged her close and bounced her playfully. "And you'll be right there with me, won't you?"

"Yep yep! I love riding on the float and throwing candy out to the other kids." She leaned in and whispered to him. "But I'm keeping a couple pieces for us to have after dinner."

Mornak pretended to be shocked. "Are you now?"

"Just a couple," Dara assured him with a wink. She looked back out over the balcony.

"It's perfect today. The sky is clear blue ... except for that one little cloud over there," she said, pointing toward it.

When Mornak followed her gaze, the smile left his face. A single dark cloud floated out there, which normally wouldn't be cause for alarm, but it hovered over Shadow Wood. And while it looked small to Dara, Mornak knew the distance deceived her perception. It covered the entire forest.

He put Dara back down. "You should go get ready," he told her as cheerfully as he could. "I have many duties to perform before the parade."

"Papa, you're always working!" she scolded. "And today's a holiday!"

"I know, Little Rose, but I'll finish as quickly as I can."

"You'd better!" she insisted before dashing off to get ready.

Mornak looked back at the cloud. *The timing couldn't be worse*, he thought.

Minutes later, he rode off on his stallion, its enchanted horseshoes letting it charge at more than twice the speed of any other animal in the realm. The Axemen urged Mornak to let them accompany him, but their horses didn't have magical shoes. Mornak didn't want to spend time or magic to make some. He might need both soon.

Despite his speedy mount, several hours passed before he arrived at Shadow Wood. His horse grew uneasy when they finally arrived—a bad sign. He dismounted in front of the first few trees, and with a smack on its rump, he sent the steed home. He'd be using a spell of recall to get home himself. Still, the journey to the center of the forest would last a few more hours. If this were anything more than a normal cloud, he might miss the parade.

The cloud hovered directly above the Shadow Wood, but only the Wood—blocking the sun and making its name hold true. Soon Mornak had walked well into the forest with a magic ball of light floating just above his hand to push back the shadows around him. His senses warned him that something was wrong. The place was too quiet—no crickets chirping, no lightning bugs sparking. The air seemed to press on his skin, and the smell of old wet leaves filled his nostrils.

His years of training took over, instinctively making Mornak mutter a shield spell without even realizing it. The area around him shimmered a pale yellow just when a dark blue magical bolt shot out from the shadows at him. It bounced harmlessly off his shield but startled Mornak, causing his light to go out and his body to break into a cold sweat. He could feel his heart beating quickly, but it felt as if it were in his throat. He swallowed, shook away the fear, and readied himself. A few quick gestures strengthened his shield, and then he readied a Net spell to capture whoever attacked him.

"The Great Mornak," he heard a voice say. He looked in the direction it came from, but he couldn't see anyone. "The Predictable Mornak is more like it."

"Do I know you?" Mornak asked, trying to see through the gloom.

"Not as much as I know you. On the Day of Peace, I knew you'd be reckless enough to come here alone. We don't want the common folk to think something is wrong now, do we? Canceling the parade and bringing the Axemen out would have been the wiser course of action."

"I can always go back and get them," Mornak replied, trying to sound more annoyed than worried.

"Go right ahead," the voice challenged.

Mornak held his ground for a while, trying to sense movement around him, trying to feel magic at work. Then he started through the trees. A giant spider web appeared between two trunks just as he was passing between them; one of his hands got stuck in it before he could stop. The strands seemed as strong as steel but as flexible as a normal spider's webbing. He stretched away from the web so that he wouldn't accidentally get any other part of his body caught in it.

Another bolt of magic raced toward him, breaking through his blue shield, but he stopped it with a smaller magic shield he conjured with his free hand. He quickly cast a small ball of fire at the web, which burned up like tissue paper. Then he ducked just in time to avoid another magic bolt.

"You're quick for an old man," the voice joked.

"Enough of this," Mornak grumbled. With a wave of his arms, the area lit up as though the sun hovered right above them. In front of him, just to the right, Mornak saw a man's shadow. Then he realized that the man *was* the shadow. The shadowman gestured, and suddenly three more shadowmen stood facing Mornak. The wizard-king knew the spell. The three new enemies were decoys, just illusions. When all four cast out magical beams, Mornak dived behind a tree, not knowing which beam to dodge. He jumped back out, sending a magic net flying at his enemies. It wrapped around a shadowman who immediately vanished, and then fell to the ground in a heap before disappearing as well.

Wrong guess, Mornak thought as he brought up a new shield. He expected another assault, but the shadowmen were running away. *No*, he realized, *not away, just out of the light*.

Mornak ran after them, leaving the brightened area while sending a paralyzing beam into a shadowman's back. The man popped out of sight when the beam shot through him.

Two down, thought the wizard-king. *It won't be long now*.

The other two shadowmen stopped briefly to cast spells. Two ghostly wolves appeared and charged at Mornak. Mornak cast a spell while running; in the next instant, a huge bear was running with him. The wolves skidded to a stop at the sight of the bear before running into the woods on Mornak's right. The bear chased after them.

Mornak dashed around trees and hopped over bushes as he pursued the last two shadowmen. Around him, the shadows of the woods distracted him. He would dodge what looked like an arm, only to realize it was a swaying tree branch. Sometimes, the darkness at his feet hid a hole or a rock. He knew he needed more light, and then—suddenly—all the light went away. Mornak quickly realized he had run into a spell of darkness. Before he could stop himself, he tripped over a big tree root and knew immediately why the darkness had been placed in that particular spot. As he tumbled to the ground, Mornak began to cast another ball of light to counter the darkness, but his body cleared the area of darkness before the spell activated.

He found himself sitting in a clearing, holding a harmless ball of light, which made him an easy target in the forest's gloom. On either side of him stood the shadowmen. Glowing green energy surrounded each one's right hand—a Death Bolt spell ready to cast. Mornak knew he could only block one of them, and he only had a second to decide which. But they looked exactly the same. His ball of light became his saving grace though, because only one of the shadowmen cast a shadow. Two Death Bolts raced in. Mornak brought up his shield to stop what he hoped was the right one. One green energy bolt splashed against his shield and dissipated. The other hit him in the back and just disappeared. Mornak countered with a searing beam that burned into the "real" shadowman's arm. He screamed and dashed off again. Getting off the ground, Mornak resumed the chase, only to arrive in an all-too-familiar clearing. He had arrived at the heart of Shadow Wood. It was here that he had buried the Hall of Shadows so no one would accidentally come across it.

"Well done," he heard a voice say, but again he couldn't tell where it came from. "This was only a test, you realize. I had to see how strong I was and how strong you were. The next time we meet, I will be your better, and I relish the thought of how much you are going to worry until that day comes. And it will come, Great Mornak."

Mornak stood in the clearing focusing on the voice. It seemed to be coming from below him, but that was impossible. He cast his magic downward. The Hall of Shadows still lay buried there, its magic still strong. Nothing could escape it. So who was that shadowman then? Why did he choose to fight here? Mornak had to find out somehow. He had to prepare for what he knew would be the fight of his life.

I

A large square room glowed in the light of several torches spaced evenly on the walls. Tapestries depicting humans, dwarves, and elves being killed and eaten by ogres hung between the torches. On the far side of the room stood a sacrificial altar, and just in front of it, a pedestal held up a statue of the ogre god. In its hands lay a golden key. Dressed in animal skins and wielding clubs, a dozen ogres stood between the heroes and the key, all frozen in place. "What's the plan, Axeman?" Dax asked.

"Cast a Confusion spell," Alex replied. "Then I'll rush in and chop down the ones that aren't attacking each other."

Dax pointed at the floor in front of the pedestal. "They're avoiding that area. I'm thinking trap."

"I'm thinking you're right," Alex agreed. "I'll try and avoid it during the fight. Then you can use your magic to disarm it."

Dax shook his head. "Still looks too easy."

"I know, but we need that key. You ready?"

"Yep."

Alex pressed the pause button, and the video game resumed. Dax hit his controls, making his wizard cast the Confusion spell. Icons appeared over most of the ogres' heads, indicating that they had been confused. Then each ogre attacked the nearest thing to it, which, at the moment, was another ogre. Alex's Axeman rushed into the battle at once. He defeated the first ogre easily with a Power Attack and then used his Whirlwind feat to make his character spin like a top to chop into three more ugly foes. By then, Dax was firing lightning bolts into the battle. Alex had to guide his character carefully to avoid the altar until a well-placed Bash Blast sent an ogre flying onto the trapped area. A bed of spikes rose up from the floor impaling it.

"Ouch!" Alex laughed. "That *had* to hurt!"

He quickly checked his stats. He remained at seventy-five out of one hundred health after killing half the ogres. Suddenly, a magic portal appeared on the far side of the room, and a huge, fancily dressed ogre stepped through.

"Should have seen that coming," Dax said. "What good is temple without a cleric?"

"Watch my back!" Alex yelled as he used a Fatal Fling to throw his axe across the room into the cleric's chest. The cleric died before he could cast his first spell, but the special feat left Alex unarmed with six ogres around him. To make things worse, the Confusion spell ended right then, and the remaining ogres focused their attention on the Axeman.

"Are you crazy?" Dax complained. He cast a Slow spell to buy Alex some time. The spell slowed the ogres to half their speed for a few seconds. Alex rushed through the big hairy beasts to get at his axe, but even slowed, the ogres hit him enough to take his health down to fifteen. Dax tried to even things out by using Fingers of Fire to burn the ogres between him and Alex. Arcs of flame shot from his character's fingertips into the group of monsters. Two died. Two kept after Alex. Two turned and went after Dax.

A worried look came over Dax's face. "Uh ... Alex, a little help here?"

"You wizards," Alex laughed as his character picked up his axe. "Hand to hand, you'd lose against a paper bag."

Alex chopped into his ogres, dispatching them easily before rushing to save Dax. Alex's health had dropped to seven, but Dax had gone from one hundred to thirty-three after just two hits. Alex slammed into the last two ogres from behind, finishing them off before they could turn to fight. As they fell, both teens sighed.

"Why did you throw your axe at him?" Dax asked.

"We didn't know how powerful he was," Alex explained. "I didn't want to risk it."

"I can't believe you can only carry an axe. I mean, if I were a real weapon master, I'd still have a dagger or something as backup."

"It's called a weapon master for a reason. You get to master *one* weapon. I chose the axe because I'm an Axeman!" Alex was referring to the name of his band, The Axemen, in which he was the lead guitarist and unofficial band leader. "Besides they wouldn't give me Fatal Fling if I could, like, use it and then just pull out another weapon. I could just Fatal Fling at every enemy until I ran out of weapons to throw. The character would be too powerful."

"Yeah, you're right. But, man, I've never seen someone use an Axeman like you. You're crazy, but the stuff you do works. And you never seem to use the same moves twice."

"Always keep them guessing," Alex explained. "People, and a lot of the games nowadays, figure out your habits. So I always try to do something different. But you're right. I got da mad skillz, dude!" Alex laughed, and Dax laughed with him.

"It shouldn't really surprise me that you do so well at these games, I guess," Dax commented. "You've seen, like, every movie, played every RPG, and you've read what ... like a thousand books?"

"Don't exaggerate," Alex teased. "It's only like nine fifty."

Alex, an eleventh grader, stood at above-average height with a slim but sturdy body. His straight blonde hair hung evenly around his head almost like a skirt, and his long face usually held a smirk since Alex tended to be a wise guy. A T-shirt, blue jeans, and sneakers made up his typical outfit along with his red wristwatch on his right arm and a studded leather cuff on his left. On this day, Alex wore his orange shirt with the band's logo—a yellow *A* with lightning bolts on either side that looked almost like wings. Behind the *A* lay Alex's instrument—his guitar—in red. Alex loved his music but not as much as swords and sorcery. He'd been a fan of the latter since the age of six and had collected enough books, cards, movies, and toys to open his own store.

Slightly shorter than Alex, Dax stood at about the same height as most of the girls in their grade, which he hated since he preferred shorter women. His mother kept his brown hair in a kind of crew cut, which made him look like a cross between a soldier and punk rocker. At least it gave him character.

Dax owned the game console, so the guys typically hung out at his place. His room was one large mess, and getting set to play video games usually involved shoving clothes off Dax's double bed first. These clothes were usually a mixture of one or two day-old shirts and pants, and the neatly folded pile of clean clothes that Dax's mom had left to be put away. The floor was a minefield of dirty underwear and socks that visitors were careful to avoid. The light blue walls of the room hid behind the multitude of posters and pictures that Dax had pinned, tacked, and even stapled on them. Most were movie posters like *Spider-Man* and *The Lord of the Rings*, but some pop stars and video game ads hung scattered among them, as well as magazine cutouts of the movie stars, TV shows, and toys he liked. Dax essentially surrounded himself with one big commercial for everything every kid had ever wanted to see or own.

Alex stared at their two video game characters on the TV screen. They stood patiently in the room with ogre bodies all around them, occasionally glancing up to look out at Dax and Alex as they waited for commands. "That would be a great life, you know."

"Fighting monsters every day?" Dax asked. "It could get boring."

Alex quickly responded. "Not just fighting monsters, not even fighting monsters. The adventures, the fame, the freedom to be out exploring. Wouldn't you love to have that kind of life?"

"Me? Not really. I like my life. I like my video games. I like my thirty-inch flat screen, and I get, like, a billion channels on cable. Things are pretty good the way they are."

"I dunno," Alex sighed. "I just think I should be doing something more. You know, like I'm destined for something big."

"I thought that was the plan," Dax replied. "Your band gets a contract, puts out an album. Next thing you know, you're on a world tour."

"That's assuming my parents let me go on a tour. Can you imagine a rock star with like a ten o'clock curfew?"

Dax chuckled. "Yeah, that'd suck."

"I hate that my parents are so strict. I want to go on a big trip to someplace I've never even heard of—no restrictions and no parental supervision. I keep having this feeling like something big is gonna happen, but the only thing in my future right now is that history exam tomorrow morning."

"Speaking of which, did you bring the notes from last period?"

"Do you ever take notes?" Alex asked as he reached into his book bag and grabbed his notes. "Or do you just copy everyone else's?"

"Copy pretty much," Dax smiled. When he saw that Alex wasn't smiling back, his grin vanished. Alex looked depressed. Dax needed to cheer him up.

"Look, Alex, it's not that bad. You gotta look at it the way I do. We're only sixteen, and we've got it pretty good right now. After this exam, we're off for summer vacation and can do whatever we want for two months. (You till 10:00 PM, me till 11:00 PM.) Would it be cool if, say, a spaceship landed in my backyard and took me away for a Star Wars kinda adventure? Or wouldn't it be cool if I had aliens living in my closet? Sure. Is it likely to happen? Nope. Seriously, how many sixteen-year-olds out there are off on grand adventures of any kind? And who knows? Sometime soon, someone could come running in and tell you you've got the audition of a lifetime, and it could make you a star."

Just then Tanya Krowski burst through the door of Dax's room, startling both boys. Tanya was the keyboardist of The Axemen. A slim, petite, spunky girl with short spiked red hair and blue eyes, she had a love of tight jeans and cutoff shirts.

"Dax!" she exclaimed. "Have you seen—oh, Alex! You're here. You'll never guess what happened. Actually, don't even try. I'll just tell you. We got an audition with Shadowland Productions. It's our big break, the one that could make us stars!"

Alex and Dax sat silently, mouths opened, exchanging glances for several seconds before Dax yelled, "Damn, I'm good!"

Alex jumped off the bed, rushing to Tanya and grabbing her arms.

"Are you serious? When did this happen?"

"Just an hour ago," she replied. "I tried to call you on your cell."

"I turn it off during game time," Alex explained. "No distractions."

Tanya gave him that video-games-are-*not*-that-important look that girls usually give.

"Anyways," Alex continued. "When's the audition?"

"Tomorrow morning. 9:00 AM."

"You're kidding?" Dax jumped in.

Tanya looked confused. "No. Is that a problem?"

Alex let her go and dropped his head. "Our history final is tomorrow morning at 9:00 AM. Can we reschedule?"

Tanya then gave him her are-you-kidding-me looks and said, "You want me to tell a producer from Shadowland Productions, 'I'm sorry, but tomorrow morning just isn't good for us. Would you mind rescheduling? How's next Tuesday?'" She glared, adding, "Are you nuts?"

Dax lay on his stomach on the bed with his chin propped up on his fists, smiling at the situation. "Dude, you're screwed."

*   *   *

"That's it, Little Rose," Mornak encouraged while the energy collected between Dara's hands. She knelt on the grass in the palace gardens; her yellow floral dress spread around her like a sunflower.

Dara was proving herself a good student, but she still had a few years to go before she could be properly trained. Nonetheless, magic was in her blood, passed down to her from her parents just as her father's power had been passed to him from both his parents. Some said that Mornak's powerful potential came from the mix of wizard blood. Most wizards did not marry other wizards, and while they could become friends and allies, a rivalry almost always developed between spell casters that prevented them from getting too close to one another. They feared having their secrets stolen or being seen as *number two* in the pair. Because of this, most wizards chose to practice the arts alone and only took an apprentice to carry on their legacy. Fear also made them train only one apprentice at a time. Jealousy could spark if one student considered the other the master's favourite. (Few did not know the tale of Kelnarr's students—Tash and Zarod, and the fate to which their jealousy led them.) Mornak's parents were different though. Just like Mornak and his wife, Elanni, they loved each other unconditionally; they kept no secrets from each other; and they helped each other grow as a people as well as wizards.

Mornak saw much of his wife in Dara: her curiosity, her sassiness, the way she saw the beauty in everything around her. He still missed Elanni greatly. She died defending the realm from evil, and her death drove Mornak to create the Hall of Shadows. He did not want anyone else to lose a loved one to evil as he had. More precisely, he feared that one day he might lose Dara in the same way if he didn't do something. But now, it looked as though his precautions may have been for nothing. He didn't know who or what this shadowman was, but if he was trying to unlock the Hall of Shadows—if he could find a way to get inside or let what lived inside it out—then the realm would be plunged into darkness again, and it would, most likely, be worse than before.

Almost a year had passed since Mornak's encounter with the shadowman. Since then, he had been hard at work preparing. He had trained in the art of divination, the ability to see other places and sometimes other times. Through it, he had searched the realm for the shadowman, but he found no trace of him. That did not make Mornak feel any less worried. The shadowman made it clear that his powers were growing, and one particular vision of Mornak's made him believe that he may someday be defeated by his mysterious enemy. He saw himself in what must have been the distant future, for he looked old and withered, chained to the floor of a dungeon.

Mornak could not let that come to pass. He needed to increase his own powers so that when they met again, he would be the victor. To that end, he had created an elemental staff to augment his magic. He could cast his spells through it, and it would magnify their power. More importantly, with the staff, he could create creatures from the elements at hand—such as bears made of fire, snakes made of water, and even sand soldiers. The staff could only be used this way once a day, and the elementals would only last a few minutes. But they behaved just like the creatures they looked like, and they obeyed all Mornak's commands. To make sure he didn't face the shadowman alone next time, he also created magic horseshoes for all the Axemen's steeds. If the knights were needed, they could accompany Mornak to Shadow Wood.

And then there was Dara. A wizard didn't usually start training another until the apprentice reached the age of thirteen, but Mornak did not know if or when he might need Dara's assistance. That was why she had a small colourful magic ball of light in her hands. Seconds later, it became a butterfly. Mornak smiled. The girl was a natural summoner.

"I love making butterflies!" Dara giggled as the insect took flight through the garden.

"Remember, you didn't make the butterfly. You summoned it from somewhere else. When you grow up, you'll be able to summon a book, or your horse, or even a person. Just remember that it's easier to summon people who want to be summoned. If they don't, they can usually resist and stay right where they are," Mornak explained, as he pulled a scroll out from an ornate box. "Now, I have something special for you. Wondrous magic ... if you can read it." He handed her the scroll, which she eagerly opened.

Her face scrunched up as she looked at the parchment. Its words made no sense to her, but she'd done this before. The words were tones of power. Pronouncing them correctly, and in order, either cast a spell that they formed or unlocked magic stored in the scroll. She mouthed them first, trying out the sounds in her mind. Then she spoke them. "*Ana shi ka rei ful. Shumen ro sakra mali.*"

The scroll began to glow as its magic activated. The glow then pulled away from the scroll like a huge teardrop of purple water to splash onto the ground, disappearing in a bright flash. A glowing purple puppy happily wagging its tail sat where the teardrop had landed.

"A puppy!" Dara exclaimed. "Can I keep—" She caught on then and pouted. "Aw, he's not real. He's not summoned. He's conferred."

"Conjured," Mornak corrected, chuckling to himself.

"Conjured," Dara repeated. "How long is he here for?"

"For one day, Little Rose," Mornak answered.

Just then a knight walked up to them. "I've have returned from the Wood, my king," he announced. "I am happy to report no unusual activity."

"Very good, Senufer," the king replied, "but I told you to call me Mornak in private. Have we not been friends for two decades?"

"That would be improper, my king," the man replied with a wink.

Senufer Praxis was the leader of the Axemen and Mornak's right hand. Next to Mornak, he was probably the most respected man in Aspiria, respect gained through his deeds as well as his outstanding skill. A mountain of a man, Senufer stood a head taller than Mornak and was very muscular—but not so much that it restricted his movements. He kept his head shaved so enemies could not grab his hair during battle, and he sported a tightly trimmed goatee. Like all Axemen, he wore armour of brown leather with a bronze chest plate, as well as bronze knee, ankle, wrist, and elbow guards. This gave him great freedom of movement while protecting vital areas. Engraved in the chest plate shone the Axemen insignia: an axe with two lighting bolts on either side, almost like wings.

The man was an imposing individual except to a certain few.

"Hi, Uncle Senufer!" Dara exclaimed, hugging his waist.

The Axeman picked her up and hugged her back. "Hello, Little Rose. Are you having fun?"

"Yep yep," Dara answered. "I made a puppy!"

"So I see," he remarked. Though Dara and Senufer had no blood relation, she had known him all her life, and they treated each other as family. "You are becoming quite the little wizard. Maybe next year your father can step down, and you can take over as queen."

"I'm too young, Uncle Senufer," Dara giggled. "Besides, I've seen what Papa does. It's far too much work. I'm going to stay a princess forever!"

Senufer laughed. "I wish you could. In any case, I doubt you'd make a good queen."

Dara looked at him in shock. "Uncle Senufer, that's mean! Why would you say that?"

"Real queens are very proper," Senufer explained. "They don't giggle when you do this." He began tickling her tummy, making her laugh and squirm in his arms.

"Uncle Senufer!" Dara squealed through her giggling. "Stop. I give up. I give up!"

Senufer placed her back on the ground. "When you can pass the tickle test, you will be ready to be queen," he announced with an official tone as he placed his hand to his heart.

"Yes, Sir Knight," Dara curtsied with the same seriousness before both of them broke into laughter.

Dara's puppy whined then, drawing their attention.

"Go play with him," Mornak told her. Needing no further prompting, Dara and the puppy rushed off together at once, running through the gardens.

Mornak and Senufer watched her go.

"I don't ever want her to grow up," Mornak sighed, "and at the same time she's not growing up fast enough in the face of this threat."

Senufer nodded. "Her skills are surprising for her age."

"Indeed," Mornak agreed. "I only hope I have the time to teach her offensive and defensive spells."

"It has been months since you saw the shadowman," Senufer stated. "Are you sure he will return?"

Mornak nodded. "I could sense it was no idle threat. He is preparing himself, and so, I have been as well."

"I have not seen you so unnerved since some time before the Hall went up," Senufer commented.

"Because this man has some connection to it, but what it is, I cannot imagine."

"And you fear defeat so much you that feel Dara must be trained so early?" the knight questioned.

"I am being prudent," Mornak stated. "It is better to err on the side of caution. Magical fail-safes are in place to give Dara access to my spell books and magical items. She will have all she needs if the worst should come to pass."

"While I always trust in your wisdom, King Mornak," Senufer commented, "I hope, this time, you are being overcautious."

"As do I, my friend," Mornak agreed.

Senufer saluted and then returned to his duties. Mornak turned his attention back to Dara. He smiled as he watched her and her magical puppy, and then he smiled to himself. He'd been using his powers to help her focus hers. She still lacked enough experience to do proper summoning on her own. The scroll spell, however—she did that naturally. If it came down to it, she would be his fail-safe—the realm's fail-safe.

*   *   *

At 6:00 PM, Alex rode his bike home from Dax's place. The end of June meant long warm days and no more school. Classes had ended already, as had all of his exams, except history. A few hours ago, he had been looking forward to a great vacation for the next two months. Now he could only think about tomorrow. The Black Eyed Peas played on Alex's iPod Nano as he rode, but he didn't even hear it. His mind was trying to deal with his dilemma. If he went to his exam, he'd make it through another year of school—a year closer to freedom (unless he went to college, in which case it would be a year closer to another four-year sentence and then freedom). If he went to the audition, he might be able to bypass all that and become a rock star right away. Of course, if the audition didn't go well, then he would have failed the exam for nothing and would have to repeat a year of school—as well as endure the wrath of his parents.

Alex wasn't unintelligent, but this year his mind had often drifted with thoughts of a bigger purpose, which had brought his grades down. Many of his teachers recommended that he repeat the year since all his marks so far were just above the passing level; some marks reached that level only because his teachers liked him. His parents had made a deal that if he could show renewed focus on this next exam, he would be allowed to move to the next grade. Passing, and his parents' trust and respect, now hinged on this exam, and Tanya had just told him that he should skip it.

On top of that, this audition might be the big thing he felt approaching. He had the nagging feeling that he was meant to be somewhere else and that he could do it if he could just get out of—out of—*Out of what?* he wondered. *School? The city? The country?* He felt trapped, trapped in a life that should be so much more. It had been this way for three years now—a hollow feeling. He knew what caused it—everyone knew. It was why his teachers were so lenient, but he thought that by now, the feeling would have gone away or at least faded. It only felt stronger.

He pulled into his driveway and parked his bike in the garage of his house—a typical two-storey, four-bedroom suburban home that looked almost exactly like every other house on the street. He walked in to be greeted immediately by his mother's voice.

"Alex!" she called from somewhere upstairs. "Take out the trash before you get settled in."

"Yes, Mom," he called back. "Bigger purpose ... greater destiny ... trash boy," he mumbled as he carried the bags to the curb.

He returned inside only to hear his mom again. "Did you remember the recycling?"

"Crap," he muttered as he went to find the recycling bin.

A while later, he entered his room. His history books lay on his desk. He needed to study. His guitar leaned against the wall. He needed to practice. A warm summer breeze wafted through his open window. He needed to escape. He went with studying. Surprisingly, Alex enjoyed this year's history course so much so that he'd gone out and gotten some books from the library on his own. One in particular, which he had just started reading, examined figures from different eras and different places around the world and cited evidence that some of these legendary and mythical people may have really existed. In *Legend and Lore,* he had just begun reading the life story of a Roman legionnaire named Scorpius who had a knack for strategy. A portrait of him appeared at the beginning of his chapter. He looked to be about the same age as Alex, perhaps a year older. With short brown hair and a sturdy yet not-too-muscular body, Scorpius had a serious look about him that said, "All work and no play." His armour consisted of a chest plate and bronze shoulder guards. A leather kilt protected his upper legs while tough leather boots protected his shins and feet. He wore bronze wrist guards and held his sword, a gladius, and his large rectangular shield, a scutum; he was ready for battle. Alex couldn't wait to see how Scorpius applied his tactical talent as he grew up. He picked up the book, knowing he shouldn't read it now. He had his texts to study, but he still felt drawn to this book. In a hundred years, or a thousand, would he be in a similar book, or would he be forgotten by history like so many millions of others? Then he chuckled to himself. *What would his story be? The Taker Outer of Trash ... and Recyclables!*

He tossed the book aside, deciding to reread his class notes. He was lost in the war of 1812 (and wondering what it would be like to experience a war firsthand) when his mom called him down for dinner; he welcomed the break.

Unlike many TV generation families who watched while eating, Alex's father insisted they eat at the table so that they could connect as a family each night.

"Just one more exam, eh, Alex?" his dad mentioned.

"Yeah. Tomorrow," Alex answered. "History."

"I'll bet you can't wait until that exam is history!" his dad said, laughing at his own joke.

Alex and his mom rolled their eyes.

"And after that, I guess it's band practice and video games every day?" His dad continued. "Who knows? Maybe you'll become a rock star, and then your old man can retire and live off your success."

Alex knew he was joking, but he hoped some truth hid in the statement. "You'd be okay with me becoming a rock star?" he asked.

"A rich rock star, yes," his dad replied.

"Now, James," his mom interrupted. "Don't go giving him ideas. He's got to finish school before he even thinks about something like that."

"Why?" Alex asked. "Aren't I just going to school to, like, get a career and make money so I can live comfortably? If I become a rock star, then I'll have plenty of money to live comfortably off of—and so will you."

"Kid's got a point," his dad noted before he shoved some mashed potatoes in his mouth.

"Stop it, James!" his mom scolded. "Alex, it's not that easy to become a famous musician or actor or something like that. If it were, then everyone would be doing it. And the thing about fame is it can go as quickly as it comes. What if you just have one hit and that's it?"

"Yeah," Alex's dad agreed. "Remember those New Kids in the House? Whatever happened to them? You never hear about them at all anymore. They can't still be kids. And don't even get me started on that Britney girl. Now Celine—"

Before his dad could veer off topic, Alex's mom jumped in. "The point is," she said, "you need a solid career to fall back on if the rock star thing doesn't work. We don't want to see you out of work at forty with no money and no job prospects because your music career fell through."

"And we sure don't want you living here!" Alex's dad laughed.

"James!" his mom scolded again and then turned back to Alex. "Honey, you know you're always welcome here, but—"

"But we'd prefer if you got your own place by then!" His dad jumped in. "No offense," he added with a wink. "I don't know why we're even worrying about it now. It's not like you've got some record producer offering you a deal."

Alex did his best not to choke on his food.

2

*L*etting out a sigh, Mornak welcomed another Day of Peace. A full year had passed without any sign of the shadowman. In that time, Mornak had journeyed to the Hall of Shadows almost two dozen times and reinforced its magic on many of those visits. He also had placed wards around it as an extra precaution although he was certain that nothing could break in or out.

Mornak readied himself in his chambers for his duties in today's celebration. He knew he should be enjoying this day, but now it marked the anniversary of the day he met the shadowman. He felt that if something somehow were to happen, today would be the day.

As if on cue, one of the Axemen entered. "Sir, you asked to be informed if anything occurred at Shadow Wood."

A cold chill went down Mornak's spine. "What has happened?"

"Nothing, sir," the Axeman replied. "Nothing serious, but you said you wanted to be alerted about *anything* unusual."

"And?"

"And, well, there's a storm cloud over the woods. We thought it was just a passing storm at first, but it doesn't seem to be moving. Shall we send riders to have a look?"

"Ready all the Axemen. We ride out within the hour."

"All, sir?"

"Yes, and let us hope that I am being excessively cautious," Mornak answered and then left to prepare.

After quickly changing from his formal clothes to his traveling ones, Mornak gathered some items and went in search of Dara. He found her in the gardens covered with dirt, playing with her latest puppy—this one blue. He called her over and sat her down for what would be the most important and, possibly, the last talk they would have. Not knowing the significance of the situation, Dara's attention stayed focused on the puppy.

"Dara, you must listen," he said, turning her head toward him and locking his gaze with hers. "This is very important. I am going out to Shadow Wood, and I don't know when I'll be back." From his pocket, he pulled out a small ring made of silver. A pearl, set in the ring, glowed with a soft white light. "Put this on," he said as he placed it on Dara's finger. "If the light in the pearl goes out before I get back, then you will need to act quickly. I want you to open this scroll and activate its magic," he said as he handed it to her. Unlike the other scrolls Mornak had given Dara to practice magic with, this one was not just a piece of parchment. It wrapped around two rollers, making it look more official, although the old yellow paper and the plain wooden rollers said otherwise.

"What does it do, Papa?"

"I can't tell you that yet, but it is very important. You will do this for me, won't you, Little Rose?"

Dara immediately caught on to his demeanor. "Are we in danger, Papa?"

Mornak could not lie to her, not now. "We may be. I have to go to make sure that we are not. You will be safe here, though."

Dara's face showed a little worry, and she broke his gaze. "What if I can't make it work?"

Mornak smiled. "I have no doubt that you can make it work, Dara. I have watched you practice and have complete faith in you. I need you to tell me that you will do what I need you to do if the time comes."

Straightening up, she looked him in the eye. "I promise, Papa."

He hugged her fiercely. "That's my Little Rose." He wanted to hold onto her forever, but time was important. "Go lock the Scroll in the chest in your room. Keep it safe there until I return or you need to use it." He kissed her forehead and then rushed out to meet the Axemen.

Minutes later, he and the knights were riding with all speed toward Shadow Wood. Mornak glanced at the ring on his finger, the twin to the one he gave Dara. Through it, he sent a tiny bit of his magic into Dara's ring to keep it lit. It required as much effort to maintain the connection between the rings as it did to breathe. And like breathing, he could stop it at will, or it would stop if something very bad happened. However the connection broke, it would then be up to Dara to do her part.

A few hours later, the small army pulled up in front of Shadow Wood. Thunder rumbled in the clouds above although no lightning flashed. When the Axemen dismounted, Senufer ordered them to form ranks in front of Mornak. They put up a brave front, but Mornak could see that most were worried. Worse, he knew they should be.

The sight of this elite force always impressed Mornak. They were a unified force and yet quite diverse at the same time. Even though the Axemen all used axes, the type of axe varied from man to man. Most sported two-handed battle-axes, some throwing axes, and others double hand axes; a few used huge great axes that could only be wielded properly by very strong large men. Of the strong men, Senufer was the strongest. The lead knight wore two magical great axes strapped crisscross on his back, but his axes had no blades. Senufer would draw the heavy metal handles like swords from their scabbards. Once free, though, his right axe burst into a burning yellow axe head while his left axe chilled into a frozen blue head. He called them Sun Stroke and Bone Chiller. Most of Senufer's opponents tended to back down when he just drew them—at least the smart ones did.

Senufer inspected the ranks before reporting to Mornak. "Do you wish to address the men, my lord?" he asked.

"Yes, Senufer. Thank you," Mornak answered. Senufer moved out of the way to give his king the stage. Mornak seemed more imposing with his magical staff in his hand.

"Many of you men have been with me for years since before the time of peace. You know the dangers that we once faced. You know the friends that we have lost. I fear that a new evil may have surfaced. I encountered it a year ago, and while I was able to defeat it, it escaped. Now it seems it is back, and if its promises are true, then it is even more powerful. Our enemy is a wizard of sorts. I believe he is seeking a way to open the Hall."

Murmurs went through the ranks. They all knew the danger of opening the Hall of Shadows. Senufer felt embarrassment for the undisciplined display. "Axemen! Attention!" he yelled.

Mornak held up a hand to him. "It's all right, Senufer. I know how they feel." He turned back to the Axemen. "Men, you are the best of the knights in the realm. You have met every challenge thrown at you and come out victorious. Our new enemy is quite dangerous and his plans disastrous, but I have confidence that we will overcome him. I have faith in the magic of your blades, the skills in your bodies, and the strength in your hearts. You are Axemen. Let's chop this enemy down."

A great cheer went up from the crowd. Mornak smiled. They had been worried before. He needed them to march with confidence, so he told them what they needed to hear—even if he wasn't sure of it himself.

* * *

They advanced cautiously through the woods, weaving around the trees while trying to maintain their formation. The farther they traveled, the gloomier it became. It did not grow dark so much as it grew hazy. The Axemen seemed as much like shadows as the shadows they cast, as the shadows the trees cast.

"Keep the ranks tight," Senufer ordered, though at this point he could not see enough knights to tell how well the formation was holding. He could make out less than a dozen men; so trusting in their skills, he put his focus on Mornak who seemed to move with purpose.

"How do you know where you're going, my lord?" he asked. "Do you even know where this wizard is?"

"No, I don't," Mornak replied, "but I can feel the magic of the Hall. I'm simply following it. The ground above the Hall is the most likely place for him to be."

"That seems logical," Senufer agreed. He turned to relay the information to his men, but stopped at what he saw—or rather, what he didn't see. None of his men were behind him. He took a few quick steps back and peered through the gloom, but there were no men, only shadows. He turned back quickly to stop Mornak to inform him of the turn of events, but Mornak was no longer ahead of him either.

"My lord?" he called. "King Mornak?"

Senufer did not have his lord's skills. He could not tell which way led to the Hall. Right now, he could not even tell which way led out. He decided to follow his last course and try to catch up with Mornak. If he couldn't find him soon, he'd have to pick a direction and move until he got out of the Wood. He did not like the idea of abandoning his lord or his men, but what other choice did he have? However, if his men were as good as he thought, they would take similar actions, and he would regroup with them at Mornak's location or on the perimeter of the wood.

*   *   *

The moment he realized that Senufer was not with him, Mornak cursed himself for a fool. He had been so focused on getting to the Hall that he had missed the immediate threat. The Wood had been enchanted with a spell of misdirection. Because he followed a magical link to the Hall, the spell had not affected him, but by now, all his men were wandering around lost—some probably within a dozen paces of one another—unable to find each other or a way out.

Of course the shadowman had prepared for him, he realized. The storm clouds above weren't a sign of trouble. They were an invitation! The shadowman had turned Shadow Wood into an enormous trap, and Mornak had led his best men right into it. He could try to counter the spell, but that would use up much of his magic just before he needed it. That was the shadowman's intent, no doubt. No, he had come this far. He would see this through. He had to.

Soon he reached the clearing. Above him the clouds seemed to hang unusually low, and sheet lighting lit them up every now and then. In the center of the clearing stood the shadowman, waiting; his hand was surrounded by a bright green glow. A Death Bolt, Mornak saw. *Same tricks as last time*, he thought. *Stronger magic though*.

"Welcome, Great Mornak," the shadowman greeted as he took a deep bow.

"And your name?" Mornak asked.

The shadowman tilted his head to the side. "Hmm, you know, I haven't thought of one yet."

"I suppose it won't matter once I rid this world of you," Mornak threatened.

The shadowman laughed. "I truly doubt you are capable of that."

"We shall see," Mornak said as he sent his magic downward, feeling for the Hall of Shadows. It still lay buried beneath him, closed, its wards still in place.

The shadowman seemed to sense his actions. "Yes, it's still locked up," he said. "It's not yet time."

"Time?" Mornak asked.

"You have to be defeated first."

"Then that time will never come," Mornak promised.

"We shall see," the shadowman challenged as he let loose the Death Bolt.

Mornak didn't even try to block it. He'd been waiting for the strike and simply moved out the way. He cast his own Searing Light spell, channeling it through his staff as he moved. It spread out in a cone toward the shadowman, allowing no room to dodge its effect, its immense power. Mornak wanted to end this battle quickly.

The spell struck the shadowman, essentially erasing him on contact. Mornak looked at the area where the man once stood. The spell had burned the grass beneath him and some of the trees behind him. He knew almost immediately that he had won too easily. The shadowman had, most likely, been an illusion. Mornak began to put a shield spell up when something struck him from behind, not painfully but hard enough to knock him to his knees. The large sticky strands of a Web pushed him down and held him fast. Mornak cursed, angrier with himself than the shadowman. Twice he had let his opponent get the better of him. He wouldn't let it happen again.

Still the same tricks, he thought. Again, he channeled his energy through his staff. His body caught fire, burning up the web. Getting to his feet, Mornak stated, "Enough of this, wizard. Your tricks won't work on me."

"Perhaps not the old ones," the shadowman snickered, "but the new ones ..."

Just then a hand reached out of the ground, grabbing Mornak's ankle. When he looked down, another grabbed his other ankle. He tried to raise his staff to cast, but another hand seized it, too. Shadows rose out of the ground and took shape into more shadowmen. They reached out, taking hold of Mornak's arms and legs, his waist, his neck. Soon he could not move any part of his body as a dozen shadowmen held him securely.

"No movement, no spells," the shadowman taunted.

Mornak smiled. He had created the staff for this very reason. Its main power didn't need him to move, only think. The ground shook and shifted before him. Then a dozen earthmen rose and attacked. The shadowmen who held Mornak were soon pulled off, and what followed resembled a barroom brawl. The shadows and earth punched and kicked, grappled and threw each other. Both groups felt the blows of the other, but neither seemed to be hurt for long; as each individual was knocked out of the fight, it would pick itself up and jump back into the fray.

When Mornak looked around for the lead shadowman, he found him standing safely to the side of the battle. The two opponents locked gazes.

"That's an impressive weapon," the shadowman admitted. "Would you like to see mine?"

Again the earth rumbled and shook. This time men did not rise from it. The ground erupted, throwing shadowmen and earthmen alike across the clearing. Mornak's eyes went wide with shock when he saw what was coming up: the Hall of Shadows.

Mornak had not seen the Hall since he buried it in this place ten years ago. To see it now was frightening. The Hall, a huge rectangular stone building, stood a dozen storeys tall and over one hundred meters long. When it had been created, it had been perfectly smooth and made of whitestone. Now its surfaces were warped and had turned gray and black. It seemed more organic, as if the stone were somehow alive. Warped faces and skulls had formed—*no, were forming*, Mornak realized—across its surface as if the souls inside were trying to push free but couldn't. The Hall was transforming, mutating—but into what, Mornak could not tell.

As if to accent its arrival, lightning flashed across the sky, followed by a thunderclap that deafened the wizard-king for a moment. Mornak felt the pressure change and detected the smell that comes just before a storm. This would be a terrible storm indeed.

The wizard-king stared at the building before him wanting to believe it wasn't real, hoping it was some illusion the shadowman created, and yet feeling its familiar presence, which told him his worst nightmare had come true.

"H-how?" he asked more to himself than the shadowman.

The shadowman answered anyway. "It is alive now, powered by the ones it holds prisoner, and it has chosen to release me."

"You are *from* the Hall?" Mornak asked, not believing the words as he spoke them.

"I *am* the Hall!" he yelled. "I am its voice and its hand. I am its Shadow Lord. Now, feel its power."

The Shadow Lord, as he called himself, sent a powerful beam of pure darkness at Mornak. Mornak countered with a shield of light. The beam struck the shield hard but could not break through. Black sparks flew in all directions. Both men grimaced with effort; neither let up.

*　　*　　*

"How'd things go with your parents?" Dax asked Alex over the phone.

Shocked, Alex replied, "What? You think I told them? I haven't even decided what I'm going to do yet."

"If it were me," Dax suggested, "I'd go with the audition. Fame, fortune, money!"

Alex rolled his eyes as he replied. "Okay, I'll go take the exam. You go to the audition for me. Oh, wait. Do you have any musical talent? That's right. No!"

"Dude, that's harsh," Dax shot back.

"I'm not in the best mood right now," Alex explained.

Dax decided a change of subject might help. He didn't pick the new subject very well though. "Tanya was looking extremely hot today."

Alex sighed. "Yeah." Alex had a huge crush on Tanya, but he didn't want to tell her. He feared she'd leave the band if she didn't feel the same way.

"Ask her out, dude," Dax prodded. "She likes you."

"As a friend, sure, but I think she's into Scott," Alex countered, referring to the other guitarist in the band.

"Well, Scott is way cooler than you," Dax joked.

"I didn't know you were in his fan club," Alex shot back. "You sure *you* don't want to date him?"

"Ha, ha," Dax replied sarcastically. "Hey, if you don't know what you're going to do tomorrow, then what did you tell everyone else?"

"I told them to go to the audition anyways. Scott can do my riffs. They should be able to pull it off without me."

"I don't think any of them are going to be too thrilled with you. If they get the gig, will they even include you?"

"Include me?" Alex repeated, suddenly realizing the implications. "I never even thought of that."

"Hey, I'm not saying they won't, but ya never know."

Alex felt a knot forming in his stomach.

"Do you really think they might ..." He couldn't finish.

"Tanya—no." Dax said. "Glenn—probably not. But Scott and Bamm, they might see this as you abandoning them."

"But I'm not. I'm thinking about my future."

"Hey guy, Scott and Bamm have history with us," Dax reminded Alex. "They're skipping the same exam without a second thought."

*   *   *

White magic shot from Mornak's staff, smashing into the black magic coming from the Shadow Lord. At first, the two seemed equally matched, but then—slowly—the white energy moved toward the Shadow Lord. Mornak smiled, his confidence growing and adding to his strength with each passing moment. This would be over soon; then he would deal with the Hall though he had no idea how. If it had truly become sentient, then his troubles were just beginning.

The black beam continued to shrink as the white beam grew. If the Shadow Lord could sweat, he would be now. Then, suddenly, Mornak was grabbed again. The magic of the staff had worn off; his earthmen had fallen back into the ground, but the shadowmen had not been conjured. They, too, were from the Hall. They quickly took hold of Mornak again, this time tearing the staff from his grasp. Caught once more, he saw little chance of escape this time.

Black fire suddenly coursed through his body, making him cry out in pain. When it stopped, tendrils of smoke wafted up from his body. He looked up to find the source and saw the Shadow Lord holding his staff. "It amplifies magic," he said, admiring it. "Very impressive!"

Then the Shadow Lord walked up to him. For the first time, Mornak could make out his features, or perhaps, for the first time, he had features to make out. The Shadow Lord stood at the same height as Mornak, but he wore a gray and dark red fez with a golden gem at his forehead. The fez made him seem taller. The features on his bluish gray skin looked as though they had been carved from stone. His robes—black and dark blue with red trim—seemed to be partly made of shadows. They moved like something alive and changing. They reached out and merged with other shadows the Shadow Lord approached and seemed to melt off and separate from shadows left behind him. Long thick straight black hair hung from the Shadow Lord's head to just below his shoulders, and a beard in the style of the Egyptian pharaohs started below his lip and reached past his chin.

He stood above Mornak, holding out the staff.

"You don't mind if I keep this, do you?" Then he hit Mornak over the head with it, knocking him out. The Shadow Lord looked at the staff, smiling.

"Makes a good club, too."

* * *

Dara looked out to the storm from her balcony. She had seen the bursts of magic and knew that her father was fighting to protect her, to protect everyone. Her hands gripped the railing tightly as she nervously watched, hoping her father would win. Then the ring went out.

At first, she didn't do anything. She just stared at it. Then she suddenly understood that its light going out might mean that her father may have died. She could not believe that anything could defeat her father. She brought her hand closer to her face and shook it, hoping the ring's light would come back on. She tapped it with her finger and shook it again. Nothing happened. Then she remembered her father's words: "You will need to act quickly."

She ran back into her room to the chest that held the Scroll. The key to it hung on a chain around her neck. Grabbing the key, she tried to put it in the lock, only to yank her neck down in the process. She silently scolded herself, took the chain off, and tried the key again. She pulled the Scroll out in an instant and opened it to find out what her father's instructions were. To her surprise, the Scroll was blank.

* * *

Senufer realized that the woods were bewitched. Every now and then, he heard the call of an Axeman lost like him, but he could never locate the voice before it disappeared again. He would be lost in these woods forever unless he found a way out. Then it occurred to him that he didn't necessarily have to *find* a way out. He unsheathed Sun Stroke and Bone Chiller. With a few swipes from Sun Stroke, the tree before him fell in flames; a few taps from Bone Chiller put the flames out. The Axemen chop down all their enemies. This forest had just become his enemy. He was going to cut a path straight out of it.

*   *   *

Alex reread the same notes for the fifth time. He was getting nowhere. His mind kept wandering. He kept thinking about missing the audition and losing the gig—and maybe losing his friends. He kept thinking about missing the exam, losing a year of school, and really angering his parents. *If I were Scorpius, I could come up with some strategy to get out of this*, he thought, but that line of thinking didn't help the situation. He wasn't Scorpius, and he was never going to meet the guy to ask him what he'd do.

Alex was startled by the phone ringing. It was Tanya.

"So?" she said when he picked up.

"I dunno," he replied.

"You're gonna tell me before you go to bed, right?" she asked hopefully.

"I'll tell you when I know. For now, assume I'm going to the exam."

Tanya sighed. "Alex, a chance like this only comes along once in a lifetime."

"I know. I know. But even if we get the gig, my parents might not let me take it just because of what I did to get it. How did you set this up anyway?"

"Shadowland producers were at the bank to work out a deal with my dad," Tanya explained. Her father was the president of a major bank—Alex could never remember which one—so it was not unusual for Tanya to see or meet important executives and even stars when she visited her dad at work. Sometimes she'd visit because she knew they'd be there. Alex figured that she had done so here.

"I *ran into him* in the elevator," she told Alex, "and got him to agree to listen to us by the time we reached my dad's floor."

"A real elevator pitch," Alex noted. "Tanya, you're amazing."

"Yes, I am. And you had just better take advantage of my amazingness."

"Amazingness?"

"It's a Tanya word. Add it to your vocabulary!"

Alex laughed. Statements like that were among the reasons he liked her so much.

Then her voice took on a more serious tone. "Alex, it ... it just won't be the same if you're not there."

"I know. The sound won't be as—" Alex started to say.

"No! You big dope!" Tanya cut in. "It's you. It's not the sound. We can always get another guitarist, but the Axemen won't be the same without Alex Logan."

Alex felt like she was trying to say more, like she was holding back on something. Maybe Dax was right. Maybe she *did* like him, but she was afraid to tell him—maybe for the same reasons he was afraid to tell her. Then he shook his head. No, that was just wishful thinking.

"I'll call you as soon as I know," Alex said at last.

Tanya huffed. Alex knew that if she were in the room, she'd be giving him her I-know-what's-best look.

"Okay, okay," she relented. "Call me when you know. I hope you can't study. I hope you spill Coke on your texts. I hope ... I hope you're there tomorrow, Alex."

"Will you hate me if I'm not?"

"Never," she swore.

"Thanks. That's important to me."

"Damn! I should have said yes then!"

Alex laughed again. "Okay, I'll talk to you soon, Tanya."

"Good-bye ... Axeman," she said and hung up.

Alex sighed. She was right. If she had said she'd hate him, then that probably would have tipped the scales. He found it amazing that a decision, so hard when based on the facts, became a no-brainer when a girl was thrown in mix. However, this girl was so great that she didn't let her feelings influence his decisions, leaving him back where he started.

He returned to studying, feeling a little better and leaning toward the exam. He fell asleep at his desk somewhere in the late nineteenth century.

* * *

When he awoke, Mornak found himself chained to a wall with his hands spread apart above his head. He looked around to see a large chamber with an arched ceiling. Torches lined the walls, making the room light enough to see everything, but it still remained gloomy. Drawings, like those in ancient caves he had explored, covered the walls; pictures of people in despair and pain being tormented by shadows surrounded him. Mornak avoided looking at them as much as he could. A score of shadowmen stood in two lines leading away from him—dark, dangerous, and armed. They did not appear wispy and insubstantial as before. They were solid, threatening Shadow Warriors. Reclined on an ornate throne on the other side of the lines, the Shadow Lord eyed Mornak with a smile.

"Welcome back," the Shadow Lord greeted.

"Where—" Mornak began to ask, but the Shadow Lord expected the question.

"You are in the Hall of Shadows, of course," he said. "I knew you'd want to see it, and we wanted you awake for all the fun."

Mornak had trouble believing the situation. He had created the Hall, so he knew what was in it. He had never made this chamber or a throne for that matter. Had the Shadow Lord done this or had the Hall, now alive, reshaped itself? He doubted he would get all the answers and decided to focus on buying some time for himself.

"What *fun* is that?" Mornak asked.

"Tearing the life force from your body, of course," the Shadow Lord answered. "As you know, killing you now would cause the Hall of Shadows to fall apart, and as wonderful as the resulting chaos would be when all the evil in it is released, that's not what we want. The Hall wants to live and control the evil around it. In fact, it needs more. It has consumed some of the evil inside it to get this far, and it needs dark emotions—hatred, fear, despair, you know—to feed on.

"To make sure it lives on after we kill you, we first need to strip all your power from you. So we've brought you inside the Hall to do just that, and I imagine it will be a long painful process."

The Shadow Lord paused to let the words sink in. "It is only fitting that the thing you created to imprison us now becomes your own prison."

* * *

She remembered her father's lessons. *Some items are keyed to a specific magic or person and cannot be activated without them.*

"It's protected," Dara whispered to herself, "so that only I would be able to use it." She summoned the magic inside her, letting it flow into the Scroll. Soon, words appeared on it, and even though she did not know their meaning, she somehow knew they didn't form a spell. They activated magic within the Scroll. As she began to recite them, the Scroll began to glow with power.

* * *

The Shadow Lord shot dark energy into Mornak, making the wizard-king cry out in pain. His chains held him tightly and kept him from collapsing on the ground, but they also prevented him from casting any spells. Luckily, he didn't need to. He had only to hold out until he felt the call he was waiting for. He hoped Dara's abilities were up to the task. If not, Mythos would soon become worse than some of the mythic hells.

"You were so predictable, Mornak," the Shadow Lord taunted. "I knew you'd come to reinforce the Hall's power, and each time you did, you unknowingly added to mine. And this staff you've created will make me a more powerful wizard than you ever were." He strutted around confidently, enjoying his victory. Then he addressed the Shadow Warriors around him.

"We have our jailer, and soon we will suck his powers from him, making us more powerful than anything the realm has ever seen. We will spread through Mythos and plunge it into darkness. Glory to the Hall!"

The Shadow Warriors cheered in hollow, eerie voices.

The Shadow Lord turned his attention back to Mornak. "And you will watch it all happen from a cell in the Hall of Shadows."

Then Mornak felt a pull on his magic. He smiled. "You may have me, Shadow Lord, but you will never have my powers!" Mornak vowed. Then he screamed as the energy within him ripped away from his body. As he had planned, his powers were sucked out and sent across the distance to the waiting scroll. Even though he let it happen, even though he wanted it to happen, it was still agony.

"No!" the Shadow Lord screamed in anger, as loudly as Mornak cried in pain. He knew what was happening, but he had no idea how to stop it.

*　*　*

Dara closed her eyes as the Scroll lit up with a golden white light almost as bright as the sun. She held it as far away from her as she could until, at last, the light dimmed. To Dara's surprise, the Scroll did not appear as it had before. The parchment had thickened and become cream coloured with a silvery shine. The rollers, now solid gold, had runic designs engraved in them. It felt heavier. It felt powerful. Her father had once told her that powerful magical items had to be made from materials of the highest quality to hold the magic properly. Impure or defective items could leak magic or function incorrectly. She realized then that what she had seen before had been an illusion. This was the true Scroll. She stared in wonder as some writing inked itself on the parchment.

Thank you, Daughter.

"Father?" Dara asked.

The words faded off the Scroll, but more seemed to write themselves.

You are reading my thoughts. While you hold the Scroll open, we can communicate.

"Where are you? What's happened?"

I have been captured and am in a place where magic cannot help me. I have transferred my power into the Scroll, and only you can use it.

"But I don't know how to use your powers. I've only just learned a little from you."

I will teach you in time, but right now, time is short. You are in danger. You must leave.

"Leave? Leave the palace? But you said I was safe here."

They will think that I have sent my powers to a safe place in the palace. It is the first place they will come to look. You cannot be there when they do. If they get hold of the Scroll, the entire realm will be lost forever. There is a secret passage in my room behind the statue of your mother. It will take you out beyond the city walls. Go to the town of Kashla to the north and hide there. The leader of the city, Harrod, knows to help you. Do not try to get me out. After what just happened, they will ensure that I am shielded from magical means. My only link to the outside world is this mental tether with the Scroll. I will be with you again in time, but you must protect yourself until then. Be brave, Little Rose. Run, hide, and defend the Scroll.

Dara waited, but Mornak wrote no more. She stared at the Scroll, now blank again, and then closed it. Quickly gathering her clothes, some bread and cookies, a water skin, and some gold coins, she rushed to her father's chambers. It took some searching to find the switch that moved her mother's stature, but soon Dara was racing through the escape route.

*   *   *

Senufer had cut a path a hundred meters long. He hoped it was straight. Since he could only see a short distance in front and behind him, he kept moving back and forth along the path to try to make sure it didn't bend. His plan seemed to be working. He also hoped that some of the other Axemen might stumble into the path and follow it to him. The only problem might be if other Axemen had the same idea and were cutting their own paths. Then they would be unwittingly creating a maze of paths within the forest, only making matters worse.

He swung hard at the next tree, but before Sun Stroke connected, its flaming blade blew out. The handle of the axe hit the tree, and the impact sent a shock up Senufer's arm. He recovered quickly, spinning around into a defensive stance, thinking that someone nearby had dispelled the axes' enchantments. He waited several minutes before realizing the truth. Mornak's magic was gone, and to Senufer that meant only one thing: Mornak was gone as well. He dropped to his knees in hopelessness. Not only had he lost his king and best friend, but he and the Axemen would also be trapped in Shadow Wood forever. Who would protect the realm now?

*   *   *

The alarm clock blared, and Alex's head shot up from his desk. Drool covered his arm. He had managed to get bed head without being in bed, and his body ached from being bent over all night. So far, the day had not started well.

He had an hour to get ready and go to the audition or the exam. He still hadn't decided which. A quick shower later, he sniffed his Axemen shirt and decided it was clean enough to put on. Wearing the logo was important to him. During breakfast, he tried to go over history facts in his head but frowned at what he'd managed to store up there. Slipping his history books into his book bag and grabbing his guitar, he left his house and jumped on his bike for school. As he rode, he mentally drilled himself with questions and facts. The closer he got to school, the fewer facts he seemed to have in his head. It all seemed so clear last night, but maybe that was the imaginings of an exhausted mind.

His bike skidded to a stop at an intersection. *I don't know if I can do this*, he thought. *I really have a good chance of screwing this up.* He turned his head to the right, to the street that would take him to the audition. Then he looked back down toward the school a few blocks ahead of him. As he considered his choices, he ran his hand over his head, pushing his blonde hair back and then pulling it forward again.

A chance like this only comes along once in a lifetime, he remembered Tanya saying.

Alex knew better. Several of these chances would come along, but this may be the one that shot them to stardom. Having talent didn't mean automatic fame. You had to get the right person to listen to you when that person was in the right mood and socializing with the right people. Many variables, other than being good, came into play. That's why corporately formed groups topped the charts while extremely talented people had yet to get their big break.

Alex swung his bike around and shot up the street toward the audition. *Why wonder if you're going to fail an exam?* he thought. *Just fail it and get it over with*.

"Grade eleven, here I come again," he sighed.

Unless something special happened at this audition, he was about to lose most of his friends to the twelfth grade and spend the summer grounded. As the studio came into view, he hoped he had made the right decision.

3

*E*veryone in the realm felt it. A wave of darkness washed over the land, and as it passed, it chilled the spine. The sky darkened. The trees took on an eerie appearance. Flowers shriveled up and died. The howl of the wind seemed to be alive and suffering. Dogs and wolves howled back at it. Other animals ran away from it. The celebrations immediately stopped in every city in Mythos. People looked around at each other and up at the skies to find the source of the darkness. It did not show itself. Across the realm, evil creatures, hidden for so long, sensed the change as well and emerged from their holes. Some people panicked and swore the end of the world had come. They didn't realize that the world ending would be a blessing compared to what was about to come.

In Aspiria, many people flocked to the palace of Mornak only to be told that he was not there. They did not take the news well. Some tried to force their way in, and the palace guards had difficulty trying to stop them without seriously hurting anyone. Rumours of the cause circulated until, inevitably, someone suggested that the Hall of Shadows had been opened. Then a city, once united in celebration, united in panic. The city guards moved in quickly to try to stop it. People were told to return to their homes, but many did not listen. Fighting quickly broke out, and the guards were forced to hurt innocent people to keep them from harming each other.

The mention of the Hall did not go ignored, however. Guards took to the walls immediately; their sights set in the direction of Shadow Wood. For a time all they could see was a gloomy sky accented by the occasional lightning bolt striking the ground and destroying whatever it had struck. Tensions mounted when a lookout spotted movement in the direction of the Wood. Eventually, their fears were realized when an army marched from its direction. Legions of Shadow Warriors approached in formation, but not alone. From the fringes of their ranks, other creatures began to appear—dark creatures attracted by the scent of evil from the army. Ogres, trolls, ettins, and lizardmen soon joined the troops. The army grew as it approached, and the nerve of the guards slowly diminished. The walls of the city stood tall and strong, however, and the army brought no siege weapons. They felt safe, for now.

At the head of the army strolled the Shadow Lord. Beside him marched the general of the Shadow Warriors, Askar. Askar had gray skin like the Shadow Lord, but with a bluish hue. Blue beetle-like eyes peered from a wide face with a curved nose and crooked elflike ears. His dark brown hair ran in strips along his head from front to back where it merged into a short ponytail. Stocky and muscular, Askar had hands almost like claws. He wore blood red clothes over which hung plates of blue gray armour with golden trim. He had a sword sheathed in a scabbard on his hip, but he also held a large spiked mace with a rectangular head. The mace's metal handle hinted that it should be difficult to heft, yet he carried it as easily as a torch.

The army halted before the city—just out of range of the archers and catapults. Askar ordered a halt, but a few monsters on the outer edges, anxious for battle, began a charge of the city. Arrows cut them down in seconds, and a cheer went up from the defenders on the walls. The Shadow Lord shook his head in disgust.

"A foolhardy attempt, my lord," Askar agreed, "but without siege weapons, how are we to get any closer?"

"Stay with me," the Shadow Lord ordered. Then he and Askar left the ranks to approach the city.

Following tradition, two others—in this case, the captain of the city guards and a city diplomat—exited the city to meet them in parley.

"You would do well to turn your army around and leave this place," the diplomat began. "No army has ever penetrated our walls." He gestured around to the fallen monsters. "And that is what happened to all those who have tried."

The Shadow Lord smiled. "I have come to make you an offer. Open your gates to us, and the lives of most of your people will be spared. We do not wish to destroy this city. We only seek something within its walls. Be wise and spare the lives of your people."

The captain laughed at the absurdity of the statement. A hundred archers had their bows aimed right at the Shadow Lord and Askar. A dozen wizards also manned the wall with spells readied. Even with siege weapons and magic, it would take days, if not weeks, to breach the wall if such a feat were even possible. "Why in the hells don't you—" he began, but the diplomat cut him short.

"We wish no conflict with you. We wish only to live in peace. Please turn your army around and leave this field, or we will not be responsible for what happens to them."

"Clear a path to the palace," the Shadow Lord ordered.

"We will not!" yelled the captain.

"I wasn't talking to you," the Shadow Lord stated.

The great wall of the city then shook. The diplomat and guard turned to see what caused the disturbance. A section of the wall thrust out, taking the form of a great stone arm, and soon so did another. The wall above the arms crumbled to the ground, taking with it the men who had been standing there.

A giant head pulled free, its body following. It quickly became apparent that an entire section of the wall from top to bottom had come alive. Once free, it had an oddly comical look—almost like a giant cardboard cutout of a four-armed man—but this stone cutout towered five storeys high. The Shadow Lord had used the pretense of parley to get close enough to the wall to use the magic of the staff on it.

The stone giant left a great hole where it had been—easy access for the Shadow Lord's army into the city. But the army did not move. No one was willing to get in the giant's way. The guards on top of the walls ran in blind panic as sections around the giant collapsed as well. Screams of fear emanated from inside the city, and Askar smiled when he saw the fleeing citizens. Not everyone ran though. Wizards cast spells that melted or burned small sections of the stone giant, but the damage did little to slow it. Sergeants rallied their men to bring catapults to bear on it. Some even tried to attack it with swords and spears. The giant ignored them as it smashed open an even greater hole in the wall, taking out some wizards it seemed to find annoying. Then it began to make its way toward the palace, clearing a path as the Shadow Lord had ordered. People dashed about, trying not to be trampled by the giant, but it paid them no heed. It merely swept trees, buildings, and anything else out of the way so that the Shadow Lord could proceed unhindered.

While the captain and the diplomat stood stunned by the spectacle, Askar leapt forward, dispatching them both. Then he raised his mace high, and the army of the Shadow Lord surged forth.

*   *   *

Dara ran for as long as she could and then collapsed. She didn't know about pacing herself. She didn't know about moving stealthily. She was only eleven, and she was scared. So she stuck to the road to keep from getting lost, but that made her easy to spot, and knowing that only added to her fear. Mornak had meant for her to be accompanied by guards, not for her to go on her own without protection. He thought she would have summoned several of them to escort her. She knew they were trustworthy. But he had told her what to do, not what he meant for her to do. In her urgency, she had not thought it through. She had done what he had said, not what he had meant, and so, alone and frightened, she fled through a world that had just become a realm of shadows.

Hearing a cart coming up from behind her, she dashed off the road. Staying low, she didn't even check to see who drove the cart. She wouldn't even look up from the ground. She was too frightened. If someone had jumped off the cart, he could have walked right up to her, and she wouldn't have seen him looking down at her. Luckily, no one did. Her heart raced in her chest. Her stomach seemed to flip inside her. She knew she could not make it to Kashla on her own. She needed someone to protect her.

Making her way farther from the road to some nearby trees, she pulled out the Scroll again.

"Papa, I'm scared. I need help," she said to it but received no response. She sat against one of the trees and cried. She cried as quietly as she could, but she couldn't stop for a long time.

Then she remembered her father's words. *I have transferred my power into the Scroll, and only you can use it.*

Perhaps she could use the Scroll to protect herself. The problem was that she knew only one spell. *Maybe that's all I need*, she thought. She could summon butterflies, and her father said that one day she would be able to summon people. With the power of the Scroll, perhaps she could do that now. But whom could she summon? Who would be strong and wise enough to protect her other than her father? The answer came at once. She placed the Scroll in her lap and began to cast, pulling its energy into herself. Focusing her thoughts, she summoned the leader of the Axemen.

*   *   *

When Alex arrived in the studio, everyone stopped what they were doing and stared at him. Tanya broke the silence yelling, "You made it!" as she ran up and hugged him.

"'Once in a lifetime,' you said," he told her as he hugged her back.

Tanya smiled, kissed his cheek, and then rushed back to her keyboards. Alex followed her onto the stage. The full studio was the size of a classroom, only with a higher ceiling and a stage set against the back wall. A glass wall down the middle of the room separated the sound stage from the recording booth, in which the producer, a techie, and what looked to Alex like the producer's personal assistant sat. The assistant, a stocky nervous man, looked as though his main job was to suck up to his boss. The producer, a big man with a large gut, wore jeans, a dress shirt, and sports jacket. He hadn't shaved this morning.

Maybe we weren't considered worth the effort, Alex thought but then pushed the negative thought from his mind. He climbed onto the stage and knocked fists with Glenn, the drummer, a small Filipino with short hair and a goatee. He nodded to Scott. With his height and broad shoulders, Scott looked more like a teen heartthrob than did Alex. Dark brown hair hung to his shoulders and framed chiseled features that made the teen look a few years older. He wore the same clothes as Alex, but he also sported a black leather jacket over his T-shirt. Big Bamm, a Jamaican-born bass guitarist, towered over the other members of the band. He dressed like a cross between a hippie and a Rastafarian. His large Afro lifted skyward, pushed up by a large red headband. Bamm patted Alex on the back as the lead Axeman took center stage and plugged in his guitar.

Alex checked the microphone and then addressed the producer. "I'd just like to say thank you for seeing us on such short notice ..." He realized he didn't know the man's name. "Sir."

The producer nodded slightly but didn't say anything. It suddenly occurred to Alex that this guy might only be listening to them to gain points with Tanya's dad. He looked as though he didn't really want to be here, and from the expression on his face, he didn't expect much from them. Alex realized that if he didn't play his heart out, they had as much chance of getting a contract as he had of passing the history exam. Worse, he just realized that he didn't know what song to play. A trickle of sweat ran down his back, giving him a wet tickling sensation. He turned back to Tanya, who mouthed "Little Rose." He nodded and addressed the others.

"Ready, guys?" Alex asked. The others nodded.

"One, two, three, four!"

Alex struck his first chord hard so hard that the amp shorted out. An electric surge raced through his guitar, throwing Alex back with surprising force. He tumbled off the stage, somehow getting his foot caught in his book bag. Despite the shock of the current in his body, he had enough sense to know the fall would hurt. He braced himself for the expected impact. It never came.

The next thing Alex knew, he was tumbling through some sort of vortex. The studio pulled away from him into the distance as his body seemed to stretch out toward some unknown destination.

I've been sucked into a black hole! he thought.

He saw Tanya's concerned face in the distance, but she already seemed a world away. He reached for her anyway, but by then, there were only swirling colours and a feeling of nausea. Then, just as suddenly as things had started, they stopped.

Alex hit the ground—actual ground—not the floor. He sat on his butt outside somewhere—no longer in the studio, no longer even in the city.

"What the heck just happened?" he exclaimed.

Alex stood up and looked around. He realized that he was alone and saw no familiar landmarks of any kind. Even the sky, which had been clear blue on his bike ride in, was a cloudy metal gray now; the area seemed unusually dark for midmorning. His guitar hung around his neck with two broken strings. His books littered the ground around his bag. He stood in a small grove of trees just before a dark forest that shot off in either direction as far as he could see. The woods made him nervous, so he took a step away from them. The branches of the trees almost seemed to be reaching out toward him.

Not a good place to go, he thought and turned around. Behind him in the distance, he thought he could make out a dirt road across a small field. Something in this place—other than the fact that he couldn't possibly be there—felt wrong; something made him shiver, even though it was not cold.

"This has to be a dream," he said aloud. "That's it! I was knocked unconscious by the power surge. They're probably trying to wake me now, or I'm being rushed to the hospital. I just have to ride this out until I wake up. Why doesn't it feel like a dream, though?"

Then the reality of the dream sunk in. "Oh man, I just shocked myself out of the audition! Now I've blown it *and* the exam!" he yelled.

"What's an exam?" he heard a voice ask. He jumped, hearing the sound, and searched for its source. From behind a tree, a little girl poked her head out and stared at him. "You're not the leader of the Axemen," she said disappointedly.

"Yes, I am!" Alex argued.

"Then where's your axe?" she asked.

"I don't use an axe. I use a guitar."

"Warriors don't use musical instruments," the girl argued.

"Who said I was a warrior?" Alex argued back. "Wait a sec. Who are you?"

"My name is Dara. I am the princess of Mythos."

"Of course you are," Alex said sarcastically. "And you've summoned me here to protect you from the evil overlord and save the world, right?"

"What evil overlord?"

"Come on. There *must* be an evil overlord. Where there's a princess, there's always an evil overlord or, like, a witch or a dragon or something."

Dara assumed that Alex spoke from personal experience. "You must be very powerful to have dealt with so many dangers," she said, feeling better about the mix-up already. She came out from behind the tree and approached him.

"Yeah, sure," Alex said uninterestedly. "I'm the most powerful weapon master in all the world. Villains tremble before my might. Yada yada yada."

Dara glowed with admiration. "Please, sir … sir …?"

"Alex."

"Please, Sir Alex—"

"No, just Alex."

"Please, Alex, my father has sent me to a city north of here, but I got scared and tried to summon the leader of my father's Axemen. I got you instead. Will you be my protector until my father can escape his prison?"

It's just a dream, so just play along, Alex told himself. "Of course I will, Princess Darla."

"It's Dara, sir."

"Oh, sorry." He rubbed her head. "Now point me in the direction of this city, and we'll be off."

Dara pointed up to the road in the distance, and they began to walk.

"So, summon people often?" Alex asked.

"You are the first person I've ever summoned. I didn't even know if I could do it," Dara answered.

"Lucky me," Alex said.

The snapping of a branch drew Alex's attention back to the forest. A guttural growl followed as a pair of glowing yellow eyes appeared in the trees, and then another set appeared. Slowly, a large canine head pulled free from the darkness with a second head close by it. Both snarled at Alex, and only when they came a few paces farther, did Alex see that both heads shared the same body—a body as big as his own.

"Now I know I'm dreaming," he muttered.

The chink of metal sounded as the dog's chain was pulled back. Someone was holding it, someone big. As his huge legs came into view, Alex thought it was an ogre. Twice his height, it was certainly big enough to be one. The hairy creature wore animal-skin clothes and had an ugly, caveman-like face with two

big fangs protruding from its lower jaw. When Alex saw that it too had two heads, he corrected himself. "Ettin. Crap."

"I'll need a sword," he said, and then he willed one to appear in his hand. This was a dream after all. But no sword magically sprang forth. Things began to feel far too real for Alex. Dream or not, they needed to get out of there.

"Dara?" he checked. She had moved herself right behind him.

"Yes, sir?"

"Run!"

They turned and bolted. In response, the ettin let loose his pet and readied a large club. Alex could have easily outrun Dara, but he kept pace just behind her. The dog closed quickly, and Alex knew it would take them both down. So he turned and stood his ground holding his guitar like a bat. As the beast leaped for him, he swung hard. The guitar smashed against one of its heads, snapping off at the handle, before the dog barreled into Alex. They both went down, but Alex scrambled quickly to his feet. The dog shook one of its heads, but the other head, the one the guitar had struck, hung unconscious.

Then the dog saw Dara, still running, and turned toward her, but Alex threw what was left of his guitar at it to get its attention. It turned back to him, snarling.

"Way to play the hero, Alex," he told himself, and then he bolted away again.

To Dara, Alex seemed insane because he was running back toward the ettin that was now marching toward him. Alex wasn't trying to get to the ettin though; he was trying to get to his book bag. He hoped that if he stuffed those heavy texts back in the bag, it might make a decent weapon. The dog was too fast though, and clipped Alex's calf just as he reached the bag and the books. As Alex tumbled down, the dog launched itself on top of him. He grabbed the nearest book and smacked the beast in the face with it. It let out a small yelp but then got even angrier. When it moved in to bite him, Alex stuffed the book in the animal's mouth. It ground the book and spat it out. Alex grabbed another book and opened it to try to shield as much of himself as he could.

"Help!" he muttered.

Suddenly a flash of light came out of the book, startling the dog but not Alex, whose eyes were now closed tight with fear. When the dog's bite did not come, Alex opened his eyes. The animal had turned its attention to someone else, and Alex couldn't believe who it was—Scorpius.

Dressed in his red leather armour with its silver chest plate and bronze shoulder guards, the Roman legionnaire stood in a battle stance that showed years of training as he faced off with the dog. Unlike Alex, Scorpius had a sword and a shield. Alex looked at the book he was holding. It was *Legend and Lore*, and he had opened it to the page with Scorpius's portrait on it. Only the page was now blank.

The dog lunged at Scorpius, but the Roman easily dodged the attack and drove his sword into the creature's side as it passed. It yelped as it crashed to the earth, whimpering from the pain. With a final effort, the dog tried to get back up, but the wound was fatal. The second head went as limp as the first, and the dog fell dead on the ground. Scorpius then turned his sword toward Alex.

"You!" he threatened. "Why did you attack?"

"Not me!" Alex interrupted and pointed at the ettin who was now bearing down on them and who seemed very upset that his pet had been killed. "Him!"

The Roman's eyes went wide when he saw the huge creature. The ettin roared and charged Scorpius. Scorpius yelled and charged the ettin. Alex could not believe his eyes. The ettin was twice Scorpius's size. The Roman could not hope to win a clash like that. He didn't.

The ettin swung its club at Scorpius, but instead of countering with his sword or blocking with his shield, the Roman dived down and used his body to trip the monster. When the ettin fell, its club went flying from its hands. Scorpius leaped up from the ground and attacked the monster at once. He stabbed its leg, but then had to jump back to avoid a kick. The ettin tried to get up, but Scorpius moved back in, slashing its side. The ettin howled and swung at him, but its hand connected with his shield, which made it scream in pain. Scorpius swung again, slashing its arm. Then the monster lunged up, but not at Scorpius. It moved off to the side and limped off back into the woods, whimpering as it went.

Scorpius turned back to Alex and began to speak, but as mysteriously as he appeared, he vanished. Alex opened the book again and looked at the page. The portrait had returned.

*   *   *

The Shadow Lord grew impatient. The ransacking of the palace had revealed nothing so far. The vault contained only useless gold and gems. What secret rooms he found held no trace of Mornak's missing powers although the magical traps in them had destroyed several of his Shadow Warriors.

He was about to lash out at a palace servant just to release some of his anger when he sensed it. He recognized the feel of Mornak's magic at once. Someone was using it for powerful casting, but not in the palace—not even in the city. The magic was north, somewhere north. He would move his men out of the city and comb the countryside. Finding the holder of Mornak's magic was all that mattered.

4

"X-men!" Alex grunted as he tightened the bandage (made from part of his shirt) around his calf. It hurt like hell, and the pain alone told him that this might not be a dream after all. He'd been hurt in his dreams before, but never had the pain been so vivid, so real.

Alex and Dara had returned to the small grove of trees to stay out of sight while Alex figured out what to do and just how to wake himself up. Dara sat in front of him, watching him curiously.

"Are you a wizard?" she asked.

"No," Alex replied. "Why?"

"You conjured that warrior to save us," Dara answered and, after a pause, added, "and it is very obvious that you're not a warrior."

"Oh, really?"

"Any real warrior could have killed that beast, but you made us run."

"I didn't have a weapon."

"But when the thing had you pinned down you screamed like ... like ... well, like a little girl."

"Can we drop the subject please?"

"But—"

"I said drop it!" Frustrated, Alex yanked his bandage tight and screamed from the pain he caused himself.

"You sounded kind of like that, only higher," Dara commented.

Alex's glare made Dara shut up, finally.

He picked up *Legend and Lore* and examined it. Then he opened it to the page with Scorpius and held it out. "Scorpius! Come forth!" he commanded.

Nothing.

He shook it and tried again.

Nothing.

He closed and reopened it.

Nothing.

He lay down on the ground in the same position as when the dog had pinned him.

Nothing.

He tried just holding it and willing it to work.

Nothing.

"We have to find out how this works," he said to himself as much as Dara. "You enchanted it when you brought me here, right?"

"I don't know."

"Did you enchant me then?"

"I don't know."

"Okay, how exactly does the spell work? And don't you dare say, 'I don't know.'"

"I'm not sure."

"Oh, that's *much* better."

"I'm sorry, sir."

"I said, 'Call me Alex.'"

"I'm sorry, Alex, but my father only taught me that one spell, and I've only used it to summon butterflies until you."

"Then let's go find your father."

"But he's a prisoner."

"Yeah, but where?"

"I don't know," Dara replied and winced, expecting Alex to yell at her.

He was about to do just that, but the helpless look on Dara's face drove the anger from him. He let out a big breath and calmed himself down. Yelling at the little girl wasn't going to help him.

"Okay, your father is being held by some evil people somewhere, and we need to rescue him, right?"

"No, he says he will find a way to free himself. We just need to stay safe until he does."

"Hold up. How could he tell you that, if he's a prisoner and you don't know where?"

"He can talk to me through this magic scroll," Dara said, holding it up.

"What?"

"I said—" Dara began, this time speaking more loudly.

Alex stopped her. "I heard you. Girl, don't you think I could have used that little piece of info right off? Open the Scroll, and let's talk with him."

"I tried earlier, but he didn't answer."

"Hmm," Alex thought aloud as he remembered various books he had read and movies he had seen. "I'll bet there was probably someone, like, in the room, and he didn't want them to catch him. Try again."

Dara opened the Scroll and let her magic flow into it. "Papa?"

I am here, Little Rose.

"Little Rose," Alex read, his stomach churning all of a sudden. *Now I know this a dream*, he thought. *Old memories surfacing from my subconscious.* He looked at Dara. She was so different and yet—

He pushed the thoughts from his mind and focused on the task at hand, on the Scroll. "Excuse me, sir. My name is Alex, and I need to ask you some questions."

The words on the Scroll faded away. Alex and Dara exchanged glances.

"Maybe he doesn't want to talk to me," Alex guessed.

Dara focused again. "Papa? Will you not answer Alex's questions?"

I can only hear you, Dara. Who is this Alex?

Dara explained what had happened to her father and then acted as a go-between for Mornak and Alex to communicate, mentally repeating everything Alex said for him.

"So how does this book work?" Alex asked, referring to *Legend and Lore*.

I could not tell you for certain. The spell Dara cast was far beyond her level. The magic must have caused some unforeseen effects. The book may have either conjured the warrior for a short time or geas summoned him. Or perhaps he was just a powerful illusion.

"Geas summoned?" Dara asked Alex since he seemed to understand.

Alex smiled. He liked knowing more than *someone* around there. "Summoned to perform a specific task and then returned."

"You must be a wizard to know such things."

"You don't have to be a wizard to know things, Dara." He went back to talking to the Scroll. "So the other books may be enchanted, too?"

Quite possibly, but they may not be enchanted the same way.

"Yeah, I get it. Hold on a sec."

Alex got up and walked over to the books. He knew exactly what he wanted—the book on military history. He was going to summon an army. The creatures of this world would be no match for tanks and heavy artillery. When he found the book, he cursed. Torn and shredded, it was the one he had stuffed into the dog's mouth. He stared at it a while and then began to laugh.

"What is so funny?" Dara asked.

"That dog ate my homework," Alex said and laughed louder.

Dara just stared at him like she thought he was losing his mind.

He stopped laughing and sighed. "All my jokes are going to be useless here."

Alex was left with two books, *Historic Inventions* and *Historical Moments in Time*. He knew the second book would be useless for summoning, but perhaps it could serve some other purpose though he had no clue what that might be. He placed the two books, along with *Legend and Lore*, in his book bag. Then he went back to talk to the Scroll.

"So, what about some muscle? Any warriors you can hook us up with?"

"Hook you up?" Dara asked.

"Introduce us to."

The Shadow Lord defeated my city guards when he invaded Aspiria, and my Axemen are trapped in Shadow Wood.

"Trapped how?"

There is a spell of misdirection on the wood preventing them from finding each other or the way out.

"But these Axemen are good warriors?"

The best knights in the realm.

"I say we get them out then."

If you enter Shadow Wood, you will only get lost yourselves, and you cannot take the Scroll to the lair of our enemy. It is what they seek, and at that distance, the Hall or the Shadow Lord would surely sense it.

"So, if they get this scroll, then they become, like, all-powerful, and the realm is doomed. What if we just destroy the Scroll?"

Then the magic that binds the Hall of Shadows would come undone, destroying it.

"But that's a good thing, isn't it?"

The Hall is a prison to the evil in the land. If it were to be destroyed, then all the evil would escape uncontrolled, and the world would become a veritable hell. What you see around you is a controlled release of the Hall's power. As bad as things seem, they could be a great deal worse. Also, the release of energy from destroying the Scroll would incinerate everything around it for hundreds of meters.

"Okay, we won't destroy the Scroll. Good safety tip. So we just have to keep it from them? For how long?"

A powerful wizard, using the magic of the Scroll, could defeat the Hall without unleashing its evil. There are several in the realm. Dara has the potential, but I fear she is still too young and inexperienced to do anything now.

"Hold on. Hold on. Hold on. If they just need this Scroll, then why are they keeping you around?"

The Scroll contains my magic, and I am tied to it. If the Hall were to kill me, the Scroll would be destroyed as well.

"And then the Hall, too," Alex concluded. "I get it." Glancing over at Dara, he knew he couldn't ask his next question with her listening. "Mornak, is there any way I can talk to you privately?"

Hold the Scroll while Dara holds it and think to me. Have Dara close her eyes or look away.

Alex turned to her. "Dara, look away, please."

Dara shook her head. "What do you have to say to my father that I cannot hear?"

"Grown-up stuff."

"You're not grown-up!"

"More than you. Now turn away."

Dara finally turned in a huff, and Alex grabbed hold of the Scroll, making sure that Dara wasn't peeking.

You told Dara you'd escape, but with your magic in the Scroll, there's no way you can, is there? Alex thought at it.

No.

So why tell her that then?

So she would have hope. So I could direct her to others that may be able to help. If she thinks for a moment that I am lost to her, I fear that she will not be able to handle it.

She's gotta be told at some point.

We have not yet reached that point. You seem a good soul, Alex. Please watch over my daughter. She is my light, and she holds the hope of the realm.

Alex didn't really want to commit to anything right then. He really just wanted out of this crazy world, but what do you say when an imprisoned man asks you to look after his helpless eleven-year-old daughter?

I'll do my best, sir, he replied in thought. Then an idea occurred to him. *Could you defeat the Hall if you were free?*

Now that I know what has happened, I believe so.

Can the Hall ... um ... see? Alex asked.

No. From what I have been able to determine, it needs the eyes or spells of others to see anything outside of itself.

So someone could walk right up to it, and it wouldn't know. Does it have guards outside?

I believe it sent all its warriors to conquer Aspiria.

Then if we could find a way to, like, remove the misdirection spell, we could gather the Axemen and strike at the Hall while its warriors are away.

A bold plan, but risky. The Shadow Lord has returned to the Hall to better direct all his men. His magic is formidable.

What do you suggest then? We can't just keep running.

I have allies in the city to the north. They will already be watching for Dara. Go there and

And? And what?

No response.

"He's gone," Alex said aloud.

Dara turned back to look at the blank Scroll. "What should we do now?"

"We head north."

Just then more writing appeared on the Scroll.

The Shadow Warriors are getting close to you. You must run! Now!

*   *   *

A section of the wall of the chamber shimmered and displayed an image of Dara and Alex reading the Scroll. The Shadow Lord stood before it, watching the scene, although he could not make out the writing on the Scroll or hear what was being said.

Is this strange one a wizard?

The voice of the Hall of Shadows seemed to come from everywhere in the chamber.

"No," the Shadow Lord answered. "I do not sense any magic in him. His bag and the Scroll both emanate strong magic, however. The Scroll, especially. I believe it is the receptacle of Mornak's power."

Wise. The Scroll is powerful yet fragile. We cannot simply incinerate them with a fireball or drown them in the sea for fear of destroying it.

"Agreed," said the Shadow Lord. "We must be ... delicate. The girl seems to be the keeper. It is tied to her life force or her magic, no doubt. We may need to capture her as well as the Scroll. For now, we dare not risk killing her. Mornak has thought this through carefully, ensuring the safety of his magic and his daughter in one action."

Where are your men?

The Shadow Lord gestured, causing the image to zoom out. He could see a line of his warriors less than a kilometer from the pair.

They will close with the children in a few minutes.

The Shadow Lord smiled.

"Get Mornak," he ordered a guard in the room.

* * *

Mornak sat chained to the center of a large circular room. He no longer looked like a man of forty but appeared over twice that age. His hair had whitened; his skin had wrinkled and showed dark spots here and there. He wasn't any thinner, but his muscles were worn. His spell had not only sucked out his current power but also the life force within him, which would have created more power over the course of his life. It held more power than anything in the realm, except possibly the Hall of Shadows, but the Hall's power was still growing. Mornak was but a shadow of his former self—fitting, considering where he was. With his power and life force drained from his body, all that kept him going was his will and his love for life, especially his daughter's life. He would last as long as he needed to ensure her safety. He knew the Shadow Lord would not kill him—not intentionally—but he also had to hold onto the desire to not want to die, no matter what the Shadow Lord put him through. Dara's safety gave him that desire.

Five equally spaced torches hung along the wall around him. Each one cast a shadow of Mornak on the ground. Each shadow moved of its own accord. They spoke in eerie voices and reshaped themselves for brief periods.

One mimicked the shadow of Dara and said, "Oh, Papa, how could you leave me all alone? I'm so scared, Papa." Then it reverted to Mornak's shape and added, "Papa doesn't love you, girl."

One pretended to be a helpless man pleading, "Please, Mornak, save me from the Hall of Shadows."

Another hissed, "Save you? I'll send you there myself!" and dived onto the first shadow.

All five shadows continued to torment Mornak without pause, without rest. For a time, Mornak feared that they may achieve their goal and drive him mad, but then he felt Dara's call. He sat on the floor, closed his eyes, and tried to block out the sounds around him as he spoke to her in his mind. The shadows did not like that, but being only shadows, they could not touch him.

The door to the cell opened, and the guard came in, disrupting Mornak's thoughts while he still held the link to his daughter. The guard detached Mornak from the floor and pulled him into the audience chamber where he saw the shimmering magical wall.

The Shadow Lord looked to him with a smile. "My warriors are not far now. They will have your daughter in just a few minutes."

The Shadow Lord enjoyed the look of worry on Mornak's face when the wizard realized how close Dara was to being captured. As the Shadow Lord turned back to look at the wall himself, Mornak sent a final message and broke the link. A moment later, the two youths in the scene were running away from the troops, and the image faded.

What happened?

"I lost them," the Shadow Lord explained. "They must have stopped using the Scroll. No matter. The warriors are upon them. It won't be long now."

*   *   *

Alex and Dara saw the Shadow Warriors—scores of them—far to the south, heading their way. They began running north, but as Alex looked at the open ground with no real hiding spots, he didn't like their odds of escaping that way. He stopped suddenly and looked back east toward the forest. Dara skidded to a halt when she noticed that Alex wasn't moving. She followed his gaze to the trees and hoped that the ettin hadn't returned. That was the last thing they needed. Then Alex grabbed her hand and pulled her toward the forest. "This way!" he said.

Dara pulled back. "But the ettin is that way!"

"Exactly," Alex smiled. Dara didn't like that smile. It told her trouble was coming.

They picked up the ettin's trail easily enough. Broken branches, blood, and crushed plants clearly marked his route.

As they moved, Alex's plan became clear to Dara. "You mean to lead the men to the ettin."

"Yep."

"But he's badly injured already. They'll defeat him in seconds and be after us again."

"Ettins are tribal," Alex explained. "He's most likely heading home."

Dara pulled Alex to a halt. "Alex, that's crazy! We have no weapons. We'll be caught between a cliff and a stampede."

"A cliff and a ..." Alex started to repeat, but then he got the reference. "Oh! Caught between a rock and a hard place."

Dara shot him a puzzled expression. "That's hardly the same thing!"

Alex yanked her, and they started off again.

"I don't plan on us being between them," said Alex. "We'll use Scorpius to attract the ettin tribe. I'm sure they'll be eager for revenge. He'll lead them right to the guys following us."

"But you still don't know how to summon him!" argued Dara.

"Details, details."

Several minutes later they came in sight of the ettin village. Alex handed the book to Dara. "Here. Find Scorpius's page," he told her. "And see if you can figure out how to summon him while I check things out." Then he snuck close to the village for a better look.

The ettin village was made up of wood and stone shacks with a large fire pit in the center of the homes. Several dozen ettins milled about, all dressed in animal skins. Most had clubs, but some had swords and shields—no doubt acquired in battle since the village didn't have anything resembling a forge. Many of the tribe had gathered near the wounded ettin as he, Alex guessed, told them what had just happened to him. The others did not seem pleased.

"Good," whispered Alex. He went back to Dara.

Dara had the book opened, but not to Scorpius's page. She held it up for Alex to see.

"What about her?" she asked.

Alex saw a picture of an Amazon archer, her long hair almost black, but with a touch of dark red in it.

"What about her?" Alex asked.

"I was afraid Scorpius could get caught or killed by the men or the ettins, so I looked to see who else was in the book. This girl can shoot arrows from a distance to make them attack each other and still be able to get away."

Light flashed from the book, and the Amazon stood before them. Her mocha skin and thick straight hair revealed her East Indian heritage, which struck Alex as strange since Amazon women supposedly lived in Turkey. At sixteen, her cheeks still held a little baby fat in them, making her face more cute than beautiful. Her body was lean and muscular though. She wore a tan warrior's dress with boots, a belt, and an archer's glove all made of brown leather. A tan headband kept her hair out of her face, and gold armbands and a necklace accessorized her body. She had a slightly upturned nose, full lips, and big brown eyes. Despite the cuteness in her face, she had an air of wildness about her. Her long hair accentuated that wildness. Alex could sense that in his world, she'd be into fast cars and extreme sports. Now, though, she had the same confused look that both Alex and Scorpius had when they first arrived. Spotting Alex, she grabbed an arrow and raised her bow, aiming for Alex's head.

"Um ... sorry," Dara whimpered. "I didn't mean to."

The Amazon turned quickly to Dara's direction but kept her bow trained on Alex. She calmed down when she saw the little girl, quickly turning back to focus on the male threat again.

"We're friends," Alex said.

"You are a man," the Amazon stated. "That makes you no friend of mine. How did I get here?"

Alex pointed at Dara when he answered. "She accidentally summoned you. Um, sorry?"

The girl glanced quickly at Dara again. "She is a witch?"

"Wizard's apprentice, actually," Alex corrected, "but that's not really the issue here."

The Amazon nodded. "Yes, the issue is that you are a fool to kidnap me when you have no weapons with which to challenge me."

Alex sighed. "Look, we didn't mean to bring you here," he explained, "but now that you're here, you need to help us out if you wanna get back home."

"I need to do nothing," she hissed.

Alex could hear the bow tighten, but despite the threat she posed, another greater danger concerned him. The Shadow Lord's men were closing in on them with each passing second.

"We don't have much time, so I'll explain quickly," said Alex. "Dara, here, summoned you to distract some two-headed monsters called ettins, over there, into fighting some bad guys over there," he said pointing each way. "You're stuck here until you do that, and then you'll automatically be returned home."

"Auto-matic-ally?" she asked.

"Instantly. Right away," Alex explained.

She mulled over the words, and as she did, she knew them to be true. The summons had placed the goal within her. She could feel it. She lowered the bow. Alex visibly relaxed again.

"Where are the ettins?" she asked. As an Amazon, she knew what the creatures were, although she had never actually seen one.

"In a village just over there," replied Alex. "Just give us some time to get clear of here."

"You expect me to do this alone? I'll be caught between men and monsters."

Alex smiled. "You mean caught between a rock and a hard place?"

"No," she said flatly, "you just told me I'll be caught between men and monsters."

"Oh yeah," he said, feeling stupid. "Look, as soon as they're distracted, you'll be sent home, so you don't have to worry."

"And if I'm not?"

Alex had to think for a while. Finally, he took the book from Dara, pointed south and said, "We'll be this way. Catch up to us." He held up the book. "If your picture appears on this page, we'll know you were sent back. If it doesn't, we'll wait for you. Okay, Maya?"

She looked at him untrustingly. "How do you know my name?"

Alex pointed at the text in the book. "It's written right here."

Then they heard noises eastward from the ettin village and then westward from the approaching warriors.

"We have to go," said Alex.

"Fine. Go," Maya replied coldly.

Dara and Alex moved south quickly but carefully, trying to leave as little trail as possible. Maya moved toward the village, soon spying a wounded ettin being cared for by two others. Nearby, some warrior types chatted with each other in their native tongue. Several prepared for battle while a few others relaxed. One was eating a leg of meat with one head while drinking a mug of ale with another. Maya smiled. She took aim, timed her shot, and let loose an arrow. It shot through the leg, then the cup, and into a tree. One head of every ettin stared in shock at the skewered items on the arrow while the other head scanned the area for the shooter.

"Two heads can be useful," Maya commented. She smiled, waved to them, and then ran off toward the Shadow Warriors, spotting them quickly. She was only supposed to distract them, but they were men, so she thought she might as well get some enjoyment out of this adventure and drew her bow. Her shot hit a Shadow Warrior between the eyes. His head jerked back, and he fell. To Maya's surprise, just before the man hit the ground, his body dissipated into shadowy smoke. The others locked in on her location and charged. She dashed away, taking her position right between both groups. She looked at her hands.

"I don't seem to be disappearing," she thought aloud as she took cover behind some trees.

The groups closed in, and she waited for them to see each other. Suddenly, a hand grabbed her shoulder and spun her around. A Shadow Warrior, who had been flanking the main group, held a sword ready to swing. He paused, obviously confused by her. He had expected the boy or the little girl they'd been ordered to find.

"Who are you?" he challenged. "What are you doing here?"

Just then Maya felt herself being pulled away from reality as a short distance away the Shadow Warriors and ettins clashed. The warrior in front of her saw her stick out her tongue at him before his sword cut through the air where she once stood.

5

*H*ow?!

The room shook when the Hall heard the news.

How could they escape?

"We do not know," the Shadow Lord stated. "Askar just reported that they were unable to find the children. A strange female archer was seen, who apparently disappeared into thin air. She may have aided them in some way. Also, we lost some warriors to a group of ettins," the Shadow Lord stated.

Inconsequential.

"No," the Shadow Lord argued. "You cannot simply create new warriors at will. And with your power spread out so far to darken the realm, you cannot enact any magics outside of yourself. You can only feed until your magics are replenished."

I have fed on the fear and despair of the people of Aspiria, and greater numbers of people around the realm are now adding to my power.

"You are still vulnerable—and you will continue to be so—until we get that Scroll. You still have a limit to your power, and only the Scroll can remove that limit. It's a good thing we've taken ... precautions."

The Shadow Lord could see that the Hall, as powerful as it was, thought itself invincible. That was not a good thing. Still fairly new to this world, the Hall was a child in some ways—but an extremely powerful one. He needed to guide the Hall without making it feel as if it was being mentored. Invincible beings didn't like that.

Where are the children now?

"I don't know. I can only track them when they use the Scroll. We may have to wait until they do so again, but the warriors are searching regardless of that. It is only a matter of time before they are found. They were heading north, probably for Kashla. We will take the city and be there when they arrive."

* * *

Alex and Dara neared the edge of the forest, and Alex was happy to get out of there. The place gave him the creeps. He felt like the trees might have reached down and grabbed him at any time. Looking out at the landscape, he didn't see much improvement. The hilly expanse looked decayed and treacherous. To the west, a mountain range ran north and south like a giant wall, its tallest peaks capped with snow. Scattered in several places to the south were patches of trees and bushes. If they moved in a zigzag pattern, they could use them for cover in case someone followed from the north. To the southwest, Alex could just make out wagons moving along the road that he guessed Dara had taken from her city. He doubted that the people driving the wagons could spot them but decided to move southeast, just in case. Checking the book again before starting off, he was relieved to see Maya's picture. "She's back," he told Dara.

Dara nodded and smiled. They walked a bit longer before Dara asked, "Why did she say you were no friend of hers?"

Alex smiled at the thought of having met an Amazon. "The Amazons are a group of warrior women who hate men and live without them."

Dara cocked her head at him. "No men? At all?"

"Yep."

"Their home would be a paradise," Dara cooed.

"Why do girls always think that? I know quite a few of you. You're not perfect."

"But imagine a world without men to start wars or rule unjustly—"

"You don't think a woman can rule unjustly?"

"Far fewer than men. Men focus on power and conquering. Women would never aspire to that."

"I think you underestimate the aspirations of some women," Alex smirked.

"I would very much love to visit their home."

Alex laughed. "Most girls say that. Some guys, too."

"Why would men want to visit a place that only had women?"

"I'll tell you when you're older."

Dara wanted to say more but decided to let it go. "What kind of warrior was Scorpius?" she asked instead. "I've never seen a warrior dressed like him."

"He's a Roman legionnaire," Alex answered. "In my world, the Roman Empire once spanned most of a continent called Europe and some of Africa, and it lasted several hundred years.

"The Roman army was an extremely wicked fighting force, and its legionnaires were highly disciplined and trained to fight using coordinated tactics. It was harsh, though. A whole legion could be punished if they didn't fight good enough in a battle ... even if they won! Training was brutal and tough, but ya can't deny the results."

"So Scorpius has had a hard life?" Dara asked.

"I wouldn't say that, so much," Alex replied. "It's more like he's used to his commanders being strict and harsh—but not just toward him. They're like that with everyone. And he's training to be just like them.

"That sword he's got is called a gladius. It's razor sharp. Even a small cut from it is painful. And his shield, that's a scutum. When a bunch of legionnaires are together, they can interlock their shields to make what's called a tortoise formation, which gives wicked cover from arrows and rocks and stuff."

"When you say 'wicked,' you mean 'good,' don't you?" Dara asked.

"Um, yeah."

"I'm just making sure. Scorpius is used to working with a team then," Dara realized.

"Sure."

"Is he going to be okay on his own?"

Alex smiled. "You saw how he busted up that ettin. He'll be fine. Besides, he's a natural born leader. We'll be his new team."

"But we can't fight."

"Maybe he'll train us," Alex shrugged.

"I don't think I want to go through that kind of training," Dara decided. "My father's training was difficult, but still fun."

They walked in silence for a while longer before she asked, "Why are we heading south when Kashla is north of us."

"The Shadow Warriors are searching north for us and probably figure we're heading to Koshla."

"Kashla."

"Whatever."

"But my father's allies—"

"Are cut off from us and probably under attack as we speak. You saw the men back there. That wasn't just a few warriors. That was, like, an army, and it looked like more were heading north to join them."

"But what good is going south? We have no place to go to. Aspiria has fallen."

"I have a plan. While they're all up north, we're going to get the Axemen out of Shadow Wood and then have them rescue your father."

Dara turned to him in shock. "Alex, you know what my father said! We cannot go into Shadow Wood," she insisted.

"*The Scroll* can't go into Shadow Wood," Alex corrected.

Dara got very scared. "You are going to leave me alone to go there?"

"No," Alex assured. "You said yourself, I'm no warrior. Luckily, I know of some others we can send instead." He smiled and patted the book. "Do you think you can guide us close enough to Shadow Wood?"

Dara nodded. "It's due east of the Fork."

"The Fork?"

She smiled. "You'll see as soon as we clear these trees."

They continued south for several hours, keeping to the woods for cover, before stopping to rest by a small stream. They both drank their fill of water from it. Their adventure had left them exhausted and thirsty. Dara guessed that they had already passed Aspiria and now approached Shadow Wood although they were somewhere east of it.

Alex looked around at the gloomy world under its red sun.

"The sun looks like blood," he commented. "It's yellow where I come from."

"Our sun was yellow, too ... this morning," said Dara.

"The Hall turned the sun red?"

"And darkened the land."

Alex could not believe that anything was that powerful. "It's probably, like, filtering the light coming through the atmosphere, so it seems red."

"I don't understand what you're saying," Dara stated.

"Don't worry," said Alex. "It's just technical stuff."

Alex realized that while he could easily believe in magic, he was trying to apply understandable limits to it, but in this world, that may not be the case.

He sat down and leafed through the book. It contained three other legends: a Japanese samurai named Genjuro, swift as the wind; an African warrior named Bantu, whose size was dwarfed only by his strength; and Tenzin, a Shaolin monk of near inhuman skill.

"What is a samurai?" Dara asked, looking over his shoulder.

"The name *samurai* means 'to serve.' They are the servants of their lords," Alex answered. "Although they're most famous for their skill with the sword, for most of their history they referred to themselves as the followers of 'the way of bow and horse.' This guy doesn't have a bow or horse in his picture, so I'm guessing he doesn't come with them. We probably have to buy an expansion pack for that."

"Pardon?"

"Nothing," Alex chuckled. "Samurai carry two swords: a katana and a wakizashi. The katana is a long sword used in combat. The wakizashi was mainly used for decapitating beaten opponents or—"

"Decapitating?" Dara asked.

"Cutting the heads off of," Alex explained.

"Oh," she said, regretting having asked.

"*Or*," he continued, "for ritual suicide."

"They keep a sword just to kill themselves with?"

"A samurai would rather die by his own hand than be captured by an enemy," Alex told her. "And, if he really screws up at something, he would rather die than live with the shame."

"Shouldn't he just try to make up for his mistake?"

"I guess it depended on the mistake."

"I think it's a silly rule," Dara stated.

"You can tell him that when we summon him," Alex suggested.

Dara shook her head.

"I didn't think so," Alex smiled.

Dara flipped the pages to Bantu. "He's a Nairobi," she said. "They are fierce warriors and skilled hunters and trackers. Papa has entertained delegates from their lands at the palace. They're big men. They live in the realm to the south. It's very hot there, Papa says."

"That's pretty much how I would have described Bantu, too," Alex said, "except the place he lives is called Africa in my world, Kenya specifically. His people are called the Masaai." He flipped to Tenzin. "What about him?"

"He looks like an acrobat," Dara guessed.

Alex laughed. "Well, to watch him fight, you may think so. He's a Shaolin monk. They're skilled with many weapons but are deadly even when unarmed. The Shaolin spend years disciplining both mind and body. I saw a demonstration by a group of them once. They can break bricks with their heads, do a handstand on two fingers, and throw a needle so hard it cuts through glass!"

"They must use strong magic," Dara assumed.

"No magic," Alex corrected. "Focus and discipline. Apparently anyone can do it, but it's way too much work and dedication for most people."

"Like becoming a wizard," Dara realized. "All people have magic in them, some more than others because of bloodlines, but even if powerful magic flows through your veins, it requires dedication, discipline, and years of training to become a great wizard. Papa admires the students that train to be wizards who have little magic in their blood. He says they show the most strength of character because the hard training yields fewer results for them, yet they still persevere."

Alex flipped through the book one last time before closing it. "I think these warriors should be enough to find the Axemen," he said.

"But we still really don't know how to summon them," said Dara. "We've only done it by accident so far."

"I'm pretty sure it's just a matter of giving them a task to do when you summon them. Like you did when Maya appeared."

"I did?" Dara asked.

"You were like, 'This girl can shoot arrows from a distance to make them attack each other.'" Alex repeated. "And she did. At least, I'm assuming that's what she did. We heard them start fighting."

"But I didn't mean to summon her. I was just saying that."

"It looks like you just have to, like, say the words, even if you don't mean them. I guess we'll have to be careful what we say when the book is open then."

"You use that word a lot," Dara commented.

"What word?" asked Alex.

"'Like,'" she stated. "And you don't even use it correctly."

"What are you? The grammar police?"

"It's a bit annoying," Dara told him.

"Sor-ree! I will try and use proper grammar when speaking in your presence, milady," Alex mocked.

"Try to," Dara corrected.

"Huh?"

"You'll try *to* use proper grammar, not try *and* use proper grammar. You shouldn't use bad grammar when promising to use good grammar."

"Oh, man, this is going to be the best road trip *ever!*" Alex cheered sarcastically.

Dara thought about what Alex had told her for a while and then said, "You didn't give Scorpius a task. He just appeared."

"Actually, I did," Alex said, blushing.

"You did? I didn't hear you. All I heard was you screaming—"

"Enough about the screaming!"

"Sorry."

Dara's "I'm sorry" face was far too cute for Alex to stay angry. He composed himself and started again. "I said, 'Help.'"

Misunderstanding, Dara replied, "I'm trying to help, but—"

"No," Alex stopped her, "when Scorpius appeared, I was holding the book open, and I said ... okay I yelled *help*, and he appeared and helped. He disappeared when I didn't need help anymore."

"Then why didn't he appear later when you ordered him to?"

"It was a useless request. I was like ... I said, 'Come forth.' If he appeared then, the task would have been finished, and he would have just disappeared again."

"So you can make him appear now and do something?"

"Maybe, but I want to wait until we stop for the night."

"Why?"

"Magic items usually have limits on them. We may only be able to summon one warrior at a time or only use the book three times a day or the warriors may only last for like ... ugh ... this is harder than I thought ... for a limited time. I don't want to take any chances until we're in a safe place and have time to really test this thing out."

They set out again a little while later, walking until the sun began to set. As they cleared the trees, Alex noticed the unusual mountain far off in the range to the west. It had two peaks.

He pointed at it. "The Fork?"

Dara nodded.

"It's called the Fork in the World," Dara explained. "I can see it from my bed chamber at home. The whole mountain range is impassable except by traveling through the middle, up, and over the Fork. Taking it can save you weeks of travel time, but the climb is dangerous. The temperatures are cold, and travelers sometimes come across monsters up there. So, no one really uses it unless it's really important."

"So you've never been over the Fork?" Alex asked.

Dara laughed. "I've never been out of the city."

"You've spent your whole life in one city? What about seeing the world? Even just exploring the countryside?"

"You haven't seen my city," said Dara. "There are gardens and parks so big you feel as if you're out in the countryside. I've gotten lost more than once. And I've studied maps of the realm. I have some in my bag. That's how I know where things are. I have a big map in my room with pins in all the places I want to visit. Papa promised he'd take me traveling when I'm old enough." She sighed. "I suppose I'm old enough now."

Then she moved into Alex and started to cry. "Oh, Alex, I don't know if I can do this! I'm so scared. Papa's always been there for me and now he's gone, and so is my home! It's like my whole world has been taken away!"

"It's okay, Dara," Alex said softly. "We're going to make it right. We're going to find your dad, and he's going to kick the Hall of Shadows' butt, or its backdoor, or whatever part of a Hall you kick."

Dara giggled and looked up at him, her face soaked in tears. "You're silly."

"That's me. Alex, the silly Axeman."

"I know you're not a warrior, but I'm glad you're here with me," she said and hugged him tightly.

"Thanks, Dara," Alex replied, returning the hug. They just stood there for a while, Alex letting Dara take comfort in his arms. Her words eventually soaked into him though. She had said it was as though her whole world had been taken away. For Alex, that wasn't how it seemed. That was what happened. Hours ago, his biggest problem had been whether he should go to an exam or an audition. Now he was in a magical realm facing life or death situations. His parents' wrath would be something he'd gladly welcome if he could get home right now. At the same time, however, he couldn't just leave Dara—even if he could figure out how to send himself back home. Besides, he probably needed a wizard to send him back, and Mornak was the only one he knew of so far. Therefore, rescuing him was their best option, and the sooner they did it, the better.

They started moving again, still heading roughly southeast. After a while, the land to the east seemed to just drop off. When Alex asked Dara about it, she explained that they were close to the sea and were nearing a series of cliffs that led down to it. If they could find one of the roads down to some fishing towns or a trading port that lay along the coast, they might be able to stay the night. Alex didn't want to go to any place where there were people. He didn't know whom to trust in this world yet.

He guided them toward a series of rocky outcroppings farther inland among more groves of trees. As he hoped, they found a cave to spend the night in. Alex checked the dirt around the entrance and found no signs of tracks made by man or animal. He hoped that meant the cave was empty. By now, they both were hungry, and it was getting cold. Sitting down, he flipped through *Legend and Lore* by the light of his Nano. He smiled at Dara who was listening to his music over the headphones with a look of wonder. He had already decided that the Nano served better as a flashlight here than a music player (as long as its batteries lasted), but that didn't mean they couldn't listen to music while using it. He soon found the page with Bantu's picture.

"Bantu, build us a fire and find us some food," he said, holding up the book. After a flash of light, the great African warrior stood before them.

To say Bantu was big would be an understatement. If Dara sat on Alex's shoulders, he could look her in the eye. The African warrior wore a red tunic trimmed with gold and had matching armbands around biceps thicker than

Alex's legs. The rest of his muscles were equally large, though his well-fed belly showed that muscle alone did not make him big. Many necklaces made of beads and bone and gemstones adorned his neck while bracelets and anklets hung around his wrists and feet. Completely bald, he had a wide nose and thick lips. His face, arms, and legs were painted with red lines—tribal markings put on before battle. As if he wasn't overwhelming enough, he held a spear as tall as he was and almost as intimidating. Designed differently than typical spears, it did not have an arrowhead tip. Instead, the top third of the weapon was a long blade resembling a double-edged sword. Alex did not want to be on the receiving end of that thing.

Both Alex and Dara leaned back to look up at the warrior. Despite his size and presence, Bantu's look was one of fear. He brought up his spear defensively as he looked around the darkening cave. Alex nudged Dara.

"Excuse me, sir," Dara said.

They had decided that Dara put the warriors more at ease, so she should start the conversations.

Bantu looked down and noticed them finally. Dara waved. "Welcome to our cave."

"How ... how did I get here?" his voice deep boomed. Alex thought he'd make Darth Vader say, *Wow, he's got a deep voice.*

"Strong magic," Dara replied, "but do not fear. You will be returned safely in a little while. We just need you to do us a favour."

"What favour is that, little one?" he asked, still on guard.

"Could you please make us a fire and find us some food?"

Bantu thought about it. "It is already dark," he said.

"Yeah," Alex replied. "Sorry about that."

Bantu leveled his spear at Alex, and Dara smacked Alex's arm for speaking.

"Please, Bantu?" she asked.

Bantu could feel that he had to do as she asked, as though it was his reason for being there. Relaxing, he nodded and exited the cave.

"I thought you said you weren't going to talk?" Dara scolded Alex after Bantu left.

"Sorry, it slipped out."

"Why is it that none of these warriors seem to like you?"

"I don't have that cute adorable factor working for me," he replied, then grabbing her cheeks added, "or these chubby little cheeks."

"Stop it!" she said, pushing him away but giggling at the same time.

Alex opened the book again. "Now comes the first test," he said.

"Test?" Dara asked.

"We're going to find out if we can summon more than one warrior at a time," he explained. "Genjuro, guard us until we wake up in the morning."

The young Japanese samurai appeared wearing brown clothes under deep blue armour with large shoulder guards. He was short, halfway between Dara and Alex's heights; his face was wide but angular; his Asian eyes were sharp.

A red headband kept his hair out of his face, and a similar red cloth tied his ponytail behind him. He wore tabis on his feet, socks in which the big toe had its own section, and wooden sandals under them. His sword flashed out in a second as he looked around the dark cave. The speed of the motion shocked Alex and Dara. Then the Nano caught the samurai's attention.

"What evil sorcery is this?" he yelled.

"Not evil," Dara replied. "I'm sorry, brave warrior, but we need your help."

"What manner of people are you?" he challenged. Then, regarding Alex, he asked, "Why is your hair that colour? And what is wrong with your eyes?"

They explained the situation to Genjuro, and after his initial skepticism, he became fascinated by the thought that he had been transported to another world filled with magic. Alex and Dara were filling him in on their adventure when Bantu returned.

Genjuro moved to the cave entrance in a heartbeat. Again, the boy's speed stunned Alex and Dara. Bantu dropped the wood and food he carried and brought out his spear defensively.

"Whoa! Whoa!" Alex yelled. "He's a friend. Genjuro, Bantu. Bantu, Genjuro."

The two lowered their weapons and relaxed, and then Genjuro helped Bantu bring in the supplies. Soon a small fire burned as Dara explained to Bantu which of the various plants he found were edible.

"No meat?" Alex asked.

Bantu shook his head. "I looked for some game, but it seems the animals have fled this place."

"Smart animals," Alex remarked.

Alex was about to thank Bantu for the food when the warrior disappeared. Genjuro jumped back, his sword coming out instinctively.

"Relax, Genjuro," said Alex. "He's just been dispelled. That's just what'll happen to you when we wake up in the morning."

Alex broke open a strange-looking fruit that looked like a melon with a white center. When he tasted it, his face lit up in surprise. "This is really good."

"Allo," Dara told him. "Papa says it's good for building muscles."

"It tastes like cream," Alex stated. "Bantu would love this. His tribe drinks lots of milk."

"We can save some for him," Dara suggested.

"You'll be summoning him again, Alex-san?" Genjuro asked.

"We'll be needing all of you to find the Axemen," said Alex.

"When will you be needing me again?"

"Probably tomorrow morning."

"But I will be awake all night."

"It doesn't matter," Alex said. "You're not real. The book will bring you back in perfect health the next time we need you. At least, I think that's how it works."

"What do you mean 'I'm not real'?" argued Genjuro. "I am here! I know I'm real!"

Alex shook his head. "I know this may be hard to accept, but *this*," he said, holding up the book, "is a book about legends. There's no proof that any of the people in here actually existed. And since your picture disappears from the book when I summon you, I'm guessing the magic creates you from it. We're not really summoning you from some other place. We're conjuring you from the book."

Genjuro sat back stunned by what Alex had said. He couldn't come to grips with the fact that he might not be real. "But I can remember my life, the village I live in, the daimyo I serve."

"Would you like me to read about them to you?" Alex asked showing him the text in the book.

Genjuro jumped up and moved about the cave in a near panic. Alex wondered if he would lash out at them. Then the samurai pulled out his sword, and Alex threw himself in front of Dara. To their surprise, the boy did not attack them but held the blade against his own hand and cut. Dara cringed as the boy's blood began to flow. He held up his hand. "If I were conjured, would I bleed?" he asked.

"Yes," answered Alex, but then he finally started to sympathize with the boy. "Look, maybe you are real. I could be wrong, you know. We'll just have to find out."

Genjuro lapsed into silence for a while and then finally asked, "How do I find out if I am real or not?"

"Well," Alex guessed, "if we summon you again right away and you're not tired, that would be a sign that you're not real—or, if you were injured and your wounds were healed ... unless the book heals you each time. Hmm, if you don't remember us, that would be a definite sign that you're being made up each time." Alex didn't believe Genjuro was real though. He was sure that the book was just creating these warriors. More so, he needed it to be that way. Sending them into Shadow Wood could be dangerous. If the Hall noticed them, it could destroy them. If they were not real, then they'd just be returned to the book to be used again. If they were real, though—

Then a look of worry came over Alex's face. "Crap!"

"What is it?" asked Dara.

"We don't know if we can even summon someone more than once! We may have used up our chances to use every warrior except Tenzin!"

"Do you want to try to summon someone again now?" Dara suggested.

"No," Alex decided. "We'll see in the morning. I don't want to risk any unnecessary summoning." He looked at Genjuro. "Would you like me to summon you back right away or wait in case you need to sleep?"

"I would rather find out right away if I am real or not, Alex-san," Genjuro answered, bowing.

"If I were you, so would I," Alex agreed.

They finished dinner and talked a bit more, but Genjuro's earlier happy mood did not return. Dara fell asleep while Alex and Genjuro talked about their worlds. Finally, Genjuro moved to the entrance of the cave where he simply sat and stared out into the night. Alex looked at him as he tried to get comfortable on the cave floor, wondering what was going through the boy's mind. Alex wanted Genjuro to be real for the samurai's sake, but he wanted him to be magical for theirs. He fell asleep trying to decide which was better.

6

$\mathcal{A}$ beam of morning light woke Alex. He looked to the cave entrance and saw Genjuro sitting just where he had been the night before, which made him wonder if the samurai had even stood up to stretch his legs. Alex got up and walked over, feeling the stiffness that comes from sleeping on sand and stone. "I'm awake," he said. "Why don't you take a break before I wake up Dara?"

"Please, do not wake her right away, Alex-san," Genjuro asked. "If I am not real and this is the end of my existence, then I would like to enjoy this world a little longer."

"Not a problem," Alex replied understandingly.

Genjuro got to his feet and walked away from the cave until he could see the morning sun rising behind it, its red light penetrating the haze of this shadowy realm. "It is a beautiful morning, Alex-san. I think I will take a walk." He bowed and walked off through the trees.

Alex looked around at the foreboding, shadowy world and thought, *Beautiful? I guess if it's your last moments, any place can seem beautiful.*

He stood for a little while, watching Genjuro walk away, marveling at this strange new world. Only when Alex turned to look for some place to pee did he see the dead bodies of the six lizardmen piled to the side of the cave entrance, all killed by a sword. Alex looked back to Genjuro, but the samurai had wandered out of sight.

"He didn't even wake us," Alex said with wonder. Then his bladder yelled at him, and he rushed off into the bushes. When he returned, he thought, *Oh, man, I'm gonna have to do a "number two" eventually, in a world with no toilet paper. Dax was right. Things were great the way they were.*

He waited until Genjuro returned. When the samurai was ready, Alex woke Dara up. Genjuro vanished as she opened her eyes. Alex held out the book and said, "Genjuro, help us rescue the Axemen from Shadow Wood."

The samurai reappeared. Looking around, he yelled, "Banzai!"

"You remember everything?" Alex asked.

"Not only that," Genjuro exclaimed. "For a brief moment, I was back in my world, I believe, at the moment I left. I saw it clearly. My life is not my imagination! Now let us rescue the Axemen so that I may return with tales of great adventure!"

"Can it wait a while?" Alex asked. "We'd like to wash up and eat first."

"Of course, Alex-san," Genjuro agreed.

"You should get some sleep," Alex suggested.

"I am too excited. I shall be outside."

Genjuro bounded out of the cave, leaving Alex and Dara smiling at each other. They ate some more allo and some berries for breakfast and then found a small lake nearby to wash up in. Now it was Alex's turn to be worried. If the warriors were real and being summoned, not conjured, then they could really die here if they were killed. Alex wanted to call off the mission, but he did not know how to cancel the summons and return Genjuro. He didn't know if it could even be done. The best option was not to let the samurai go alone. He would summon the rest of them to help.

When Alex and Dara returned, they found Genjuro farther back in the cave in deep meditation. In the light of day, they could see that the cave was bigger than they had thought. The roughly dome-shaped section they had camped in was large enough to sleep twenty people, but a natural tunnel extended out the back, sloping downward into a black hole. Not wanting to disturb their new friend, they went outside where Alex took out the book.

"Who first?" he asked Dara.

"Scorpius," she answered.

"I thought you were going to say Maya."

"She kind of scares me."

"And Scorpius doesn't?"

"No, he's more ... heroic."

Alex felt a twinge of jealousy. Yesterday, he thought he was becoming her hero.

"Okay. Scorpius it is," he agreed. He opened the book to the right page and said, "Scorpius, help us rescue the Axemen from Shadow Wood."

Scorpius appeared in a flash, and the moment he got his bearings, he lunged at Alex, knocking him over and punching him repeatedly.

"Tormenter!" he yelled. "You are demon spawn, aren't you? I will kill you with my bare hands!" He punched and punched and punched.

"Scorpius, no!" Dara yelled as she rushed in.

Scorpius held Alex down by the throat, his hand cutting off Alex's air, as he turned to address Dara.

"Do not think I think you are any less evil than he. The two of you sent me there! You placed me in that purgatory!"

At that moment, Genjuro flew out of the cave, weapon ready. Scorpius's blade flashed out immediately, stopping at Dara's throat.

"Make no move!" he warned the samurai.

"Scorpius," Dara pleaded. "Please, we don't know what you're talking about."

Scorpius tightened his grip even more. Alex made a gurgling sound as he struggled, his efforts dwindling with each second.

"You deny placing me in that ... hell?" Scorpius hissed.

Tears flowed openly down Dara's cheeks.

"Please let him go," Dara begged. "He ... we meant you no harm."

Scorpius stopped and stared into her eyes. He could see she was telling the truth. He could see she was scared and sorry and confused. He turned back to look down at Alex, whose right eye was puffing out. Tears ran down his bruised cheeks, blood dripped from his lip, and his jaw looked out of place.

"Please," Alex whispered.

"You really do not know?" Scorpius asked. He released his grip a bit.

Alex tried to shake his head and then moaned from the pain of it. Scorpius realized a demon would not be so easily subdued. He lowered his gladius, got off Alex, and helped him to a sitting position. Dara rushed over and tried to help, but she didn't know what to do. Genjuro moved in cautiously, his sword still at the ready.

"Wh-wud hah-pund?" Alex asked Scorpius through his swelling lips.

"Did you not return home?" Dara added.

"I did," answered Scorpius, "but my world was frozen."

"In ice?" Dara asked.

"In time," Scorpius replied. "I was returned to the exact moment I left, the middle of a great battle. My uncle, a general, had just been slain in front of me. The world had stopped at that moment."

Alex and Dara looked to Genjuro.

"I was only back a moment," he answered, guessing their question, "but now that I think about it, the world did seem ... odd."

"You cud see bwut not moob?" Alex asked, wincing as he tried to talk.

"No, I could move," said Scorpius. His head hung down as he remembered it. "I wandered around the battlefield, seeing men frozen in combat, some locked in the moment of their deaths, others about to be slain. I spent hours looking at them. I even tried to kill some of the enemy, but I could not cut them. I could not change anything! Do you know what it is like to see your friends dying or about to be killed and not be able to do anything?" He stared at the ground for a while. Then his body began to shake. His hand curled into a fist, and he slammed it into the earth. "Why?" he yelled. "Why was I made to endure that? Was it not enough that my uncle was slain in front of me?" Then he looked up at Alex with hate. "Your magic is evil, wizard."

"Um nob a wizard!"

Dara placed her small hand on Scorpius's fist. "We are sorry," she told him, the emotion in her voice emphasizing her honesty. "We didn't know. If we had, we wouldn't have ... by the gods—"

"What is it?" Scorpius asked.

Dara turned quickly to Alex. "The others! If they are going through the same thing ..."

Alex grabbed the book off the ground and quickly flipped through the pages, forgetting his own pain. When he reached Maya's page, he handed it to Dara. "Say wut Ah said," he told her.

She did and soon they repeated the process, apologizing profusely. Maya would have shot Alex the moment she appeared if she did not see how badly Scorpius had already beaten him. All of them had been sent back to the moment they had left and had been trapped there. Alex could not even guess why, but he knew someone who might.

They soon had the Scroll out, and after Alex and Dara filled them in on the situation, the group of teens sat gathered around it. Alex explained to Mornak what had happened to the others and asked for his advice. His thoughts wrote themselves across the parchment.

It is possible that they cannot return to proper places and times because the overall geas summoning has not been completed.

"Wud overall geas summoning?" asked Alex.

Yours.

Alex's jaw dropped, and it hurt.

"But I was bwought here accidentally. I wasn't eben summoned for a spespific mishbon."

Are you sure?

Alex grabbed Dara by the shoulders and turned her to him. "Dawa, when you twied to summon the leader ob the Axemen, dib you thay abbithing else or dib you just ask him to appear?"

Worry came over Dara's face. "Alex, I ... I ..."

"It's okay, Dawa. I won't be mad, bud I need to know."

"I asked for the leader of the Axemen to be brought here to protect me ... until my father escapes his prison."

Alex slumped. In the back of his mind, he had thought he might be able to find a way out of this world if he really didn't like the way things went. That hope just vanished. Further, there was a good chance that they may not be able to free Mornak, in which case he would be bound as Dara's protector forever.

"So you are as much a prisoner here as we are," Scorpius reasoned. "Both prisoner and jailer."

Alex lifted his head. "Jailer?"

"How else would you describe the one who holds our lives in his hands, quite literally."

Alex hadn't thought of it that way.

"So what do we do now?" asked Maya.

Alex brought himself to his senses. "We wescue the Axemen. Mornak, ib there any way to dispwel the enchantment on Shadow Wood?"

I could give Dara a counterspell to cast, but that would mean her going into the woods, and the spell would need to be powerful. The Hall would surely detect it. You would be too vulnerable.

"Is there any food left from last night?" Bantu asked, making everyone turn his way. He blushed. "Sorry. I'm hungry."

"I would think a person your size is always hungry, Bantu-san," Genjuro commented, smiling. Bantu winked back.

Alex shot them both a glare. "Guys, pwease." While it was gradually getting easier to talk, he didn't need distractions. He turned back to the Scroll. "What about getting the Axemen out? Id there a way to overcome the spell, get awound it?"

It affects both your sight and your hearing, limiting and twisting both, to make sure you are thoroughly confused.

"So you were completely lost in the Wood?"

No, I could sense the Hall's position and used it as a guide.

"I don't suppose you could arrange it so one of us could do that?"

Only Dara has the innate ability.

Suddenly, Alex's face lit up.

"Hold up!" he exclaimed but then immediately winced from the pain his excitement caused. "Does the spell affect items or only people?"

Living beings.

Alex grabbed his bag excitedly and then moaned as the movement caused him severe pain. He reached in and pulled *Historic Inventions* out of the bag. Flipping through it quickly, he stopped on a specific page. "I need this to find the Axemen!" he exclaimed.

After a small flash of light, a compass sat in Alex's hand.

"What is it, Alex-san?" asked Genjuro.

"A compass," Alex replied, examining it. "There are arguments about when it was first used, but the first incontestable reference to one is in Chinese literature around 1086 AD in the *Dream Pool Essays*, written by a scientist named Shen Kuo. Since then, it has been used in navigation in pretty much every vehicle and on foot." Alex looked up to see the blank expressions around him. He sighed. "It always points north," he stated.

As one, their faces lit up in understanding.

"Magnetic north may be different here," Alex continued, as he turned the compass around to see what the needle did. "Nope, it's the same."

"That gets us through the forest," Scorpius commented, "but it doesn't mean we can find the Axemen. Mornak said that the spell limited what you could see and hear. We need a way to extend our vision or bring them to us somehow." He stroked his chin with his fingers in thought.

Alex looked around. "Where's Bantu?" he asked.

"He went into the cave to grab some food," Genjuro stated. "He could smell the berries from here."

"Smell!" Scorpius yelled.

"Smell?" Maya asked.

"Perhaps we could lure them out with a strong scent," Scorpius explained.

"That's right!" Alex exclaimed. "The spell doesn't affect smell, and smells can carry pretty far. As hungry as they are by now, the Axemen will follow the right scent in a hurry!" He touched the Scroll.

"Mornak, do you have a spell that can create a strong scent? We want to lure the Axemen from the forest with it, kinda like a Siren lures men with her songs. Only we'll be bringing them out from danger instead of luring them to it."

There is a Siren spell as you mentioned it. I can alter it to use smell instead of sound. You will need a vessel.

"Um, I don't think we're going to find a ship anywhere around here," Alex warned. "And, besides, how would we get it to Shadow Wood?"

Scorpius rolled his eyes. "He means vessel as in a container."

Alex turned red. "Oh."

Then he reached into his book bag, this time pulling out a clear plastic energy drink bottle that he packed for the exam. "Okay, I have one."

The others stared at the strange clear bottle filled with a blue liquid.

"What is that?" asked Genjuro.

"A vessel!" Alex said, as though it was obvious.

Fill it and give it to Dara, and I will guide her through the spell.

Since it was already filled, Alex handed the vessel over to Dara. She scrunched her nose at the look of the drink.

"It tastes good," Alex insisted. "Really!"

Mornak gave Dara instructions on how to cast the spell, her hand gestures, and what to do with the bottle. Then he sent the words to the spell itself. Dara followed the instructions, and soon the blue liquid in the bottle pulsed with light.

"So how does it work?" asked Alex.

When the bottle is open, it will release a magical scent that will smell to a person like his favourite food. The person will follow the scent back with great longing, but a small sip of the liquid will break the spell. Closing the bottle will also break the spell until it is opened again. The scent will fan out and carry a great distance on the wind, so it should prove very effective. You will each need to take a sip from the bottle, or the spell will affect you while you search for the Axemen.

"Sounds like we're good to go!" Alex exclaimed. He lifted his hand for a "high five" from Scorpius. The Roman looked at him for a moment and then mimicked the gesture, but he did not slap Alex's hand.

Alex shook his head. "I have so much to teach you guys."

"I'm not sure I understand," said Genjuro. "We're going to walk up and down a forest waving around scented bottle?"

"When you put it like that, it sounds stupid," Alex commented.

That was not Genjuro's cause for concern, however. "Won't the smell also attract animals? Perhaps dangerous ones? Are we sure they have all left?" he asked.

"There are no animals in Shadow Wood," said Dara, and everyone turned to her. She shrugged. "My father told me that. They avoid it just like people do. There are only bugs."

"Feel better?" Alex asked Genjuro.

He nodded, bowing.

"Why do people turn to smoke here?" Maya asked suddenly.

"Who turned to smoke?" Alex asked back.

"A warrior," she replied. "I shot one and he turned to smoke."

Dara repeated the question to her father.

They do not turn to smoke but to shadow. The warriors are shadows from the Hall, given substance by its power. They are Shadowlings. When they die, they revert to their true form. Be mindful. Warriors are not the only shadows that were imprisoned in the Hall.

After thanking Mornak for his help, Alex had Dara close the Scroll, and then he stood up to address the group.

"Okay, here's the plan. You guys'll go to Shadow Wood, rescue the Axemen, and then bring them back here. Stay out of the center. That's where the Hall is. According to Mornak—"

"Stop right there," Maya demanded. "Did you just say that the Hall of Shadows is in the center of Shadow Wood?"

"That's how it got its name," Dara told her.

"So we're going to walk into the home of the source of all evil in this place?" Maya said in disbelief. "Does anyone else think this is plan is insane?"

"According to Mornak," Alex reminded, "its men and its attention are other places in the realm, so it shouldn't even notice you're there unless you, like, attack it or something. I'll summon this last guy to help you."

"It *shouldn't* notice?" Maya repeated. "So you don't know."

"I'm going by what Mornak said, and he built the thing," Alex argued.

"And then lost control of it," the Amazon argued back.

"You guys'll be fine," Alex insisted.

"Then, you're not coming?" Maya asked with her hands on her hips.

"I have to stay and protect Dara," Alex stated. "It's my job."

"It's your excuse," Maya huffed. "You can barely protect yourself! I think you should come with us to show us how safe this place is. Bantu can protect Dara."

Scorpius disagreed. "Alex should stay. He'd only slow us down, but Bantu should also stay to protect the girl."

"I have a name!" Dara said, annoyed.

Scorpius ignored her. "Summon the last warrior," he ordered Alex. "He can help us."

"So, you think you're in charge now?" Alex challenged.

Scorpius smiled. "If you want to be in charge, why don't you lead the rescue?"

Alex backed down immediately. "I'll summon Tenzin."

"Coward," Scorpius muttered under his breath.

Moments later, Tenzin stood in front of them. The young Tibetan monk with a shaved head, who was pulled from his calisthenics, wore a blue gi with beige leg wraps and black tabis on his feet. His top hung off one shoulder, exposing the tight, rippled muscles on his bare upper body, which were an impressive sight. He was just a touch shorter than Alex and had an oval face, sparkling slanted eyes, and a smile that seemed to brighten the area. They all waited for the reaction of surprise, shock, and fear. It didn't come. Tenzin merely looked around curiously before smiling at them.

"Which of you summoned me?" he asked calmly.

"I did. I'm Alex," Alex replied.

"I will grant you three wishes, Master Alex," he stated.

The jaws of the others dropped while Alex grinned from ear to ear. "Really?" he asked.

Tenzin laughed. "Of course not! I'm no genie."

There was a moment of silence, and then everyone laughed.

"Now let us be off to rescue these Axemen," Tenzin urged.

"You know why you're here?" Genjuro asked.

"Yes, when one is summoned, the task becomes a part of them."

"So you've been summoned before?" asked Alex.

"No, but I know of the ability, and since this is not my home and I can feel the task within me, what other conclusion could I draw?"

"Oh, yes," Maya said sarcastically. "We all realized *that* right away."

"I'm sure nothing escapes those fiery eyes, beautiful lady," Tenzin replied.

Maya blushed and wondered how a man could disarm her so. She did not like being in the company of men. She especially did not like being the only woman among them. (Dara was too young to count in her opinion.) If what her people taught her of them was true, then they would try to enslave her when the opportunity presented itself. She kept her guard up to prevent that, but for some reason, she was immediately comfortable with Tenzin. The boy had an energy about him that felt good and pure. Scorpius had a look of fierce determination; Alex had one of nervousness. Genjuro was in awe of the world around him; Bantu was awkwardly unsure of everything. But Tenzin stood with a casual smile as though everything was—and always would be—wonderful.

"I like him," Dara said to Alex about Tenzin. Alex nodded in agreement.

"Let us be off then, Master Alex," Tenzin said.

"I'm not going," Alex said.

"But you must," Tenzin insisted.

"No, we decided—" Alex started to explain, but Tenzin stopped him.

"You do not understand. I was summoned to *help you* rescue the Axemen as were these others, I imagine. If you do not come along, then we are not helping. We are doing. The magic will not let us do it ourselves."

Alex sighed.

Scorpius chuckled and then said, "Maya, you'd better stay here then."

Maya was insulted. "You think that *he* is equal to me?"

"No, but I want two people here with the girl."

"Dara!" Dara exclaimed.

"She's apparently the hope of the realm," Scorpius continued. "And I doubt we'll encounter anything too dangerous while we're walking through an empty forest waving a scented bottle."

Maya nodded.

Alex knelt in front of Dara. "You'll be okay with them?"

She nodded and then hugged him. "Yep yep, I'll miss you, though." She touched his bruised and swollen face gently. "You look awful," she said, but smiled.

"It's not as bad as it looks," he told her, but then he winced as her fingers brushed a cut and quickly pulled her hand away. "Okay, it is. I'll be fine, though."

Alex looked west to the distant trees of Shadow Wood. It was at least a dozen kilometers away. "Be good, Little Rose. We should be back by nightfall," Alex told her, hoping it was true. Then the small group began their journey.

*   *   *

The image on the wall of the Hall faded when Dara closed the Scroll.

He must be a wizard. He summoned those warriors and that device.

The Shadow Lord still did not feel that that was the case. Alex was exactly as he looked—something that not only did not belong in the realm but also defied it somehow, far more so than the others with him. Not a wizard, more like a being from another plane. That made him unpredictable and dangerous.

"He is something," the Shadow Lord stated, "but he still looks disoriented by this world. We had best eliminate him before he masters his abilities."

They are near the Eastern Sea. It seems he summoned the others to help protect the girl. They will likely try to cross the seas in hopes of escape. They may be a formidable force, especially if they possess magic of their own.

"Yes, we best not take chances. I will send Askar himself with a legion of Shadow Warriors from Aspiria to eliminate them and retrieve the Scroll."

7

Down a grassy hill, Scorpius led the way with Tenzin beside him. Scorpius's determined march greatly contrasted Tenzin's carefree stride. Neither boy spoke, each lost in his private thoughts. Alex and Genjuro followed just behind them, with Alex mesmerizing Genjuro with his tales of *Samurai Jack*. He didn't tell Genjuro that it was just a kids' cartoon, not the life of a real samurai stuck in the distant future. He was enjoying the look on Genjuro's face far too much for that. Explaining the concept of androids took some doing though.

After a couple hours they came over a rise, finally seeing the valley that contained Shadow Wood. The sight did not make them happy. Shadow Wood was shaped roughly like a football field running north to south—however, instead of being only a hundred meters, it was at least a dozen kilometers long.

"I expected it to be much smaller," Alex commented.

"Why?" asked Tenzin.

"It's called Shadow Wood, not Shadow Vast Forest," Alex answered. "It'll take us days, maybe weeks, to find all the Axemen."

"I doubt that," said Scorpius.

The others all turned to him for an explanation.

"You said Aspiria is north of Shadow Wood. The Axemen would have entered from the north end then. Since the spell causes you to become disoriented, the men are most likely wandering in circles in the northern section of the forest. We also have a breeze blowing southward. So if we just open the bottle there," he said pointing just north of where the Wood started. "The breeze will blow the scent into the woods, and many of the men will be able to use it to get out without us even going in."

Alex smiled. *Master strategist,* he thought. *Good thing he's here.*

They reached the northern end of Shadow Wood, and Alex removed the bottle cap. The strength of the urge to drink from the bottle surprised them. Alex swore he smelled his mom's roast turkey with mashed potatoes and gravy that he only got to eat at Thanksgiving and Christmas. The others had similar visions of the foods they craved, from eel sushi to smoked oxen. Alex could only imagine how strong the desire would be if he were hungry. He quickly poured himself a cap of the energy drink, drank it, then refilled it, and passed it on to each boy in turn. The nature of the drink combined with the magic cast on it, making each drinker feel refreshed and energized, effectively wiping away the exhaustion they felt after the long journey from the cave.

Then they waited. Ten minutes passed with no result.

"It's not working," Alex complained.

Scorpius shook his head. "The men have to realize they can follow the scent, and they also have to reorient themselves each time the spell turns them around. It could take some time."

They waited another twenty minutes before the first Axeman emerged. He moved almost desperately. When his gaze connected with the bottle, he charged.

His axe waving wildly in the air, the knight came at Alex. Scorpius and Genjuro moved to intercept, Genjuro reaching him first and trying to block his way. The Axeman swung at the samurai, who spun out of reach before making his own attack. He didn't mean to hit the man but simply engage him in battle until they could subdue him. The Axeman countered Genjuro's attack with remarkable skill and moved on toward Alex with only Scorpius in his path. Genjuro reprimanded himself. Alex had told him that the Axemen were the best knights in the realm. Seeing this wild-eyed, unshaven man had made the samurai think he had the skills of a vagabond. He was lucky not to have gotten himself killed.

Scorpius did not make that mistake. His goal was not to engage but simply to block. He matched every move as the man tried to get around him, his shield blocking every attack. But just watching the man's movements, Scorpius knew he could never beat him in a fight. He realized that even trying to use his sword against him would likely result in the Roman losing the weapon or his arm. However, as the Axeman pounded against Scorpius's scutum, Tenzin snuck in behind him and grabbed the knight in a headlock. Scorpius moved in at once, locking the man's axe up with his sword. Tenzin pressed down on a nerve cluster in the back of the man's neck while keeping him busy with the choke hold until the man finally dropped, unconscious. Alex came up and poured a tiny bit of the drink into the man's mouth so that he would swallow it when he woke. A few minutes later, his eyes opened, and after the initial distrust of the strangely dressed and strange-looking characters, he listened to their story and finally agreed to help subdue the other Axemen as they appeared.

Only a few minutes later, several more arrived. This time Alex had the sense to close the bottle, breaking the spell just as the teens prepared for battle.

Scorpius turned and growled at him. "Why didn't you do that the first time?"

"Sorry," Alex apologized with a shrug.

The Axemen were on guard, but without the spell amplifying their hunger and with assurances from their fellow knight, they allowed themselves to be restrained while Alex reopened the bottle and poured capfuls of the energy drink. Again, the teenagers explained who they were, and the Axemen thanked their rescuers. Their only complaint was that the food they had been tracking did not really exist.

Nine Axemen had been recovered when the wind shifted westward.

"We'll have to move east and set up again," Scorpius said when they noticed the change. "We'll stay here a little while longer in case there are stragglers."

A few minutes later, the ground began to shake. Everyone looked around and at each other, hoping someone would know the cause.

One of the Axemen suddenly called out, "We have to move!"

"Is it an earthquake?" Alex asked.

"No! It's—"

The ground erupted between the Axemen and the teens, and a giant furry animal emerged. Its head looked much like a bear, but its body was shaped more like a mole. Though half of it still remained underground, it appeared to Alex to be the size of a school bus. Its claws were the length of Alex's arm, an inky liquid filled its black eyes, and the noise it made sounded like something between a bear's roar and an elephant's trumpet. It lashed out with a claw, barely missing Genjuro who leaped out of the way.

"What is it?" Genjuro asked.

"Bulgor!" many Axemen yelled. "Run!"

The Axemen sprinted away while Alex and the others stood in confusion. What they had been told about these men seemed to be a lie. They were running off like cowards.

"Where are you going?" Scorpius yelled after them as he drew his gladius. "Together we can defeat it!"

"No!" an Axeman called back. "You don't understand!"

Before he could finish, the earth erupted in several more places between the Axemen and the teen heroes. Five more bulgor burst forth, one knocking the youths from their feet.

Tenzin sighed. "I believe he was trying to warn us that they travel in packs."

"Ya think?" Alex asked sarcastically.

* * *

Dara swung from Bantu's arm with a "Wee!"

The African warrior laughed as he spun her about. Maya was not as amused. She did not like being stuck in a cave playing babysitter. Besides, the baby seemed a bit uneasy with her. Dara seemed a good child, and Maya felt sorry for her being caught up in this whole business. But that didn't mean that she had to be dragged into it, too. There had to be a way to be free of the book. She just had to figure it out.

Maya was, however, relieved to be out of the company of so many men. Although they seemed peaceful enough toward her, she had seen the deeds of many men in her life. They were always bent on conquest. They hungered for power and often more. Some of her Amazon sisters had been captured as slaves by invading men. Many had died in battle against them. Now, through some magical mix-up, Maya was working beside some men, virtually a slave to one of them thanks to that damn book. She didn't know if she could get used to this. She did not want to get used to this. She doubted that she could ever truly trust any of them, except perhaps that Tenzin. She could not believe how often he crept into her thoughts after such a brief meeting. Maya shook her head. *He is a* MAN! she thought. *He doesn't deserve this much of your attention. Think of something else.*

Unfortunately, she didn't know what else to think about, and sitting around only made her anxious. She wished she was outside, maybe even looking for those Axemen—or better yet, fighting those Shadow Warriors. Wasn't that why she was summoned after all? She needed a little action. She got up, brushing a lock of her reddish black hair away from her face. She slung her bow and walked toward the cave entrance.

"Where are you going?" Bantu asked.

Maya stopped, confused. "I ... I don't know," she answered. "I was lost in thought and then just got up and walked this way." She started back in the cave but stopped again as a slight feeling of nausea came over her. She pulled her bow off her shoulder and used it to steady herself.

The other two noticed her expression at once. "What's wrong?" asked Dara.

"I don't know," Maya replied. "When I started back in, I just felt ... sick."

"I can feel it, too," Bantu told her.

"You're both sick?" asked Dara. "Will I get sick, too?"

"I don't think it is that kind of sickness," said Bantu.

"What do you mean?" Maya asked.

"I have been feeling a pull ... toward Shadow Wood," he explained.

"Yes, I wish I was out there, too," Maya stated but then added, "no offense, Dara."

"It's okay," Dara replied.

Bantu shook his head in disagreement. "I think we're being called."

"By the others?" Maya asked as she moved back to Bantu and Dara.

"No, by the book," Bantu answered. "Alex summoned us to help rescue the Axemen. We're not doing that by staying here. I think the magic is urging us to do what we've been summoned to do, and since we are not, it is making us sick. I've been trying to distract myself by playing with Dara."

"So the longer they take, the stronger the pull will get?" Maya asked.

"Or the sicker we will get," said Bantu. "I don't know much about magic. I am only guessing, but you cannot deny the urge to go to the Wood."

Maya nodded. "But we cannot leave Dara, so we will have to deal with it." She knew she couldn't just sit around and endure this feeling. "I'm going to need something to distract me," she decided aloud.

"Stay where you are and drop your weapons," warned a voice from behind her.

Maya looked back to see four Shadow Warriors—three swordsmen and an archer—standing at the cave entrance. The archer had her in his sights.

She smiled. "That will do."

She winked at Bantu, who nodded back. Then in a flurry of movement, she stepped to the side while nocking an arrow in her bow. Bantu picked up Dara, shielding her with his body, as he moved for his spear. The other archer shot, but his arrow flew into the space where Maya had been just a moment ago. Maya's arrow raced away and hit the man in the chest. The force of the impact threw him back, and he collapsed against the cave entrance dropping his bow as he clutched the arrow and struggled to breathe.

"Missed!" Maya cursed.

"You hit him!" Bantu corrected.

"I was aiming for his heart," she replied.

"Oh."

The other three men charged in. Maya had time to nock another arrow and take out one swordsman who dissipated into shadowy smoke. Only his sword remained.

Then the other two charged her, but before either could attack, Bantu pushed Maya down and barreled into both men, his spear out front horizontally in both hands. Both warriors fell down from the impact. One recovered quick enough to swing his sword at Bantu's foot, but Bantu merely lifted it out of the way and rammed his spear down into the man's gut, turning him to smoke. The other didn't move. His focus was on Maya, who had another arrow aimed at him.

A groan from the cave entrance distracted everyone. They turned to see the archer finally fall and become smoke. His quiver and bow fell to the ground. The remaining Shadow Warrior used the opportunity to dash for the exit. Maya walked out after him in no hurry. She moved casually to the entrance and aimed her bow at the running man. The arrow flew out, hitting him in the back. For a moment smoke hung in the air in the shape of his body before it dispersed. What Maya saw beyond him stole the smile from her face. Off in the distance marched dozens of warriors. She realized that the ones they had just faced had been scouts. The Shadow Lord's men had come.

*   *   *

Genjuro slashed at one of the paws of the bulgor. It yanked its arm back and roared, but it then swung back at the young samurai. He managed to duck under it and pull back. Nearby, Scorpius moved quickly under the bulgor he faced, right between the front and hind legs on its right side. From there it could not attack him, and as it moved to solve this dilemma, he moved with it. Another bulgor attacked Tenzin, but he simply stepped out of the path of each attack, claw, or bite as though he were taking a stroll in the park. Alex

could not believe the grace of the monk. The bulgor swung its claws quickly, but it looked like Tenzin was dancing out of harm's way. He even kept his hands behind his back.

The roar of a nearby bulgor got Alex's attention. Unlike the others, Alex had no fighting skills or weapons. Sure, he could handle himself in a schoolyard showdown, but this was a giant mole with razor talons and a bear's head. Running seemed to be the smartest choice, and he was about to do so when Tenzin called to him.

"Close the bottle, Master Alex," he said, "and do not move."

"But—" Alex protested.

"Trust me," Tenzin assured him.

Alex quickly put the cap on the bottle and held his position. The bulgor stopped a moment, swinging its head back and forth and sniffing the air around it.

"Look at their eyes," Tenzin told him. "They are blind and tracking by sound and scent. The bottle has attracted them. They must have followed it when the wind shifted. Now that it is closed they will only attack that which moves."

As if to confirm this, the bulgor bolted toward Tenzin; unfortunately, Alex stood directly between them.

"Now you should run," Tenzin said calmly. Alex ran, but the other teens—all engaged in battle—could not. Luckily, that's when the Axemen got back. Dividing themselves up so that each bulgor faced two opponents, the warriors laid into the monsters. Alex could only watch from the sidelines as the action took place. He had to admire the teamwork of the Axemen. They coordinated their attacks with looks and slight gestures, making small cuts on the beasts that kept them off balance and on the defensive. However, Genjuro and Scorpius appeared to be the only ones trying to kill the bulgor.

"Watch yourselves," an Axeman warned. "They'll get frustrated and leave fairly quickly as long as ..." A bulgor slashed Genjuro in the arm, sending him flying. His sleeve quickly turned red. "They don't smell our blood," the Axeman finished, sadly.

Then all the bulgor went into a frenzy.

*　　*　　*

Maya rushed back into the cave. "We have to get out of here!" she urged.

"More?" asked Bantu.

"Many more," she confirmed.

Bantu looked around the cave. "Is there a back way out of here?" he asked.

Maya's hands went on her hips. "Did you see me get up and explore what is back there at any time? No? Then what makes you think I would know?"

The cave extended back at least a hundred meters, but how much farther, they didn't know.

"You decide," Maya told Bantu. "If we go out the front, they'll see us. If we go out the back, we may be trapped."

"The back," Dara said suddenly.

"Are you sure?" Maya and Bantu asked together.

Dara nodded, though there was clearly some worry in her eyes.

Scooping Dara up into his arms, Bantu shot toward the tunnel at the back of the cave. Maya rushed to the cave entrance, grabbed the fallen quiver full of arrows, and then followed after them.

*   *   *

They're like sharks in a bloodlust, Alex thought as he watched things get very bad. The bulgor lashed out with renewed fury, one of them kicking an unlucky Axemen with its hind legs. He flew over several others and did not get up after he landed.

The bulgor that Scorpius was attacking suddenly rolled sideways, forcing the Roman to dive toward it to slip under it before it crushed him. A short distance away, Genjuro still put up a good fight even though he cradled his left arm to his side. Alex worried that if Genjuro did not stop fighting soon, he would bleed to death. Tenzin was altogether something else. An Axeman fought a bulgor with him, but Tenzin told him to go help Scorpius. The man was skeptical at first, but seeing Tenzin's casually effective dodging ability, he did what the monk told him. When the man had gotten far enough away, Tenzin stopped moving; his muscles tightened all over his body. The bulgor lunged at him; its bear head snatched him up in its jaws. There was a loud crunching sound as it bit down, followed by a yelp. It spat Tenzin out, along with a few broken teeth. Then it burrowed into the ground and was gone. Landing gracefully on the ground, unharmed, Tenzin moved toward the next bulgor.

Scorpius came up from under the bulgor as it rolled on its back. He turned around, just managing to block a flailing claw with his shield; he then leaped onto its stomach, driving his blade in. The Axemen with him leaped in, too, hacking away. Soon, the monster stopped moving.

A cry of pain from one of their comrades sent the Axemen rushing off. The man had been slashed, and a bulgor opened its mouth wide to eat him. Luckily, before it could, several axes flew into the side of its head. It screamed in pain and turned in the direction of the other Axemen. Having thrown their weapons to save their friend, they were unarmed.

"This is familiar," Alex said to himself, remembering using Fatal Fling in his video game a few days ago.

The bulgor charged through the Axemen, knocking them aside as it passed. The beast trampled one unfortunate Axeman's leg. Two others broke some bones after being knocked into trees.

Scorpius looked at the fight around him. He had heard what Tenzin said about the bulgor, and those words had been nagging at him. He knew he should jump back into the fight, but he needed time to think this through. Finally, he noticed it. The bulgor cocked their heads at every small sound. Their ears were that sensitive. Throwing his shield on the ground, Scorpius dragged the tip of his sword across it hard. The high-pitched scraping sound made the men around him shudder and sent shivers up their spines, but the effect on the bulgor was far more dramatic. They howled, as if in pain, and broke away from the fight, digging fast and deep into the ground.

Scorpius continued to scrape his shield until the sound of the burrowing faded away, leaving the area quiet. When they were sure the creatures would not return, the men helped each other up and went about the business of bandaging each other and setting bones.

Alex came up to Scorpius. "Smart move," he told him.

"No thanks to you," Scorpius spat back. "You are useless in a fight, aren't you?"

"I didn't have a weapon," Alex argued.

"Would it have mattered?" Scorpius asked. "Besides, Tenzin didn't have a weapon."

"He *is* a weapon, apparently an invulnerable one, too." Alex turned to the monk. "How did you do that?"

Tenzin gave him that gentle smile. "When the mind and body are pure and focused, one can become harder than steel."

"Sure," replied Alex. "I knew that."

"We have to set up so that the wind blows straight into the forest again," Scorpius stated. "Alex, *this time* close that bottle if the wind shifts in the slightest. Everyone, be wary of those creatures. I will make that sound again if we feel them approaching."

Alex slumped for a moment, a wave of nausea coming over him.

"Whoa," he said.

"Are you ill, Master Alex?" Tenzin asked.

"Just felt sick there for a moment," he said, reassuring the monk.

"I fear you have been away from your charge for too long."

Alex cocked his head. "Excuse me?"

"Your summons binds you to be Dara's protector. Since you are not protecting her now, it is inducing a response from you to do what you are supposed to do."

"But you told me I *had* to come along."

"That I did, but you must also protect Dara. In the future, do not create tasks for us that directly contradict your own."

"Gee, thanks. Good tip."

*   *   *

A Shadow Warrior emerged from the cave and presented Askar with the recovered weapons.

"I told them to scout, not attack," Askar said, disgusted with their actions. "This was no less than they deserved. Where is the child?"

"We're not sure, sir," the warrior replied. "There are several tracks leading toward Shadow Wood, but the fight obviously took place inside the cave. There are more tracks leading off toward that lake and back."

"The child," Askar said flatly. "Where do the smallest tracks lead?"

"There are some in the cave, but they do not go into the back tunnel with the others, and there are some that lead off to the lake."

"The lake is our best bet then," Askar decided. "Leave ten men here to guard the cave entrance. The rest of you come with me."

* * *

The Nano really wasn't much of a lantern, but it kept them from walking into walls and falling into holes as the tunnel weaved its way down into the earth. They were forced to travel slowly, but Dara still appreciated the device that Alex had left with her. Without it, they would be walking completely blind.

The tunnel was wide enough for three people to walk side by side, but fallen rocks, stalagmites, random ditches, and holes made doing that difficult. Water dripped from the walls, and the slight odour of saltwater wafted at them from somewhere far ahead. Dara hoped she'd guessed right, and that this tunnel ended at the sea like several others in the area. Bantu had put her down, and she now led the way. Behind her, she heard both Bantu and Maya begin to breathe strangely. Moving away from Shadow Wood seemed to be making things worse for them.

They continued for what seemed like an hour before Maya leaned to the side of the tunnel and vomited. Things were getting very bad.

"Can't do this," Maya whispered breathlessly. "Must get to the Wood."

She turned to go back, but Bantu grabbed her. As weak as the African was, he was still stronger than her in her condition.

"There could be an exit nearby," he suggested. "Then we can double back and head west."

It was wishful thinking, but Maya nodded and they moved on.

* * *

Seventeen Axemen had been rescued before they were forced to go into the Wood. Senufer arrived with the latest men, and the spirits of the warriors soared when he exited the forest. The boys were awed by the size of the man.

"Thank you for rescuing me and my men," he told the young warriors, and Alex.

"We're not done yet," Alex replied. "Thirty-three to go and now we have to go in there."

Seeing Alex's face and the condition of some of the warriors, Senufer noted, "You have seen battle."

Alex blushed, not wanting to tell the man that Scorpius was the cause of his injuries.

Scorpius jumped into the conversation. "We'll move back to the north and then move in straight south," Scorpius said. "The Axemen can cut a path as we go so that the remaining men can follow it out if they come across it."

Alex wondered if Scorpius spoke up to stop Alex from telling Senufer who was responsible for his wounds, or because the Roman saw how uncomfortable Alex was.

Senufer nodded. "I had a similar plan until my axes lost their enchantment. We may come across the path I began to carve."

Scorpius did not seem pleased. "I hope not. Intersecting paths could make things worse."

"I know," Senufer agreed.

They moved back to the site of the bulgor carcass where they began to chop their way into the Wood.

Alex showed the others how his compass worked and led the way in, finally feeling useful to the group but sicker by the moment as well. The men tied themselves together to keep the misdirection spell from separating them. Alex thought they looked like a kindergarten class on a field trip, having to hold the rope, but the precaution was necessary. The forest's haze limited their vision to ten paces in any direction. Many men could not see others tied down the line, but they ignored the problem as best as they could, determined to find their friends. Tree after tree fell before them, and the logs were lined straight on the ground pointing the way out.

Another seven Axemen soon found their way to the group. The speed of the search increased with each man while Alex's confidence soared.

"Don't worry, Senufer," he said. "We'll soon have the rest of the men out and then ... then ..." Alex ran to the side of the path they had carved where he threw up. "Oh, man! This is getting worse fast."

"Dara must be moving away from you," Tenzin surmised.

"That doesn't make sense," Alex said. "Why would she be moving that way ... unless she's on the run!"

When the others went silent with shock, Scorpius jumped in.

"Alex, take Genjuro and Tenzin and head back. I'll stay with the Axemen and finish the search. One of us has to stay and *help* find the Axemen as you ordered us."

"Take five of my men with you," Senufer added. "We will meet up with you when we've found the rest."

Alex, Genjuro, Tenzin, and company rushed back down the tree trail. Alex's nausea vanished the moment they started.

*   *   *

Askar returned from the pond to the cave, greatly annoyed that no trail had been found there. He moved into the cave angrily and soon found the footprints inside. Looking at the ones leading down the tunnel, he called the Shadow Warrior who had reported them to him.

"What do you see here?" Askar asked him.

"Two sets of footprints," he replied. "A large man and a woman, but no child's, General."

He dragged the man by the ear into the cave's center. "And what do you see here?" he asked.

"The large man's footprints, General. I don't see—"

"Fool!" Askar yelled. "These footprints are shallower than those! He was carrying the child! You've just cost us hours!"

"My apologies, General. I will not make that mistake again."

Askar's arm swung out without warning, his mace smashing into the man's chest and crushing it. The man dissipated into smoke.

"Well, at least you were right about *one* thing," Askar commented. He addressed the ten men who had been guarding the cave entrance.

"Stay here in case they manage to get around us. The rest of you grab wood for torches and follow me," he told them, and then turned and moved into the tunnel. His blue eyes began to glow as the tunnel darkened around him.

*   *   *

With Bantu and Maya both staggering, Dara now slowed down for them instead of the other way around. Finally, Dara heard a thud behind her and turned to see that Maya had collapsed. Bantu fell moments later.

"Maya? Bantu?" Dara cried, shaking them. They only moaned in response. "No, please. Don't leave me. I can't do this alone!"

She froze then as a distant sound echoed through the tunnel toward her. Footsteps. Dara quickly pulled the Scroll from her travel bag. *Papa?* she thought to it. *Papa?!*

No response.

She wanted to try another summons but feared what could happen this time. All she could summon effectively were butterflies. *No, not butterflies*, she thought, *something else small.*

She took a deep breath and let it out, relaxing like her father had shown her. The Scroll sat in her lap as she cast. It began to glow as she pulled a small bit of its power from it to help her focus. Her summons began with, "Please work. Please work. Please work."

*   *   *

They set a good pace across the countryside, but it didn't seem nearly fast enough. Alex resisted the urge to run, knowing he would only be able to keep it up a little while before he'd be moving at a pace slower than they were now. Almost every minute, Alex opened the book and checked Bantu's and

Maya's pages. He figured if something happened to them, then their portraits would return or something. So far nothing had changed. That didn't make him feel better though. Just because Maya and Bantu were alive—*if* they were alive—that didn't tell him what state they were in or what had happened to Dara.

"I hope they're okay," Alex said. "Maybe they've found a place to hide. Do you think Bantu and Maya can handle whatever it is that's making them run?"

"I will scout ahead," Tenzin said, and then he set his pace to double that of the rest of the group, leaving them shaking their heads.

"That guy's a wonder," said Alex, "and with the rest of the Axemen bringing up the rear soon we should be able to ... to ... oh my god! I'm an idiot!"

"What is it, Alex-san?" Genjuro asked.

"We should have told them to postpone the search!"

"Why?"

"What happens to you when they find the last Axemen?" Alex asked.

"My task is complete, and I return to the book," Genjuro answered, "but then you can just summon me again for—"

"You return to the book!" Alex exclaimed. "All of you!"

Genjuro's expression turned to one of worry. "Including Bantu-san and Maya-chan. Leaving Dara-chan ..."

"Alone," Alex finished.

* * *

The path cut several kilometers into the forest now, and fifteen more Axemen had joined the ranks either because the group had cut their way to them or they had followed the scent of imaginary food. Scorpius kept glancing over at Senufer and finally had to ask the question, "Why are you here?"

"Same as you," Senufer replied. "To rescue my men."

"But why are you still here? I thought Dara was the daughter of your king," said Scorpius.

"She is," Senufer confirmed.

"They why didn't you rush off to rescue her?"

"Because this path we're making leads directly to my king, and I want to be there when we get to the end. He was defeated because of my inadequacies. Do you know how that feels?"

Scorpius had a brief flash of his uncle falling in battle because he could not help him in time. "I do," he replied. The two exchanged a look of understanding.

"If there is a way to save him, I will find it," Senufer swore.

* * *

Askar led his troops through the tunnel at a good pace. After an hour, he could sense that their chase was nearing its end. The tracks of their prey had become awkward, as though they were tired and nearing collapse. Their scent grew stronger as well, confirming that they had almost caught up. That's when they heard the humming. The tunnel distorted the sound of it, but it was familiar. Neither Askar nor his men could place it, however. They set a more cautious pace but continued on. Soon a blue light could be seen in the distance around a bend. The humming, much louder now, vibrated their bodies, its sound accented by a crackling within it. Askar drew his mace and stepped around the corner. As he did, the hairs on his body stood up from the static in the air. He dreaded what it might mean.

The passage was well lit for the next fifty paces, and where the light ended sat Dara, her eyes glowing with power; the Scroll sat in her lap as she cast a spell. On the walls and ceiling between them and her hovered the source of the light—hundreds of lightning bugs. Askar froze. The lightning bugs of his world looked much like large hornets. Instead of a yellow and black striped abdomen, their abdomens had black and translucent stripes with blue electricity sparking inside them. They did not stab you with a stinger but shot you with a small bolt of electricity. The bolts of two or three hornets could disable a person. Five could kill. They filled the tunnel, crawling and hovering, as if they were waiting for something.

A new lightning bug appeared in Dara's hands. As it took flight, she looked up in Askar's direction, the glow fading from her eyes. Behind him men pushed up to see the source of the light and sound. Askar made no move whatsoever as he tried to think of a way to back out quietly—despite the congestion of bodies behind him.

Dara looked right at him. "Get them," she said.

The lightning bugs shot straight at the Shadow Warriors. Just before they reached him, Askar twisted the top of his ring, activating a spell of Recall, which transported him in an instant to the Hall of Shadows. He vanished from sight, and the bugs moved in after his men. The warriors turned in a panic, and many tripped over each other in their desperation to get out. Some swung their swords ineffectively at the insects before being jolted by them. The unlucky few who managed to strike a lightning bug discovered that swords acted as excellent conductors of electricity. Soon the screams of the Shadow Warriors drowned out the humming in the hall, and the light of the bugs dimmed slightly as the smoke of dead warriors filled the air. The men at the back managed to run, but the lightning bugs, following Dara's order, pursued them relentlessly.

Farther back in the cave, Dara shook her protectors. "Bantu! Maya!" she urged. "The way is clear. We can go to Shadow Wood now."

As if hearing the news somehow healed them, both warriors opened their eyes and slowly got to their feet. Using the fallen torches of the Shadow Warriors, they moved back down the tunnel. With each passing step, their strength returned and their heads cleared. Soon Bantu carried Dara on his shoulders as they jogged back to the entrance. They were so focused on getting out that they didn't notice the figures behind them, matching their pace.

* * *

"The *girl* defeated you?" the Shadow Lord asked incredulously.

"She was using the Scroll!" Askar defended. "It is a formidable force. You know this to be true."

"I still find it hard to believe that she could cast a spell powerful enough to wipe out a legion of Shadow Warriors," the Shadow Lord remarked. "Even a third-year apprentice could not summon that many lightning bugs at once—if there were as many as you say."

"There were, my lord!" Askar insisted. Then he remembered the bug appearing in Dara's hands and realized what had happened. The Shadow Lord did not miss the expression on his face.

"What is it?" he asked.

"I believe she summoned them one at a time."

The Shadow Lord opened his mouth to argue the point, but stopped and then nodded. It made sense to him. Small magic, used effectively, could have devastating results. It is one of the first things a wizard is taught.

Askar decided to press his advantage. "Send me back now, my lord," he begged. "There were but two warriors with her, and they had collapsed on the ground."

The Shadow Lord shook his head.

"I cannot send you to a place I have not been, and it will take far too long for you to journey from here. They will likely have moved to a safe place."

"They have been on the move all day," Askar said. "They will need to rest for the night."

"Still the distance ..."

Can be overcome.

Both men looked over toward the throne where the voice of the Hall seemed to come from this time. Hovering in the air was a black ball of magic. It rotated and pulsed, seeming to breathe. Black appendages thrust out to the sides and widened, becoming wings. Talons clawed their way into view near its bottom, and soon its shape coalesced into a giant black falcon, larger than both men. Its form was not completely solid. Much like the Shadow Lord's cloak, it melded with and melted off the shadows around it. When it hovered right in front of a shadow, it completely disappeared. Suddenly, energy surged from the Shadow Lord's eyes, making him scream. His arms came up as if to cover them, but he could not lift them all the way. Twin red and blue ribbons of power spiraled away into the falcon's head until glowing blue eyes appeared. Just as suddenly, the transference ended; the Shadow Lord staggered, almost collapsing. The falcon landed on the floor and screeched in a booming voice so loud that Askar winced.

Behold. Specter.

"What? What did you do to him?" Askar asked referring to the Shadow Lord.

I gave him a gift.

"Gave? It looked more like you took—"

"No," the Shadow Lord replied, regaining his strength and straightening up. "Its eyes are mine. What it sees, I see." He smiled at the opportunities this presented.

Ride it back, Askar. Grab the girl while she sleeps. Kill any who defend her.

"Yes, O Great Hall of Shadows," Askar replied, bowing low in submission.

"And to better help you against your enemies," the Shadow Lord said as he cast a spell. Energy crackled around Askar's mace. He pulled it from his belt and held it in front of him. He could feel the power coursing through it. Small arcs of electricity danced between its spikes and then jumped up to his face. Askar's head jerked back as he expected the pain of an electrical shock. Instead, he felt a slight tickle pressing above his eyes. A blue gem formed on his forehead, glowing with the same light as his eyes.

"The gem will protect you from electricity of any kind and let you channel it," the Shadow Lord told him. "Go. Do to her warriors what she did to yours."

Askar smiled. "With pleasure, my lord."

*   *   *

Tenzin crouched behind a small grassy rise, looking at the guards at the cave entrance who stood with little attention. He sized them up and determined that he may not be able to best them by himself. With the others, however, the fight would be over swiftly. Looking northward from the cave, he noticed the tracks of the Shadow Warriors who had come. Many more men had been here than the ones he could see, but where had they gone? Suddenly, the men broke away from the cave and rushed to the south. Tenzin looked that way, thinking they had spotted his comrades, but nothing lay in that direction except a small lake just past some trees.

Movement and flashes of light brought his attention back to the cave, and he realized the men weren't running to something. They were running from something. A small swarm of bugs emerged, crackling with electricity, and pursued the Shadow Warriors. Tenzin watched as the men dived into the lake as a group. The bugs followed, and a giant spark of energy shot up as they touched the surface of the water. Soon after, the Shadow Warriors reemerged from the lake, wet and uncomfortable, but otherwise unharmed. Tenzin struggled to suppress his laughter. He thought about sneaking in the cave, but Alex was waiting for his report. He turned and jogged back the way he came.

*   *   *

"Hey!" one Axeman yelled at another.

"Hey yourself!" the other replied. "You walked into me."

"What's going on?" Senufer demanded, not liking dissension in his ranks. He knew the men were tired, hungry, and on edge, but they had to press on. They only had two more men to find.

"Jonas can't walk straight," the first said.

"It was Malik that walked into me!" Jonas countered.

"Let it go!" Senufer demanded. "Move on."

The two did as they were told. Grabbing their axes, they moved forward toward the next trees. They took only two steps before smashing into each other.

"What is wrong with you?" Malik shouted. "Can't you walk straight?"

"I did!" Jonas insisted.

"Neither of you did!" Senufer yelled to stop the coming fight.

With a nod from Senufer, Scorpius walked up to their position and focused on the compass in his hand. He took a step forward and the needle turned. When he looked up, the other men seemed to have moved as well. He realized that the needle hadn't turned, he had.

Senufer smiled. "It doesn't want us going any farther."

"Then we're there," Scorpius realized.

Senufer nodded.

"But if we can't walk any farther ..." Scorpius said, trying to determine the next move.

Senufer was ahead of him though. He threw a rock toward the trees, and it flew unerringly. "The spell affects our minds, not our bodies. If we leap in that direction ..." he prompted.

"We'll go in a straight line," Scorpius finished.

Senufer tied a rope around himself and handed it to Jonas. "Just in case we need you to guide us out," he said.

Scorpius and Senufer backed up several paces from where the magic grew stronger and then ran hard. When they jumped, the world spun around them—one way then the other as though a whirlwind flung them about. When they landed, they had come out of the trees into a clearing. The trees arced away from them; a series of giant wooden pillars—the bars of a cage for something too dangerous to let escape—defined the boundary of the clearing. The dull gray sky above them lit up occasionally with sheet lightning, and a light drizzle fell in the clearing—but only the clearing. Having been here before, Senufer knew they stood in the right place, but the only thing before them was an immense crater. The Hall of Shadows was gone.

* * *

Dara, Maya, and Bantu quickened their pace when they saw daylight around a bend ahead. They had passed many dead lightning bugs as well as lost weapons along the way. They had hoped the way out would be clear, but

Bantu quickly put out his torch when he saw the silhouettes of the enemy by the mouth of the cave. They kept behind the bend, and Maya watched the entrance carefully for several minutes. The men kept glancing in warily but seemed uncomfortable and distracted. She soon realized that they were all wet for some reason; yet the ground outside was dry, and it hadn't rained. She finally turned and said, "I count eight, assuming more aren't outside the cave. I think we can take them."

"Eight?" Bantu considered. "That is too many."

"If we stay here, we are only going to get sick again," Maya reminded him. She twirled a finger around a lock of her hair. "We should be able to defeat six with no real difficulty."

"You just said there were eight."

Maya smiled and stepped out around the bend, nocking two arrows at once and tilting her bow almost sideways. The guards ahead had just noticed her when she loosed the arrows. Two guards disappeared into smoke. The others took cover, three shooting arrows back at her. She slipped back around the wall.

"I must have miscounted. There are only six," she winked.

Bantu sighed. Dara giggled.

* * *

Tenzin ran up to Alex, Genjuro, and the others.

"I believe they have our friends trapped in the cave."

"Did you see them, Tenzin-san?" Genjuro asked.

"No, but enchanted insects flew out from the cave and attacked the warriors. I believe the magic of the Scroll was involved."

"How many?" Alex asked.

"Ten outside the cave. I don't know how many inside."

"Ten against seven," Alex thought aloud.

"We are eight, Master Alex," Tenzin pointed out.

"I don't count," Alex stated.

"You greatly underestimate yourself," Tenzin warned. "We are only as great or as small as we allow ourselves to be."

"I have no weapons," Alex argued.

"You have a very powerful weapon," Tenzin countered, tapping Alex's head. "You must just make use of it."

"Scorpius is the strategist," said Alex. "He figured out a way to get the Axemen out of the forest."

"Yet you had the wisdom to know to rescue them," Tenzin pointed out.

"But I made myself sick and put Dara in danger in the process."

"Lasting experience comes from making mistakes," the monk lectured.

"And if I screw up again?" asked Alex.

"If we anticipate losing, we have already defeated ourselves."

"You're going to counter everything I say with something insightful and profound, aren't you?" Alex guessed.

Tenzin gave him a playful smile. "That is my plan."

Alex couldn't help but smile, too. "Okay already," Alex said in resignation but almost laughing. "Let's go rescue that kid! High five!" he said, holding both his hands up for Tenzin and Genjuro to slap.

They both held their hands up where they stood but did not know to slap Alex's hand. Alex put his hand to his face and shook his head. So did Tenzin and Genjuro.

* * *

"This cannot be!" Senufer exclaimed.

"It can move?" Scorpius asked.

"I did not think it possible," Senufer replied. "But, if it gained enough power, then a spell of transportation might have been possible."

"So it can go wherever it likes?"

Senufer shook his head.

"If what Mornak has taught me about magic is correct, then such a spell would greatly tax its energies. It would be impossible for it to do such a thing while keeping the realm darkened. Even now, darkening the realm must be limiting its abilities severely."

Scorpius nodded, stroking his chin as he thought it through. "So it moved first ... to hide. Then it waited a while to regain its power before it darkened the realm."

"And now it could be anywhere and with it ... Mornak," Senufer concluded.

Scorpius walked up to the edge of the crater. It extended down several storeys with a diameter a couple hundred meters wide. He guessed that the Hall must have risen at least as high as it was deep. Even in its absence, the Hall's size impressed him. The Roman Colosseum could fit inside its crater.

Senufer seemed to sense his thoughts.

"There was much evil to be put in there," he said. "The realm was tearing itself apart. Even good people were forced, or persuaded, to do immoral things. I should know. I was one of them."

"You? What immoral things had you done?" Scorpius asked although he wasn't sure he wanted to hear the answer.

"I prefer not to speak of it," Senufer told him. "Let us just say that I am sometimes surprised I didn't end up in there. Mornak was my friend from before my descent into darkness and the one who saved me despite my actions. Were I he, I would not have been as forgiving. To this day I cannot believe the mercy he showed me, the mercy he showed so many. He saved thousands, perhaps millions. He should not be the one trapped in that damned Hall.

"It does not matter where it is hiding. The Axemen will search the realm for it. We will rally wizards and warriors to our cause and break down the walls of the Hall of Shadows and free our king! It will be as historic a moment as when the Hall was created. You can be a part of it if you wish ... as an Axeman."

Senufer turned to Scorpius to see his reaction to the offer, but the boy was not there. Alex's compass sat on the grass where the young Roman had stood.

*   *   *

Every time Maya tried to peek around the corner an arrow shot her way. She fired back periodically to try to keep the men at bay, but her shots struck either high or wide because of her angle. She thanked herself for grabbing the extra quiver earlier, since she had already exhausted its contents. "They won't give me time to sight my shot," she complained.

"Perhaps if you asked nicely," Bantu suggested sarcastically. "Did you really think it would be that easy?"

"It was before," Maya remarked.

"The first warriors we faced didn't expect us to be a threat," said Bantu. "We surprised them. These men won't make that mistake. Your first shot let them know that they're dealing with an expert marksman."

"Thank you," Maya said playfully, "but if you really want to get on my good side, you'll help in some way."

Maya poked her head out again. Just before she had to duck back, she saw two Shadow Warriors approaching with their shields locked. They'd be up to the bend in moments, and her bow would be useless in a close-quartered fight.

"Come out, woman!" one yelled. "All we want is the girl. Give her up, and you can go unharmed."

They hadn't seen and didn't know about Bantu, Maya realized. She pointed at herself, then the ground, and then at Bantu and the men. He got the message.

"All right," she answered resignedly. "Don't attack. I'm coming out."

Stepping out from behind the wall, Maya pretended to trip. As the others watched her go down, Bantu jumped out from around the bend and swung his spear into the faces of both men. They flew back onto the ground. Before he could do anything else, though, an arrow pierced his leg and another embedded in his spear. Maya shot from her position on the ground, taking out one archer, but then she took an arrow in her left shoulder. She yelped from the pain as her bow fell from her grasp. Bantu reached for her to pull her clear and took another arrow in his side. He cried out and slumped to the ground, but he would not give up. Maya reached out to him with her right arm but then grunted as an arrow pierced her stomach. She knew she was going to die, but she would not give up in the face of her enemy, especially this enemy.

"Hera, I hate men," she cursed.

Then Bantu had her by the wrist and prepared to yank her from the line of fire. She glimpsed the smile on his face from his accomplishment before they both vanished from sight. Dara broke into a cold sweat when she saw what had happened. She had no idea where Bantu and Maya had gone and was too scared to even try to reason it through. She only knew that the Shadow Warriors were getting up off the ground—and now she had no defenders.

8

Alex, Tenzin, Genjuro, and the Axemen peeked over the same rise where Tenzin had been at earlier. They counted five Shadow Warriors at the cave entrance. The men battled with someone or something inside the cave—a distraction they intended to use fully. They moved ahead quickly, Tenzin reaching the men first and leading with a flying kick to the nearest man's head. The monk vanished just before connecting. Alex turned to Genjuro to get his reaction, but the samurai had disappeared as well. The Axemen had also halted their attack with the unexpected event. Only then did it click with Alex what had just happened. All the Axemen had been found.

Noticing the movement behind them, the men at the cave entrance turned to see Alex and the five knights with him. The Shadow Warriors with bows dropped them, drawing swords instead. Then the two groups faced off silently, sizing each other up while waiting for the other to make the first move. Keeping his movements as subtle as he could, Alex opened the top of his book bag.

Dara's scream caused everyone to burst into action. Shadow Warriors and Axemen clashed in a flurry of steel on steel while Alex bolted toward the cave entrance, praying he was not too late. Unarmed and seemingly harmless, the Shadow Warriors ignored him as he slipped inside.

Seeing movement at the back tunnel, Alex rushed onward, picking up a discarded sword from the ground as he went. A heavily armoured Shadow Warrior stepped out, confronting him with sword and shield. He skidded to a stop.

Oh, this is fair, Alex thought, but he raised his sword defensively, prepared to do whatever it took to save Dara.

Then a second warrior came into view, holding a frightened Dara with a knife at her throat.

"Crap," Alex muttered as he dropped his sword and put his hands up. The warriors grabbed him and pushed him outside.

"Surrender or we kill them!" one yelled.

The Axemen looked up to see Alex and Dara's predicament. Realizing they had no choice, they stopped fighting and dropped their weapons. The Shadow

Warriors moved in, quickly scooping up the weapons before restraining their prisoners.

Soon Alex and the Axemen were kneeling on the ground, their hands tied behind their backs and their ankles bound together. Alex silently cursed himself for his earlier actions. He had rushed in because of Dara's scream.

I should have summoned the warriors first, he told himself, but that move would only have been wise if he knew that Dara was being held and not fighting for her life. The time to summon them could have been fatal for her.

Dara sat nearby with her hands and ankles bound in front of her. The men had taken Alex's and Dara's bags and emptied the contents. The leader of the group had the Scroll tucked in his belt.

"Where can Askar be?" he asked aloud.

"How do you know the lightning bugs didn't get him?" a warrior asked.

"Askar?" the leader challenged. "Are you joking? It would take much more than bugs to defeat him. If he's not back by nightfall, we kill the Axemen. As much as I know Askar would like to torture them, they're too dangerous to travel with. In the morning, we'll head back to Aspiria with the girl. The Shadow Lord will reward us greatly for bringing her and the Scroll to him."

One man flipped through Alex's books. He obviously couldn't read. He just looked at the pictures. He had scanned *Historic Inventions* and now worked through *Historic Moments in Time*. He stopped on a picture of a giant mushroom cloud.

"Fellas, come look at this," he said.

"Is that a cloud?" one asked.

"Real weird looking," another commented. "Looks like a mushroom."

The book holder turned the book toward Alex and asked, "What is it?"

It was the Hiroshima explosion. "It's an atomic bomb," Alex answered.

"What's that?" the man asked.

Alex realized that there was no way these men had ever seen a bomb, let alone an atomic explosion.

"It's the name of the spell. Atomic Bomb," he lied. "It's a fireball so powerful it destroyed a city of thousands. That's the cloud of ash it produced." Alex knew the bomb killed over a hundred thousand people but doubted these men would believe cities could be big enough to hold that many people.

The men reacted with awe. "A city of thousands, you say?" the man asked. Several of the men crowded around to look at the picture.

"Wouldn't you have liked to have been there to see that happen, eh, men?" he asked.

They all nodded. A second later, they were sucked into the book.

Alex cringed. "They're gonna feel that in the morning," he mumbled to himself.

Only three men remained. The leader lunged at Alex, putting his sword against the teen's throat. "Bring them back now, wizard!" he demanded.

"I can't!" Alex cried.

"You will, or I will kill you right now."

"If you kill me, then they'll never be freed," Alex threatened, not really knowing what would happen if he died.

"Fine," the leader said. He turned to one of his remaining men. "Every minute he delays, kill an Axeman. Kill one now to let him know we're not bluffing."

The Shadow Warrior moved over to one of the Axemen and drew his sword. The Axemen looked at him defiantly but did not move.

"No! Please!" Alex yelled as he picked up the book. Unseen by the others, ash fell from between its pages, quickly turning to shadowy smoke before vanishing.

The Shadow Warrior raised his sword over the Axeman, but before he could swing, a crossbow bolt struck him the in chest; then he, too, turned to smoke. Everyone present turned toward the source of the bolt to see a half dozen figures in black running from the cave entrance with swords drawn. As one, they charged into the remaining Shadow Warriors with a level of skill that awed Alex; soon only the newcomers remained.

"Thank you!" Alex exclaimed, holding up his bonds for one of them to cut. "You couldn't have timed that any better."

He looked over to the Axemen expecting to see relief on their faces but found suspicion, anger, and caution.

Alex turned back to take a good look at the people who saved them— five men and a woman. All of them wore light, tight black leather armour and boots over black shirts and pants. The black armour was studded with small sharp metal spikes along the outer arms and legs, on the shoulders, and on the gloves. When one of them made a fist, the spikes would be the first things that would strike whatever was punched. Alex did not want to be on the receiving end of such an attack. Even the bottom of their boots had tiny metal spikes, almost like cleats on baseball shoes—only much smaller and sharper. All wore cutlasses with black scabbards; the curved blades were of polished silver. A couple had small crossbows slung over their shoulders; these were black like the rest of their attire and weaponry. Most of the group wore black daggers with black blades at their hips, but one had a bandolier across his chest with ten black throwing knives in it. All the men and the woman looked built for speed and agility—not sheer strength and power—although not one appeared weak by any means.

The new black-clad warriors had what appeared to be Southeast Asian features, suggesting to Alex that they were of Filipino or Malaysian heritage. He could only tell this because the cowls of their outfits were currently drawn back. Their long hair was tied in the back, and the men sported tiny goatees. They wore smiles after their small victory, but Alex realized that he did not like those smiles. There was a sinister feel to them.

"Pirates," Brasius, an Axeman, spat.

Pirates? thought Alex. *They look more like ninja. Whoa! Ninja-pirates!*

The woman walked up to him. Her confident and sultry motions suggested authority as well as a deep-seated vanity. A tattoo of a spider's web surrounded her left eye, accenting both her beauty and her deadliness. Alex noticed small blades that looked like fingernails at the end of her gloves. The woman looked down, taking in Brasius's uniform.

"Axemen," she said with loathing.

"You have much nerve showing your face here, Helena," Brasius said angrily.

"You know me?" Helena replied, pleasantly surprised by the recognition. "I would have thought that my men and I would've been forgotten by now. I'm flattered."

"We've not forgotten the deeds of Captain Helena, the Black Widow of the Sea," he told her. "Kill us and get it over with."

"I don't think so," she replied. "Kill an Axeman in cold blood, and the rest will not stop until you're dead or in the Hall. Besides, we saved your lives. I like knowing that you will all have to live with the fact that you owe us one."

She turned to her men. "Take what's worth taking."

The pirates removed the weapons from the Axemen while Helena picked the Scroll up from where it had fallen in the battle and put it in her belt. Alex's books were placed in his book bag and added to the loot, along with Dara's bag.

"You can't take the Scroll," Alex warned. "The realm is in danger and we need it to—"

"To restore things to peace and harmony?" Helena asked. "Is that what it does? I don't think so. You Axemen are always trying to restore peace and harmony. We've been exiled for ten years by your damned sorcerer-king, Mornak. And if this," she said shaking the Scroll, "keeps things the way they are now, then we're keeping it and ending our exile."

"You were given a chance to redeem yourselves," Brasius argued.

"And what?" Helena snapped back. "Become merchants? We are pirates! We live for the adventure of the seas, the thrill of the hunt, and the luxury that comes with the spoils." The others gave nods, and some even said, "Aye!" as she spoke.

"When we saw the skies darken over the realm yesterday," she continued, "we figured something *bad* must've happened. From the looks of things, the Hall has been opened, hasn't it?"

"No," Brasius answered.

"You lie," she accused.

"He doesn't lie," Alex insisted. "The Hall has somehow become alive. It's trying to take over the realm."

Helena paused and considered his words. Then she burst out laughing.

"That is perfect! It is no less than you all deserve! I suppose Mornak has his hands full right now, fighting his own creation."

Their reaction to her statement was not what she had expected.

"Say what you know, Axemen," she ordered. "Is Mornak not concerned with this problem?"

The others looked at each other but did not reply.

Helena did not like being answered with silence. She grabbed Brasius by the neck. He thought her grip felt quite strong for a woman. She seemed to sense the condescending thought and squeezed harder. Her "nails" dug into his neck, and lines of blood appeared.

"Speak, Axeman!" she demanded.

"He's been captured!" Dara yelled, fearing for the man. "The Hall of Shadows is holding my father prisoner."

"Your fath ... Dara!" Helena exclaimed as she released the Axeman and moved over to Dara. "Oh, little one, what a pleasure to meet you!" Her words dripped with venom. "You must be *so* upset about your father. I can't say that I am. Well, a little perhaps. If Mornak were free, I'd kidnap you for the ransom, but I suppose there's no point in that now. I thank you for the information, however. It has proved highly valuable."

"If you help rescue him, my father will reward you!" Dara promised.

"Now that's an amusing thought," Helena laughed. "Rescue our most hated enemy from the hands of the weapon he used against us. I really don't think so, dear. We'll just be off with this booty and the knowledge that our piracy will not only be permitted here but possibly encouraged."

"I don't get it," Alex thought aloud.

"Excuse me?" Helena asked.

"You said you've been exiled for the last ten years. You mean they allowed piracy before the Hall was built?"

"Of course not, boy," she answered, "but there's a big difference between the fear of being captured or even killed as opposed to being imprisoned and tormented forever in a man-made hell. We felt it better to take our business to other realms, but the booty in those other realms hasn't been near what we used to collect here. It seems that that will all change now, especially once our wizard unlocks the secrets of your magic tomes, and this golden Scroll will fetch a fortune from a foreign wizard.

"Now," she said turning her attention to the Axemen, "I want your word that none of the king's Axemen will pursue us, or I shall slay his daughter right now."

"No!" Alex yelled as he lunged forward. With his wrists and ankles tied, he only succeeded in throwing himself on the ground near Helena.

"You evil witch!" Brasius spat.

"Witch?" she laughed. "I wish! Can you imagine how powerful I'd be if magic ran through my blood? Now swear. If there's one thing that can be counted on, it's the word of an Axeman." She playfully grazed her fingers under Dara's neck. "Well?"

Brasius hung his head. "By my word, not one of the king's Axemen will pursue you or your men."

"Good enough," she said. "We're taking the girl with us, just in case."

"Leave her alone!" Alex yelled. "Take me if you want a hostage!"

"Take you?" Helena laughed. "Who *are* you? A stranger by your garb. You are of no worth to me."

"Please," Alex begged. "Don't take her ... or take me, too. I'm ... her guardian."

"And a fine one you turned out to be," Helena scoffed. "We'll put her on the next ship we loot and instruct them to bring her back to port. On that you have *my* word," Helena stated.

The pirates gathered their loot and returned to the cave.

Three hours passed while the Axemen waited in the dark for their comrades to arrive. The entire time Alex just lay on the ground, staring at the cave, weeping and mumbling "no."

*   *   *

Scorpius waited in place for almost an hour for Alex to summon him, all the while growing angrier with his jailer. Scorpius wondered why he hadn't been summoned yet now that Alex knew what happened when the legionnaire returned to the book. Could it be that since they didn't get along well, Alex was trying to minimize the time they spent together by keeping him in the book? He could see Alex doing that and cursed him for it. How could that boy leave someone trapped in time like this?

The world remained suspended around him. He slipped between arrows stopped in midflight and walked on grass that would not bend beneath his weight. A slight lack of colour in the world accented the fact that he was not really a part of his surroundings. Amid the chaos of friends and enemies, he was completely alone; he knew that if he spent enough time here, he would go mad.

What was he to do though? He could not force his way out of this situation, or if he could, he had no idea how to go about doing it. Then something else occurred to him. What if the reason Alex hadn't summoned him was because he couldn't? What if Alex was dead? He shuddered at the thought. Would Alex's death really result in locking Scorpius and the others in time? Was he so attached to Alex that he would have to put his life on the line for him just to keep from being stuck in this place, or was he already too late and already stuck? He could do nothing but wait to find out the answer.

Around him the battle seemed evenly matched. Scorpius knew that could change when time started again. His uncle, the general of their forces, had just fallen. Someone new would have to take charge of the battle, or the enemy would gain the advantage and defeat them. Unfortunately, the men directly below his uncle in rank were yes-men. They excelled at agreeing with superiors and relaying orders, but none could truly command. Someone else would have to take charge. Looking around at the men, Scorpius wondered who it would be.

*   *   *

Bantu walked through the grasslands of Kenya, heading back to his village. He had found the lion he had been hunting, the one that had killed several of their sheep. One of his duties in the rituals to attain manhood was to kill a lion, and this one volunteered when it attacked their livestock. He did not look forward to the next ritual, the circumcision, but it was Maasai tradition; he would make his parents proud of him when he went through it. He had laughed when he came upon the lion, frozen in time, and thought he would have an easy kill, but he could not harm the animal in this suspended world. So he decided to return home.

The silence of the usually noisy environment was eerie. He passed by animals that seemed like statues and had to climb over areas of tall grass that would normally give way before him. The world seemed made of stone, just coloured in to look like a grassland. Even those colours were slightly washed out. At least his wounds had disappeared when he had found himself back here, but while he was thankful for that, being here still disturbed him.

After a great deal of meandering, Bantu saw the loaf-shaped wooden huts of his village. He thought he would feel more comfortable once he arrived home. However, as he entered the village, the sight of his people, frozen like statues, had the opposite effect. Two women prepared a meal over a cooking fire. The smoke hung in the air, unmoving. The fire glowed, but the flames could well have been red crystal. Bantu tried to pass his hand through it, but it felt as solid as a tree; no heat came from the flames. He realized then that the air held neither heat nor humidity. Neither cold nor hot—the world stayed a temperature that went unnoticeable until he focused on it.

Many warriors in his village were preparing weapons. They would go to war with a neighbouring village soon. Bantu did not like the idea of war, but the tribe was growing too large for their current livestock to sustain them. The junior elders had decided that they would take what they needed from villages to the south and scatter those people into the lands. While Bantu understood that the needs of his people were important, he did not know if he could stomach battle for any reason other than defense.

Bantu looked around to see some women building a new hut, his older sister among them. He tried talking to her, hoping to see the expression on her face change in understanding, but nothing happened. He wanted to tell her that he was fine, that he was not lost, until he finally came to understand that she did not even know that he was gone.

It had taken him a few hours to walk home, but no time had passed. The concept was difficult for him to get his head around. He had never heard stories about such things, so he had no references from which to draw upon, but he now realized that if time started again, no one would even know he had been whisked away on an adventure in another world. They would not believe him if he told them about it, and he had no way to prove his story.

Then he wondered what would happen if time did start up right then? It would look to them as if he just appeared in the village. What would he do if someone appeared before him in such a manner? He would be frightened.

He would think the person a spirit, likely an evil spirit. Bantu did not wish to be seen that way in his people's eyes. He looked back to the plains and then began to make his way back to where he started. He didn't know what he would do with himself when he got there, but it seemed the best thing to do.

*   *   *

Maya had done all she could think to do. She had hung from the arrows suspended in the air that were flying toward the buck that she and her sisters were hunting for dinner. She had fired arrows at rocks, then animals, and then her sisters' butts only to see them bounce off and fall. She had walked across the surface of a nearby lake, which felt as solid as the ground. You could only amuse yourself so many ways in a static world. Unlike Scorpius, Maya never thought that she might be stuck this way. Her conversations with the others led her to believe that she just had to wait to be summoned. Nevertheless, it had been hours. Perhaps the others had gone to sleep for the night. She thought about sleeping, too, but she was neither tired nor hungry since arriving. Her wounds had disappeared, and when she tried cutting herself, she found that no blade could hurt her. She was impervious and immortal. However, she was very, *very* bored; for Maya, that was like being in hell.

Not even after her third pass by the buck did Maya notice that one of her Amazon sisters had started to trip. That in itself would not be an issue, but Maya, in her cockiness, had shot an arrow between several of the girls to hit the buck. The girl would fall right into the path of her arrow. When time started again, Maya would kill one of her sisters.

*   *   *

Genjuro walked around the samurai of the rival daimyo, who had arrived for a meeting with Genjuro's daimyo to discuss matters of territory. They had chosen a large field for the meeting so neither party could place archers nearby. Each leader had brought twenty samurai who all sat kneeling in mirrored protective positions around their leaders, ready to spring up when needed.

The sun hung directly overhead in a sky that held only a few puffy white clouds. There should have been a soft warm breeze, but the air hung deathly still. Despite the beautiful day, tensions were high. Genjuro could see it in the face of every man as he walked around the field; each man carefully watched the movements of his counterpart. Since this was his first mission with his own daimyo, he wanted to prove himself and show his honour. The samurai across from him had cast a disrespectful look at his master, and Genjuro was about to spring out to deal with him before he had been yanked into another world. Now the expression of that man was fixed on his face; the longer Genjuro looked at it, the more it bothered him. Such man must be dealt with. When this was over, the man would die quickly, and the others would learn not to insult the honour of his daimyo.

* * *

Tenzin arrived home to a frozen sunset. The temple he lived in rested halfway up a mountain, carved into its stone. Pagodas containing the living quarters, kitchens, and a temple surrounded a tiled courtyard where the monks observed their daily practices. The courtyard was empty now as everyone prepared for dinner. Many pillars with lessons inscribed on them bordered it. Tenzin moved to the western landing, which looked out from the mountain, giving a heavenly view of the world. He sat there for a while, admiring its beauty before testing his limits of interaction with the world.

When it became clear to him that he could not affect or be affected by anything in his world, he decided that he best not waste the time afforded to him in a quiet, peaceful place. He meditated for two hours before beginning his daily practices, fascinated by the fact that he did not sweat or grow tired. *A monk could train very quickly this way*, he thought.

* * *

"You can't be serious!" Alex yelled. "We *have* to go after them!"

"I gave my word," Brasius replied. "Axemen are bound by their word."

"But the rest of you didn't," Alex insisted, looking around at the others.

"He spoke for us," Senufer stated. "Any one of us would have made a similar pledge to protect innocent lives."

"What about the lives that'll be lost now that those pirates have the Scroll? What about Dara's life?" He grabbed Senufer by the shoulders and shook him. "We have to do something!"

His panic continued to mount, his feeling of helplessness as well. He would not let it happen again. His irresponsibility—the naive actions of a stupid kid—had made them lose her.

"I did not say we were not going to do anything," Senufer assured, "but the Axemen themselves cannot be involved in the pursuit."

"Who are you sending then?"

"You."

Alex's jaw dropped. "Me? Alone? Haven't you been paying attention? I have no skills. I have no weapons. I have no idea where those pirates have gone."

"That is where you are wrong," Senufer replied. "Where is Dara?"

Alex waved his hand toward the cave. "She's off there somewhere," he said, frustrated, useless.

"No, Alex," Senufer said. "You are Dara's protector. Now relax. Reach inside and tell me where Dara is."

Alex let out a big breath, half in relaxation, half in exasperation. He held up his arm and pointed to the cave. Then, feeling an inner pull, his arm shifted left several degrees. Surprise and wonder came over his face.

"There," he said, now sure that he pointed in the right direction. "She's right there."

"You must go after her and the Scroll."

"How?" Alex asked. "I want to, but I don't have a ship. And even if I did, I couldn't sail it."

Senufer smiled. "*That* is something we can help you with."

* * *

They had only walked a few hundred meters farther than the place where Maya and Bantu had collapsed when Dara heard the distant ocean waves and smelled the salt air. At that point, the tunnel slowly grew in diameter as they continued until, less than an hour later, they emerged in a huge oblong cave several hundred meters in diameter. The floor sloped down from the tunnel opening to a large pool of water surrounded by some small wooden buildings and a sturdy dock on which sat many crates. Dara could make out the details of the dock and the cave well thanks to dozens of torches set around the water, along the dock, and up the pathway from the dock to the tunnel the group had just exited.

In the water, a menacing black ship was tied to the dock; it was a triple-mast war galleon with inky sails. Ballistae poked out from several hatches on her side. Oars hung out of openings set a level below. Blood red paint accented its features, making it appear all the more menacing. Instead of a figurehead on most ships, its bow sported a huge curved blade that ran down to the water line. Dara could only imagine the damage that blade did when the ship rammed another.

"She's called the *Shuriken*," Helena said proudly. "Using both sails and oars, she can outrun and outmaneuver any merchant vessel and most naval ships."

Dozens of men moved crates back and forth from the ship to the dock and worked on the rigging. They were preparing to set sail. It suddenly occurred to Dara that they had nowhere to sail to.

"The far wall of the cave is an illusion," Helena revealed, reading Dara's puzzled expression. "It's a permanent one that my wizard, Cyrus, set up years ago. Cost a small fortune. Only he can see it, or rather, not see it. So only he can navigate a ship in here from outside. Impressive, isn't it?" Helena looked for an acknowledgment from Dara, but the little girl only shrugged and walked silently ahead. Helena tried not to let it show that the display wounded her pride a little. "I guess if you've seen the Hall of Shadows go up, there's not much in the world that can impress you anymore, is there?"

Noise from behind them startled Dara, and she turned to find the cause. A couple of the pirates who had lagged behind emerged from the tunnel.

Helena smiled. "The shape of the tunnel amplifies the sound of anything in it. It's a wonderful early-warning device. We heard you and your friends and went in to see who was trespassing. I loved what you did with the lightning bugs by the way. We caught up with you just in time to see the show."

Dara could not believe that these people had been right there—right behind her when she faced the Shadow Warriors. It gave her the shivers.

Helena escorted Dara onto the *Shuriken* and down into the hold. They passed a few rooms, including the sleeping quarters and the mess, before arriving near the stern at an ornate door. Helena knocked but didn't bother to wait for a response; she simply opened the door.

The room beyond was both foreign and familiar to Dara. Several shelves held books and bottles, scrolls and statues. Lanterns illuminated the chamber, yet no open flames could be seen anywhere. Two tables stood near the room's center—one covered in books and scrolls, the other in various items from bones and vegetables to idols and ornate boxes. A few wooden chairs circled the tables, and a large cushioned chair sat not too far off with a small table next to it. On the table sat a book and a goblet of wine. Off to the right, a curtain was pulled back slightly to reveal an unmade bed and a closet full of clothes.

It's a wizard's lab, Dara thought, *or rather, a wizard's quarters*.

At the table with the scrolls sat the wizard busily writing a new one. Dara had met many wizards in her young life. No two were quite the same, but they all were fairly similar. Most did not care much about their appearance, especially their hair, which typically hung loose and was unkempt. All of them wore loose-fitting robes that allowed them to move their arms quickly for spell casting. Pockets and pouches adorned their clothes for easy access to wands, gems, and other magical devices. And with a few exceptions like her father, they were usually quite large or quite skinny.

Cyrus was none of these things.

He sat at the table in black pants and boots, matching the garb of the other pirates. His shirt was what shocked Dara, especially when she realized that he didn't have one. A lean muscular man, Cyrus's hairless body was covered in mystic runes and colourful pictures. Dara could not see any bare skin from his neck to his wrists. Paint also adorned his shaved head with the designs creating a hood around his face on which dark lines formed the image of a skull. Dara felt as though she were looking at death's face.

Cyrus looked up, at first annoyed, which made Dara back up a step. Upon seeing Helena, however, he relaxed and put down his quill. Dara noticed that the ink was red—if it *was* ink.

"Don't tell me this little girl was the source of all that noise," he smiled.

"The catalyst, actually," Helena replied. "I will explain it all to you later, but first I have some gifts for you."

One of the pirates placed Alex's books and the Scroll on the table. Cyrus immediately reached for the golden Scroll. When he touched it, lightning seemed to erupt between them. Shielding her eyes, Dara felt the small shock wave from the blast. When her eyes adjusted after the flash, she saw Cyrus on the floor against the back wall; a blue field surrounded him. One of his tattoos had disappeared from his right shoulder. Dara realized that he carried all his spells on his body, with some set to work given the right conditions. While she could sense the evil in him, she suddenly respected the man.

Cyrus did not seem the least bit embarrassed that he had landed on his butt. He picked himself up and walked back to the Scroll. "It's shielded from a wizard's touch," he stated.

"Not this one," Helena disagreed, yanking Dara forward. "Mornak's daughter, Dara."

"You placed a scroll of Mornak on my table and didn't warn me?" Cyrus asked angrily.

"I like to surprise you," Helena replied playfully.

Cyrus shook his head. "Any more surprises?"

"One of those books can suck you into it. It's like a miniature Hall of Shadows. I don't know anything about the other two."

Cyrus touched a small tattoo of an eye on his forearm, and his eyes turned a milky white colour that swirled as though being stirred. He gazed upon the books and the Scroll and nodded. "The books have strong magic," he confirmed, "but the Scroll ... it has more power than I've ever seen. I am wary just having it here."

"I thought you were a powerful mage," Helena teased.

"Powerful and wise," he corrected. "I know enough that the power of this scroll is beyond my abilities to experiment with, especially when I don't know its purpose." He glanced over at Dara. "Is having her here wise? What if Mornak should—"

"Relax," Helena cooed. "If the Axemen are to be believed—and they always are—then Mornak is now a prisoner ... in the Hall of Shadows."

Cyrus whistled in awe.

"You are just full of surprises today. One trip ashore and you encounter Axemen, Mornak's daughter, and the most powerful magic item I've ever known."

Helena laughed. "I told you coming back every year on the Day of Peace was a smart move. I knew that one day there wouldn't be a celebration, and on that day we'd be free to pirate these waters again. Now that day has come." She spun one of the books around so she could look at the cover. "*Historical Moments in Time,*" she read. "A slightly redundant title, wouldn't you say?" She looked at Cyrus. "How long until you know how to use these?"

"I don't know. Their magic isn't ... right," he replied frowning. "It's skewed."

"Skewed?"

"Yes, I'm not sure how to explain it, especially to a nonwizard. It's like if two people paint a tree, and one paints it exactly as you see it while the other gives his own interpretation—slightly off colours, an elongated shape, or something. The paintings have all the same elements, and if you saw either picture, you'd recognize the tree. But at the same time, one really is not the tree. The books are like that. The magic is there and stable, but it's not quite right."

"What could cause that?" Helena asked.

"A miscast spell, interference from another wizard, the wrong spell components used in casting," he suggested, "but those things usually result in the spell failing unless they are deliberately applied."

Just then a large man entered the room. Dara could feel the air of arrogance about him and the hint of danger—not for herself alone but for anyone around him.

"I thought you were going to come see me when you returned," he said to Helena.

"We have only just returned, Landis," Helena replied in an annoyed voice. "I was just giving these items to Cyrus. Don't worry. I haven't forgotten you."

Her tone made it sound as if she was addressing a child. Landis could see the smirks on the faces of the others. He tried to save face by walking over to the table and examining the items.

"Books?" he scoffed. "A mighty plunder," he said with sarcasm as he picked one up and read the cover. "*Legend and Lore*. I can see why a wizard might be interested in these, but they won't benefit the crew in any way." He flipped through the pages quickly, seeing mostly text until he found the picture of Bantu. "A Nairobi," he stated. "Big, too. He'd make a productive slave."

"He's not a slave!" Dara exclaimed. "He's a warrior, and if you don't mind your tongue, he'll show you just how powerful he is," she swore.

"Will he now?" laughed Landis. "And just how is he going to do that? He going to jump out of the book and stab me with his big spear?" he asked in a tone that someone might use talking to a baby.

Suddenly light flashed out of the book. Landis looked at the others in the room, whose faces were stunned in surprise—everyone's but Dara's. Her face held a smile. Landis felt a sharp pain in his back and then his chest. He looked down to see the tip of a spear protruding from it. In his last moments of life, he looked back at the book and saw that the page with the picture of Bantu was blank. All the pirates in the room drew their swords, but as Landis coughed up blood and fell dead to the floor, Bantu disappeared again.

Helena shook her head. "A shame," she said sadly.

"My condolences on the loss of your lover, Captain," Cyrus said, bowing.

"The only loss I feel is that I didn't get to kill him myself," Helena smirked. "Landis had gotten too full of himself since I made him my first mate."

Cyrus smiled. "I didn't want to mention it."

She smiled back.

"My dear, Cyrus, you should know by now that you always have the captain's ear."

Dara was both horrified and intrigued. Their comrade had just died in front of them, and they didn't seem to care. They were, in truth, happy about it—not that Dara held any concern for the man either. Also, Cyrus, obviously a powerful wizard, fully respected and somewhat feared this woman. *What makes her so powerful that she leads these men?* Dara thought.

"I guess we know what this book does now," Cyrus stated. "You said that one of these other books can suck people in?"

"Yes," Helena answered.

"Do you know which one?"

"No, we were too far away at the time." She turned to Dara. "Which book is it?"

Dara shook her head, a scared but defiant look on her face.

Helena shook hers disappointedly. "Listen to me, little one," she said, kneeling in front of Dara and running a metal fingernail along the little girl's neck. "If you do not tell us what we need to know, then I will cut out your tongue—since you feel you don't need to use it."

"You won't harm me," Dara huffed. "You gave your word."

Helena's smile stole the heat from Dara's body. "I never said I wouldn't harm you, my dear. I swore to put you on the next merchant vessel we raid. I never said what condition you would be in—alive, dead, whole, in pieces."

Dara gulped.

"Now which book can imprison people?"

"The one about time," Dara whimpered.

"There, was that so hard?" Helena patted her head and stood up.

Cyrus picked up the book and leafed through it. "How did the men get sucked in? What was said?"

Helena thought about it. "One man held the book open and said, 'Wouldn't you have liked to have been there to see it?' or something like that, and the others agreed."

"See what?"

"An explosion of some sort."

"It was a question, just like Landis asked?"

"Yes, I'm sure it was."

"Hmm," the wizard thought aloud, "maybe the books respond to questions, or perhaps they don't understand that they are questions, just words. They respond to the suggestions of whoever is holding them or, perhaps, just near them."

"Let's find out," Helena mused as she moved a chair to an open area in the room. "Devlin," she said to one of the pirates, "hold that book and say, 'Destroy this chair,'" she said pointing to *Legend and Lore*.

After seeing what happened to Landis, Devlin did not like that idea at all. "Me? Why don't you make the girl do it?"

"I don't trust what she'll say," Helena replied.

"But—"

"Do it!" she snapped.

Devlin nodded his head submissively, and Cyrus handed *Legend and Lore* to him. It was still open to Bantu's page. The man gulped as he looked at Bantu's picture.

"Destroy this chair," Devlin said, pointing at the chair in question.

Bantu appeared again, and everyone jumped back. He held up his spear defensively. "Who are you people?" he asked.

"Do as you were ordered," Helena commanded.

Bantu glanced over to the chair, feeling the order within him. "You want me to destroy a chair? To what end?"

Cyrus smiled. Bantu had just confirmed that he knew what he had been summoned for, but why wasn't he doing it?

"You killed my first mate quickly enough," Helena stated.

"He reeked of evil," Bantu replied, grimly. Getting a sense of those around him, he added, "As do you all." Then he saw Dara. "Dara! Are you all right, little one?"

"Help me, Bantu!" Dara cried.

Bantu moved toward her, but the men around her held their weapons up. The African kept his distance, but he showed no sign of being intimidated by the men or the odds.

"Tell him again," Helena said to Devlin.

"Destroy that chair," Devlin ordered.

Bantu felt the compulsion to obey increase. The illness he felt before began to seep in again as he resisted. Devlin noticed the look of discomfort and decided to see if he could increase it.

"Destroy that chair now!" he yelled.

Bantu spun around and smashed his spear into the chair. As it crumpled on the ground, he disappeared again.

Helena rushed over to Devlin and grabbed the book. Flipping through it, she saw the pictures of the other heroes. "We may have lost our first mate," she mused, "but we just gained an advanced fighting force."

*   *   *

Askar quickly realized that he did not like flying. The wind roared in his ears, and every so often, a bug smacked into his face. He continuously worried about falling from Specter's back. The bird didn't purposely try to dislodge him, but it didn't seem worried about his comfort or safety either. Askar had no harness or saddle and was forced to grab skin and feathers to keep from flying off. The sudden bursts of speed only made things worse. At first, Askar could not figure out what caused them. They would be flying smoothly; then there would be a jolt pushing him backward. The world would go black. Then, just as suddenly, they'd slam back to normal speed—the world would come back into focus, and he'd almost pitch forward over Specter's head.

Finally, he figured out the pattern. It was the shadows. What he had seen in the Hall when Specter seemed to move into and out of the shadows had not been an illusion. Incredibly, the bird merged with shadows, traveling along them at great speed, before emerging at the far end. It only worked for single shadows, however. They could enter the shadow of a house and emerge on the far side of the shadow, but even if the house's shadow merged with trees, bushes, and other houses, they couldn't travel along the entire length at once. They'd pop out after the house and then slip in and out a bush and then another house, making the flight quite jerky. Specter didn't seem to notice it. It was the creature's nature, the way it functioned. To Askar, it was becoming nauseating.

9

*L*amp oil, fish, and saltwater smells permeated the nighttime air at the huge wharf of East Port, but within it, the odour of sweat from the multitude of sailors newly arrived in port lingered. Easily one hundred ships had docked in the harbour, each of which could hold around one hundred men. East Port was a major port of call, a city half the size of Aspiria, and a main supply center for the realm.

Lanterns hanging from tall posts—this world's version of streetlights—lit up the wooden walkway of the harbour front. More lanterns hung in front of each establishment to spotlight the signs over the doors. Alex read signs like "The Cracken's Corner," "The Third Mast," "East Coast Mermaids," and "The Muddy Duck." Sailors, many of them drunk, moved from bar to bar dressed more like the medieval seafarers that Alex had seen in movies. People of all races cavorted here, in port from the many different realms of the world. All races did not mean races of man either. Elves, dwarves, and other classic races that Alex recognized were present along with others he had never seen before: furry ones, scaly ones, and even walking plants. After getting looks from several "people," Alex wondered if his clothes—despite the cloak he wore over them—made him somehow stand out among the myriad of beings. Senufer let him know what was really going on.

"Stop staring," the Axeman told him.

"What?" Alex asked, partially distracted.

"You are being rude by staring at people because of their appearances," Senufer stated. "We are all created in the images of our gods. We all have the same rights to our appearances. We should not be singled out, judged, or hated because of them. Is this philosophy not practiced in your world?"

"Yes ... well ... mostly," Alex answered, "but there are only humans in my world. I've never seen a lot of these races before, and the few that I have, well, I thought they were only imaginary. I'm sorry. I'll try my best not to stare."

Alex moved his gaze to the buildings around him but thought that he must now look as though he was trying not to look at anyone. He looked out southeast to the sea, to Dara, but he sensed her moving away; that only increased his worry. He decided it would be best to distract himself by talking.

"So who are we meeting anyway?"

"Asuro, a pirate hunter," Senufer replied.

"That makes sense. He's good, I suppose."

"The best. He patrols the Mythosian waters. No ship has been successfully pirated in our waters in almost a decade because of him."

"He must be bored by now," Alex guessed.

Senufer chuckled. "A little. The king finances him, keeping him and his crew comfortable, but because of their reputation, there is not much for them to do here, except let others know they are still out here." Senufer leaned in and whispered, "He slips out of our waters now and then to attack pirates in other realms. Technically, it's illegal, but no one knows he's doing it."

"It's illegal to stop pirates in other realms?" Alex asked, amazed.

"The pirate hunters of those realms are assigned by their rulers. Doing their job would shame them and quite possibly decrease their budget from their sovereigns."

"Messing around in someone else's jurisdiction. Got it," Alex said. "We have similar rules in my world."

Only Senufer and Alex had come down to the wharf so as not to draw attention. Both wore hooded cloaks over their clothes. Senufer walked purposefully, knowing his destination. He didn't acknowledge anyone around them as he steered through the wooden streets to an establishment called Buccaneer's Dive.

The place consisted of a large square room with a square bar in the middle. The outside of the room had booths, which sat up to ten people. A staircase led up to a balcony area directly above the booths, where men and women of different species watched the amusement below. Two old women played the piano and fiddle while men laughed, sang, drank, and arm wrestled around the room. Alex expected it to be so much different. In all the movies he'd seen, the atmosphere in these places was dangerous with cutthroats and pickpockets lurking about. It wasn't until he remembered that all evil had been trapped in the Hall that the happiness around him made sense. Even with darkness around them, these men enjoyed themselves. Every now and then, however, someone passed by who wasn't quite so jovial and was even uncomfortable to be around. These were the foreigners, Alex realized, from other realms—realms where dealing with evil was still a part of daily life.

Senufer went up to the bar and spoke briefly with the bartender who pointed to the back. The Axeman gestured to Alex before moving off in that direction. They found who they were looking for in a small booth just big enough for four people. A man, sitting on the left side of the booth in a black cloak with its hood up, drank what looked to Alex like tea in tiny cups. His hood moved slightly toward them as Senufer and Alex slid in on the right, but he then turned back to watch the festivities around him.

"Why are you here, Senufer?" he asked, not bothering to look at them.

"We have need of you, Asuro," Senufer said.

"What cargo do you need shipped this time?" he asked uninterestedly.

"This boy," Senufer replied.

"To what port?" Asuro sighed.

"No port. To a ship."

"And what ship would that be?"

"The *Shuriken*."

To Alex it looked like the man had just been hit by a Japanese throwing star of the same name as the ship. His head jerked up and then turned left to look at Senufer. They seemed to have his attention now.

Senufer nodded to the man. "Helena has returned. She has kidnapped Mornak's daughter and stolen some items of great importance."

"Has she lost leave of her senses? Mornak will—"

"Mornak is a prisoner in the Hall of Shadows."

Senufer and Alex told him the tale of their adventures so far. The man listened carefully, especially to the part concerning the pirates. He glanced several times at Alex as if sizing him up. Alex still could not see his face. When Senufer finished, the man sat silently for a long while. At one point, Alex opened his mouth to prod him, but the Axeman placed his hand firmly on Alex's arm, silently urging him to be patient.

"If she stays true to her word, then they will ship out tonight, if they haven't already. But they'll stay fairly close to this port and hit the first ship they encounter. We must set out immediately."

Minutes later, Alex and Asuro sped along the docks while Senufer rushed off to rejoin the Axemen and retake Aspiria. When Alex returned, Asuro would send word to the Axemen using a messenger bird. Alex was eager to see the vessel that kept Aspiria's waters safe. His jaw dropped when it came into view.

A single mast fishing boat, twenty paces from bow to stern, sat in the dock. It was only large enough for an eight-man crew. Asuro slowed as they approached, looking to see who was around. Alex could see no one in this remote corner of the wharf. Following Asuro's lead, he then rushed over and boarded the boat. Alex noted the name when they had crossed the gangplank, *Fishbait*.

Appropriate, he thought.

"Does this boat take us to your ship?" Alex asked, not believing that this was Asuro's vessel.

"This way," Asuro ordered.

The man walked over to a wooden hatch on the deck, which seemed odd to Alex since it would likely open into the water and flood the boat. He was wrong about both. The hatch revealed a ladder that went down to a lower deck that shouldn't exist. Alex followed him down into a hallway, a very large hallway. He stopped, pulled off his hood, and checked the distance. He wasn't imagining things. End to end, the hall was three times as long as the outside of the ship, but that was impossible. Furthermore, the inside of the ship was metal.

Asuro saw his confusion. "Most of the ship is below the water. On the deck below this one, the crew has crank stations that drive large propellers on the stern. They move us quickly and quietly. Welcome to the *Dark Wave*."

The *Dark Wave* was unlike any boat Alex had ever seen in fact or in fiction. A hybrid sailboat and submarine, its iron hull was something Alex hadn't seen on any other ships docked in East Port.

Someone figured out buoyancy, he thought.

The front of the vessel was essentially a giant spear that could puncture the hull of any wooden ship easily. The deck they stood on had the ship's quarters, mess, and bridge. The level below, as Asuro had stated, had crank stations much like oar stations on other boats. The ten crank stations on each side of the vessel could each seat three men. Large metal crank poles could be turned in the same motion as oars. All the cranks connected through pulleys and gears to the propellers on the stern. With sixty men cranking, those propellers became powerful.

Asuro explained that the boat and subsections could detach so that the former could be used as a decoy or a lifeboat. Both engineers and wizards had worked together on its design. A permanent illusion hid the size of the sub from anyone looking from above.

"How deep can it go?" Alex asked.

"Deep?" Asuro asked, not understanding at first. "Oh, no. It cannot dive under water. It simply travels just along the surface. We could run out of air otherwise!" he said laughing.

Alex figured he'd tell the man about submarines later.

As they entered the bridge, Asuro announced, "Prepare to set sail, men. We're going after the *Shuriken*."

Several men started at the words, and only then did Alex note that these men looked very much like Helena's pirates in appearance and dress.

"The *Shuriken* seems to be a big deal to everyone," Alex said. "Is there a reason for that?"

Asuro pulled back his hood and removed his cloak, allowing Alex to finally see his face. He was a handsome man or would have been if not for the four scars crossing his face from left to right on a downward diagonal. Built bigger than the other sailors who had bodies like Tenzin, Asuro had thick muscles that seemed to stretch the black leather armour he wore. The number of weapons he carried was frightening—twin swords on his back, shuriken down his chest, small sickles and many daggers at his sides, and a sai, a kind of three-pronged dagger, in his boots. Those were just the weapons that Alex could see. Asuro was an arsenal onto himself. Alex pitied anyone who crossed his path. He didn't realize the man had already been crossed.

"Yes," Asuro answered. "The *Shuriken* used to be mine."

* * *

Dara stood in the corner watching Cyrus experiment with *Legend and Lore*. She wanted to grab hold of it and summon the warriors to kill the man, but a spell of holding kept her where she was with her arms at her sides and unable to move. All she could do was speak, and Cyrus only allowed that because he needed her to answer his questions. Tears soaked her cheeks— tears that Cyrus didn't seem to notice. She wished she was back in the palace and that her father was with her. She wished the realm was a beautiful safe place again. She wished she could just wake up, and this would all have been a dream. She also wished she didn't need to pee so badly.

The Scroll lay on the table on top of the other two books. Cyrus had one of the pirates place it in a water-tight bamboo tube. Similar bamboo tubes in the room held other scrolls to protect the scrolls from water damage. In this case, however, putting the Scroll in the tube protected Cyrus—not the Scroll—allowing him to pick it up without getting hurt. He couldn't open the tube or affect the Scroll inside, but it served until they could sell it to another wizard.

Dara had been watching intently for hours as Cyrus applied his magic to *Legend and Lore*. She was amazed at how quickly he learned to manipulate it. Cyrus had tried to summon Maya to be his slave, but that didn't work. The book required that a specific task or tasks be stated, which didn't go on forever. Knowing that, he then summoned Scorpius and ordered the Roman to demonstrate his swordsmanship. Scorpius tried to demonstrate on Cyrus, but the wizard had the foresight to put a shield in front of him before the summoning. Scorpius spent his energy striking a glowing blue shield surrounding Cyrus who stood ready with a lethal blast just in case the Roman got through. Afterward, Cyrus examined the residual magic, spending some time contemplating it, before making notes.

He summoned Maya next, ordering her to pull the arrows from her quiver one at a time and then to replace them without shooting. Cyrus funneled some of his magic into the book when he summoned her to gain more control. Nevertheless, she nocked her first arrow immediately and aimed at him. However, try as she might, she could not let loose the shot. Dara urged her on, but it was an impossible task. In the end, she swore many curses at the man as she pulled out and replaced her arrows. She did it as quickly as she could to end the task and get out of the sight of the wizard who now ranked highest on her list of hated men.

This time Cyrus was able to examine the magic while not worrying about being killed. He took more notes, and when he was ready to summon Genjuro, Dara could see that the energy of the magic he used had changed slightly. Cyrus ordered Genjuro to run around the room five times. The samurai didn't even question him but set about his task, disappearing as soon as he finished. Cyrus smiled evilly as he watched and took notes in his journal.

Dara took notes in her head. She listened carefully to what he said, noted what the magic looked and felt like, and marked when the warriors disappeared. Alex would need to know all this when he rescued her. She wholly believed that he would rescue her, but not because the magic of the Scroll bound him to do so. Despite his lack of any real skills, Dara believed that Alex was a hero. She saw it in him. She also felt a connection to him, though not one of magic. She could not explain it, but she knew he would not give up on her. She smiled at the thought of him and the Axemen boarding the ship, defeating the pirates, and rescuing her. Cyrus caught the look.

"What is so amusing?" he asked.

"Nothing," she answered.

Cyrus did not like being the object of a joke, especially by a little girl. He channeled his magic into the book again, this time summoning Tenzin.

"Punish the girl for mocking me," he ordered.

Tenzin appeared and strode purposefully over to her. The smile quickly left Dara's face.

The monk kneeled in front of her, eyes serious, and he curled his hand into a fist. Then he extended one finger out and said, "Now, Dara, was that nice?" a smile forming across his face.

She wanted to hug him, but she couldn't move.

"I said punish her!" Cyrus yelled.

Tenzin turned to him. "I am trying. It would be easier if you didn't interrupt."

"How are you resisting him?" Dara asked.

"I'm not," Tenzin replied. "I'm doing what he ordered me to do ... at my own pace."

"Can you free me?"

"Sorry, no."

"I'm so scared, Tenzin."

"I know. It's a scary situation, but I know you're a brave girl and a resourceful one." He leaned in and whispered, "You just might need some help with some of the resources." Then taking on a more stern and much louder tone, he asked, "Now, Dara, are you sorry for mocking the evil wizard?"

Dara giggled. "Not really, no."

Tenzin sighed. "Then I'll have to punish you! For starters, no dinner! Then I will watch you write, 'I will not mock the evil wizard' one hundred times."

Cyrus's expression almost made the ordeal worthwhile to Dara. His body shook as his face turned red with anger.

"What foolishness is this?" he screamed. "Hit her!"

"My pardon, sir," Tenzin replied. "You did not specify the method of punishment. This method works well with children in my home country."

Cyrus stormed forward to hit Dara himself. Tenzin intercepted. The wizard stopped, surprised at the seemingly free will of the monk.

"I did not say you could attack me," the wizard growled. "You are only to punish her."

"Yes," Tenzin agreed. "*I* will punish her, not you. I will not let you interfere with my task."

Cyrus went back to his table and channeled more magic into the book. "Punish her physically."

"Very well," said Tenzin. He turned and pushed Dara back unexpectedly. Unable to stop herself, she tumbled into the bookshelf behind her.

"Hey!" she exclaimed.

Tenzin moved in, picked her up, and knocked her against the shelf repeatedly, though the impact didn't seem as hard as she expected from the motions his arms made. He was easing up at the last possible moment, making it look much worse than it was. It still hurt, and Dara cried out. Cyrus was finally smiling until books and scroll cases began to fall off the shelf from the repeated impacts. His smile left again.

"I said punish her, not mess up my quarters," he complained.

Tenzin dropped Dara to the floor and then reached down and picked up the fallen items, shoving her around unceremoniously to get at them. As the monk shoved the things back in the shelves, Dara realized that he had placed her on a scroll case.

"Have you learned your lesson?" Tenzin asked, angrily.

"Yes, sir," Dara answered. She saw him wink as he faded from sight.

Cyrus smiled. "The next time I will word the command better, and it will be far worse for you. Do you understand?"

Dara nodded sadly and then asked, "Can I go pee yet?"

"No. I have a more tests to run. Hold it until then."

"He hurt me, and I can't hold it any longer!" she whined.

"I said, 'Hold it!'"

Her whine became a pout. "I'm going to pee any second, and if you don't take me to the privy, then you'll have to clean up your floor."

Looking at her a moment longer, Cyrus realized she wasn't bluffing. He got up, released the spell, grabbed her by the arm, and headed for the door—not even looking back at her in his frustration. As she was yanked off the floor, Dara slipped the scroll case in her dress and followed.

*　*　*

Specter touched down at the entrance to the cave. Askar jumped down, thankful to be off the bird, and took a moment to savour the feel of the ground beneath him. He was about to scout the area when his animal-like senses picked up a familiar scent. He smiled.

Senufer.

The Axeman was free of the Wood and helping the girl, it seemed. Dara's scent was there, too—fresher than before though older than Senufer's—leading back into cave. Senufer's scent circled around north along with many others—Axemen. Askar began to move north when Specter hopped in front of him, blocking his path.

"Out of my way, stupid bird," Askar ordered.

The air in front of Specter shimmered, and an image of the Shadow Lord appeared. "Where do you think you are going?" he asked.

Askar cursed under his breath before answering. "After the Scroll."

Specter's eyes glowed brightly. A moment later, fire flared around Askar, making him cry out in pain. The flames were not really burning his flesh but felt as though they were.

"Have you forgotten so soon that I can see everything through the bird's eyes? You're after something else. I can see it in your face. What is it?"

"Senufer," Askar grunted.

The flames around him flickered but did not go out, as the Shadow Lord's expression changed to from anger to shock. "Impossible. The Axemen are trapped."

"I can smell many of them, maybe all."

"And the girl?" asked the Shadow Lord.

Askar looked back defiantly. The flames assaulted him again. He gritted his teeth against the pain.

"The girl?" the Shadow Lord prompted.

Askar pointed. "In the cave."

"Then you're going in the cave after her. Your little vendetta can wait."

"Yes, my lord," Askar replied.

The flames around him dissipated.

"Get the girl and the Scroll. *Then* you can have your fun with Senufer."

As the image vanished, Askar growled angrily but started for the cave. He turned to Specter when the bird didn't follow. "Well?"

Specter cawed and shook its head.

"Fine," Askar grunted. "It probably comes out by the coast. I'll follow it in and see where it leads. You scan the East Port and the shoreline for the Scroll. Look for my signal to pick me up." The air around Askar crackled with electricity as he summoned the power of his mace. He held it up, and a small ball of lightning shot up like a signal flare. Specter cawed again and took flight, arcing over the cave toward the ocean.

"Great falcon," Askar muttered, "more like chicken."

He walked into the cave, his eyes allowing him to see clearly in the darkness. He would find the girl and take her to the Shadow Lord. Then he and Senufer would have their reunion.

*   *   *

Alex stood at the bow of the *Fishbait*, staring out at the ocean. Dara was directly ahead of them *somewhere*. He couldn't tell the exact distance, but he knew that they were closing in. That gave him comfort. Stars filled the night sky. As a city boy, Alex had only seen this many stars on his uncle's farm or when he had been camping, but the constellations of this world mesmerized him. He could clearly see the multicoloured clouds of nearby galaxies and wondered if one of them was his. Was he on another planet, or was this a parallel world or Earth in the past? Or should he go back to considering that he was dreaming or in a coma? Whatever the situation, he needed to treat this as real and important. He was going to save Dara somehow. With this crew, he felt that he had a good chance of succeeding.

He turned at the sound of the hatch opening to see Asuro emerging from the *Dark Wave*. They nodded to each other as Asuro came to stand beside Alex. Alex wanted to ask about the scars on Asuro's face. Asuro wanted to ask Alex about the bruises on his. Neither thought it polite to bring it up. For a time, they simply stood next to each other, each one lost in his personal thoughts. Alex decided to break the silence.

"Helena stole your ship?" he asked.

Asuro smiled. He liked Alex's directness.

"Yes and no. When the Hall of Shadows was created, we were all given the opportunity to reform. Helena not only refused to reform but was outraged at the insinuation that she was evil."

Alex raised an eyebrow, and Asuro chuckled. "It's not as uncommon as you might imagine. We all have an image of ourselves, and for most of us, that image is of a good person. Have you ever seen a child poke a small animal with a stick or a bully tease another person?"

"Sure."

"Do you think that they think they are evil? They don't. They're just having fun. They're seeing what they can get away with. Conquerors do not consider themselves evil. They are just trying to get what they feel they deserve. They often consider those who stand in their way to be evil or just ignorant to the grand scheme of things."

Alex shook his head. "But she's a pirate!"

"As was I," Asuro stated. "I was raised in a world where you did what you had to do to survive. It started as stealing food to eat. How could I be evil if I'm just trying to fill my belly? But then you consort with the wrong people. You take things you feel life has denied you. You hurt people who seem to think they're better than you. The next thing you know, you're the captain of a ship, stalking the ships of wealthy merchants who wouldn't give you a coin when you sat with a cup on the street. And you smile when you unload the booty, thinking, 'This will show them.'

"Again, you're not evil. You're doing what you have to. You're getting what you deserve. It doesn't matter that you had to kill some men on the raid. They shouldn't have resisted. They brought it on themselves. You begin to confuse fear with respect, and you try to make people *respect* you as much as you can. Believe me, I was shocked when I realized how large a part of me had become evil, but I accepted it. I came to terms with it. Then I got rid of it."

"But Helena didn't," Alex prompted.

"No, and neither did much of my crew. They chose exile rather than face the Hall. They took the *Shuriken* and sailed off, and then, having been branded evil, they embraced it. The *Shuriken* does not only plunder ships now, but it sinks them as well—sometimes with the crew tied to the railings. The members of the crew that the pirates don't kill, they sell as slaves in other realms. They will torture men for information or just for fun. They embrace the fame and the fear they have earned from their deeds, and orchestrating all of it is Helena who was my first mate and is now their captain."

"Isn't that unusual?" asked Alex. "A female captain."

Asuro smiled. "Your world *must* be different. As far as captains go, I am the exception. Here almost all captains are women. I don't know what the reason is exactly, but I think it is because of the tides."

"The tides? You lost me."

"The tides are caused by the moon. Women's bodies work in cycles of the moon. I believe that there is some link there that gives women a natural connection with the ocean. Their instincts are sharper. They can read the sea and even the weather. Women seem to be better at naval tactics, too. Again, I am considered an exception, just as ruling queens are considered the exception on land, but when the *Shuriken* was mine, I always relied on Helena's advice."

"I'm surprised that pirates aren't all women," Alex commented.

"That wouldn't work. Pirates are still pirates. If they were all men or all women, there would be infighting to get up the in the pecking order and become captain. It's difficult to be captain when you're constantly watching your back for fear of assassination. Now, put a woman in charge of men who respect and trust her—one who doesn't have to waste energy looking over her shoulder all the time—and you get an efficiently run pirate ship. While merchant ships can be filled with female sailors, and usually are, rarely is there more than one woman on a pirate ship—and that one is always captain."

"Have you been hunting her all this time?" Alex asked, bringing the subject back to Helena.

Asuro shook his head. "After she left, she never came back to the realm again as far as I know, but I hear tales of her exploits from the sailors that put into port. Trying to hunt down the *Shuriken* in the dark is impossible unless you have some sort of beacon pointing the way." He smiled and patted Alex's shoulder as he spoke. "Tonight we have one."

Alex suddenly cocked his head. "They're moving off to the left."

"How far?"

"I have no idea."

"Point, as precisely as you can."

Alex pointed out to the sea, slowly shifting his finger leftward. Asuro stood behind him, watching. He knew how fast the *Shuriken* could travel given the night's breeze, and from that, he calculated how far away they'd have to be for Alex to move his finger at the speed he was. "Two kilometers at most. If it were day, we'd be able to see her. Let's get below. I'll need that finger at the helm," he winked.

They returned to the hatch, and as Asuro began to descend back into the vessel, Alex asked, "Why would you pick a first mate called the Black Widow of the Sea? Isn't that inviting trouble?"

"She earned that name when she did this to me," Asuro explained, pointing at the scars on his face.

"That had to hurt," Alex said.

"She meant for it to kill."

"So then, you and Helena, were you two ... you know ... a couple?"

Asuro nodded sadly. "She was my wife."

"Ouch," Alex said to himself. "On top of life-threatening situations, I'm going to have to deal with the emotional baggage of an ex-wife. This should be fun."

*   *   *

Shadows danced around Mornak as he sat chained to the floor of his cell again. They laughed at him and threatened him. They mocked him and tormented him. They didn't need to.

It had been too many hours since he had spoken with Dara. He had felt her desperate call when the Shadow Lord was trying to get information out of him, and struggled to pretend that he could not hear it. The interrogation had gone on far too long. When they finally threw him back into his cell, he tried to respond to his daughter, but she was no longer in contact with the Scroll.

Then he felt the wizard.

Evil magic had touched the Scroll, and its protective wards had reacted. That frightened Mornak. Even without his guidance, the Scroll would protect itself from the touch of evil wizards. However, given enough time, a wizard could learn how to get around or neutralize the wards and gain access to the Scroll's power. Very few wizards in the world would be capable of such a deed, but Mornak was fairly certain at this point that the Shadow Lord was one of those wizards.

He knew the evil that had touched the Scroll was not the Shadow Lord, but that still meant that Dara had lost the Scroll. As frightening as that was, Mornak was more concerned about what had become of his little girl. Had Alex already fallen? Were the warriors in the book of no help? He was trapped and blind to the outside world. The torments of the shadows around him seemed unimportant compared to his worry for his daughter.

He was in hell.

*   *   *

Askar arrived in the main cave. He saw the supply sheds and the dock. He noted a passageway that headed in the direction of East Port. Seeing how the water moved along the far wall, he recognized the illusion instantly and immediately came to a conclusion.

"Pirates," he spat.

They had, no doubt, taken Dara and the Scroll out to sea, and even on Specter, he could not find them without knowing their general direction. He powered up his mace and sent a ball of energy though the illusion. Soon after the first, he sent another. Specter flew in moments later, having spotted the light show.

Askar mounted the bird, and they flew out over the ocean, but he had no real idea which way to go.

"Now what?" he muttered.

10

*I*rritated, Cyrus shoved Dara back into his cabin, knocking her down to one knee. He was growing tired of playing babysitter, but he had yet to examine the other two books, and this girl knew something about how they worked. The wizard had long ago realized that any source of knowledge is valuable, even that of an eleven-year-old girl. Besides, he sensed the magic Dara possessed. If she had received any training in her gift, then she may have some useful insight in the workings of the books' magic. And so, Cyrus resigned himself to watch over her until she was of no use.

Dara had other ideas about her role in their relationship. She shot up from the floor and dived over the work table, scattering books, scrolls, quills, and parchments until she fell over the other side. Cyrus rushed around to find her flipping through *Legend and Lore* for a hero to summon. His first instinct was to burn the little imp, but he knew better than to release fire in his lab. Instead, he touched a tattoo of a hand that grew into a ghostly form as big as a man. The magic hand flew across the room at Cyrus's command and grabbed Dara, lifting her right off the ground and holding her in the air. She struggled against the apparition; though its form was transparent, its grip was solid. When she finally stopped struggling, she looked up at Cyrus who held his hand out in exactly the same position as the hand that held her. He tightened his grip slightly, making Dara cry out.

"Now," Cyrus said smugly, "are you going to behave, or do we find out how much pressure it takes to crush a little girl's ribs?"

"I ... I'll be good," Dara sobbed.

Cyrus eased his grip a little, and Dara took in a big breath of air. The wizard tidied up the mess, doing a quick inspection to make sure all books and scrolls were accounted for. Satisfied, he turned his attention back to Dara. "The next book we're going to look at is *Historic Inventions*. I'm sure you have much to tell me about it, don't you?"

"I ..." Dara began, but just then a pirate entered the room excitedly.

"Cyrus!" he exclaimed. "You're needed on deck. We have a mark."

Cyrus flicked his hand, causing the giant magical hand to throw Dara across the room into the pirate. He made an awkward catch but held onto the struggling girl.

"Throw her in the brig until this is over," Cyrus ordered. After grabbing *Legend and Lore* and a small duffel bag, he walked out the door.

Helena was waiting for him on deck, watching a ship through a spyglass. "Merchant vessel from Kalbirr, most likely carrying silks and silver. She'll make port by morning."

Cyrus smiled. "Oh, I seriously doubt that."

Helena smiled back, nodding.

"Fog?" she asked.

"Done."

Cyrus waved his arms and chanted. Soon a fog formed in the air around them, which then moved forward toward the merchant vessel. It wasn't very thick, so as not to alarm the crew of their target. It was just light enough to mask a black ship in the night as it approached.

Several pirates stood nearby, waiting. A long time passed before anyone spoke, but none grew impatient. They had been doing this for years. They knew the routine.

Finally, Helena broke the silence.

"Boarders at the ready."

Men relayed the order across and below the deck. Soon fifty pirates stood ready, their black cowls on to hide their faces. Each wore an enchanted smoke coloured visor that allowed them to see in darkness as if it were daylight.

"Are our new recruits ready?"

Cyrus patted the book.

"Let's find out."

Out of his duffel bag, Cyrus retrieved one of the visors he had brought for the warriors as well as a special arrow. He opened the book and said, "Maya, silence their lookout."

After a flash of light, Maya stood before them. Cyrus handed her the visor and arrow. She donned the visor, nocked the arrow, and moved to the ship's bow. Helena did not miss the look of anger on the Amazon's face. She obviously hated what she was doing, but she was compelled by the book and Cyrus's magic to obey.

It must be torture for her, Helena thought. *How delicious.*

* * *

"A flash," Asuro commented as he gazed through the periscope at the *Shuriken*. "Careless. The merchant ship may have spotted it."

"How far?" Alex asked.

"Too far," Asuro replied. "They'll reach the merchant ship before we reach them."

"That gives us allies," Alex said, confidently.

"That gives them hostages," Asuro countered. "Our only hope is that the flash was spotted and the ship tries to outrun them. That may buy us the time we need."

Asuro picked up a funnel with a tube attached to it that went into the floor. "Double speed," he ordered.

Below in the rowing room, a crewman heard the command from a similar funnel and repeated it. As the *Dark Wave* sped up, Alex noticed that Asuro had changed their course slightly. They were heading for the merchant ship ... at ramming speed.

"What are you doing?" he asked.

Asuro gave him a knowing glance. "I think we can board her without them knowing."

"The merchant ship?"

"No, the *Shuriken*. Just watch." He turned to a nearby crewman. "Stand by to loose the *Fishbait*."

Alex looked through the periscope, finally getting a good look at the *Shuriken*. Its size shocked him. "Um, how many men on that ship?"

Asuro knew where the question was going. "Three times our number."

"But your men are more skilled, right?"

Asuro only stared back.

Alex couldn't believe what the response meant. "Whoa, whoa, whoa. Dude, just how do you expect to take them out?"

"We are trained as pirates. We use stealth and surprise to overcome our enemies."

"So do they!" Alex exclaimed.

"What matters is who surprises whom."

Alex groaned, "I've got a bad feeling about this."

*   *   *

The pirate had thrown Dara in one of the brig cells, locked the door, and left, also locking the brig door. Apparently a small girl did not deserve guarding. Dara reached into her dress and pulled out the scroll case. Opening it, she pulled out the Scroll. She hadn't been sure she could switch the scroll cases when she dived over the table, but it had been easier than she hoped. Grabbing *Legend and Lore* and trying to summon help had thrown Cyrus off her real actions perfectly. She only wished she had managed to summon one of her heroes before he got to her.

She checked the small window of the brig door for movement outside before she called to her father. She hoped that this time he would answer.

Dara!

"Papa!" she squealed. "I miss you so much!"

I miss you, too, Little Rose. Are you all right?

"Not really. I'm in a prison cell on a pirate ship. The pirates have Alex's books and are using the warriors to attack other ships. I managed to steal the Scroll, but they'll find out I have it eventually. I'm scared, Papa. I don't know what to do."

What has happened to Alex?

"They took me from him and the Axemen. Alex got them out of the forest, some of them at least, but the pirates ambushed us after we fought some Shadow Warriors. I know he's trying to find me, but I don't know how he'll do it."

We need to get you off that ship. I am going to send you some spells. I need you to read them exactly and do the motions I instruct.

"Yes, Papa."

First, let's make you a little less conspicuous.

*   *   *

Specter soared over the water with Askar on his back. The great bird did not see a sign of anything but merchant ships in the waters. Askar looked up at the moon as it emerged from behind a cloud. Specter had been using the shadows of the clouds to cover more territory more quickly, but the ocean was vast. Askar held no great hope of finding the Scroll this way. Meanwhile, he feared Senufer may be moving out of the area of East Port. Askar knew that the longer this search took, the less likely the Axeman would be there when he returned. The general wanted to just abandon this seemingly futile quest, but he also knew that the punishment the Shadow Lord would extract would be worse than death.

Specter called out in that screech that made Askar's ears hurt, so he looked down, thinking the bird had spotted something, but saw only empty water below him. Then Specter suddenly changed course, flying purposefully in a straight line, no longer in the arcs of the search pattern they had been using. The bird knew where to go. That could only mean one thing—someone was using the Scroll.

Askar smiled. "Foolish pirates. You're messing with things you don't know about and can't possibly control. Soon you'll discover just how dangerous possessing that Scroll can be."

*   *   *

The lookout on the *Sea Maiden* was bored. They had entered the waters of Mornak's realm. A pirate attack here had not occurred in years, and the waters from their position to East Port held no obstacles or dangers. Her hardest task was simply staying awake. As the fog rolled in, her alertness picked up a little. Fog meant danger of collision with other ships. Even though light fogs could be expected this close to land this close to morning, an inattentive lookout could be the cause of disaster for her ship and another. She waited patiently for a few minutes until she heard the captain ring the ship's fog bell. She would ring it each minute to alert any ships out there of their presence. Other ship captains knew enough to do the same. At least, they should know.

When she saw the spark in the distance—almost at sea level—she didn't know what to make of it. She could not make out the source, only blackness. She almost wet herself when the arrow appeared out of the darkness from the same direction. It struck the mast a hand's width from her head. A few seconds passed before she broke out of the shock the incident caused, and a few more passed as she realized the arrow did not make a thud when it struck. She tried to yank it out of the mast while she yelled a warning to the crew below. She expected the word *pirates* to spur the crew into action, but no sound came from her mouth. She tried again, only to scream in silence. It was the arrow, she realized. She pulled on it as hard as she could, but it was buried deep in the mast. Worse, when she tried to let go, she found that her hand was stuck fast to it, trapping her and preventing her from warning her crew while the pirates closed in on them.

*   *   *

"She missed the lookout," Helena grumbled.

"Perhaps she is not as skilled as we thought," Cyrus replied. "Still, the arrow has trapped her and silenced her. We can continue undetected."

"Rowers," Helena ordered.

The order was relayed, and below deck, dozens of men grabbed oars and began to row in rhythm to a softly played drum. The *Shuriken* sped up, its devastating blade aimed at the unsuspecting ship ahead.

Cyrus held up the book for Helena to hold. She took it with a curious expression, since she thought he would be the one summoning the warriors, but then she realized that he only wanted her to hold it up. Cyrus flipped through the pages, marking each one with a different finger until four of the warriors' pages were slightly opened.

With a steadying breath, he let his magic flow into the book. "Board the merchant vessel and secure the main deck. Eliminate any who oppose you."

Helena blinked from the flash of light and then marveled at the group before her. They were strangely dressed individuals—even to each other, she imagined—but there was no doubt that each was a skilled warrior. Cyrus handed each of them an enchanted visor. Then they moved immediately without a word to the rail where they gazed out at the ship that the *Shuriken* quietly closed on.

"I thought there were five," Helena checked.

"There are, but I don't trust the monk. He seems able to manipulate my commands. It will take more research before I can control him properly without using a great deal of magic."

As the ship grew closer, they heard sudden yelling from its crew. They had been spotted, but it was too late. Even as the ship started to turn away, the forward blade of the *Shuriken* smashed into its hull, tearing a wide gap and ripping its way to the right. That struck both Helena and Cyrus as strange, as did the feel of the impact. They supposed it could have to do with the fact that the merchant ship was turning when they struck it. But it felt as though, at the moment they struck its side, something struck their side. They glanced left over the port railing, but there was no ship to be seen.

* * *

"We're in!" a crewman relayed.

Alex rushed after Asuro as they moved to the front of the *Dark Wave*. The semisubmersible had punctured the side of the *Shuriken* at the same time the *Shuriken* had rammed the *Sea Maiden*. The spearhead of the *Dark Wave* had torn a man-sized hole between the two vessels before opening up like a bird's beak, creating a portal through which Asuro's men poured into the *Shuriken*.

Alex could hear the sounds of battle through the hole but could not see anything. The men fought in complete darkness. Asuro handed him a pair of goggles and explained, "We put out their lanterns with a spell when we boarded. These goggles allow us to see in darkness. Helena's men have similar goggles, but the surprise bought us some time to attack before they could don them. Remember to shield your eyes when I get hurt."

Asuro then dashed into the fray.

"When you get hurt?" Alex asked after him. "When are you supposed to get hurt?"

Asuro was out of earshot and already fighting fiercely against the pirates. Alex put on the goggles and then looked in the hole. The room seemed to light up as though the sun shone above. The scene appeared very much like a martial arts movie being filmed. The crews of the two ships punched, kicked, cut, leaped, and yelled "ki-yah!" at each other in a chaos of movement. They were dressed so similarly that Alex couldn't tell who was on which side. The combatants seemed to know, however. He could see two and three man groups working together. Still, he could not tell which side either of the groups fought for.

While the fight had been evenly matched when they arrived, as greater numbers of Asuro's men entered through the hole, the tide of battle slowly turned. Alex wondered why reinforcements weren't coming in for Helena's men until he saw that the only way in or out was a ladder leading to a closed hatch in the ceiling far above them. Anyone on that ladder became a perfect target for the knives and shuriken flying around the room. The storming of the *Sea Maiden* going on above them probably preoccupied most of Helena's crew. Even so, they wouldn't stay preoccupied.

Water flooded into the ship around the edges of the hole they made. They had to find Dara quickly and get out before the *Shuriken* sank and dragged the *Dark Wave* down with it. Alex wondered how much it would hurt Asuro to sink his own ship or if that had been his goal since his wife and crew left him.

He looked over at Asuro who had moved deeper into the fight. Wielding twin cutlasses, he was a whirlwind of action. Every man of his old crew recognized him, and none would face him alone. His blades cut and blocked. They deflected flying knives and put on an intimidating show. Despite their training, his opponents found themselves focusing on the swords and forgetting that Asuro himself was a lethal weapon. A fist or foot, sometimes even his forehead, took out unwary opponents. Around him, men on both sides dropped, but far fewer of his men had lost their battles since he had joined the fight. His presence inspired them while disheartening the others.

Alex has seen "Leadership & Inspire" skills available for characters in the video games he played, but he had never thought such skills useful. He always sought to do the most to improve his character, not to aid others. To see the effect of inspiration in real life made him realize the strength of the skill. That a single man could turn the tide of a battle simply by being there was a kind of magic in itself. Alex wanted to grab a sword himself and join the battle, but common sense told him he wouldn't last a second. These men fought at Tenzin's level of skill, all of them. Instead, he did what he was there to do. He focused on Dara and located her above them. When they had control of the room, he would lead them to her.

Suddenly Asuro screamed in pain. Alex turned to see what had happened, and that's when the flash bombs went off. The goggles everyone wore magnified the light so much that it blinded everyone in the room who hadn't shut their eyes—the pirates and Alex.

Alex swore to himself as he remembered Asuro's warning. Around him the pirate hunters quickly dispatched many of the disabled pirates while Alex stumbled around, hoping not to get killed.

* * *

Maya was firing arrows into the deck of the *Sea Maiden* before anyone had a chance to jump across and board her. Genjuro, Bantu, and Scorpius crossed first and not without reason. The pirates were waiting to see what they could do. The teens were magical beings. The crew wondered if they had magical powers as well, and if so, they wanted to see those powers work.

Most of the men of the *Sea Maiden* scattered and ran, but on a ship, they had few options of where to go. Scorpius and Genjuro faced off against the few who opposed them while Bantu hefted crates and whatever he could find in front of the doors to seal off the deck.

Back on the *Shuriken*, it quickly dawned on Helena what was wrong. "They haven't killed anyone," she noted.

Maya's arrows had not hit a single person but had come incredibly close to doing so. Instead of killing, she was inspiring fear and clearing an area for the others to operate. Bantu had limited the amount of men on the deck with his barricades while Scorpius and Genjuro forced the rest back, either to jump into the sea or to surrender. While impressive, the sight was disappointing, and not just to Helena. She saw the reaction of her crew. There was no bloodshed. There were no screams of agony and terror. For a pirate, there was no fun.

"Board her!" Helena ordered, and her men surged forward. But the energy that usually accompanied a raid had seeped away. Once her men secured the *Sea Maiden*, the warriors disappeared. A quiet fell upon the scene that lasted almost a minute. Then they heard the thumping against Bantu's barricades. The crew below had armed themselves and wanted to regain control of the ship. The men smiled, and some began to tear some of the barricades down. They were going to have some fun after all.

* * *

Dara read the words on the Scroll and touched the lock with her finger, which proved difficult since she couldn't see that finger. The first spell Mornak had her cast made her invisible. If anyone had walked in right then, they would have seen only a silvery gold scroll floating around the room. Mornak told her she would remain that way for an hour as long as she didn't attack anyone. Dara laughed at the warning. Who would she possibly attack?

The lock to the brig door popped open. Dara had already escaped her cell. Opening the door slightly, she peeked out. The hall was clear.

"I'm going after the books first, Papa."

Be careful, Little Rose. They may not be able to see you, but they might hear you, and if they accidentally bump into you, they will know what has happened.

"I will, Papa."

I will leave another spell of invisibility on the Scroll for you for your bags. Take care.

"I love you."

I love you too, Dara.

Dara rolled up the Scroll. It was a challenge to slip it into the now-invisible scroll case, but as she did, it too disappeared. Sneaking out the door, Dara made her way down the hall as quietly as she could. She was scared but not nearly as much as she had been when she was first on the run from Aspiria. She had a couple of advantages now. Invisibility was one. The general confusion was the other. Something was going on that had the attention of the men, something other than the raid taking place above her. She saw several men rushing down the hall to gather around a hatch to a lower deck. She didn't know what lurked down that hatch, but from the way the men stood around it, she guessed something dangerous.

She pressed herself against the wall as two pirates came rushing by, holding her breath until they passed. She couldn't concern herself with their problems. Turning the other way, she retraced her steps to Cyrus's room, finding it with little trouble.

That was easy, she thought as she grabbed the door handle. Suddenly a pulsing screech sounded that made Dara try to cover her ears. She couldn't. Her body was frozen. The same spell that Cyrus had used to hold her in his room held her now. She scolded herself. Her father was a wizard. She knew he never left his valuables unguarded. Now she could only wait to be discovered. She would soon be put back in her cell, this time without the Scroll. Tears started to flow down her face again, and again she couldn't wipe them.

*   *   *

The water had risen only knee-high in the oar room. Alex, his vision slowly returning, wondered why the ship wasn't filling any faster. A few things didn't add up, such as how Asuro's men managed to put out the lanterns in the room. He pushed the thoughts aside. The important thing was that the pirates had been dispatched. All eyes shifted to the hatch at the top of the ladder.

"How many do you figure are up there?" Alex asked.

"Many," Asuro replied.

"Then I hope your stealthy-surprise-boarding plan covers this."

"I had hoped to secure this deck in less time. It has been a while since we battled pirates of their skill. Still, we defeated three of them for every one of us."

"You realize that, at that rate, there will be no one left on either side?"

Asuro nodded. "If that is what it takes."

Alex glanced around to see how Asuro's men felt about that statement and was surprised to see them all nodding as well. "That's a noble, if suicidal, attitude."

The statement angered Asuro. "Helena's men have killed thousands in the past ten years. Thousands. If, in dying, we stop the slaughter of thousands more, then our sacrifice will be well worth it."

The men around them cheered at the sentiment.

"All the same, how about we do this without the suicidal attitude?" Alex suggested.

"Don't worry, boy. We value our lives greatly."

Alex looked up at the hatch again. "There's no way we're getting through that."

"Have faith," Asuro told him.

Just then a man emerged from the *Dark Wave*. Dressed in black but unlike the others, he wore robes with many pockets. Skinny and far less fit than the rest of Asuro's crew, he radiated a surprising amount of confidence and, more importantly, power.

"You have a wizard?" Alex exclaimed.

"Every wise captain employs a wizard," Asuro stated.

"Then why haven't you used him until now?"

"We have. You'll notice we're not underwater. And, currently the men above do not suspect that a wizard is down here."

Everything clicked for Alex then. Asuro had been using him subtly, aiding his men without exposing his advantage and without giving the enemy cause to summon their own wizard.

"Ready, George?" Asuro asked.

George? Alex thought. *Mornak, Senufer, Brasius, Asuro, ... George. Heh.*

"As always," George replied as he began casting. The air around him wavered as if looking at heat across the desert sands. Alex could feel a suction toward the man. A shimmering globe of what Alex was sure was compressed air soon hovered in front of George. He waved his hand up, and the globe shot up toward the hatch. Then, with a quick incantation, he knocked on the air in front of him. The hatch above flew open just before the ball reached it. The men above started at the sight, hesitating just long enough for the ball to pass through the opening. Then it exploded.

It was not an explosion of fire but of air. The powerful concussion sent every man in the hall flying. Many hit walls and then dropped to the floor unconscious. Several broke bones on impact. The blast hit so hard that it broke the ribs and noses of most men while it knocked the wind out of everyone.

Asuro and his men rushed up the ladder in an instant, attacking the men who could still fight. Alex shook his head in wonder as he followed after them.

"Dara is this way," Alex said, pointing.

Asuro nodded. "I will accompany you with a few men to find her. George, take the rest up to the deck and assist the merchant vessel."

"Aye, sir," George nodded, and then the two groups parted.

*   *   *

The battle for the *Sea Maiden* had become fierce. Cyrus found himself engaged with the opposing wizard while the pirates fought the *Sea Maiden*'s defenders. Colourful magics arced between the two spell casters, sometimes catching an unsuspecting pirate or sailor in their courses. The wizard was very good, Cyrus realized, but she was still losing the battle. His many tattoos reacted instantly to counter the spells thrown at Cyrus, leaving him free to cast offensive spells at twice the rate of his opponent—most of them Death Bolts.

It was the wizard who killed herself in the end. She cast Unerring Arrow, which sent a deadly magic arrow toward Cyrus. A tattoo keyed to that specific spell activated and sent the arrow back at its caster. She fell with a look of disbelief on her face. Cyrus looked down at his own body. Well over half of his skin was clear of tattoos. The battle had been fierce indeed, but now he was free to rain deadly magic on the other sailors.

The sound of the alarm from his quarters stopped him before he started. He turned toward the stairs that led down to the lower deck to see a pirate rushing up to him and Helena.

"We have boarders in the oar room!" the man exclaimed.

"Boarders?" Cyrus spat. "Impossible! There is no other ship."

"They are there, sir," the man insisted, "being led by Asuro."

The colour drained from Helena's face.

Cyrus chuckled. "It's different when you're the one being surprised, isn't it?"

Helena quickly recomposed herself.

"I think you should be more concerned. That's your alarm going off."

Cyrus turned to the pirate with worry.

"Have they breached my chambers?"

"No, we have them trapped in the oar room," the man replied.

"Then who could be trying to get in there?"

"The girl?" Helena suggested.

"In the brig," Cyrus replied offhandedly. "It could be a lone spy. The attack below may just be a diversion. I must see to this at once, especially with your husband on board," he grumbled.

"Don't call him that!" Helena snapped.

Cyrus stormed off but cast a lightning bolt into the battle as he left. It selectively struck only those not allied with him. A dozen men and women fell. Helena watched him go, pitying whoever it was that tried to get into his quarters. Then she looked around for a defensible position. If Asuro made it up this far, she would be ready.

*   *   *

Unable to turn her head, Dara watched Cyrus approaching from the corner of her eye. He was not in a happy mood, and she knew that when he discovered her, she would be put through a great deal of pain. She wanted to cry out as he stepped up right beside her, but she couldn't even move her mouth. Cyrus stood a finger's width away from her, looking at the door and around the hall. He saw no one, and the door was still closed and intact. That made him wonder why the alarm was even going off.

With a disgruntled huff, Cyrus waved his arm. The alarm stopped, and Dara, suddenly able to move, slipped her hand away from the door handle just as Cyrus reached out to grab it. Before he could open the door, a group of men appeared down the hall. Cyrus recognized them immediately: Asuro's men. He smiled.

He had wanted to kill them for a very long time. Knives and throwing stars flew up the hallway toward him. Dara gasped when she realized that she was in the line of fire as well. Cyrus gestured quickly, causing a gust of wind to scatter the small missiles. Dara then ducked when she saw him casting a counterspell. Green darts of magic flew from his fingertips over her head. The enemy tried to scatter, but the hallway confined them. Several men doubled over in pain when the darts struck them. Others pulled them out of the hall to safety.

Dara didn't know what to do. She didn't know who those men were. They looked like more pirates, but they were attacking Cyrus. Were they good pirates? Could she take the chance to find out?

Behind her, Cyrus used the respite to pull out the book. He forced more energy into it than he had before.

"Kill Asuro's men!" he yelled as he slid his fingers in the correct pages. The warriors appeared. Their eyes glowed with magic. Maya immediately brought up her bow, nocked two arrows, and shot at two men who had popped out to throw their knives at Cyrus. One managed to duck back out of harm's way. The other skillfully caught the arrow. When she grabbed another arrow, the man ducked back around the corner.

As a group, the warriors stalked down the hall after their targets. Dara pressed herself against the wall to let them pass. She knew she couldn't stop them physically, but if she had the book—

She had to get it away from Cyrus, but if she tried to grab it, she'd become visible and then Cyrus would have her for sure. She wished Alex were here to show her what to do.

*   *   *

Around a corner at the end of the hall, Alex heard the order clearly and peeked out to see his new friends coming to kill him.

"A samurai," Asuro noted as he peered around the corner.

"You know what a samurai is?" Alex asked.

"From tales I've heard in other realms. I thought they were fictional."

"I could say the same about you."

"No matter. We will kill him and the rest."

"You can't," Alex argued. "They are the friends I told you about. That wizard is just controlling them."

"I thought the book controlled them."

"Is this really a time to argue semantics?"

"They mean to kill us," Asuro stated.

"No," Alex realized. "Not us. Listen carefully ..."

A few moments later, Asuro and Alex charged out around the corner. Asuro held his twin blades while Alex sported a crossbow. He hoped he could aim well enough. *Just point and shoot*, he told himself.

They rushed up the hallway toward the warriors who neither sped up nor slowed down at their approach. Cyrus watched with joyful anticipation. Even Asuro could not match the combined skills of the warriors he faced. The two forces met—and passed by each other. Cyrus gasped in shock as he realized his error. Neither of these two were Asuro's men! The warriors ignored them and continued on their determined march while Asuro's men backed off, trying to keep their distance.

Alex fired the crossbow as Asuro charged in. Alex's aim was close. The bolt clipped Cyrus in the shoulder making him drop the book but didn't seriously harm him. Asuro's aim was better. His swords arced out before coming together on either side of Cyrus's neck, jarring as if they struck steel. For a split second, Asuro stared eye to eye with the smiling wizard, his blades still trying to push through the man's neck. He glimpsed a tattoo of a sword striking a shield vanish from the Cyrus's body just as magical force blew the pirate hunter back into a wall. He recovered quickly, but before he could attack again, black tendrils of energy shot out from Cyrus's fingers. They connected with Alex and Asuro, and the two grimaced in pain. It felt as if their very souls were burning. The skull design on Cyrus's face began to glow with power. Through the agony, Alex noted that the black energy now flowed back toward Cyrus. He was draining their life forces! Alex dropped to his knees, his insides burning. Asuro marched angrily toward Cyrus, knowing the wizard's spell and watching the tattoos reappear on his body as he replenished his spells with their life forces. The pirate hunter was only able to take three steps before he collapsed to one knee. Behind him, his men saw the predicament. They had no choice but to engage the warriors if they wanted to give their leader any hope of living, so they moved forward. As Cyrus's laugh echoed through the hallway, Alex realized he may be about to die. His only thought was that he failed Dara.

That was when Cyrus screamed. Alex's pain suddenly disappeared, but his heart beat like a jackhammer; he panted as he tried to recover. In front of him, Asuro shook his head to clear it and began getting back up, only to stare in wonder at the sight before him. Blue flames engulfed Cyrus's body. His back arched, and he seemed unable to do anything but scream. His hands clenched and opened in spasms, and Alex winced as the man's face started to burn away. A moment later the flames stopped as the wizard's form had become only ashes, which fell lightly to the ground. As they did, they revealed Dara, who had snuck her way behind Cyrus and placed the Scroll against his back. Down the hall, no longer bound by their summoner, the warriors disappeared to the surprise of the men who attacked the area they had been just in.

Dara kicked the ashes in front of her.

"Don't you dare hurt Alex!" she said to them.

Alex rushed up and hugged her. She hugged him back fiercely.

"Rosie!" he exclaimed.

"Rosie?" she said, pushing him back.

"Little Rose. Rosie," Alex explained awkwardly.

"Oh," she replied and hugged him again.

After a minute or so, he pulled away and held her shoulders, shaking his head at her.

"Just who is supposed to be protecting who?" he asked.

"Whom," Asuro corrected.

* * *

By the time Alex, Asuro, Dara, and the men got to the top deck, the pirate hunters and the *Sea Maiden*'s crew had bracketed Helena's men, but Helena herself was nowhere on deck. What had been a clear victory for her only minutes ago had changed to an even match. However, everyone was so engaged in the battle that they did not notice the dark shadow flying above them.

"Will you have control of your warriors if you summon them now?" Asuro asked Alex.

Alex turned to Dara who nodded back.

"Yes," Alex replied.

"I believe we can turn the tide of battle with them on our side."

Alex opened the book, but before he could start reading, Asuro's hand shot toward his face. Alex thought the man suddenly meant to kill him, but the hand stopped just short, having caught a shuriken aimed right between Alex's eyes.

All eyes turned in the direction it came from as Helena stepped out of the shadows.

"Your reflexes are as quick as ever, Asuro," she said. "Did you miss me?"

Asuro threw the shuriken back with deadly speed, but Helena slipped out of the way just in time.

"Apparently," Asuro replied.

"Come, lover," she said, pulling out a single sai and a sword, "let's dance."

Alex held up the book again, but before he could say a word, one of Asuro's men grabbed his shoulder. "Do not summon your warriors to aid Asuro. This is something he needs to do alone."

Alex sighed. "Why do warriors always need to settle these things alone? It's stupid. Outnumber her and take her out. End of story."

"You would deny him the revenge he's sought for ten years?"

"No, he can kill her in the end," Alex explained.

"Where is the honour in that?"

Alex shook his head. "Sometimes you gotta place common sense in front of honour if you want the good guys to win."

While Alex and the pirate hunter argued, Asuro and Helena fought a battle of incredible skill. Despite her smaller size, Helena's strength almost matched Asuro's, and what she lacked in strength, she made up for in agility. She blocked one of his swords with her sai while his other sword blocked hers. She ducked and dodged around his more powerful strikes, even managing to get him on the defensive from time to time. Unlike the other men who had fought Asuro, she anticipated when he would kick or punch rather than cut, but likewise, he seemed to guess her attacks.

"They have the exact same fighting style," Alex said in awe.

"They practiced together for years," the pirate hunter explained, "and they trained every man in our original crew."

Helena went in for a killing thrust with her sword, and Asuro was ready with the block, but she shifted the attack at the last moment to score a glancing blow on Asuro's arm. Although the wound was only superficial, Helena winked and smiled. "First blood."

"All that really matters is who bleeds less," Asuro countered and then moved in again.

The battle of the two weapon masters, as fierce as it was graceful, mesmerized Alex, Dara, and the pirate hunters. For a time, it seemed that neither would win, but eventually, Helena's confident smile began to fade. She found herself more often on the defensive. Asuro scored a hit on her arm and then immediately afterward on her thigh. Helena's balance went off, and as she tried to correct it, Asuro spun her sword out of her hand with his own sword. His elbow came in, hitting the side of her head. She fell down to the deck.

"Now," Asuro swore, "for all the pain and suffering you have caused this past decade, I sentence you to death."

Helena dropped her sai and raised her hands pleadingly.

"Asuro, do not! You have bested me. You have shown me that good is stronger than evil. Please, I renounce evil now. I pledge to dedicate my life to doing good as you have."

Asuro held his strike as he tried to determine the truth of her words.

Alex knew right away.

"Oh, come on! That's the oldest trick in the book! Just kill her!"

"I speak the truth!" Helena countered. "I need but the chance to prove it. Let me up, and I will show you."

Asuro, unsure and wary, reached out his hand to help her up. As he did, Helena readied her nails for the kill.

"Don't do that!" Alex yelled. "She's just baiting you. She'll stab you when you get close enough! I mean, how many movies has that happened in? It's the oldest trick in the book!"

"What's a movie?" a pirate hunter behind him asked.

"Keep her right there," Alex said as he opened the book, surprised to find bookmarks in it. "Maya will deal with that bit ..." He glanced down at Dara. "Pirate."

* * *

High above the chaos riding on Specter, Askar charged his mace. Around him, clouds formed and gathered in response. A storm brewed directly over the battle, and no one noticed. In the Hall of Shadows, the Shadow Lord watched through Specter's eyes. He reached out with his powers through Specter to the minds of Helena and her men.

"The battle is lost if you continue this way, but there is still a chance for victory. The Hall of Shadows is no longer a prison for evil, but a conduit for it. Give yourself over to the Hall, and it will increase your power tenfold."

Askar heard the words, too, and looked down to gauge the reaction. The men looked around at each other, waiting for someone to make a decision. He decided to make it for them.

"Behold the power that awaits you!" the Shadow Lord exclaimed.

Askar took the cue and jumped from Specter's back. He fell to the bow of the *Shuriken,* landing with a thud to the surprise of everyone around him.

"I am Askar! General of the Hall of Shadows. Embrace the Hall!" he yelled. "Gain its might as I have!" He thrust his mace in the air as he called on its power. Lightning blasted down from the sky through the mace and Askar, ripping across both ships. All about him sailors, pirates, and pirate hunters cried out as electricity seared through them.

Alex and company, just outside the range of the blast, watched the spectacle before them in awe. Distracted, first by the fight, and now by Askar, Alex still had not summoned any of the warriors.

Helena suddenly snatched her sword and scrambled away from Asuro toward Askar.

"I embrace the Hall!" she yelled. "Grant me its power!"

Asuro stormed out after her, but before he could reach her, Specter swooped down and screeched at her. The sound carried magic waves that struck Helena, making her cry out in joy.

"Yes! I feel it! I feel the power!"

Asuro stopped in his tracks, blinking his eyes at what couldn't be happening, what he must be imagining. Helena was growing; her body shone with an eerie blue and white light. She turned back to Asuro, now twice his height, and looked down at him. Her smile returned, and she beckoned him with her sword.

"Let's finish this, lover," she purred.

To her surprise, Asuro did not hesitate at the challenge. He gritted his teeth and marched in toward her.

Over on the *Sea Maiden*, the other pirates similarly called out to the Hall. Specter went to them as well, its screech blanketing them all.

"This can't be good," Alex warned.

Askar called another lightning bolt, but sent this one through himself into the deck of the *Shuriken.* A huge section of it exploded. Both ships lurched, throwing everyone to the deck. Some pitched over into the sea, including Helena.

Asuro screamed as she went overboard, "No! I will not be denied!"

Alex and the others followed him to the railing. In the water below, they could see the glow of Helena's body.

"She can swim, right?" Alex asked.

"Of course," Asuro stated. "She's a pirate."

"Then I'm pretty sure this is not over," he said assuredly and then added, "but seriously, you should have killed her when you had the chance."

Asuro started to climb the railing, but Alex pulled him back.

"Later!" he yelled over the wind, which was picking up. "Your men need you now!"

Asuro looked over to see Helena's men all growing and glowing with power.

"Get to the *Dark Wave* now!" Asuro told Alex. "We will follow soon."

"The warriors can help you," Alex argued.

"We will be right behind you. Have no doubt."

Alex took no chances. He opened the book and called the warriors forth.

"Make sure Dara gets safely to shore," he ordered each of them, and then they all quickly descended to the lower deck.

"George!" Asuro yelled. "Repulse!"

The wizard immediately ran around the battle into position, making sure the spell would reach all the pirates. Askar, recognizing the potential threat, moved toward George, his mace ready to crush the wizard's skull, until he felt the small sting of a blade in his back. When he turned around, a shuriken hit him in the chest although this one didn't get through his armour.

"Come deal with me," Asuro challenged.

"With pleasure," Askar smiled.

Just then George got his spell off, creating a wave of force that moved out, pushing the pirates and Askar across the deck and over the railing, but leaving all others alone.

"Men! To me!" Asuro yelled. His men leaped from the deck of the *Sea Maiden* to the *Shuriken* and gathered around him. George moved to the bow of the *Shuriken*, focused on the *Sea Maiden*, and cast the spell again. The ships separated.

"Make for shore!" Asuro told the other crew. "We'll help if we can."

The *Sea Maiden*'s upper decks were torn, but she was not taking on much water. Below, the pirates moved about in the water, their bodies glowing. Some tried to climb the side of the *Sea Maiden*, but shuriken, knives, and crossbow bolts shot by Asuro's men dropped them back into the water.

Strangely, many of the pirates did not even surface, but instead, gathered under the water where Helena had originally fallen.

"What are they doing?" a man asked.

"Nothing good," Asuro replied. "Let's get to the *Dark Wave*."

They had almost reached the stairs leading down when the bow of the ship, from the point where Askar's lightning bolt had hit, wrenched free, causing several sections of the *Shuriken* to collapse in on themselves. The entire ship tilted, forcing the men to hold onto the deck and to each other to keep from falling into the sea with the pirates.

"Over the side!" Asuro yelled.

He climbed the angled deck to the side where the *Dark Wave* had entered, his men close on his heels. "I hope those kids made it back in time," he muttered.

* * *

Knowing the way to the lower decks, Alex ushered Dara and the warriors down the hall.

"The books!" Dara exclaimed before they got very far. "They're in Cyrus's cabin. It's just down this way."

They rushed down the hall until they reached the door. "It was trapped before," Dara warned.

They stood for a moment wondering what to do.

"We don't have time to be careful," Scorpius stated. "Bantu, can you break it?"

The African warrior charged the door. It shattered when he struck it, but no alarm went off. They raced into the room. Dara retrieved the other books and her and Alex's bags. Seeing what was in the room, Alex quickly grabbed some items off the shelves. Then he snatched some parchment and jotted something down quickly. The others could not believe he was taking the time to make notes.

"What are you doing?" Maya asked, looking annoyed.

"Taking precautions," Alex replied as he shoved the items in his bag.

Then they were running down the hall again. Suddenly the ship shook violently, seemed to fall for a second, and then stopped. The hallway now tilted almost forty-five degrees. They didn't know what it meant until they got to the hatchway to find water seeping up through it.

"Crap," Alex said. "We're not going that way."

"Back up," Scorpius decided. "Over the side."

"Over the side?" Genjuro exclaimed. "There is a storm outside. We could drown."

"If we stay in here, we *will* drown," Scorpius stated.

The others didn't argue. They turned and headed back up to the deck, trying their best to run at an angle. Alex reached the stairs first, looking up to see that a storm now raged outside. Lightning flashed of its own accord while rain pelted the deck above. The howl of the wind outside flowed into the hallway. Alex stopped in his tracks, forcing the others to stop behind him.

"What is wrong?" Scorpius asked. "Why don't you go up?"

Lightning flashed again, drawing Scorpius's gaze up to the top of the stairs. Standing between them and the deck was Askar.

II

*T*rembling with anger, crackling with electricity, and soaking wet from his dunk in the ocean, Askar did not look in a mood to be argued with.

"The Scroll!" demanded the general.

Alex glanced back down the hall. Water slowly filled it up. *Great*, he thought. *The only way out is through the guy with the mace that can fry you.* He figured that if he was going to face the Hall's general, he might as well be flippant about it.

"Get your own scroll, Oscar!" Alex yelled.

"Askar!"

"Whatever."

Alex braced himself for a jolt of electricity, but it didn't come.

"Why doesn't he use the magic weapon on us?" Genjuro whispered.

Glancing down at Dara, Alex knew.

"He can't risk frying the Scroll."

Scorpius muscled his way in front of Alex. When he raised his shield, Genjuro stepped up beside him, the samurai guessing his plan and eager to fight. Nodding to each other, the two of them charged up the stairs. Askar swung his mace, and the impact of it on the shield jarred the human battering ram. Electricity stung the teens, but they gritted their teeth and plowed into Askar. All three tumbled across the deck when they cleared the doorway.

The others ran up the stairs right after them. Genjuro rose in a heartbeat, his katana slicing down at Askar who managed to roll to the side just in time. The general tripped up the samurai and then got up to one knee when an arrow struck him in the shin. As Maya nocked a second shaft, Bantu charged in with his spear. Rather than dodging, Askar grabbed the shaft of the spear, stopping it just short of his gut. His move effectively turned Bantu into a shield from Maya. Unfortunately for him, the other teens had gotten up and now charged in.

They all stopped and ducked when Specter strafed them, assaulting their ears with a powerful screech. Maya immediately changed targets and let an arrow fly at the bird as it passed. The wind gusted, causing the arrow's path to sheer just off from its target. Meanwhile, Askar displayed his strength when he lifted Bantu with the spear and threw him into Scorpius.

Alex looked around the deck to check the state of the ship. The *Sea Maiden*, now barely visible, moved away in the storm. The pirates of the *Shuriken* weren't anywhere in sight, but in the water by the lower side of the ship, dozens of forms moved about, glowing with a blue white light. They moved toward each other, their light merging into an increasingly bigger glow. Alex wondered what the Hall was doing to them.

Asuro's men were also missing. Alex hoped they hadn't fallen overboard and drowned, but at the moment, that seemed most likely. The only good thing was that the deck was leveling out as the boat sank—not that sinking was a good thing, but at least it was getting easier to stand and fight.

His attention snapped back to the fight when Tenzin forced Askar back a few steps with a flying kick. Unfortunately, the man (if he was a man; he looked more like a beast) seemed more angry than hurt from the blow. Genjuro moved in at a surprising speed and swung his katana, but Askar deftly blocked it with his mace. That gave Tenzin an opening; he struck hard with his fist into Askar's side. Askar grunted and swung his free arm at the monk, who flipped back out of the way. Then Bantu grabbed Askar from behind as Scorpius readied his gladius, but before the Roman could attack, he had to use his shield to block Specter's talons as the bird swooped in again. Maya shot another arrow at it, this time clipping its wing, but the bird seemed to hardly feel it. The distraction gave Askar the chance to break free of Bantu's grip.

"This fight could go either way," Alex said to Dara.

"If Askar starts to lose, he'll just use his ring to disappear," Dara said.

"He can become invisible?" Alex asked.

"No, I think it transports him somewhere safe."

"The Hall," Alex guessed.

Just then Askar's mace crackled with energy that spilled out over the deck, shocking all the teens. Bantu and Genjuro became dazed and fell to their knees around Askar who lifted his mace to crush their skulls.

"Dara, give me the Scroll!" Alex yelled as he grabbed her bag and rifled through it.

Askar stopped and turned when he heard Alex's words. He grabbed Genjuro by the neck and held him up. "Give *me* the Scroll or your friend dies."

"Come get it, Nascar," Alex challenged and then whispered to Dara, "Hide now."

Livid that Alex mispronounced his name a second time, the general roared. "It's Askar, you ... you're doing that on purpose!"

Alex stuck his tongue out and the others were forgotten as the general's anger erupted. He dropped Genjuro and stormed toward Alex.

Tenzin moved in and grabbed the samurai, checking to see if he was okay. He and Bantu had taken the worst of the electric blast. Genjuro was conscious, but barely, and Bantu was getting up, though with great difficulty.

Maya hit Askar with two arrows. They struck hard, but he just grunted and moved on. Alex held up the scroll case and yelled, "Scorpius! Go long!"

Alex then threw the scroll case toward the Roman. Scorpius could not believe what Alex had just done. He rushed to get in place to catch the Scroll. Askar too watched it fly, giving Alex the opportunity to slip away. As Scorpius reached up to catch the Scroll, Specter intercepted it, catching it with its talons. Askar laughed at the turnaround.

"Alex, you fool!" Scorpius yelled. Before he could say more, however, Askar let loose with another blast from his mace as the warriors charged in at him. They tumbled when their legs convulsed from the electricity.

"Specter!" Askar called, and the bird swooped in to him. He jumped on its back, and they flew up into the storm. Askar held his mace up, and Alex knew the man was going to use the storm's lightning to finish them off, but then Askar paused when he glanced down at the water. Smiling, he twisted his ring. He and Specter vanished from sight.

All the teens stood up, wondering what had just happened.

"Why didn't he finish us?" Genjuro asked.

"He expects we'll drown," Scorpius stated, "and he's probably right."

The deck of the *Shuriken* floated just above sea level, and the glow off the starboard side grew larger and brighter. Without warning, a creature rose up from the water. Looking like some sort of giant slug, its blue torso and white underbelly—the same shades as the light that had surrounded the pirates—towered above them. Alex knew at once that these were the pirates, twisted by the Hall's evil magic into an abomination that served it. It opened its mouth, showing row upon row of razor sharp teeth, and howled out at the storm around it.

"I think," Bantu said, "that he expects *that* to kill us."

"First prize in 'How we're gonna die' goes to the African warrior," Alex commented.

"Move!" Scorpius yelled, and they all ran to the port side of the ship. A skiff hung there, though whether they could launch it in time remained in question.

The slug bumped against the broken bow of the ship and then rose up high in the air.

"Grab hold of the railing, tight!" yelled Alex.

The slug dived down, smashing into the other side of the ship. The side the group stood on lurched up violently. If they hadn't been holding onto the railing, they would have been thrown over the deck and into the sea. The skiff was not so lucky. Snapping free of its lines, it arced through the air to land by the slug.

Alex looked up at the sky and asked, "Is *one* break asking too much?"

They had gone as far as they could. The slug would soon smash what was left of the ship, and then they would either drown or be eaten.

"Rock and a hard place?" Maya asked Alex.

He nodded looking up at the slug. "Big friggin' rock."

"What's that?" Dara yelled, pointing off the port bow.

"A small boat," Maya noted.

"*Fishbait!*" Alex yelled. It had drifted toward them in the storm.

"Yes, we are," Maya said.

"No. That's the name of the boat. We can swim to her."

"In this?" Maya asked incredulously, gesturing at the storm around them and the large whitecaps in the water.

Alex pointed back at the slug as it smashed another section of the sinking *Shuriken*. "Stay here and face that then."

"I see your point," said Maya as she jumped in the sea.

Alex was about to jump in after her when Scorpius grabbed his arm.

"The book," he said.

Alex glanced at his book bag. It would provide some protection, but the books inside would eventually get soaked.

"Put it in my bag," Dara offered. "It keeps things dry no matter what."

"It's enchanted?" Alex asked.

She nodded and held up her finger and thumb close together. "Just a little."

Alex stuffed all three books into the bag along with some of the other things in his book bag, then slung Dara's bag over his shoulder with his own, and moved to jump in again. Dara grabbed his arm, stopping him.

"We're in a hurry," Alex said. "Can it wait?"

"I can't swim," Dara stated.

Before Alex could say anything, Bantu scooped her up. "That is not a problem, little one. Just hold tightly to me." And with that, he jumped in.

Genjuro almost jumped next until Alex reminded him that he was wearing armour and would sink like a stone. With his impending death at hand, it had slipped his mind. Scorpius also had to lose his chest plate. They hoped the items would return to the book when they returned.

Soon all the teens were swimming hard toward the *Fishbait*. Dara clung to Bantu's neck and kept her eyes shut. The sound of smashing wood made them glance back to see the slug destroy the remainder of the *Shuriken*.

Tenzin reached the boat first and climbed, almost like a spider, up its side. A moment later, a rope dropped down, and the others used it to pull themselves up. Dara hung onto Bantu as he climbed on. He was surprised by how heavy she felt until he realized that her hair, which was almost as long as she was tall, was soaked, creating the extra weight. Bantu had to smile, looking at Dara, when he put her down. Soaked to the bone and miserable, she looked like a wet kitten. The rest did not fare much better. Their clothes clung to their bodies, and they had to wipe their hair and the rain from their faces constantly as the storm assaulted them.

"Anyone know how to sail?" Alex asked.

"I do," Scorpius stated. He took the helm and tried to turn the boat around.

Alex couldn't see any sign of land in any direction. "How do you know which way to go?" he asked.

"I don't," Scorpius replied. "I'm just heading away from that," he said, pointing at the slug, which now moved toward them. It was easily as large as the *Shuriken* had been.

"We're gonna need a bigger boat," Alex mumbled.

Lightning exploded across the sky, lighting up the night for a brief second before plunging them all into darkness again. If not for the glow of the slug and the frequent flashes of electricity in the sky, they might not be able to see at all.

"It is a shame that we cannot command lightning like Askar," Genjuro stated. "A powerful blast could certainly destroy that thing."

Alex's eyes went wide with realization. He lifted off Dara's bag and opened it up. Pulling out the book *Historic Inventions*, he flipped through quickly, hoping too many pages didn't get wet before he found what he was looking for. The slug was almost upon them. He needed more time. Maya shot arrows at it, but they felt like tiny pinpricks to the huge beast. Scorpius turned the boat sharply just as the slug dived toward them. It just missed. The wave it caused pushed them away from it, giving them a few more moments. To everyone's surprise, Alex pulled a long metal pole out of the book before quickly stuffing it back in Dara's bag.

"What good is a metal pole?" Scorpius asked.

"Invented in Europe by Vaclav Prokop Divis between 1750 and 1754 and in the U.S. by Ben Franklin. This one was patented by Nikola Tesla in 1919 because it actually ionizes the air around itself, increasing the chance of a lightning strike."

"It what?" asked Maya, thinking she had heard right but checking to make sure.

"It's called a lightning rod. It attracts lightning!" Alex exclaimed, handing it to Bantu. "Spear guy, think you can hit that thing in the head?"

"It will be hard to miss," Bantu replied, smiling. He held up the rod, but to everyone's surprise, the slug was gone. They searched the water, but found no sign of it until, ahead of them, the water glowed blue.

"Scorpius!" Alex yelled.

"I see it! I'm turning!"

The slug shot up from under the water ahead of them. The wave it caused knocked everyone over. Bantu dropped the lightning rod when he fell while Scorpius flew away from the wheel. Maya slipped over the side, but Tenzin caught her by the wrist and yanked her back. The slug loomed directly over them. This time it would not miss.

Suddenly, the slug convulsed and raised its head up, roaring in pain. A metal rod popped out of its lower torso and then slid back in as that torso arched up. Alex recognized the end of that rod.

"The *Dark Wave!*" he exclaimed.

"That was the name of Asuro-san's ship, was it not?" Genjuro asked.

A black ooze seeped out of the slug's torso, but it was far from finished. It twisted around, trying to get at the vessel behind it. Then it screamed in anger when it bit down on metal. With its head down and body twisted, Bantu had as good a shot as he was going to get. He picked up the lightning rod and threw it with all his might. It penetrated the side of the slug's head. Lifting its head, the slug swung back around at the *Fishbait*; its maw opened for the kill. Alex could see right down its throat into its glowing gut.

Even if I woke up this morning, knowing I was going to die, Alex thought, *there's no way I would have seen this coming.*

Then lightning hit the rod. The slug didn't even have time to scream. The power overloaded its magic, and its body exploded into thousands of pieces that, in turn, puffed out into shadowy smoke. Lightning flashed once more, and in it, Alex thought he saw a shadow flying quickly away but figured it must be a trick of the light. The storm immediately began to die down; the magic that sustained it, gone. Within minutes the sea calmed.

The Dark Wave surfaced under the *Fishbait*, and the two vessels linked up. When the hatch opened, Asuro climbed out.

"You made it!" Alex exclaimed.

"You did not," Asuro admonished. "You had enough time to get to the ship. Why did you not reach her in time?"

"We had to stop off in Cyrus's room for my books," Alex explained. "You don't want to know what happened after that. The important thing is we made it."

"Is your memory so short?" Scorpius yelled. "Askar has the Scroll. You practically handed it to him. The Hall of Shadows will steal its powers and take over the realm now. Are you proud of yourself?"

"Yeah," Alex smiled. "I kinda am."

* * *

Askar screamed in agony as the Shadow Lord's black magic coursed through him.

"How could you be so incompetent?" the Shadow Lord hissed as he burned Askar with one hand while holding a completely nonmagical scroll in the other.

"It ... it wasn't me! The bird grabbed it! I thought you could see through its eyes. You didn't say anything!"

The Shadow Lord stopped his attack. Askar was right. He had been tricked just like the others. He just needed someone to take his frustrations out on. Specter kept quietly to the shadows, happy that Askar was the focus of the Shadow Lord's wrath.

You tricked those pirates into being your weapon.

The Shadow Lord frowned, thinking the Hall was scolding him.

"I could not have cast such a powerful spell through the bird if the subjects were not willing."

I am not admonishing you. I am praising your ingenuity.

"I chose the wrong form. The slug was powerful but slow," the Shadow Lord complained. "And they defeated it with a metal stick. A metal *stick*. The whelp is tricky," he hissed. "He even sent us a message although I'm not sure what it means. I believe it to be an insult of sorts."

"What ... what does it say?" Askar asked, catching his breath.

The Shadow Lord threw the scroll at him, and Askar held it up.

Dear Shadow Lord,

You suck.

The Defenders

* * *

"He sucks what?" Maya asked.

"It's an expression," Alex explained. "If you suck at something, that means you're bad at it, incompetent. If you just suck, you're bad at everything. You're a loser, that kind of thing."

Scorpius laughed. "He won't know what it means any more than we do. Your insult will be lost on him."

"I'm sure he'll get the general idea," Alex hoped.

"When did you write that note?" asked Genjuro.

"Remember when I was grabbing things in Cyrus's room? I wrote the note on a blank scroll and grabbed some others as well as a few empty scroll cases." He pulled a couple of the scroll cases out of his bag and held them up.

"Now we have decoys. When Dara told me about the ring, I figured Askar would use it to get the Scroll back to the Hall as quick as possible. So I had to give it to him without making it look like I was giving it to him."

"A wise plan," Tenzin complimented.

"Thanks," Alex replied.

"You called us 'the Defenders'?" Bantu asked.

"Every superhero group has a name," Alex said matter-of-factly.

"We are *super* heroes?" Maya asked, doubtingly. "I wouldn't even call us heroes."

"You are heroes to me!" Dara exclaimed.

Maya smiled a *thank you* at her.

"I would have called him horse dung," Genjuro stated, still stuck on the message. "That is a clear insult."

"Swine entrails," Maya suggested.

"Monkey snot," Bantu laughed.

"Unenlightened!" Tenzin exclaimed and laughed loudly. When he realized no one else was laughing, he tried, "Dog fart?"

"Good one!" Alex laughed. "How about you, Dara? What would you call him?"

"Poop face," Dara said, though more with conviction than in jest.

"It's settled then," said Alex. "The next letter I send to him will be addressed to Mr. Poop Face."

They all agreed as they laughed. Alex looked around at his friends. They were soaked, they were exhausted, but they were smiling. He smiled, too, and gazed up at the now visible stars. This was the first moment of happiness he had had since he got here. He decided he'd better enjoy it. These moments would be few and scattered, he knew. Then he noticed Asuro staring off at the sea.

"What's the matter?" Alex asked moving over to him.

"Helena escaped my grasp."

"Not really," Alex consoled. "You rammed your ship into her pretty good."

"That was a monster."

"A monster created from the pirates, and you can bet that Helena was guiding its actions more than anyone. She's gone, and you had a big hand in that. You stuck it to every one of those pirates, literally."

Asuro smiled. "Perhaps you are correct."

"That give you closure?" Alex asked.

"Closure?"

"Nothing, never mind." Alex chuckled, knowing that it did. He then said, "Can I ask you something?"

"Yes, Alex?"

"Why would you *ever* marry a woman known as the Black Widow of the Sea?"

Asuro chuckled. "I called her that after she tried to kill me when we parted ways. She liked the name and kept it."

"Ah," Alex nodded. "That makes a lot more sense. So, are your pirate-hunting days over now?"

"Not so long as there are pirates out there," Asuro winked.

12

The remaining Axemen followed Senufer as fast as their enchanted steeds could gallop. A fireball exploded just behind them, its heat singeing some of the men's backs. They headed south toward Shadow Wood but would turn west once they were sure that no one still followed them. Senufer kept one hand pressed on his left hip to slow the bleeding of his wound. Other men were similarly hurt, but they dared not stop to see to any injuries yet. Their pursuers would not let up or show any mercy.

Aspiria was lost.

They had expected help from the city guard, and even Aspiria's citizens, when they tried to retake the city. Despite not having magic in their weapons, they remained a formidable force. Combined with allies in the city, they had planned to retake Aspiria quickly and effectively. They did not count on the Hall's affect to be so overwhelming. Aspiria had become a city of purgatory. Most of its people were lost in personal nightmares brought on by agents of the Hall. Many had been killed or captured by Shadow Warriors. Still others had been brought into the service of the Hall. While the Axemen could meet the Shadow Warriors head on, fighting old friends and allies was another matter entirely—even if they now served the cause of evil.

Though its walls had been darkened, seeing the palace still standing genuinely surprised Senufer. The city of Aspiria had been the jewel of the realm of Mythos. He had expected the Hall of Shadows to have replaced the palace. He had, in a way, hoped so. It would have made their job easier in the long run. His hope had been unfounded. The Hall hid somewhere else in the realm—no doubt someplace remote, dark, and treacherous. It could very well take a lifetime to find it.

Their one small accomplishment had been finding their horses on the way to the city. The steeds knew not to venture back into the dark city after returning from Shadow Wood. They had, instead, roamed free on the grasslands just south of Aspiria. Some of them were injured when the Axemen found them; several were covered in blood that was not their own. The predators, now out and about the realm, had likely tried to capture or eat them. Those predators probably knew better than to attack a herd of the king's warhorses now.

Meanwhile, many in the city still needed their help, and Senufer's heart ached, knowing the suffering that they must be going through. But brute force would not save Aspiria. He had lost several men discovering that, and many of the others were sorely injured. One Axeman could heal, but that healing would have to wait. They needed a safe place to rest and plan how best to retake their home. They had to find a different way to cleanse the city, or else they had to find and destroy the Hall. To do the latter, they needed Dara and the Scroll and those unusual teenagers. Senufer hoped that Alex had caught up with Helena and her crew. If anyone had a chance of catching her, it was Asuro and his pirate hunters, but he would not know their fate until they could make contact.

So the Axemen rode south—trying to recover with their first defeat since before the Hall was created, trying to push aside the memories of what they had seen during their brief incursion in the city through that enormous breach in its outer wall, and trying to cope with the loss of their friends and families in the city as well as the Axemen who had just fallen in battle. One thought drove their actions now—vengeance.

* * *

"Alex, wake up," Asuro said as he shook the boy.

"I did the recycling, Mom," Alex mumbled back, pushing the man away. "Alex!"

Alex's eyes shot open. "Wha—" He looked around, at first wondering what had happened to his bedroom. Then, waking further, he realized that home was the dream, and this was reality.

"Asuro? What is it?"

"We have a problem."

Only five seconds into his day, Alex already regretted waking up. Feeling pressure on his back, he turned to find Dara curled up in a little ball pressed against him for security. The bed she had been given sat next to his, but she must have climbed in with him in the night. He smiled and carefully got out of the bed. Rubbing the sleep from his eyes while following the captain, he left the crew quarters and climbed to the deck of the *Fishbait*. His face felt a little better today although his chest still ached. His sudden increase in activity and having some of his life force sucked out probably didn't help the healing process.

The sun had already risen. Alex checked his watch to see it was almost eleven in the morning. He had set it as close to the correct time as he could guess and hoped that the days here were twenty-four hours long. They felt about right.

Pirate hunters, admiring his sword, surrounded Genjuro.

"He's quite the celebrity," Asuro remarked. "Many of the crew read about samurai adventures in fablepics."

"Fablepics?" Alex asked.

"They are thin books that have pictures on every page. Artists draw them, and wizards magically copy them for sale. It's quite a lucrative business."

"Comics," Alex realized. "We call them comics in my world."

The rest of the Defenders stood at the bow looking forward, along with several pirate hunters. Alex noted how close Maya and Tenzin stood, their arms touching. He wondered about that. Maybe it was nothing, but maybe those two had made a connection.

Asuro followed Alex's gaze and smiled. "Those two were up here talking most of the night. Ah, young love."

Alex smiled at the thought: the cocky wild Amazon and the focused, disciplined Shaolin monk.

Talk about opposites attracting, he thought. Still, Alex wasn't entirely sure that Asuro had it right. Maya hated men. She was raised to. Tenzin might be charming, but Alex doubted if even he could sweep Maya off her feet.

Chuckling to himself, he moved up to see what had everyone's attention. His smile vanished at once. East Port lay in ruins. Most of the buildings had burned down, and several still smoked. A few ships lay half-submerged in the harbour, looking like they had seen battle. The dark, shadowy port reminded Alex of Shadow Wood. Ghostlike figures appeared and vanished among the ruins, but Alex could not tell if they were hiding or searching. No one doubted that the Hall's evil had reached the city and destroyed it.

"We've been passing fleeing ships for several hours now," said Asuro. "I didn't want to wake you because I knew you had not slept in over a day, and it did not make a difference if you were awake ... until now."

"We obviously can't dock there," Alex stated.

"Obviously," Asuro repeated. "The shore is likely being patrolled. Even if you sailed in on the *Fishbait*, they will attack you wherever you try to land."

"The pirates," Alex realized.

"What of them?" Asuro asked.

"They took Dara through a tunnel to their ship or maybe to, I dunno, a secret cove or something, where they could safely land a skiff. It'd be just south of East Port."

"I have sailed these waters for years. I would have spotted any place to put in by now. There are only cliffs and treacherous rock outcroppings there."

"It's hidden," a voice said. Both of them turned to see Dara standing behind them. "There's an illusion of a wall hiding the entrance."

"Good morning, Little Rose," Alex said, mussing up her already mussed hair.

She smiled at the affection.

"Would you recognize the shoreline if you saw it?" Asuro asked.

"I never saw it," Dara answered. "They took me inside right away. I only saw the illusion from inside the cave."

"So how do we see the illusion for what it really is?" Alex thought aloud. "Hey, could George come up with something?"

"We lost George last night," Asuro replied grimly.

"I'm sorry," Alex said sadly.

"He held off Askar long enough for the rest of us to reach the *Dark Wave*. I lost many men in that skirmish," Asuro sighed, but then a small smile formed on his lips, "but they died well, the way they wanted to leave this life, saving others."

"So what now?" Alex asked.

"We drop the *Fishbait* here to keep from attracting attention and then scan the cliffs for some sign of where the entrance is."

"But if there's an illusion to make it seem like the rest of the cliff ..."

"Then we hope that we can spot the difference between real and magical," Asuro replied.

Alex didn't know that they could find it, but finding that entrance seemed their only option at the moment.

They went below, released the *Fishbait,* and set a course for the cliffs. Asuro kept the *Dark Wave* moving slowly and steadily, parallel to the cliffs. After two hours of searching, he found it.

"There," he said, looking through the periscope. He let Alex have a look, but the boy saw only water and cliffs.

"Are you seeing something I'm not?" Alex asked.

"See the three large natural rocky pillars in the water?" Asuro asked.

"Yeah," Alex replied, "but I thought we were looking at the cliffs."

"Look at the cliff wall behind them," Asuro ordered.

Alex looked carefully at the walls. "I just see walls," he announced. "There's no ... oh, wait ... the waves aren't breaking against them."

"Exactly," Asuro agreed. "They chose well. If not for the pillars, it would be easy to spot, and only a very skilled helmsman can navigate through the pillars to the cave. I'm fairly certain the Hall's agents do not know about this place."

Asuro took back the periscope and began yelling orders to his crew. Soon the *Dark Wave* glided into the cave, and the crew disembarked. As soon as Dara stepped onto the dock, the Defenders disappeared. Alex quickly summoned them again to protect Dara until she exited the other cave entrance.

A few hours later, they stood just inside that entrance, trying to determine their next move.

"Senufer wanted to hook up with us when we got back," Alex reminded Asuro.

Asuro held up a messenger bird. "I've already taken the liberty of writing a note." He launched the bird, which flew out to the west.

"How does it know where Senufer is?" Alex asked.

Asuro shrugged. "It always finds Senufer and me. We have been using it for years. Mornak's doing, no doubt."

The bird did not return that day. Asuro said it typically took a day for the bird to find Senufer, sleep, and then return, so they would have to wait the night. The group kept mostly to the cave while they waited although Bantu left to forage for their evening meal and the pirate hunters scouted the area periodically to ensure that they didn't get ambushed. At one point, the camp went on full alert when they heard a strange creature moaning and moving toward them. They relaxed when they saw Bantu, returning from his hunt. He wore Alex's iPod and sang along, or rather tried to sing along, to some funky music. He smiled when he saw everyone looking at him and yelled over the music that they couldn't hear. "I am jamming!"

To pass the time, Scorpius and Genjuro compared sword techniques. Genjuro handed Scorpius five leaves. (The Roman could not help noticing that they had become darkened and warped. This world was changing into something twisted.) When Scorpius threw the leaves up, Genjuro drew his blade and sliced each one of them before they hit the ground. The reflexes of the samurai amazed Scorpius. Genjuro explained samurai sword motions and how they applied power and speed. He then urged Scorpius to try the same feat. He threw up five leaves, and Scorpius drew his gladius and cut. Three of the leaves landed untouched despite four swipes from Scorpius's sword.

"If you practice the techniques with me, I am sure you will be able to do it as well as I, Scorpius-san," Genjuro assured him.

Scorpius doubted that. Genjuro was faster than any swordsman he'd ever seen. Scorpius didn't think even Genjuro realized that. He could probably cut more than five leaves if he tried. Scorpius knew he couldn't, but then realized that he may not need to.

"Throw five more," he told Genjuro.

Genjuro smiled. "Your technique needs work first, Scorpius-san."

"Throw them anyway," Scorpius insisted.

Genjuro grabbed five more leaves and tossed them in the air. Scorpius did not draw his gladius right away, focusing instead on the movements of the leaves. Then his blade shot out, and with only two swings, he cut all five leaves.

Genjuro smiled but shook his head. "The idea is to see how many accurate cuts you can make in the short time they fall."

"If you kill five Shadow Warriors with five cuts while I kill five with two, will you complain to me about it?" Scorpius asked with a wink.

Genjuro laughed. "Not at all, Scorpius-san. Not at all!"

Meanwhile Tenzin gave Maya basic lessons in his fighting style, emphasizing how she could use her bow as an effective weapon in close combat. Maya questioned the need at first, pointing out that several of the others could deal with close-quartered fighting. Tenzin asked if she was sure that she'd never be forced to fight by herself. She conceded and let him teach her how to use the bow as a staff. He also taught her some basic punches and blocks while telling her about her chi and how to use it. She didn't really believe that she had some powerful inner energy that could be used to break stone, but she smiled and played along.

Alex noticed an unusual amount of giggling during the lessons. He grinned. Asuro may have been right. *So much for the man-hating Amazon*, he thought.

Alex, himself, captivated the rest of the people present with tales of his world and the wonders there. He further amazed them by showing pictures of places and inventions in his books, making sure that no one spoke a word while he held them open. When they asked to see Mornak's Scroll, Dara pulled it from its case and showed them the silvery gold parchment on its golden rune-covered rollers. When she opened it, Alex noticed the writing on it.

"There's a message from Mornak!" he exclaimed.

Looking at the parchment, Dara shook her head. "No, that's a spell of invisibility. My father wrote it there so I could make our bags invisible when I found them."

"It's a what?" Alex asked excitedly.

"It's a spell of—"

"I heard you."

"Then why did you ask?" Dara huffed.

"Sorry," Alex apologized. "Habit in my world. We ask again when we're shocked by what we heard." He reached into his bag and pulled out one of the pieces of parchment he took from Cyrus's room, along with a quill and ink. He then copied the words from the Scroll to the parchment. When he finished, the words faded from the Scroll.

"Hey, where'd they go?" he asked.

Dara shrugged. "Maybe the Scroll knew you copied the spell."

Alex cocked his head. "The Scroll isn't alive. It doesn't know what I'm doing. So, what happened to them?"

"I don't know, Alex," Dara told him. "I'm not a wizard. I only know one spell."

"I thought you said you cast the invisibility spell on the ship," Alex checked.

"I did."

"Then you know two spells, don't you?"

"But I've only cast invisibility once."

Alex held up the parchment. "Well, now you can practice. In fact, I think we should start right now while it's still fresh in your memory."

The pirate hunters sighed, realizing that storytelling time was over. Sitting down, Alex held up the parchment for Dara. She reached for the Scroll, but he stopped her.

"No," he said. "You need to learn to cast without the Scroll. You may not always have the opportunity to take it out."

She pouted but did as she was told. Reading from the parchment, she tried to remember the gestures involved. On her third try, Alex turned green, bright green. Dara paled.

"I'm sorry. I'm sorry. I'm sorry," she apologized.

Alex looked at his arms, turning them over and back. He didn't feel any different, so he guessed that she had managed to manipulate the light hitting him. "You're getting close," he said calmly.

Dara could not believe he was not upset or scared or ill. "But you're green!" she exclaimed.

The conversations around them had all stopped. The others all stared at Alex now, most with looks of worry.

Alex smiled. "I'm okay," he told them and then turned back to Dara. "This is how invisibility works," he explained, "in physics anyway. Light hits things and bounces off them, and what gets bounced into our eyes is what we see. To make someone become invisible, you have to bend the light around their body so it never hits them." He held up a rock with one hand while showing the path of light toward, around, and past it with the other hand. "That way, you can't see them."

"But you're green!" Dara repeated.

"Because you're not bending the green light."

"But I don't know how to bend it. I'm just reading the words and doing the movements."

"You just have to get the movements right. I'm just explaining why I'm green, at least, why I think I'm green. It doesn't hurt. Now try again. Focus."

Dara tried but stumbled, too nervous after her mess up. The try after that Alex turned back to his normal colours but expanded. From his point of view, Dara shrunk.

He reached a hand out to her and watched it shrink as it moved farther away from him.

"Cool," he said. "That's much closer. See how the light is making things stretch and contract? That's because you're bending it, just not enough."

Dara would have been in a panic if Alex's unconcerned attitude didn't utterly confuse her.

"Are you sure you are all right, Alex?" Asuro asked.

Alex waved, his fingers weaving and stretching along the warped field of light. It was like looking at someone in a funhouse mirror.

"One more time," Alex coaxed. "You can do this."

Dara fell into herself, doing the breathing exercises her father had taught her. She thought back to the cell on the pirate ship, when she could feel her father guiding her motions somehow through the Scroll. She cast again. Alex disappeared.

"Alex?" she asked to make sure he was just invisible and had not been sent somewhere ... or worse.

"How do I become visible again?" he asked.

"It will wear off in a while, probably not long because I'm not very good at this, or you can attack someone and it will stop." She waited for a reply, but one didn't come. "Alex?"

Not far away Genjuro jumped unexpectedly. He grabbed his bottom after feeling a slap. When a figure appeared, Scorpius drew his sword but relaxed when he realized it was Alex, giggling at his prank.

"You're right, Dara," he called back. "Attacking someone *does* make you visible."

Genjuro turned to him, a mischievous smile on his face, and drew his katana. "Alex-san, you want to attack someone? I'll show you how to attack someone."

Alex bolted back toward Dara yelling, "Cast it again! Cast it again!"

Genjuro pursued. Though he could easily overtake Alex, he stayed right behind him, waving his sword while yelling, "Slap my bottom, will you?"

Everyone laughed at their antics, especially when Dara accidentally made Genjuro invisible and Alex fell victim to his first wedgie out of high school. Shortly after, Dara gave everyone a scare when she collapsed. With her powers still developing, casting a spell so many times without the aid of the Scroll had overtaxed her. Alex guessed that she could cast invisibility on a person twice at most without it affecting her adversely, although she could probably cast it more often on small objects.

As it got late, most of the people found a comfortable place on the ground to settle down for the night. On his watch, Alex noticed Tenzin and Maya leaving the camp.

I wonder what they're gonna do? Alex thought with a smile.

* * *

Nights in Mythos were almost beautiful. Twinkling stars crowded the sky, fighting for room with the rainbow clouds of distant galaxies. The moon shone brightly casting distinctive shadows across the land, shadows that some of the Hall's agents could use for dark purposes. The resulting contrast was remarkable. The sky glistened above—gorgeous, inviting, and inspiring—while beneath it lay a dark world—dreadful, foreboding, and disheartening. While gazing upon an image of hope, one remained trapped in a realm of hopelessness. Perhaps that was exactly what the Hall wanted everyone to feel.

Tenzin and Maya strolled with carefree attitudes despite the dangers around them. Staying a comfortable distance from the cave where the others camped, and being more than capable of defending themselves, they were content to wander around the sparse woods and circle the small lake into which Tenzin had seen the Shadow Warriors escape the lightning bugs a few days before.

"I really needed this," Maya sighed, breaking the peaceful silence they had been enjoying. "I don't think I could bear to be in the company of so many men much longer."

"Perhaps you should seek service on a ship," Tenzin suggested.

Maya cocked an eye at his remark. "Are you so anxious to be rid of me?"

"Not at all, my lady," Tenzin smiled, "but if women rule the seas, as Alex says, then serving with a crew of women would make you feel more at home."

"I am not one for boats," Maya told him, "and I would feel guilty if I were not taking part in the mission we were brought here for."

"And I would miss your company," Tenzin added.

"Yes," Maya replied with a playful grin, "you would."

The soft crunch of earth nearby caused both to stop their chat and turn in its direction.

"A moment, my lady," Tenzin whispered as he bowed with an open hand over a closed fist raised before him. He rushed off toward the noise, his feet making no sound as they skimmed over the ground. Maya watched him move up only twenty-five paces before crouching low and peering out from behind a tree. Moments later, he rushed back to her.

"They appear to be lizards walking like men, armed and armoured, and reeking of evil," he reported. "We should get back to camp and warn the others."

"How many are there?" Maya asked.

"A dozen at most," Tenzin replied.

Maya grinned. Tenzin sensed her thoughts immediately and frowned while shaking his head.

"That is too many, Maya," he warned.

"I need to work off the frustration of having served that damned wizard and his sea witch," she complained.

Tenzin shook his head. "We should—"

Maya readied her bow in a flash, and an arrow raced past Tenzin's shoulder, taking down a lizardman who had just stepped into view. Several more appeared, including archers. Glancing around quickly, the pair noted that the area provided little cover to avoid their arrows.

"I believe our options have just narrowed considerably," Maya said with a smile.

Tenzin shook his head but did not seem angry. He held her by the shoulders, and Maya was surprised at how comfortable she felt with his touch.

"Watch me," he said. "Feel my motions."

"What do you me—?" Maya started to ask, but Tenzin was already rushing toward the enemy.

Arrows sped toward them, but Tenzin intercepted the ones that would have reached Maya while dodging the ones aimed at him. When she realized that Tenzin's actions left her free to shoot, Maya did just that. At first, she aimed at the outer lizardmen to make sure she did not hit Tenzin. She killed three before the lizards with shields took up positions to protect the remaining archers. She was forced to shoot into the thick of the battle.

Tenzin kept on the defensive against the swords and shields. He dodged the attacks easily but could only get a few strikes in—and those were neither lethal nor crippling, only painful. He moved about quickly, leaping and flipping, pulling the lizardmen's attention away from Maya while he kept glancing back at her. Finally, she understood. She took aim as she watched the monk's actions, falling into his rhythm. She let an arrow fly.

A lizard man moved in on Tenzin, his sword held high ready to strike. Maya's arrow took him in the side below his raised arm. Tenzin flipped toward another opponent, putting himself directly between the lizardman and Maya.

The creature moved in for what he thought would be an easy kill, but the monk suddenly reversed direction with another flip back. The lizardman cut empty space and then gaped in horror as an arrow took him in the chest. Tenzin then rushed at another who held up a shield in defense. Flying in with both feet, Tenzin struck the shield, and both he and the lizardman tumbled to the ground. An arrow whizzed over them and struck the archer that the warrior had been protecting.

The dance continued with the monk and Amazon eluding and eliminating the evil amphibians. Maya read Tenzin's actions with subtle glances from him and a growing feel for his style. She could almost feel the connection between them as though they had become one weapon against these foes, but then several lizardmen managed to slip by Tenzin and close in on her. Holding her bow like a staff, she struck the first one in the head as Tenzin had shown her, calling upon her supposed *chi*. She shocked herself with the force of the blow. While she did not kill it, the creature fell to the ground unconscious despite the protection of his helmet. She had no time to think about it, however, as two more opponents moved in to attack. She ducked under the first swing and then jumped back from the next, bumping into a tree behind her. The lizardmen closed side by side, smiling. It would be an easy kill.

Suddenly, Tenzin rose up between them. His legs kicked out, catching them both in the side of the face and sending them sprawling. He reached in, grabbed Maya, and pulled her with surprising force around him. She saw an approaching lizardman and realized Tenzin's intent, stiffening her legs just before they swung into his gut. The creature curled up into a ball on the ground, moaning in pain. Maya, now standing before him, kicked him hard in the face before being pulled back toward Tenzin and narrowly escaping an overhead chop from an opponent to her right.

Maya spun into Tenzin's arms as though they were dancing. She found herself face to face with the boy as he dipped her low, taking them both under yet another deadly swing while one of his legs lashed out, knocking the attacker's sword from his grip and sending it flying into the woods. Tenzin didn't even look as the lizardman rushed to retrieve his weapon. The monk's gaze locked on Maya. Their lips touched, and her eyes closed for a moment. The battle, the world, seemed to stop.

Then she found herself standing again. She opened her eyes to see Tenzin on the attack again. His body spun, executing flying roundhouse after flying roundhouse kick, striking the unarmed lizardman repeatedly until he dropped. Maya brought up her bow again and fired at the remaining creatures who finally had the sense to turn and run off into the night.

Tenzin walked up to her, his stride confident and carefree.

"You were correct, my lady," he said bowing, an open hand covering a closed fist again. "We could defeat them." He glanced around to make sure the remaining lizardmen posed no threat. "We should return to camp," he advised with a smile, and then he strolled back toward the cave.

Maya stood for many seconds before she followed him. One thought repeated over and over in her mind. *He kissed me. Tenzin kissed me!*

* * *

Back at the cave, Alex watched as Tenzin and Maya slipped back into camp from a midnight stroll. Even in the darkness, the Amazon had a glow about her. Tenzin stopped when he saw Alex looking. Alex noticed that both teens were out of breath. He smiled and winked. Tenzin winked back and then found a place to meditate before bed. Finding a spot next to Dara, Maya fell asleep in moments.

A few hours after sunrise the next day, they received an answer to their message, but instead of a bird, a half dozen Axemen rode in on their enchanted steeds led by Brasius.

"We've come to escort you to Senufer," he said, dismounting.

"Then my part in this is done," Asuro said as he nodded to the Axeman.

"You're not coming with us?" Maya asked.

"My place is on the sea," Asuro stated. "Be assured that you can count on my help when it is needed again."

Brasius and Asuro grasped hands as though they were going to arm wrestle and then nodded to each other. Alex realized it was a warriors' handshake. Asuro repeated the gesture with each of the Defenders, including Maya. Alex could see the surprise in her face. Since he was a man, she had expected him to treat her like a docile female and try to hug or kiss her. That is what her mother had told her about how men treat women. Asuro showed that he respected her as a warrior. Maya wondered if her mother had taught her falsehoods or if the men of this world simply differed from the men of her own world. Dara got a hug from Asuro though.

Finally, Asuro grabbed Alex by the shoulders. "I thank you, Alex."

"You thank *me*?" Alex asked. "You're the one that saved my life and helped get Dara and the Scroll back."

"But were it not for you," Asuro countered, "Helena would still be out there, terrorizing the seas. I am at peace with myself for the first time in many years. I thank you. My crew thanks you. We are forever in your debt."

He hugged Alex and kissed both his cheeks. The members of the crew who had accompanied him gave Alex the warriors' handshake. Then Asuro and his pirate hunters turned and walked back into the cave.

Alex watched them go for a while before turning back to the others to find them eyeing him suspiciously.

"What?" asked Alex.

"I really don't see why you got that much more respect than the rest of us," Scorpius stated.

"I guess I just spent more time with them," Alex answered, blushing.

"Would you care to explain how Dara and the book ended up on that ship?" Scorpius continued.

"The pirates stole them."

"Why didn't you just summon us again when we returned to the book?"

"Dara was in trouble. Shadow Warriors had her. I had to help," Alex defended.

"I see that worked well. Did you defeat the Shadow Warriors before the pirates arrived?"

Brasius jumped into the argument. "Alex did the best he could."

Scorpius turned on him. "But if he had summoned us instead of trying to play the hero, do you honestly think it would have turned out the same?"

Brasius, having seen the Defenders fight, could not answer *yes* to the question. His silence was as good as *no*.

"I thought so," Scorpius stated.

"What is your point, Scorpius?" Bantu asked.

"Alex has us trapped in that book. He knows we hate to be in there, and he knows that he, the girl, and that Scroll are safer when we're around. Yet he doesn't summon us when he should. He thinks he can survive in this world on his own skills, and because of that, this time we were forced to attack innocent people. Next time, the book may get destroyed and us along with it."

"What are you saying?" Dara asked accusingly. "You can't carry the book! You're in it."

"I'm not suggesting that at all," Scorpius countered. "I'm saying, when we get to the Axeman camp, Alex and Dara can stay in the care of the Axemen and a person who can truly handle the responsibility of our lives and the protection of the Scroll should have the book—Senufer."

"No!" Dara exclaimed. "It's Alex's book! He should keep it!"

"You should be the last person to argue," Scorpius told Dara. "When you summoned Alex, you were trying to summon Senufer. You know he is the best one to guard the Scroll." Scorpius then looked around at the other Defenders. "Which of you truly trusts in Alex's abilities to safeguard our lives, especially after what just happened?"

"He got us back," Tenzin reminded him.

"He shouldn't have lost us to begin with!" Scorpius spat. "Answer honestly. Who would you rather trust your very existence to? Alex, who is ineffectual by his own admission, or Senufer, leader of the realm's greatest fighting force for over a decade?"

Alex looked at the Defenders. He could see that although they felt sorry for him, they agreed with Scorpius. He hung his head.

"If that's what you guys want. I know Senufer will be a good guardian for the book. I'll give it to him."

"Master Alex—" Tenzin started to say.

Alex wouldn't hear it.

"No, Tenzin, Scorpius is right. I screwed up, and I'm likely to do it again. I don't want to be the one that gets you used as murderers ... or worse. Let's get going."

Alex asked the others if they wanted to ride or wait in the book. Maya, Genjuro, and Scorpius chose to ride, all of them familiar with horses. Bantu opted to wait in the book, partly because the mounts frightened him and partly because he felt he would be too heavy for them, especially with another rider. Tenzin, at first, chose to return to the book to perform his daily practices, but a subtle cough from Maya made him change his mind. Alex wondered who else caught the exchange.

With that, they stepped out of the cave, and Alex recalled everyone except Bantu for the ride to the Axemen camp out west.

"Where is the camp?" Alex asked. "Not Shadow Wood, I hope."

"Farther," replied Brasius. "The foothills of the Fork in the World."

*　　*　　*

Kendrik's preferred weapons were throwing axes. He could throw several of them in a single second, each one as accurate as the next. When his belt had been enchanted, it provided him with an endless supply of axes that disappeared after hitting their target. He wished he had them now. He wished he could throw a dozen axes into the villain, Askar.

The general had arrived in the city shortly after the Axemen's failed attempt to retake it. Kendrik had not made it out. The way he had fallen in battle, he was sure the others thought him dead. He had thought himself dead. He had awoken later, healed by his enemies, but stripped of weapons and armour. He was chained to a wall in the prison that once held the ones who held him. Askar had come to pay him a visit. Since then he had been enduring the electricity from the man's mace. He had, long ago, stopped trying not to scream.

"Where have the Axemen gone?" Askar asked again. "Where? Where is Senufer?"

Kendrik shook his head. Askar let the energy flow in him again and enjoyed the screaming that resulted. The hairs on Kendrik's body had burned off. It had been over a day since the torture began. He knew it would not stop until he told Askar what he wanted to know or until he died. He prayed for death.

Askar was in no mood for such defiance, but he knew enough not to kill his only lead. The Shadow Lord had told him that if he appeared in the Hall again without the Scroll, then he would be killed on the spot. With no way to determine the location of the Defenders anymore, he managed to convince the Shadow Lord that the children would most likely try to meet up with Senufer again.

The Shadow Lord knew Askar's reasons for seeking Senufer, but in this case, it seemed the best course of action. Luckily, Senufer's attack on Aspiria made finding him easier, but Askar had gotten there too late. Kendrik was the only Axeman alive after the attack. Askar knew he would have been given a rendezvous location. Deep down, he also knew the man would never give it up through torture, but he wanted to have his fun. Besides, he had other resources at his disposal.

"General," a Shadow Warrior said as he stepped into the cell, "he's here."

Askar smiled. "Bring him in."

Kendrik lifted his head to see about whom they were talking. A Shadow Warrior walked into view. He appeared much like the others only there was something familiar about him. Kendrik knew he should know this man, and his gut began to twist with fear when the recognition clicked.

"No!" he screamed. "Not him! Please!"

The Shadow Warrior smiled as he walked up to the Axeman. Kendrik wanted to back away, to somehow fade into the wall, but it was not going to happen. The warrior placed his hands on Kendrik's shoulders, and they melted into him.

"No!" Kendrik screamed.

The man moved forward, stepping right into the Axeman. For a moment, a single body switched back and forth between two forms. Each fought for control. Then, gradually, Kendrik's form faded, and only the Shadow Warrior remained chained to the wall.

"Release him," Askar ordered.

The guard complied, and the Shadow Warrior, with some features slightly more Kendrik-like than others, rubbed his wrists as he smiled at Askar.

"Well?" Askar asked.

"Fork in the World."

13

*L*etting nothing distract them, the group raced at an incredible speed (for everyone except Alex) toward the Axemen camp. While Alex was used to the speed of cars and planes, he had to admit that he'd never traveled this fast on a horse despite many summers riding on his uncle's farm on some spirited steeds. The smoothness of the ride also surprised him. He had expected things to be quite uncomfortable in the saddle, but the magical horseshoes apparently acted as shock absorbers, too.

As an Amazon, Maya refused to ride behind any man, but when she then told Tenzin to climb on behind her, forcing two of the Axemen to ride together, the others finally caught on to the budding romance. Alex thought it ironic that the hater of men would be falling for one, but if any man could win an Amazon's affection, it was Tenzin. Within minutes, if not seconds, of meeting him, you knew that he had no ill will toward any creature. He saw beauty in everything around him and kept a positive attitude even when things seemed hopeless. Alex remembered looking at him as the *Shuriken* sank beneath them. While he was as likely to die as the rest, he offered no suggestions on how to save them. He simply stood quietly with a small smile, confident that the others would find a solution. Alex wondered if, perhaps, he *had* known what to do but had simply waited for someone else to suggest it.

Unlike Tenzin, the rest of the Defenders each had their unique idiosyncrasies and sometimes conflicting personalities. This was especially noticeable in the conflict between Alex and Scorpius. How well they would all function as a team and whether they would become real friends remained a mystery, but their biggest worry, right now, was staying alive.

The Axeman had hidden their camp in a sandy clearing among many large boulders and near a cave that led into the mountains. The Defenders were shocked to see that the group numbered only thirty-four men now, and many of the remaining men were sorely injured. Whatever had happened to them in the past few days could not have been good. One of the Axemen moved from person to person, checking bandages and splints—a single medic for so many men.

The two groups spent several hours filling each other in on what was happening in the realm. They built several campfires—small enough to not attract attention—at sunset to handle all the food needed to feed so many people. The mountains protected them to the west; many rock outcroppings, a couple storeys high and often as wide, blocked the fires' light from anyone approaching from other directions and formed several small winding paths to get to them. They functioned like uneven walls and pillars.

Upon seeing her uncle, Dara charged at him, leaping up into his arms for a welcomed hug. Senufer spun her around, threw her up, and caught her. The two of them laughed and held each other, enjoying their reunion. The Axemen smiled at the sight, some of them chuckling. They rarely saw this side of their leader. Usually the stoic, dutiful knight, Senufer's emotional display caught the others off guard. Eventually, Senufer put Dara down, but she stayed close—often holding onto an arm or a leg for security—while he attended to his duties. Alex felt a slight pang of jealousy now that Dara seemed to have so quickly forgotten him, but he reminded himself that he had only been a part of her life for a few days while Senufer had been there since her birth.

Senufer refused the book when Alex presented it him.

"Alex was summoned with these books to be Dara's protector," he insisted. "That he shall remain. Many of us are not prepared for the challenges life gives us. This does not mean that we should hand off our responsibilities to someone else. We must face our challenges and live with the consequences of our actions or inaction. Only then will we grow in wisdom and spirit."

"His responsibilities involve other people's lives," Scorpius argued.

"It is the same for all of us," Senufer countered. "No, Alex is the keeper of the books. He is the bringer of knowledge—knowledge that, as I have heard, saved you on that boat. Guard him as you would have him guard your book."

Scorpius seethed quietly with the turn of events. He did not want to be a prisoner to Alex, but he let it go, for now.

Soon after, Senufer and Scorpius began discussing the best course of action for them to take. They decided that as impossible as it seemed, the Defenders should quest for the Hall of Shadows. For one thing, it kept them on the move and made it harder for the Hall's agents to find them. For another, the Shadow Realm they now inhabited would continue to exist, and most likely worsen, as long as the Hall remained and grew in power. If it became powerful enough, it would spread to the other realms and eventually control the entire world. As much as the Axemen wanted to go back to Aspiria, that would have to wait.

Dara's journey north to Kashla would also be cancelled. The city had fallen to the Hall's forces, and Mornak's allies there had either fled or perished.

The Defenders and the Axemen would split up in small groups to search for the Hall. One group would remain on this side of the mountain range, World's Divide. The rest would journey over the Fork in the World to search the rest of the realm.

"I thought crossing the Fork was dangerous," Alex said to Senufer.

"More to some than others," Senufer replied. "I know of a safer route that will take us to the peaks more easily and more quickly than the journey up the mountainside. From there, the way down the other side is less dangerous."

The Defenders disappeared when the decision was made since Alex had summoned them to be present until then. He had considered summoning them for longer periods, but after finding out that their fatal wounds healed instantly upon returning to the book, he decided that summoning them step-by-step would be the safest way to do things. He removed the book from his bag and summoned them again—this time to protect Dara and the Scroll—until they reached the second peak of the Fork.

"Now let's see if we can get some worldly advice," Senufer suggested.

Sitting on her uncle's lap, Dara took her cue and brought out the Scroll.

Opening it, she thought aloud to her father. "Hello, Papa, I'm here with Alex and the Defenders and Uncle Senufer and the Axemen. We are at the Fork in the World."

My greetings to you all.

"We have some questions about what we should do," Dara told him.

Alex placed a hand on the Scroll. "Before we get to that, I have some questions of my own. How come we're all speaking English?"

"We are speaking Latin," Scorpius argued.

"Japanese," Genjuro insisted.

You are speaking Mythosian, Alex. You speak the language of the summoner, which was Dara, but your mind lets you hear things in your own language. Even the text you are reading is a translation by your mind.

Alex realized that while he saw letters, Genjuro saw kanji, Japanese characters. He had no way of knowing what the symbols in this world's language really looked like.

"Okay, I get that," Alex said and then moved on to his next question.

"I saw some, well, dwarves and elves in East Port, but they're not real in my world. And Asuro knew what a samurai was, but said they were fictional here. Is there a connection?"

There is a connection between our worlds. Some people can, consciously or not, see things in the other world. They often perceive their visions as things their imagination came up with. Stories, even legend and lore, are created from these visions. Few people can see the bridge for what it is. Fewer still can cross it, as you have.

"Is there a way to get back, or to send the Defenders back somehow?"

This I do not know. The geas on you binds you to your task, but returning to your world may break its hold on you. I know you long to return to your home, but please remember Dara. You promised to keep her safe.

"I would never abandon Dara," Alex said, giving her a wink. "I'm thinking more about the Defenders. I know some of them are anxious to return to their homes." Alex and Scorpius shared a cold stare with that statement.

"Besides," Alex continued, "I'm bound to protect Dara, no matter what, although the Axemen will be doing most of the protecting from now on. I'm no warrior. I don't even have a weapon." He glanced around the camp at the Axemen a moment. "Speaking of weapons, why did you take away the power of the Axemen's weapons?"

"All Mornak's magic was sent into the Scroll," Senufer corrected. "It does not exist elsewhere."

"No," Alex insisted. "Dara's bag has its enchantment. The bird still found you. The horses have magical horseshoes. He specifically removed your magic. Was it because they were weapons?"

The spell that transferred my magic to the Scroll had a large radius, and the Axemen would have been in the path between the Scroll and me as well. I did not expect this, but it is something we can correct. Dara, read carefully and focus your attention on the Axemen in front of you.

Dara stood up while the Axemen gathered in front of her. The Scroll went blank for a moment, and then the words of a spell wrote themselves across it. It was no simple spell, and Dara's face grew more worried with each new word.

Seeing her expression, Alex walked behind Dara and put his hands on her shoulders. She turned and looked up at him, her eyes giving a silent plea for help.

"Don't worry, Dara," he soothed as he smiled and squeezed her shoulders. "You wiped out a legion of Shadow Warriors and killed an evil wizard single-handedly. This'll be child's play, and, hey, you're a child!"

When she finally smiled and nodded, he stepped away and let her cast. The Scroll's glow increased as she spoke the words. Everyone could feel the energy building in the area. Soon, Dara's nervousness vanished. In fact, she showed no emotion at all, as though she now served as a vehicle for the words that moved off the Scroll and into her. Her eyes became golden orbs of power while her voice amplified and echoed into the night. Then a golden wave of magic moved out across the camp. Every person could feel its power through its wake. It wrapped itself around them and entered them, seeking out their skills, before fusing into their weapons with a memory of what it saw in each person.

Dara slumped momentarily, and Alex jumped in to keep her from falling over. Her eyes returned to normal as he sat her back up. She looked at the Scroll to see the words, *I'm proud of you, Little Rose.*

* * *

Gliding along back toward the sea, Specter suddenly felt the power of the Scroll again. Strangely, it was coming from the World's Divide where Askar and his men now headed. It seemed the general was correct. The Defenders had met up with the Axemen again. Soon, there would be another reunion. The bird banked until it saw the Fork. Jumping from shadow to shadow, Specter knew it would not take long to get there.

* * *

"Don't worry, my lord," Senufer told the Scroll. "We'll find you and get you out. On this you have my pledge."

I thank you, my friend. Just remember that if it should come to it, it is better to destroy the Hall with me in it than risk defeat in a rescue.

"Understood," Senufer replied.

Alex could see in the man's eyes that while he did understand, he was not going to let his king die in that Hall.

Dara took the Scroll to herself then and bid a thank you and farewell to her father. With their magic restored, the Axemen's mood became jovial. Furthermore, with the healer's axe now able to magically heal, everyone was soon restored to good health. Most men gathered around the campfires, eating and talking. Several walked the perimeter, alert and on guard. Bantu and Genjuro told some Axemen the story of their adventure at sea while Scorpius talked training and strategy with others. Tenzin and Maya sat with their hands clasped, listening to Bantu and Genjuro, and smiling at the way the two told the tale together—acting out the parts as though they performed a play. Maya kept sneaking glances at Tenzin, wondering what it would be like to kiss him again.

At first light, the group would set out to their different destinations, but for now, it did not look like many would sleep tonight. They were enjoying themselves too much.

While the festivities continued, Alex still found himself concerned about the future.

"Tell me about this quicker path," Alex said to Senufer. "It's through that cave, isn't it?"

Senufer nodded.

"That's why we are camped here. There is a network of tunnels under the mountain that leads up to the first peak of the Fork, but also to the Underrealm, and one can easily get lost in it."

"But you know the way."

"No."

Alex didn't like that answer.

"So we just wander around and hope to get lucky?"

Senufer gave a knowing smile. "Down the main tunnel, before things get very confusing, is the home of some special friends of mine. They hide easily from travelers, but make themselves known to friends. They know the tunnel network and can guide us up through the mountain to an exit near the first peak of the Fork. That will get us past the more dangerous part of the journey."

"Sounds perfect," said Alex. "What are these friends of yours like?"

"They are quite unusual, not at all what you'd expect." He winked with his next statement. "So I would ask you not to stare again."

"I promise. What do they look like?"

"They—"

"Shadow Warriors!" a guard yelled.

The camp sprung into action, weapons appearing in ready hands.

"How many?" Senufer called back.

"Many!" came the reply.

"Defensive perimeter!" Senufer ordered. "The rocks will force them to come to us in smaller groups. Stay alert. There are many entrances they can use."

Alex watched as many of the magical weapons, now charged again, began to glow with power. Senufer unsheathed his axes, and Sun Stroke burst into its yellow flaming axe head while Bone Chiller's blue ice blade grew from its handle.

When the first Shadow Warrior came into view, Maya was ready for him. She tried to aim at the man's heart when, suddenly, he moved right up in front of her. Maya fell back in a panic. When she looked up, the man was back where he started. A throwing axe took him down. From several openings around the camp, the Shadow Warriors charged in. The Axemen moved in to intercept the enemy.

Anxious as ever to prove his worth, Genjuro scanned the camp for enemies. Spying a lone Shadow Warrior who had come in near one of the northern openings, the samurai moved quickly to challenge the man, too quickly. He found himself running faster than he had ever run before, and in his shock, he tripped over his own feet and tumbled to the ground, ending up dazed at the man's feet. The Shadow Warrior smiled at his easy kill, but Bantu had seen what had happened and hurled his spear to save his fellow Defender. The spear shot clean through the Shadow Warrior before it buried itself, almost to its end, in the rock behind him. The warrior puffed into smoke.

"What's going on?" Alex exclaimed, seeing the unusual actions of his friends.

Senufer waded into the battle, cutting through one man with fire and freezing a second one with ice. "They were in range of the spell!" he yelled back.

"What spell?" Alex asked.

"Mornak's," Senufer called out as he chased down another man. "Their weapons are enchanted!"

Maya looked at her bow and then back at her quiver, realizing for the first time that it was empty. So where had the arrow come from? She lifted the bow into place and then reached back again. She felt an arrow waiting for her fingers in the quiver and pulled it out. She chose another target, this time expecting the illusion—or whatever it was—but still unsure of its meaning. When she aimed at a Shadow Warrior's head, the head moved closer to her until she could see nothing else. So she chose an eye. The arrow flew, hitting its mark, and the warrior puffed out as shadowy smoke.

"I understand now," she smiled as she reached back again, a new arrow waiting for her. This was going to be fun.

Lifting himself up, Genjuro began to move to another target, slowly at first, but then picking up speed. He could now run twice his already fast speed. He engaged several warriors in battle. The men could barely track his movements, but to Genjuro, they moved in slow motion. Within seconds, the Shadow Warriors were simply smoke.

Meanwhile, Bantu looked at his spear embedded deeply in the rock. "How do I get it back?" he asked aloud.

"Call it," Alex answered.

"Call it?" he questioned.

"Summon it to your hand. A lot of thrown weapons work that way."

Bantu concentrated on the spear, and instantly, he felt it in his grasp.

"Behind you!" Alex yelled.

The African warrior spun and swatted the approaching Shadow Warrior with the shaft of the spear. The strength of the blow sent the man flying to smash into a nearby rock wall, crumple to the ground, and turn to smoke. Bantu looked down at the spear and his arms. He had never felt this strong before.

Scorpius found himself facing two warriors. They worked in concert to keep him on the defensive. Suddenly, the world stopped. Scorpius was ready to scream, thinking he'd been locked out of this world as he had his own. Then he realized that he was frozen too—or rather, moving extremely slowly. He looked around at the battle, noticing that although his head didn't really turn, he could see all around his position. Then he focused on his opponents and examined their movements. One was overbalanced to the right in his swing; the other was coming in high to cut him down from shoulder to opposite hip. Scorpius then knew what to do. The world sped up again, and he moved into the overbalanced man, pulling him forward and spinning with him. The second man's blade sliced into his comrade's body. As the first man's body became smoke, Scorpius beheaded the second and then turned to find other opponents as the Shadow Warrior faded.

Tenzin faced three warriors on his own. His kicks and jumps kept them wary, but they had swords and wielded them skillfully. All three moved in to strike simultaneously at three different parts of Tenzin's body. Tenzin froze, concentrating to make his body like steel; only this time, it physically became steel, adamantine steel. The blades broke when they struck him. Tenzin reverted to flesh and then lashed out with a whip kick that snapped the necks of two of the men while he double punched the third man's heart. All three turned to smoke.

The Axemen did their part as well. Although dozens of Shadow Warriors poured in from different directions, they cut them down almost as quickly as they came. Axes flew unerringly to their targets. Magic blades of different colours caused varying effects on the unfortunate Shadow Warriors they touched. Empowered Axemen grew, sped up, turned to living stone, and even changed into animals. Still, the sheer number of enemies began to wear them down.

"Senufer!" a voice cried out over the chaos. It was Askar, standing atop one of the outcroppings. He jumped down to meet the Axeman leader who paled when he recognized Askar. This was a meeting he'd hoped he would never have to make. Electric mace met frozen axe. Then Sun Stroke sliced at Askar's stomach, but the general pulled away before it could touch him.

"I've been waiting for this a long time," Askar yelled as he swung his mace. "Remember the fun we had imposing our power, pillaging those weakling fools? You abandoned that life, abandoned me, cast me into the Hall."

"I'll cast you out of existence this time!" Senufer yelled back, trying to get through his defenses.

Alex looked down at Dara who was sticking close to him for protection. He thought the action almost pointless—what protection could he give? But they kept back far enough that the fighting hadn't reached them.

"You get the feeling that those two know each other?" he asked Dara, indicating Askar and Senufer.

Dara nodded, keeping her body behind Alex's as she watched the fight. "I wouldn't worry," Alex assured her. "There may be a lot of bad guys, but the Axemen and Defenders are cleaning up. We may actually win this."

Unseen by anyone, however, Specter had landed on one of the outcroppings, its body hidden in shadow. Watching from the Hall, the Shadow Lord did not approve of the battle's progress, so he decided to see how versatile his connection to the bird was and held up his staff.

Suddenly one of the campfires erupted outward. Everyone jumped away—Axemen, Defenders, and Shadow Warriors. The flames continued to expand, taking form, until a huge dragon composed entirely of flame stood in their midst.

The dragon's features became more defined. Nearly twice the length of a bulgor from beak to bottom with a tail that doubled that length, the beast appeared to be made of flaming bone. Its wings faded toward the outside and puffed out when they flapped only to reform when they settled. That seemed to indicate that it could not fly, but that disability did little to console the Axemen who rushed to get out of the flaming lizard's path. Several men attacked it, but their weapons passed through the flames. They only succeeded in burning themselves. The dragon turned on one such Axeman and bit down on him. Again the creature's insubstantial form kept him from being crushed by what looked like its huge jagged teeth, but his whole body was now engulfed in searing flames. Furthermore, the dragon's bones and teeth burned white hot. Their heat could cut through flesh. The Axeman screamed briefly before his body burned up in the dragon's jaws.

The rest of the Axemen tried to back out of the clearing, but still more Shadow Warriors poured in through the openings—their numbers creating a wall that left the Axemen facing a foe they could not harm.

Scorpius sliced at the dragon's side. The magic that his gladius now possessed made it flinch slightly as though a mosquito had stung it. It whipped its tail to swat him. The Roman held up his shield defensively, even though he thought the flames would pass through anyway. Surprise filled him when the dragon's tail pushed him back instead. The dragon was solid to his shield!

"Ice," Maya said, the thought seeming to come from her bow. She reached back to find an arrow made of ice in her quiver and nocked it immediately. The shot flew into the dragon, making it howl in pain. She then pulled out arrows, three at a time, and fired. With such a large target she did not have to be accurate.

Two other Axemen with cold weapons added to the dragon's grief, but their efforts were doing little to slow the beast. Senufer also wanted to attack it with Bone Chiller, but Askar kept him engaged.

Watching the battle, Alex saw the damage being done to the dragon but also saw the wounds closing up again. *Not fair!* he thought. Then he saw all the small fires around the camp. *They're healing it*, he realized. They had to ignore the dragon and put out the fires, but the fires burned *inside* the dragon.

"Fire extinguisher!" Alex said, snapping his fingers as he, Dara, and Tenzin took cover behind a boulder. When he reached in his bag, shock came over his face. "They're gone!"

"What is gone?" asked Tenzin.

"The books! They're gone."

It wasn't just the books. His bag was completely empty. Alex glanced over to see *Legend and Lore* still sitting where he had left it—near the dragon.

"Crap! The book!" he exclaimed.

"I'll get it," Tenzin offered. The monk leapt out from around the rock and snatched up the book. Before he could make it back, the dragon swung its tail at him. Instead of speeding up, however, the monk slowed down to a walk. Although the tail swept over him, he continued on his way unharmed.

"How did you do that?" Alex asked stunned.

"I became one with the fire and let its energy flow through me. Normally, I can do it with small amounts of heat, such as when I walk across hot coals, but Mornak's spell has increased my ability substantially."

"You're invulnerable to fire and weapons?" Alex asked in awe.

"Not at the same time. I have to focus on what I want to happen. When I let the fire flow through me, weapons could easily kill me and vice versa."

"Got it. Now if we just had some way to put out that fire."

Then Alex's bag got heavier. Opening it, he saw something wooden inside. He turned the bag over, and a barrel fell to the ground.

"What the—" he exclaimed.

"What is that?" Tenzin asked.

Alex saw the barrel label. "Gunpowder!"

"Is that good?"

"Only if we all want to die in a massive explosion. Where the heck did this come fro ... oh, my god! The books have merged with the bag. That's got to be what happened. My bag, it's ... it's my weapon."

"That is good," the monk stated. "You can easily access all the items."

"If I knew what they were. I didn't have those books memorized!" Alex complained.

"But every wizard knows his—"

"I'm not a wizard! Why does everyone keep calling me that?"

The dragon roared and lashed out, burning Axemen and Shadow Warriors alike. Scorpius ran up to take position in front of it. As it swung a deadly claw toward him, the world slowed again. He saw the path it was coming from and marked the speed. He let things speed up again, angling his shield so that he could deflect the claw rather than get hit with its full force. The impact jarred him nonetheless.

"Around me!" Scorpius yelled.

The Axemen listened, rallying around him to defend him from Shadow Warriors while he protected them from the dragon.

Alex peeked around the corner. "If something isn't done soon, no one from either side will be left. And this bag didn't give me an extinguisher it gave me ... an extinguisher!"

"You're not making sense," Tenzin said, shaking his head.

"An explosion will wipe out the fires and the dragon all at once. We just need to get this gunpowder to the center of its body and have everyone take cover. Genjuro-san!"

The samurai heard the call and raced up to Alex in seconds.

"Warn everyone that when Tenzin reaches the center of the dragon, there will be a huge explosion that will destroy it." He turned to Tenzin. "You can survive an explosion, I'm hoping."

Tenzin nodded. "If I am focused and aware, it will happen, yes."

Alex clapped Genjuro on the shoulder. "Go!"

As the samurai raced off, Tenzin picked up the barrel and walked toward the dragon.

On the other side of the dragon, still visible through its flames, the battle between Askar and Senufer continued.

"You have gotten old and weak," Askar taunted, "while I remained young."

"I'm not too old to finish you," Senufer spat back.

"Don't you miss the raids? Don't you miss the fear in the people's eyes?"

"You would do well to focus on our fight rather than our history."

Askar smiled. "Do you remember how it felt killing Mornak's wife?"

Senufer glanced over toward Dara to see if she heard that remark and was relieved that she did not.

Askar smiled.

"She doesn't know, does she? And she looks up to her uncle Senufer so much. Perhaps I should tell her."

"Be silent!" Senufer put all his rage into his next swing, and that was his mistake. Askar slipped in under his defenses, not with his mace but with his hand. It touched Senufer's chest and went in, much to Senufer's surprise.

Askar laughed as he melded into his adversary. As it had happened with Kendrik, the two men fought for control of the body.

"What the heck is Askar doing to him?" Alex asked, watching the struggle.

He regretted being so absorbed in the battle when without warning, Specter appeared above them and dived toward Dara. Luckily, Maya picked up the movement out of the corner of her eye and switched targets from the dragon to the falcon. Bantu raced in as well, hurling his spear skyward. The arrows and spear forced the bird away before it could grab its prey, and then the two warriors took up defensive positions around Dara.

Tenzin neared the central campfire while Scorpius and the Axemen got ready to retreat into the rocks. They delayed as long as they could to catch as many Shadow Warriors in the coming explosion as possible.

Not far away, the battle of wills ended. Senufer's form was gone, and only Askar's remained, slightly bigger and seemingly much more powerful. He looked around at the damage. Several Axemen had fallen, and many more soon would. He could see them withdrawing from the area, from the threat the dragon posed, he assumed, until he saw Tenzin walking through the dragon, carrying a barrel, somehow unaffected by the flames. Askar didn't know what it meant, but he knew it couldn't be good.

"You don't mind fire?" he grumbled. "Try electric steel." He launched his mace through the dragon at the monk. It struck Tenzin in his knee, crushing it. The monk fell, dropping the barrel, which rolled away.

"No!" yelled Scorpius, rushing in to engage Askar. Askar pulled out Sun Stroke and Bone Chiller and chopped at Scorpius, but the Roman's shield resisted both fire and ice. Then Tenzin screamed. With his concentration broken, the fire now burned his flesh.

"Tenzin!" Maya called out as she ran toward him. Bantu quickly grabbed her and pulled her back.

"You can't go in there!" he warned.

Genjuro arrived back, saying that everyone had been warned, but then he saw the monk burning alive, and he froze with shock.

While concerned as everyone else about Tenzin, Alex was the only one who realized the bigger problem of the now-flaming barrel. Though its curved surface should have made it turn circles, small stones in its path put it on a meandering path back toward them.

"Move!" he yelled and shoved everyone back toward the cave. The group ran, but to Alex it felt as if they all moved in slow motion as the deadly gunpowder barreled in. Bantu pushed Maya and Dara forward while using his body to shield them from whatever Alex had them running from. He guessed it was the dragon. Raised in the grasslands of Africa, he could not possibly expect what happened next.

The explosion deafened everyone momentarily, its heat singeing their skin. The force of the blast threw Alex and the others into the cave and caused the entrance to collapse. They had to scramble farther in to keep from getting buried as the mountain crumbled around them. Everyone began to choke and cough as dirt and dust kicked up and entered their lungs, and through it, they could still smell the burnt hairs on their bodies. Then everything quieted. They were trapped in the mountain in complete darkness, except for the gentle yellow glow of Genjuro's katana.

Maya sprang up at once, rushing toward the wall of rock.

"Tenzin!" she screamed as she started digging with her hands.

Alex grabbed her from behind.

"Let me go!" she yelled.

"You can't get through that way, Maya," Alex told her. "There're tonnes of rocks between us and them."

She struggled against him, and he could barely compete with her strength. Then, suddenly, she stopped. "The book!" she exclaimed.

"Huh?" Alex asked.

"We can reach him through the book!"

"I don't know how to. The only way to return to the book is by completing your task as far as I know."

Regardless, Alex opened the book—first to Scorpius's page, in which his portrait was still missing, and then to Tenzin's. The colour drained from Alex's face. Not only was Tenzin's picture gone, but all the text of his chapter was missing, too. The pages were all blank.

"What ... what does that mean?" Maya asked. "Why is nothing there?"

Alex guessed, but he didn't want to say what he thought.

"Maybe something's wrong with the book," he said instead. "I'm sure the text will come back. We just have to wait."

"Don't lie to me, Alex!" Maya yelled. "I can tell you're lying! What happened to his story?"

Then it hit her.

"He ... he doesn't have a story anymore, does he? He died out there!"

"We don't know for sure."

"Why *else* would the pages be blank?" She crumpled to her knees and wept.

"No, no, Hera, no. I hate this world. It's worse than Tartarus."

The others stood around not knowing what to do. They couldn't believe Tenzin was gone. Alex knelt in front of Maya and held her. She didn't resist this time. She held him tightly and cried.

* * *

Pushing the pile of rocks off himself, Askar scanned the clearing, finding it littered with bodies. The bodies of the Shadow Warriors were obviously still alive. Otherwise, they would have puffed out. Askar thought the Axemen fools for not finishing them, but he knew that their code would not let them slay a defenseless enemy.

There were no Axemen.

They would not have left any of their own here, and they would, no doubt, stay hidden now until it was least convenient for him. He hated Axemen. Scorched earth marked the area where the explosion started. There was nothing left of the monk who had been so close to it. Askar smiled, happy about that—and also happy that the Shadow Lord couldn't blame him for this mess. He hadn't summoned the dragon. He wondered if any of the Defenders survived, other than Scorpius. The general looked down at the fallen warrior. The Roman had been buried in the rubble with Askar and assumed dead by the Axemen. The youth's hand twitched as he lay unconscious. Askar grabbed him by the head and dragged him clear of the rocks. He wasn't gentle about it at all.

Then Specter swooped down to land beside him, and the image of the Shadow Lord appeared. A small amount of magic from the Shadow Lord woke Scorpius. Askar propped him up to a kneeling position in front of the Shadow Lord. Scorpius screamed as the movement ground the bones of both his broken legs.

"Listen to me, boy," the Shadow Lord said. "I have a job for you."

Scorpius tried to laugh but ended up coughing up blood.

"You are dying, boy, and only I can save you."

"And what do I have to do to be 'saved'?" Scorpius asked.

"What I know you want to do—return home."

Scorpius was stunned. *What was this man really asking?*

"And how do I do that?"

"I will show you."

An image of a dark fiery place appeared nearby, hovering above the ground. A small devilish imp scurried around picking up what looked like human bones and playing with them.

"That is a demon from one of the lower planes. I am going to summon it to serve me."

The Shadow Lord spent some time chanting and gesturing. Finally, the imp disappeared from the scene, appearing right in front of Scorpius.

"You see?" said the Shadow Lord. "He is now my servant. Any magics he possesses are also bound by my summoning."

"I don't see the point," Scorpius said.

"Think of him as your leader. What is his name?"

Scorpius wanted to argue the *leader* point but let it go. "Alex," he replied.

"Alex," the Shadow Lord repeated. "Unusual name. Like Alex, this demon possesses magic. That magic can be torn from him, even destroyed, just like your book can be taken from Alex and destroyed. The interesting thing is—if it *is* destroyed—it's gone for good."

"What else would you expect?" Scorpius scoffed.

"Ah, but I am getting to that," the Shadow Lord replied with a smirk. "What I am saying is that if you die or your book is destroyed, then your life is over."

"But?" Scorpius prompted.

"But if Alex dies ..." He nodded to Askar who pulled out his mace and smashed the imp's head in. The imp reappeared in the image of the lower planes.

"Well, then he returns home as well as his magics—in this case, you."

Scorpius stared at the imp in disbelief.

Was that really the way home?

"Now to make things even more enticing for you, your sword and shield will likely retain their enchantment when you return. Imagine what someone like you could do in your world with such items. You would become the stuff of legend."

Scorpius knew what was coming but asked anyway. "What do I have to do?"

"Your friends are going over the Fork. You, Askar, and my men will climb the mountain and meet them at the top. You will pretend that Askar has you prisoner, and he will exchange you for the Scroll."

"They'll never do that."

"No, they won't, but they will try to trick us, probably with another fake scroll. When we make the exchange, however, you will kill Alex, thus returning you and all the other Defenders, including Alex, safely home."

"What about Dara and the Scroll?"

"I will not harm the girl. She is of no consequence. As for the Scroll, you know I want it. Right now, it is only a matter of time before I get it, and truly, do you really care what happens on this world once you leave it? Don't you have duties in your own world to attend to? This world isn't even real to you.

"Now, say the word, and I will heal your wounds and send you on your way. Refuse and we will leave you here."

"You'll just leave me?" Scorpius asked skeptically.

"You are kilometers from help, your legs are broken, and you are probably bleeding inside. Yes, we will leave you here. You will die slowly and painfully. And you will discover that death here is truly death.

"Now, do we have a deal or not?"

Scorpius looked down at his shattered legs, he felt the thirst that came with a loss of blood, and then he envisioned the look on Alex's face when he rammed his blade into him.

"We have a deal."

14

*E*veryone's eyes on his plight, Tenzin screamed as the fire burned into him. He fell, clutching his shattered knee. Maya was instantly firing ice arrows into the dragon until she formed a path large enough to run down. She dashed in and pulled him out, taking cover behind a rock pillar before the gunpowder exploded.

"Thank you, my love," Tenzin told her.

Maya held him close, happy he was still alive.

"Maya," Alex said softly. The girl was quiet in his arms, her mind on Tenzin no doubt.

Since meeting her, Alex had seen her as confident and cocky. She was the type of girl who faced danger and enjoyed it. He hadn't thought that anything could break her spirit. He hadn't anticipated love. She had fallen fast, and she had fallen hard, but in a world where you could die at any moment, was there any other way?

Her hands tightened their grip on his shirt when he tried to pull her away. She wasn't ready to move, and yet they had to get going if they wanted to help Scorpius. He had to talk her through this—only he had no clue what to say.

Tenzin screamed as the fire burned into him. He fell, clutching his shattered knee. "Focus!" Maya yelled. "I know you can!"

Hearing her words, the monk raised his head to see her. Their eyes met, and he smiled. His body seemed to become transparent as he ignored the pain and let the fire flow through him again. Maya ducked around a rock pillar as the gunpowder blew. She looked back around after the explosion to see Tenzin standing there, unharmed. Smiling, she ran into his arms.

Genjuro paced the area, the light of his katana causing the shadows of the others to shrink and stretch as he moved. When he was sure that everyone's attention was on Maya and not on him, he reached back and yanked a shard of wood from his lower back. A piece of the barrel had hit him with such force that it pierced his armour. He looked at the shard. It was longer than he thought, splintered, and red with his blood. He hoped he got all of it out. Genjuro took comfort in the fact that the others would not see his injury in this darkness. He was a samurai, and he would not show weakness. The others were counting on him to be strong. He wanted to wrap the wound to staunch the flow of blood, but to do so meant putting down his sword. Then the others would know. He settled for pushing his back against the wall to apply pressure.

"Nintai," he muttered. "I will persevere."

Alex pulled his face away from Maya. Her eyes stared blankly into space. She was in shock. "Maya, please," he told her. "We need you here."

She didn't look at him. She didn't see him. Her mind was somewhere else, trying to make things better.

Tenzin screamed as the fire burned into him. He fell, clutching his shattered knee. Bantu and Alex herded the others toward the cave against Maya's protests. Just before the barrel exploded, Tenzin found his focus and became steel. Maya and the others were thrown into the cave and sealed in, but on the other side of the wall of rock, Tenzin still lived. He just had to find a way to let them know.

Bantu sat on the ground, pitying poor Maya. He could not believe what had just happened. He hoped that the Axemen had escaped, that Scorpius was not badly hurt. But that explosion! He had never seen anything like it. The force with which it threw them into the cave was incredible. He felt the heat of it searing into his back at the time. He did not want to see what his back looked like now. It felt like it still burned. Tenzin had been in the dragon and close to the barrel when it exploded. How could anyone survive that? He had no doubt that the monk had died. He mourned the loss of his new friend and honoured the deaths of the many Axemen who had died with him.

"Why doesn't she answer?" Dara asked.

"She's trying to figure out what she could have done to change things," Alex told her.

"But what will that do?"

"Nothing," Alex said sadly, "but she's not ready to accept that he's gone, so she's trying to keep it from happening ... in her mind."

"I don't understand," Dara admitted.

Alex took one hand away from Maya and put it against Dara's cheek. "I hope you never have to."

Tenzin neared the campfire, the energy of the fire flowing through him and the barrel without harm. Nearby, Askar had absorbed Senufer's form. He grew slightly bigger and seemed much more powerful. He saw Tenzin, walking unaffected through the flames. Askar didn't know what it meant, but he knew it couldn't be good.

"You don't mind fire?" he grumbled. "Try electric steel."

Seeing the fiend's intent, Maya quickly nocked an arrow of steel and fired. It struck the general in the chest, piercing his armour. He vanished into smoke before he could throw his mace. Tenzin released the barrel, and it caught fire. Seconds later, it exploded killing every Shadow Warrior in the area. When the smoke dispersed, Tenzin stood alone in the clearing. Axemen and Defenders popped their heads out from around the rock formations and then cheered at the victory. Maya rushed up and kissed her beloved, their hero.

Alex hated this. He didn't want to be strong right now. He didn't want to be holding Maya and comforting her. He wanted someone to comfort him. He wanted to curl up in a ball and close his eyes and wake up back in his bed at home and have this whole adventure fade like a dream from his memories. This world had been exciting and scary and intriguing and annoying. Dara had made it all feel real to him, but at the same time, that Little Rose made him believe that he'd wake up at home, like Dorothy, once they melted the witch and met the wizard. He wanted to wake up. He wanted to play video games with Dax, tell Tanya how he felt, pass that damn exam—even fail that damn exam—as long as he was back home. This world has been unbelievable, but now Tenzin was dead. Now everything felt acutely real.

Fighting the bulgor, the pirates and the sea slug, Askar, and the Shadow Warriors, even the dragon—Alex didn't really expect to lose. He thought they'd figure someway out, or someone would swoop in at the last minute and rescue them. That's what happened in the movies. The only time he'd been genuinely worried was when the pirates had Dara, but that had nothing to do with his feelings for this world.

He looked at Dara—young, innocent, full of life, and his responsibility, no matter what else happened. He wouldn't shirk his responsibilities a second time. He wouldn't let her be taken again. He wouldn't let her be—

He brought his thoughts back. He couldn't dwell on that now. Tenzin was dead. Scorpius was cut off from them. Maya was, well, a basket case at the moment. The others wore vacant expressions, not knowing what to do or where to go. It was up to him to get them moving, or they would all die in this mountain. That seemed such a real possibility now. Scorpius would have them moving in moments, whether they wanted to or not. The Roman could drive an army if he set his mind to it. Tenzin would have cheered them up and offered some profound advice that would make them feel silly if they didn't follow it. Alex only had bad jokes that the others didn't get and knowledge about a future they may never see. He wished he had more.

"Damn it, I hate to do this," Alex said to Maya and himself. Then he slapped Maya across the face, hard. Her attention focused on him instantly—and she lunged.

"You!" she hissed as she knocked him down and landed on top of him. "This is your fault!" She pounded her fists on his chest. "You sent him in there. There could have been another way to kill the dragon."

Alex groaned. The blast had hurt him, and he was still a bit tender from the various beatings he'd taken up to now despite a bit of healing from that Axeman.

"You didn't stop him, either," he argued as he tried to grab her wrists. "We all thought he'd be fine. No one could have known what Askar would do."

She kept hitting him, but the strength left her punches. Then she began to cry again, collapsing on Alex. Maya hadn't cried since she was a little girl. Now she couldn't stop.

"I'm upset he's gone, too," Alex told her. "He was a great guy. I could see why you liked him so much. It was pretty obvious that he felt the same way."

She pulled herself up and looked into his eyes, pulling stray strands of her hair, wet with tears, away from her face. "He did?"

Alex smiled. "You couldn't tell?"

"I thought so, but I've never known a man before. I don't know how your minds work. I hoped he cared as much, but I thought perhaps he was just having fun."

"He loved you," Alex said.

She smiled, and the tears started again. She hugged him tightly.

"Maya," Alex whispered, "Scorpius is still out there. We need to help him."

It took a few seconds for her mind to grasp what Alex had told her.

"What?" she asked.

"Scorpius is still alive, but we can't get to him. He could be hurt. He could be captured. We have to get up the mountain."

She shook her head.

"We have to find another way back out."

Alex shook his head back.

"I don't think there is one. Our best bet is to find Senufer's friends and have them guide us to the top."

"And then journey all the way back down on the outside?" she asked incredulously.

"No," Alex assured as he stood up. His body ached, and he grunted "Punisher" as he straightened himself out.

"Punish who?" Maya asked.

"Huh?" Alex asked. "Oh, no, I grunt out the names of comic book characters to push away pain. Never mind that. We have to get to the second peak of the Fork. Once we get there, you all return to the book." He didn't really want to give her false hope, but he had to get her moving, and besides, he thought he might be right about what he was about to say.

"There's also a chance that ending the task might reset everything."

"Reset?" she repeated, not understanding.

"Put everything back the way it was," Alex explained. "It could bring Tenzin back."

Maya was on her feet in an instant.

"Let's go."

* * *

"You took a great chance with that dragon," Askar stated. "What if it had burned up the Scroll?"

"The Scroll was never in danger," replied the Shadow Lord. "If Dara or the boy had moved toward the dragon, it would have backed away. I would never take such a chance, but they did not know that."

Askar walked over to the collapsed entrance. A small section of the mountain had fallen in front of it, completely sealing off the original opening.

"You can't blast through here?" he asked.

"I would risk bringing the mountain down on the Scroll. If it is crushed and tears ..."

"What about animating the rock like you did the city wall? Make it move out of the way."

"I've already used the staff today. It needs a full day to recharge. They could well be at the top by then if they avoid the dangers in there," he said, pointing at the mountain.

Askar nodded then added, "They've been communicating with Mornak."

The Shadow Lord turned to him with a look of shock. "Impossible. He's cut off from his powers."

"Not quite. He cannot use them, but he can send messages to Dara through the Scroll and she can use them."

"How do you know this?"

Askar tapped his head. "Senufer."

The Shadow Lord remembered when they first tried to capture Dara just north of Aspiria. She had run off as they closed in as if she knew they were coming. Mornak had been in the room at the time, watching the events on the wall. He must have warned her.

"He's using the spiritual link that binds him to the Scroll," the Shadow Lord surmised.

"You can't sever it?" asked Askar.

"Only by killing him, but that would destroy the Scroll as well."

"Torture him then, physically. He can't communicate if he can't think."

"I'll consider it. Constant torture may kill him anyway. Besides, whenever they use the Scroll, we can track their location. That is how the bird knew to come here. For the moment, we need that advantage."

The Shadow Lord pondered the dilemma for a moment before returning to the matter at hand. "Are you prepared for the climb?"

"We'll need protection from the cold," Askar stated.

The Shadow Lord nodded and then began an incantation. When he released the magic, it came, not from him, but from Specter. His image was only a projection, Askar remembered, and Scorpius took note of the fact that the Shadow Lord had to use the bird as a conduit. The magic fanned out, encompassing all the men there, including Scorpius. Each immediately felt a warm tingle flow across his skin.

"The spell will last a full day," the Shadow Lord told him.

"Why don't you just have the bird fly us to the top?" Askar argued.

"It is still subject to many natural laws," the Shadow Lord answered. "The winds in these mountains would buffet it and send it flying out of control. I will have it fly around the mountain range, but that will take it at least a day, even riding the shadows."

"They'll beat us to the top," Askar said, assuredly.

"I doubt that," the Shadow Lord smiled. "Don't forget that things have changed since the realm darkened. The Emils are dealing with guests from the Hall. I doubt they will be much help to the children, and the mountain holds other dangers for those not on the path."

"The brats are resourceful, though. Look what they did here." Askar said, gesturing around at the blackened rock walls and pillars.

The Shadow Lord shrugged.

"I will also summon our troops on the other side of World's Divide to bracket them, but it may take time to gather enough men. There are dozens of routes down from the other peak to the ground, and the brats could easily evade us. Just remember—the easiest way to finish this is through Scorpius, and that means you need to get to the top first. So get up there fast."

"We'll get there faster if you two would stop talking," Scorpius called out. He stood, fully healed, with the Shadow Warriors, waiting to depart.

Twenty-three of the nearly three hundred Shadow Warriors remained from the battle with the Axemen. He could feel their stares. While some applauded his betrayal, others still eyed him with distrust. He knew that if he showed a hint of uncertainty or regret in his decision, those would be the ones who would jump at the chance to kill him.

He would not change his mind though. The image of killing Alex cemented his thoughts. He would follow through with the plan.

*   *   *

Genjuro's sword led the way with its pale yellow glow. Maya walked just behind him and to the right, Bantu across from her on the left. Dara stayed safely in the middle while Alex brought up the rear. In the dim light, and because of his naturally dark skin, the others could not see the burns on Bantu's back, nor could they see the red stain on Genjuro's clothes beneath his armour. Maya limped slightly, having injured her knee when they tumbled to the ground after the explosion. It was more of an annoyance to her than anything else, yet hers was the only injury visible to everyone else.

They walked for over an hour with no sign of Senufer's friends. Maya noted that these tunnels differed greatly from the one by the sea. Whereas the other was natural and meandering with pits, stalagmites, and stalactites, these seemed carved with a flat floor. The widths of these tunnels, though they shifted in places, were fairly uniform. Even the smell differed. The air in the cave was fresh, though slightly damp, with a touch of the sea. While the air was drier here, a mustiness filled these passages as well as a slight scent of decay. Side tunnels led off in both directions at regular intervals, but they ignored them, remembering Senufer's words that his friends lived somewhere down the main tunnel. They assumed, or rather hoped, that this *was* the main tunnel, so they kept walking forward.

Alex had already spotted the wheel tracks on the floor. He guessed that they were traveling through an old mining shaft. Whatever valuable ore it contained had long ago been removed. Now it was a dark labyrinth that could imprison them forever if they weren't careful.

Though not claustrophobic by nature, Alex felt cramped inside the cave. The darkness seemed to press in on him from all sides. From their expressions, the others were having similar feelings. Both Maya and Bantu would drift in toward the center of the tunnel as they walked only to realize their shift from the sides and would then move back out again. Dara, who typically stayed close to Alex, instead stayed right behind Genjuro—or rather, as close to the light as she could. Alex felt as though the darkness behind him pushed on his back. He glanced over his shoulder repeatedly to check if something were really pressed against him, as well as to check that nothing had sneaked up behind them from one of the side tunnels. The utterly black void he saw was discomforting.

A rumble through the mountain stopped them in their tracks.

"What was that?" asked Genjuro.

"I don't think these tunnels are all that stable," Alex replied. "And that explosion didn't help matters."

Everyone looked around, expecting the ceiling to collapse right then. When it didn't, the group let out a collective sigh and continued on.

Genjuro stayed wary as he led the group. They were supposed to be meeting allies, but given their adventures to date, he was prepared for the worst. Besides that, these were Senufer's friends, not theirs. Without the Axeman leader with them, they had no way of knowing how these "friends" would react. Senufer also didn't mention whether anyone or *anything* else lived in these tunnels, probably because he figured he'd be along for the journey.

"What happened to Senufer-san?" Genjuro asked. His voice made everyone jump when it broke the near silence.

"I don't know," Alex replied. "It looked like they merged. Askar seems to be able to possess someone else, or absorb them, or something."

"Can they be separated?" Bantu asked.

"Why do you think I would know?" Alex said exasperatedly. "I'm as new to this world as the rest of you."

"But you know things," Maya stated, "from your books and movies. Has this not happened in any of them?"

Alex nodded.

"Several, in different ways, with different results. It's a lot different when you're not watching and can't see the big picture. I dunno what's going on. It could be that all the Shadow Warriors can do that. Try not to touch any in the future."

Bantu nodded. "A good ide—"

Genjuro's sudden stop caught everyone's attention. They had come up to a wall of rubble.

"Cave-in," Alex mumbled. "Crap."

"That's a bad word, isn't it?" Dara said as realization swept over her.

Alex winked at her.

"Not as bad as some of the words I could be using." He looked back at the fallen rocks and sighed. "The explosion probably collapsed the ceiling."

"No, Alex-san," Genjuro argued. "The dust here is settled. This happened some time ago."

"What now?" Maya asked, and then everyone turned to Alex for direction.

Oh sure, he thought. *They pretty much voted me out earlier, and now they're looking at me to lead.*

It reminded him of the reality TV shows he'd seen where the contestants voted one person off the show each week. The only person safe was the one who managed to win the immunity challenge. Senufer had given Alex immunity this round. With the Axeman leader gone, would Alex make it to the next round? He shook his head at his silly thoughts. This wasn't a show. This wasn't TV. Ironically, this world of fantasy was the reality, and the only way out of it was the way Tenzin had gone.

These people did not fully trust in his abilities—truthfully, neither did Alex—but they needed him as much as he needed them. He pushed his hair back and pulled it forward again as he reviewed his options.

"We go back," Alex said finally. "We take a side tunnel and try to work our way around and back into the main tunnel."

"How do we find our way?" Maya asked. "Can we use that com-pass?"

Alex opened his bag and reached in. "I'd rather have a GPS locator, but if you want a compass, I'll give you a ... light bulb?" Alex stared dumbfounded at the light bulb he had pulled from the bag. He looked inside again to check if he missed anything, but the bag was empty again.

"A light bulb?" Genjuro repeated.

Alex scratched his head. "What good is a light bulb without a—"

The bulb lit up.

"Oh," said Alex as he examined its design. "I think this is the light bulb that Edison ran his first successful test on, on October 22, 1879. It lasted ... thirteen and a half hours. Great. So we're on a time limit now? Stupid bag."

Alex handed the bulb to Bantu and tried to pull the compass from his bag again, but it gave him nothing. Frustrated, he gave up, and they turned themselves around, getting back into their marching order. With the brighter white light of the bulb, Bantu's burns became visible to those behind him.

"Bantu! Your back!" Dara exclaimed.

"You've been burned," Maya said, touching him gently with her fingertips. Bantu winced even though she only brushed against him lightly.

"Why didn't you say anything?" Alex asked.

"What can be done for it?" Bantu countered.

"A healing spell, maybe?" Alex suggested.

Dara had the Scroll out in moments and called to her father. The teens gathered around her, watching for words to appear on the Scroll.

Nothing.

"We'll try again in an hour," Alex suggested.

"Why does he not answer?" Bantu asked.

"I don't think he can right now," Alex answered as he started off again.

"Do you not care *why* he cannot answer?" Maya asked, getting annoyed with Alex's dismissive attitude about the problem.

Alex looked over at her. "As Bantu said, 'What can be done for it?'"

She opened her mouth to speak but quickly realized he was right.

"We'll keep trying until we get through," Alex assured her. "It's too bad we can't leave voicemail."

* * *

"Where are they taking the Scroll?" the Shadow Lord demanded.

"I don't know," Mornak panted out, his body smoldering again.

They had brought him back out to the throne room of the Hall and chained him back to the wall. The Shadow Lord threw more black fire at him. Mornak screamed from the pain.

"Where?" the Shadow Lord said again.

"I'm locked in here," Mornak said. "How could I possibly know what they are doing?"

How indeed, thought the Shadow Lord. He knew Mornak lied, but he did not say anything. That knowledge gave him the advantage.

"Did you leave instructions for Dara?"

"To go to Kashla," Mornak replied.

"They have not gone there."

"She always did have a mind of her own," Mornak smiled.

The Shadow Lord wiped the smile from his face with more black fire.

"They freed Senufer from Shadow Wood, you know?"

Mornak looked up at him, trying to seem surprised.

"Really?"

You're a horrible actor, thought the Shadow Lord.

"But since then we've killed him and the rest of the Axemen," he said smugly, drawing satisfaction from the sorrow in Mornak's face. "Would Senufer have told them to go somewhere? Over the Fork?"

Mornak shook his head. "Too dangerous. Too cold. I would never send her over it."

"And yet that is where she is headed."

Mornak's brow furrowed then, and at the same time, the Shadow Lord could feel the Scroll being used. They were making contact. He threw black fire at the wizard again to break his concentration while feigning anger.

"Answer me, wizard!" he yelled. "I will teach you to defy your lord."

He kept the fire up, varying its intensity, so that Mornak could not think through it. Soon the magic of the Scroll stopped. The Shadow Lord kept up with the fire a little longer to mask the fact that he knew when the Scroll was being used and because he enjoyed hurting this man.

I do not believe this method will make him talk. He would never betray his daughter, even under torture.

"This method has its purposes," the Shadow Lord said to the Hall. He had not yet informed it of Mornak's other connection to the Scroll. He needed time to decide a course of action and did not want to listen to it complain about the situation. He had already been berated about the failure outside the mountain. This news could have the Hall spitting black fire at *him*! No, he would find a way to turn this to his advantage. He would find a way to make Mornak suffer further because of this.

"Too dangerous. Too cold," Mornak muttered through his pain.

*   *   *

Genjuro thought about mentioning his injury as well, but decided that he would do so when they were able to be healed. Bantu had ignored his pain and remained strong. Genjuro would do the same. He was samurai. He would endure.

The group headed back down the tunnel, following Alex's lead—although he walked behind them all—and tried to find a way around the cave-in. Turning down an opening on their right, they soon found themselves in a tighter tunnel, so they reformed their line. Genjuro and Bantu took the lead. Maya walked behind Genjuro so she could fire arrows over him if necessary. Dara stayed behind Bantu so he could block whatever came her way. Alex remained at the back.

The light of the bulb, much brighter than Genjuro's blade, made everyone feel a little better. Genjuro even sheathed his sword, but stayed alert. At first, Alex thought to ask the samurai to keep his sword at the ready, but then he remembered how fast Genjuro could draw the blade, especially now.

Another right turn had them traveling parallel to the original tunnel. They would eventually need another right turn to get back to it, but so far, they only passed tunnels on their left. They became more anxious with every step. Compared to the quiet of the area around them, their footsteps sounded thunderous. They knew that anything ahead would hear them coming from a great distance.

Dara kept glancing over at Maya to see how she was holding up. It did not go unnoticed.

"What is it?" Maya huffed in a tone a little harsher than she intended.

"Are you okay now?" Dara asked innocently.

Maya's look softened immediately. "I am holding up."

"Did you think of a way you could have saved Tenzin?"

Maya looked at her in disbelief. "How could you possibly know what I've been thinking?"

Dara glanced behind them. "Alex told me."

Maya turned to him. "And how could you know?"

Alex shrugged. "Movies, books, TV shows," he lied.

Maya tilted her head quizzically. "Did you do anything else in your world besides read and watch your shows? I am surprised you are so skinny with all that inactivity."

"I *do* exercise," Alex said defensively. "I bike, skateboard, jam with my band, ski, snowboard, I've even base jumped. Well, that last one isn't really exercise ... but it's fun!"

"You realize that I have no idea what any of those things are, don't you?" Maya asked.

"They're recreational activities," Alex explained.

"So the only time you do something physical is for fun?"

Alex thought about it. "Yeah, pretty much."

"Yours is a lazy world, Alex. I could not imagine living in a place that didn't constantly challenge my mind *and* body. It seems a place of sloth."

"That may be so, Maya-chan," Genjuro jumped in, looking back at them, "but I, for one, would like to see a TV. It sounds like a remarkable ... Hey!—"

Genjuro disappeared. The others froze, holding back their mounting panic. A moment later, when they heard a crunch come from somewhere below them, they realized what had happened. Shining the light down, they saw a large hole in the floor.

"Genjuro!" Alex called down. "You okay?"

No answer.

"Genjuro!" Alex yelled. "Are you okay?"

Silence.

"He's not okay."

Bantu leaned in, holding the light forward to see better. The floor at his feet began to give way. He backed off, but the ground continued to crumble. The group retreated, but the collapsing floor seemed to follow them. Bantu quickly scooped up Dara and handed her the light bulb. Alex pointed up ahead at a side tunnel, for which they bolted.

Dara's scream made Alex and Maya turn to see her and Bantu fall with the collapsing floor. The light faded away with them as Alex turned into the side tunnel. Looking back, he saw Maya's quickly fading form coming at him. Her scream told him that the collapse had caught up to her. He reached out and grabbed her outstretched hand before everything went black. Alex strained at the weight of Maya's body. She was pulling him down toward a hole he could not see. He did not even know how close to the edge his feet were.

"Don't let go," Maya begged, her voice full of panic.

Alex grunted as he tightened his grip. He worked a hand up to grab her wrist. Still he could feel Maya slipping through his grasp.

"Alex, please," Maya called.

Alex shook his head, feeling himself slipping toward the edge. He couldn't see that the flap of his bag had opened. "Oh, to be on a beach even for just ten minutes right now," he wished.

Both he and Maya were sucked into the bag, which fell to the floor at the edge of the hole.

*   *   *

Bantu twisted as he and Dara fell so that he would bare the brunt of the impact. He did not expect to have to do it twice. When they hit the floor of the tunnel below them, a large slab of it gave way, and the pair fell yet another level, this one even deeper, riding the slab down. Bantu growled, trying his best not to scream from the pain of his still tender back grinding into the floor.

"Bantu, are you all right?" Dara asked, getting off him.

He could not reply immediately as he focused through the pain.

"Bantu?"

"I ... will be ... fine," he grunted. He rolled off his back and immediately felt some relief, but his nerves still felt on fire. "I need ... a moment."

"Alex!" Dara yelled at the opening above them. "Maya! Can you hear me? Alex! Bantu is hurt! We need help!" Dara paced the area, looking about nervously and checking the ceiling constantly. "Alex! Maya!" She turned to Bantu. "Why don't they answer?"

"They may be ... ugh ... too far away," he answered, every word painful. "We don't know ... how far the floor ... collapsed."

"They'll come back, won't they?" Dara asked, panic building quickly in the little girl. "They won't just go away. They—"

"Dara!" Bantu snapped, and it hurt him to yell. He softened as soon as he saw her focus on him. "Alex would never leave you."

Dara nodded.

"Bantu, where are we?" she asked, looking around. They had fallen into a room of some kind. Old tables and chairs lay strewn about, their wood rotting. Crates and barrels also littered the room, most of them opened and empty. Several large rusty pipes ran from ceiling to floor along one wall. Big valve wheels adorned each pipe, and Dara could hear a soft hiss coming from them.

Bantu shrugged—even that hurt.

"I have never been ... in a stone room before."

Just then the ground shook again. Nearby, one of the pipes cracked. Hot steam and a stream of water sprayed from it. More rubble fell from the ceiling. One chunk struck Dara in the head. She did not cry out. Instead a curious expression came over her face.

"Dara?" Bantu asked.

Then Dara toppled over unconscious. Miraculously, the light bulb did not break when she fell, but when she released her grip on it, it went out. Bantu panicked and moved to her quickly. He felt something tear in his back, and then the pain overwhelmed him. He too fell unconscious. Unknown to either of them, the broken pipe ruptured further. Scalding water, heated from an underground lava flow, poured onto the floor, slowly filling the room.

*   *   *

Genjuro woke to find himself in complete darkness, propped up against some rocks. His head hurt.

"Alex-san?" he asked. "Bantu-san?"

He reached down and was glad to find his swords on his hip. As he drew his katana, its blade lit up the area around him. The skeleton was right beside him, jaws open, staring at his face.

Genjuro cried out as he tried to scamper away backward, but then screamed when he moved his left arm. It was broken. The skeleton's arm reached out, gripping his leg. He kicked hard, sending both the hand and forearm flying away. Protecting his injured arm, Genjuro backed up into something, something too soft to be a wall. Another skeletal arm fell over his right shoulder wrapping around his chest. Genjuro looked up over his shoulder to see the thing looking down at him, smiling. He quickly reversed direction, swinging his katana and severing its neck. Its arm held onto his chest though. He got to his feet and turned around, remembering the first skeleton that had crept up beside him. He kicked its head where it crawled on the ground.

Now that he was standing, he could see the others. Two came at him from his left. He arced his blade toward them. They showed no fear even as he cut them down. He backed into the center of the passage and saw more along the walls. There were dozens of them. They were all around him, staring, smiling—not moving.

Genjuro stopped. He willed himself to calm down and really look at what was there. The skeletons were not alive. They just lay propped up against the walls. The ones he thought had attacked him had simply got caught on his clothes. He dropped to his knees and took a deep breath, happy none of the others had seen his display. He grabbed the limb attached to his chest and threw it aside and then looked up. The next level was too high to reach, and much of it had broken away. He quickly searched the debris for signs of his friends.

Finding nothing but a hole to another, much deeper level, he reasoned that they had either all gone down the hole—which seemed unlikely since it wasn't that big and since they would have had to be on top of each other to all fall in—or they had escaped the collapse and were looking for another way around. If the latter were the case, then they would try to get to him from the tunnel farther down from where he had fallen. He stood at the end of the collapse, looking around, completely unaware that he was just below Alex's bag and a few levels above Bantu and Dara. Genjuro called out but received no reply.

Feeling a throbbing pain at the back of his head, he reached up to find his hair matted with blood. He must have hit hard when he landed. His lower back hurt, too. He reached back and brought back fingers slick with blood. His *fight* with the skeletons had reopened his wound. He tore off a swath of his pants and wrapped it tightly about his waist. Tired and thirsty from his loss of blood, he knew he would get neither water nor rest for some time. He would press on and look for his friends. If he could find the way to the main tunnel, he could make things easier for all of them.

Putting his sword to the ground where he fell, Genjuro scraped it along the floor and up the wall and then dragged it along as he walked. If they made it to where he landed, they would have something to follow.

Unseen by Genjuro and attracted by the noise, several shadowy figures had arrived; they watched the predicament of the samurai with great interest. They gauged his strength and his ability to fight. He would not last long, they knew. Soon his wounds would overcome him, and he would be easy prey. They slipped through the area, dark and silent, tracking the warrior. When they were sure he could not defend himself, they would take him.

15

So far the path up the mountain had been easy going, but now the way narrowed, forcing them to march single file as they rounded the edge. The drop was sheer, but in the dark of night, you could not tell or see the height of the fall.

The torches they held lit the path before them. Only Askar could see in the dark. The rest, despite being spawned from shadow, were human in every aspect, except that they turned back to shadow when they died.

No one talked during the march. The Shadow Warriors seemed to be a single-minded bunch. Scorpius had tried a few times to talk to some of them in the hope of learning more about his enemy. They only looked at him as though he was some annoying child, then grunted, and walked on.

The path took a sharp turn, and around the bend, some boulders had fallen and blocked the way. The men ahead stopped. Scorpius, looking out and up at the night sky, walked right into the man in front of him with enough force that they both slipped off the edge. Scorpius grabbed him by the wrist with one hand and the edge of the cliff with the other. Warriors above them reacted quickly, grabbing Scorpius's forearm. The ground at the cliff edge gave away a little, so only two men could hold onto the Roman without it crumbling under their weight. They tried to pull the two up, but the armour of both men weighed them down considerably. Scorpius felt his arm slowly slipping out of the grip of the warriors above him. In another moment, he and the Shadow Warrior would be falling down the mountainside to their deaths. It really wasn't a hard choice for him to make about what he should do. He released his grip, and the man tumbled away into darkness, screaming in fear the whole way, while the others yanked Scorpius back up to safety.

Scorpius expected repercussions immediately, but the Shadow Warriors only peered over the edge to confirm the man's fate—although they found no real way to do so. Ahead, despite the situation that Scorpius had been in, several of the warriors were already clearing away the rocks. Askar glanced over at him, not angry, but a bit annoyed. Camaraderie seemingly did not exist for the Shadow Warriors, nor did a sense of loss. They simply hated good and cared nothing for each other. Only their service to the Hall mattered to them.

*   *   *

Ten minutes had passed. Alex and Maya reappeared at the edge of the pit, screaming as they lay with their hands over their heads. When all they heard was silence, they opened their eyes. Neither could see a thing.

"Alex?" Maya asked, her voice almost a squeak.

"Yeah?" Alex replied, his heart beating in his throat.

"Where are we?"

"Back in the mountain, I think."

"Where in Athena's name were we?"

"Omaha Beach, Normandy, June 6th, 1944. D-Day. That was the Second World War on earth. One hundred fifty thousand men stormed the beach attacking the Nazi forces."

"What were those ... those things?"

"Guns."

"And the—"

"Mortar fire."

Alex remembered playing *Call of Duty* and other war video games and how he and his friends had discussed how realistic it was. They didn't know a thing about real war, he knew now. His battles in the video games had been nerve-racking and tense at times, but while they could get his adrenaline pumping and the game quality seemed near photorealistic, there was always an element of fun and an assurance of safety. Real war was nothing like that.

He and Maya had been on that beach ten minutes, and in that time, hundreds of men had died around them. As scary as things had been on this world, they at least had a means to fight back. On that beach, stray bullets whipped by them, explosions went off close enough to deafen them, and the very air tasted of blood and gunpowder. Being helpless in the chaos of hundreds of thousands of men fighting and dying was far more frightening than anything they had experienced so far. Alex knew that. Even if he had a gun, he would have questioned what difference he could have made in the scale of what was happening on that beach. He wondered how many of those men thought the same thing. You didn't have to be involved in a fight to die there. You just had to be present for death to come without warning. Blood stained everything, and many men lay screaming, having lost limbs in explosions. It had been horrifying to look at, and although they had left that terrifying place, the images still burned strongly in their minds. Alex, still shaking, remembered the expression "War is hell." For the first time, he truly grasped what that meant.

He shook his head. "When I said I wanted to be—"

"Alex!" Maya barked with both fear and annoyance.

"Yes?" Alex replied.

"Before you say anything else, close your bag."

A cold sweat ran over Alex's body as he realized that he may have almost sent them back to the beach at that moment. He reached around until he felt the cloth of his bag and closed the flap.

"Done. Now what do we do about light?"

"What about your music light?"

"My what? My Nano!" Alex reached into his pocket and pulled it out. It didn't light up. "Great. I think Bantu drained the batteries. Wait! You used ice arrows against the dragon."

"What good does that do?"

"Can you draw a fire arrow?"

Maya felt around for her bow. Alex heard her getting up.

"Careful," he warned. "We don't know how close we are to the edge."

Maya got to one knee, drew an arrow, and nocked it. Its tip flared to life. She looked down to see her toes hanging off the edge of the drop and immediately backed up. Both teens noticed how pale the other was.

"What now?" Maya asked.

"We're the only ones still on the top level," Alex replied. "I think we should find Senufer's friends."

"What about the others?"

Alex opened the book and checked their chapters. "Their portraits are still here, so they're probably just stuck on the lower levels." Alex saw Maya wince at that statement. He had just reminded her that Tenzin's portrait wasn't there. He thought it best to just keep her busy by moving on.

"Bantu! Dara!" he called into the hole beside them. There was no reply, but Alex did feel a slight warmth coming from below, a moist warmth.

"They're not down there. If Senufer's friends live here, then they probably know the tunnels. They can help us search."

"Do you hear something?" Maya asked.

Alex did—something below them, almost a rumbling, but not quite. Familiar in a way, he still couldn't place it, and they couldn't sit around and try to figure it out. Their friends needed them. Getting up, they moved quickly down the hallway, leaving Dara and Bantu unconscious in the room directly below them while steaming water quickly filled it.

* * *

Every step Genjuro took was harder than the last. He had lost the strength to keep his sword against the wall and now dragged it beside him. Even like that, scraping the stone deep enough to leave a visible line became increasingly more difficult. He had found a ladder up to the next level. Now he just had to find the main tunnel.

He knew they were behind him. He could sense them. He just couldn't see them. Whatever they were, they were shadowing him. He had tried briefly to speed up, but he couldn't maintain the pace. Now walking itself had become an effort. He didn't have much time left, and he knew it. But if it was possible, then he was going to die a warrior.

He spun around quickly, regretting the action immediately as needles of pain shot through his broken arm. Gritting his teeth against it, he called out to the darkness.

"Face me, demons! Battle me with honour, and let us see who is the better!"

At the edge of his sword's light, shadows moved about. Genjuro assumed a fighting stance and waited for the attack. It did not come. The shadows backed away from his light. He moved toward them, but they only backed away farther.

"Cowards," he called out. As he turned to continue his journey, the tunnel seemed to spin. He almost fell over. The shadows reacted, moving in suddenly but then backing off when he regained his composure.

They are waiting for me to die, Genjuro thought and straightened himself resolutely. *I will not give them the satisfaction.*

He continued down to the next intersection. It opened to a wide tunnel. He looked down to his right and saw a caved-in section. To his left it continued past the light of his blade. This was it. He had found the main tunnel. Now he had only to find his friends—or Senufer's friends.

Far down the tunnel he saw a light moving about. Thinking it might be Alex's light bulb, he called out, "Bantu-san, is that you? Alex-san?"

The light stopped and hovered for a moment; then it slowly approached.

It must be them! he thought.

Adrenaline pumped into his system, and he started to move up, but something took hold of his ankle and tripped him. He felt several hands wrap around his legs before he was dragged back down the tunnel he had just exited. His sword flared with his anger, revealing inky black forms. Genjuro swung at one, striking its arm. Although his blade cut right through, the arm did not come off the creature. It was as if he had cut through mud. More hands took hold of his body.

He fought hard, but his strength was fading fast. He called out for his friends down the hall, hoping they would get to him in time. Then a slimy hand covered his mouth. The dark figures moved all about him now, wrapping him up and pulling him with greater speed from the main hall. Genjuro was born a samurai, trained to fight, honour bound to serve and protect, but he was also a sixteen-year-old boy in an alien world against unimaginable dangers—he was scared. He had never been this scared before. This was not how he wanted to die, and yet it seemed that this was how he would perish—alone and helpless in a dark tunnel. Something yanked his sword from his grip. Its light flickered out, plunging him into complete darkness. He felt his consciousness slipping away. He knew they had won, and then he knew nothing.

* * *

Bantu woke up to a new pain. His toes stung. He pulled them up toward his chest and reached down to feel them. They were wet. Then he realized that he could hear water pouring.

"Dara!" he called. "Dara, are you there?"

"B-Bantu?" Dara said in a groggy voice. "What happened?"

"Can you find the light?" he asked. He heard her shuffling around and then a shallow splash.

"Hey!" Dara exclaimed. More shuffling followed, and then the white light bulb glowed.

Looking around the room, they saw the broken pipe and the water rising. Steam filled the room and rose through the opening above. The section of the upper floor they had landed on had kept them above the rising tide until now. Bantu scanned for the door and rushed to it, wincing as his feet sloshed through the steaming water. The door was locked, but that would not stop him. He rammed his shoulder into it.

It didn't move.

He was much stronger now. *A wooden door should not pose a problem*, he thought.

He slammed against it again with the same result. Grabbing his spear from the ground, he thrust it into the door and yanked it back. The door tore from its hinges to reveal a pile of rocks behind. The room behind it had caved in.

He turned and looked for another way out, but the only one hung several floors above them out of reach. The African would not give up easily, however. He stacked several crates around him into a pile and then climbed them, holding another crate to build the pile up even higher. Unfortunately, the rotted wood crumpled under his weight, dumping him back down into the water with a splash. He immediately cursed himself for a fool. Dara may have been able to climb the crates and gotten to safety if he had let her go first.

Seeing his near-panicked state, Dara tried to calm him down.

"We'll be okay, Bantu," she assured him. "The water is hot, but I'm getting used to it. It's like the steam baths we have at the palace. We can just float up with it to the next level."

Having been to a hot spring, Bantu knew better. "No, Dara, the heat will make us pass out long before the water rises high enough. Then we will drown."

Dara thought about pulling out the Scroll, but she had no idea what all the steam would do to the parchment. She didn't want to risk getting it wet. She knew that even if they didn't make it, the Scroll had to survive at all costs. At least it was safe in her bag.

Bantu tore open barrels and crates looking for anything that might help; he finally found a length of rope. With the water already waist deep on him, Bantu had to sit Dara on a barrel to keep her above it. He quickly tied the rope to his spear and got under the opening. He pulled his arm back and heaved, pain wracking his body from the motion and taking the force from the throw. The spear landed on the next level up; he pulled it back. It fell back into the water. Now the rope was soaked through, slick, and hot.

Dara didn't know what he was doing. "Bantu, if you throw the spear up to the next level, it'll just fall back. It has nothing to hook on to."

Bantu ignored her. He braced himself for the pain he knew would come and hurled the spear up again. It passed the level above them, then the level above that, and embedded in the stone ceiling. Bantu checked the sturdiness of line before picking Dara off the barrel.

"Grab hold of my neck," he told her as he pulled her to his chest.

"Wouldn't it be easier for you if I climbed on your back?" Dara asked.

"No," Bantu replied flatly, the burns on his back still stinging.

He looped the rope around his hand and then pulled himself up. Slickness made the climb difficult, but Bantu was not climbing to save himself. He was climbing to save Dara. Soon his body cleared the water, and they approached the level above. They felt a slight jerk as the spear slipped a little from its holding, so Bantu tried to smooth out his ascent so as not to dislodge the spear.

Getting to the top level was impossible. The floor had collapsed for a good distance in each direction. If he could swing a little, however, he could reach the level onto which Genjuro had fallen.

The spear slipped a little farther, and Bantu was also finding it hard to maintain his grip. Each time he reached up and pulled, he slid back half the distance. He was weakening; he was tiring. The heat was making him go light-headed. He knew then he wasn't going to make it. The next floor stayed just out of reach.

"Dara," he groaned through the effort to hold on. "You need to climb up."

"I ... I can't."

"You must. I cannot support us both much longer. It is not far. If you stand on my shoulders you can reach the ledge."

Tears welled up in Dara's eyes.

"I'm scared."

"As am I, but I need you to be brave for both of us. Please."

Dara released her tight grip on Bantu's neck and climbed his body. The route to his shoulders was easy enough. Then she gripped the rope and tried to pull herself up. Feeling the rope's slickness, she realized the effort Bantu was making to just hold on.

"Quickly, Dara," Bantu urged. "I will be right behind you."

Dara began to climb, slipping back a bit just like Bantu had, but making progress. The spear jerked out some more. She didn't have much time. Neither of them did. Bantu began to swing, taking them closer to the ledge so that Dara could jump to it. She lifted herself up the rope a little higher, checking the spear above them. The swinging would pull it out, she knew, but could she reach the ledge before then? The spear slipped a little more, and Dara, not wanting to take any more chances, leaped for the ledge. Bantu watched her disappear onto the floor above them. He smiled, and then his strength gave out. He lost his grip on the rope and fell back, slamming onto a floating table below. His scream made Dara shake and close her eyes. After it was over, he made no sound.

"Bantu!" Dara called down. "Bantu!"

Bantu heard her voice, but it was fading into the distance. He looked up and saw the light of the bulb above him, but darkness closed around his vision as he lost consciousness.

* * *

"What was that?" asked Maya as she jerked her arrow toward a side passage.

"What was what?" Alex asked back.

"There was something there, a shadow. It was looking at us," Maya replied.

Alex strained to see farther into the darkness than the arrow's light would allow. The tunnel was empty.

"There's nothing there," he stated.

"I know what I saw!" Maya insisted.

"I'm not doubting you," Alex told her, "but there's nothing there now. Whatever it was must've run off."

Alex really hoped it ran off. If creatures lurked in these tunnels, then he hoped they were afraid of him and Maya. Otherwise, they could be in big trouble. He had felt as if they were being watched for a while now, but he had chalked it up to nerves. Now he knew he was right. Something was shadowing them, but for what reason, he couldn't tell yet.

"What do your books say about this situation?" Maya asked.

"Typically, we're okay as long as we're together. It's when you're alone that the monster or the killer gets you."

"Killer?"

"There are dozens of movies about killers taking out several victims one at a time."

"Why in Zeus's name would anyone want to watch that?"

"Some people like to get scared. It gives them a thrill."

"Are you one of those people?"

"Yeah, actually."

"So, you must really be enjoying this."

"It's a lot different when you can't just get up and walk away from it or close your eyes during the scary parts. Believe me, if this were a movie, my eyes would be shut about now."

Alex glanced back. The shadow was right behind him. He screamed and backed away. Maya turned quickly and aimed. She saw it scampering away from her light. The arrow shot through the darkness and pinned the shadow to the wall, but then its flame went out, leaving them in total darkness.

Maya immediately nocked another arrow, and its fire lit up the area. Her first arrow remained stuck in the wall a moment longer before it faded from sight. There was no sign of the shadow, however, and no sign of blood or any fluid that a wounded creature might leave.

"I hit it," Maya insisted.

"I know you did," Alex agreed.

They saw it again on their left, but it disappeared when they turned toward it. Then it was on their right.

"It can't be that fast," Alex muttered.

"It's not," Maya realized. "There is more than one."

They backed away slowly, picked a new tunnel, and moved down it, picking up their pace as they went.

"You watch front. I'll watch back." Alex suggested. A hallway opened to their left, but shadows moved within it. They kept moving on. Then shadows appeared in front of them, so they took a passage to the right.

"There're a lot of them," Alex thought aloud. "Maybe they hadn't attacked us before because they were waiting for reinforcements."

"That's reassuring," Maya commented.

"Sorry," Alex apologized.

"This way," Maya said, jogging down another turn.

They kept moving, picking up the pace. The shadows had fallen back. At least, the pair hoped they had. With every new turn, though, they became more lost. Every tunnel looked similar, and Alex was sure that they had looped at least once. They finally came to a carved hole in the floor with a ladder leading down. A white line led away from it down a tunnel they hadn't tried yet. Someone or something had scraped the stone.

"It could be a trail left by the others," Maya suggested. "They may have gotten up here."

It made sense to Alex. "So we follow it and see where it leads?" Alex asked, glancing around to see if the shadows had caught up with them.

Maya nodded. As they continued up the tunnel, Alex pulled out the book to check on the others. What he saw stopped him in his tracks. Both Genjuro's and Bantu's pages had gone blank.

"What is it?" Maya asked, seeing his expression.

Alex stared at the empty chapters in the wavering light of Maya's arrow torch.

Two more gone, he thought. *Two more friends lost ... because of me*. The strength left his legs, and he dropped to his knees.

"I can't do this anymore," he whispered, and then he yelled it. "I can't do this anymore!"

As if their roles had suddenly been reversed, Maya knelt and took hold of Alex's shoulders although her approach was not as gentle as his.

"Alex!" she snapped. "You can't give up on me now!"

"I didn't want this," Alex sobbed. "I swear I didn't. I just wanted a little adventure, a little fun. The good guys are supposed to beat the bad guys. It's supposed to be hard, yeah, but that's what makes it satisfying." His voice lifted to roar. "But we're not supposed to all die!"

"Alex!" Maya said, forcefully. "Alex, don't do this. We can get through this."

"Can we?" Alex asked her, his look disbelieving. "Dax was right. Everything was great the way it was. I just didn't see it. I wanted more. Well, I got more, didn't I? I got the quest of a lifetime, and it's already claimed three lives. Look."

He pointed at the line on the floor. "Genjuro must've made this trail, but now he's gone. Bantu was with Dara and he's gone, too."

"Think about that, Alex," Maya urged. "That means Dara is alone, and she needs your help. Alex, Dara needs your help!"

"We don't even know where she is!" Alex yelled at her. "This place is a maze! Senufer said so! Oh yeah, let's add him to the list of casualties on Alex's little fun-filled epic. And what about Asuro's crew and the people in East Port? People are dying everywhere we go, and I can't do a damn thing to help them!

"Why did Dara have to bring me here? Talk about the worst mix-up in history! I've got to be the biggest disappointment in her life. Protector of the princess, ha! I can't protect anyone—least of all myself. She'd almost be better off if I died. What good have I done? I've been useless in every battle so far!"

"But you gave us the means to find the Axemen, to defeat the sea slug, to destroy the dragon!" Maya argued. "You may not be a fighter, but without you, the rest of us would have been lost or dead a long time ago. You've gotten us this far!"

"I've gotten half of us dead!" Alex shot back.

"And could you deal with Dara's death as well?" Maya asked harshly.

Alex looked right at her.

"It's a good bet Bantu died protecting her," she continued. "Do you want his death to be for nothing?"

"But I don't know what to do!" Alex complained, tears streaming down his face.

"I thought you could sense Dara's location when you focused!" Maya reminded him. "Why don't you just sense where she is?"

Alex suddenly felt a fool. He'd been trying to look for Dara normally because he knew she was close, but the ability would work just as well here as it did on the ocean. He fell into himself and felt for her. His head turned immediately. "She's behind us! We passed her!"

"Then let's go back and get her!" Maya told him. She picked up the book, glancing at Bantu's pages before closing it. What she saw made her stop.

"Alex, these pages aren't blank."

Alex's head snapped around at her. "What?"

"The writing has faded," Maya said, showing him the book. "It's barely legible, but it's still there."

Alex grabbed the book and flipped through. Maya was right. He couldn't see it before, but with Maya's arrow right by the book, the text was visible, albeit barely. Bantu's story was still there. He flipped to Genjuro, and the same held true. He and Maya exchanged a smile. Then he turned to Tenzin's chapter, but those pages were indeed blank. They both cursed at the confirmation.

"What does it mean, though?" Maya asked, putting Tenzin's fate out of her mind again. "Why is their text so light?"

"They're dying," Alex concluded. "That's what the book is telling us. We have to find them before the words fade completely." He left off the part that they were both thinking—like Tenzin.

That's when they heard Dara scream. It came from the hole they had just passed. They turned and ran full out. Maya lowered her bow, relaxing her grip on the arrow to gain some speed. Its flame went out. She heard Alex tumble to the ground ahead of her.

"Maya!" he yelled.

"Sorry," she apologized and lit the arrow again.

Rushing down the ladder, they saw that the white line resumed below. *We followed it the wrong way*, Alex thought as he sent Maya before him.

They found Dara backed against a wall with several skeletons between them and her. Maya released an arrow immediately, which struck the bony figure closest to Dara. The skeleton fell apart. She readied another shot, but Alex grabbed her arm.

"Wait," Alex urged, taking in the scene. "They're not alive. They're just lying there."

He rushed over to Dara and held her. She shook with fear.

"Dara," Alex said softly, "are you okay?"

She looked up at him, her eyes full of tears. She was in shock.

"Where are Genjuro and Bantu?" Alex asked.

"Bantu!" Dara yelled, coming to her senses. She grabbed Alex's arm and pulled him farther along the tunnel.

They came to the ledge where she pointed over the edge, holding the light bulb out. When Alex stuck his head over, the rising steam hit him in the face. He squinted but saw the African warrior below, floating on the water—his upper body supported by a wooden table.

"I was going to try to find help when I saw the skeletons," Dara told Alex, but he wasn't listening. He was looking at the rope hanging from the ceiling above. He reached out and grabbed it and was about to lower himself when Dara stopped him.

"The spear is slipping out," she warned.

Alex nodded. "We'll have to find another rope."

Maya walked up beside him, grabbed the rope, and yanked hard and fast. The spear popped out of the ceiling.

"Or you could use this one," she said, handing the rope back to him.

Alex quickly pulled as much of the rope up as he could. The heat made them all sweat. Alex didn't want to think about how bad it was for Bantu. He hoped that the sweltering heat in the jungles of Africa had hardened the warrior to the temperature in the room below.

"Dara," Alex said, making a loop at the end of the rope. "We're going to lower you down. Loop this around Bantu, under his arms like this." Alex put the rope around himself to show her. Then he looked down again, judging the distance, and made another loop farther up the rope. This one he put around Dara.

Maya paid more attention to the tunnel they had come down than to Alex. She had her bow out, ready.

"What are you looking at?" Dara asked.

"If we're lucky," Maya told her, "nothing."

They bunched up the rope, put it in Dara's arms, and then lowered her down. It was no easy task for her to move the African's huge body around enough to get the rope on him, but she managed it. When she was ready, Alex pulled Dara back up. He helped her out of the rope and then knelt close to her.

"Dara, I want you to watch the back hall carefully while we pull up Bantu. Let us know if you see any movement, even shadows—especially shadows."

Dara's lower lip began to quiver. "Alex, you're scaring me."

"It should be okay," he said, not knowing if he was hoping or lying. "We just want to be careful."

Then Maya and Alex strained to pull up Bantu's limp body.

"My god, he's heavy!" Alex complained. "He couldn't be—"

"Don't say a word!" Maya snapped. Even though Alex's bag was closed, she did not want to chance that his constant chatter might send them on another unexpected trip.

They hoisted their friend closer. The worst, for Alex, was when Bantu was up to the ledge and he had to brace himself in position while Maya let go to grab Bantu's body and pull it over. Alex thought the big teen's body would drag him over the edge, but in the end, they had him up. Maya checked his breathing. He was still alive. They dragged him past the skeletons to the ladder where the air was cooler. Both Alex and Maya kept glancing up the ladder, adding to Dara's uneasiness.

Alex slapped Bantu's face lightly. "Bantu, Bantu, come on, big guy."

Maya opened the book. She could barely make out the words on Bantu's pages.

Bantu's eyes fluttered. He looked up and saw Alex looking down at him. "Alex?"

Alex smiled. "Thought we'd lost you there, big guy. Welcome back."

The words on the page instantly became clear and solid even though Bantu was still very groggy.

"He's back!" Maya exclaimed. She held up the book for Alex to see. "Look!"

Alex smiled and nodded to her and then turned to Dara.

"Dara, do you have a water flask in your travel bag?" he asked.

"Yes," Dara replied.

Alex just stared at her when she stood there waiting for him to say something else. Finally, it clicked. "Oh!" she exclaimed and retrieved the flask.

Alex helped Bantu to sip the water.

"Didn't your mom tell you no more than ten minutes at a time in the hot tub?" he playfully scolded.

Maya huffed. "Must you joke about everything we go through?"

Alex smiled. "Yes, I must."

"Why?"

Alex became very serious then. "Because otherwise I would have given up a long time ago."

Maya dropped the subject and nodded in understanding.

After a few minutes, Bantu struggled to his feet.

"Easy, big guy," Alex told him. "Get your strength back. We may need it to help Genjuro."

"He is not with you?" Bantu asked.

"No, but we'll catch up to him soon enough." Alex assured him.

"How can you know that?" the African asked.

Alex pointed at the white line carved in the stone. "He left us a trail."

*   *   *

The dark things carried Genjuro to their lair where they lay him across a table and stripped his armour and clothes from him, leaving him naked and helpless. Then several of the creatures began secreting a black substance over him, which eventually coated his body. The unconscious samurai lay there looking much like a larger version of the creatures around him, and they smiled.

16

*I*nsisting he was strong enough to travel, Bantu led the group as they made their way up the ladder, following Genjuro's trail. It ended at a large hall, but Genjuro was not there. A quick look around confirmed that they had journeyed back to the main tunnel, but what then had happened to the samurai?

"Perhaps he continued ahead, knowing we'd be okay from this point," Bantu suggested.

"He should have waited," Alex thought aloud.

"Patience is not one of Genjuro's strengths," Bantu stated.

Alex knew he was right. Genjuro's speed was not restricted to his movements. He was quick to fight, quick to act. Standing in one place and waiting without knowing how long would drive him crazy.

Bantu looked down the tunnel, guessing that the samurai had gone off in that direction when something grabbed his attention. Alex noticed the big African's reaction and turned.

"What is it?" he asked.

"There," Bantu whispered as he pointed up the tunnel. Far ahead a pinprick of white light moved about. They could not tell its size or its source, but it flew around in a random pattern. Dara first thought it was a lightning bug, but those bugs lived in forests, not caves, unless someone had summoned it as she had. Her skin broke out in goose bumps when she considered the possibility that Askar waited up ahead with an army of his own lightning bugs, ready to pay her back for her attack.

They stood for a while, watching until the light shot to the right and disappeared, presumably down a tunnel. The other Defenders turned to Alex who shrugged before walking down the tunnel, seeing no other alternative. They had halved the distance to the source of the light when it reappeared; it had turned blue. This time when it flew out into the tunnel, it stopped and hovered, shifting slightly left and then right.

"It's watching us," Bantu noted.

"What do we do?" asked Maya.

Alex moved up beside Bantu, staring at the light. He lifted a hand and waved. "Hi!" he said as cheerfully as he could.

The light shot off to the right again and disappeared. The Defenders looked at each other, wondering what it meant.

"I think you scared it," Maya guessed. "Maybe Dara should have said, 'Hello.'"

More movement up the tunnel caught their attention. The light had returned but not alone. A few dozen lights, each a different colour, moved about, neither approaching nor retreating.

"We're friends," Alex called out. "Senufer sent us to find you."

Several of the lights moved toward them quickly. Maya and Bantu raised their weapons instinctively.

"No," Alex warned. "Don't scare them."

"Don't scare *them?*" Maya asked.

The creatures stopped just in front of the team. This close, their forms were clear. They were pixies, but bigger than the ones Alex had seen or read about. Most pixies could easily be held in your palm, but these stood about knee-high. They still had the typical features—slim elfish bodies, butterfly-shaped transparent wings, and short wild hair. They wore tiny fur clothes over bodies that looked like they had been dipped in glitter dust. Both males and females fluttered about, every one of them beautiful. Each had a skin tone that matched the light it gave off, or perhaps the light they gave off tinted their skin. If they had been humans on Earth, they would, no doubt, be movie stars or models. Not one looked older than thirty.

"You know Senufer?" one asked in a voice that sounded surprisingly normal. Alex had expected a voice like someone on helium, but this creature's voice was like honey—sweet and smooth.

"Yes," Alex answered. "He is a good friend of ours. He said that you would guide us to the top of the mountain."

The pixies turned toward each other and began speaking in a fast, high-pitched tongue that sounded like a conversation being played at fast-forward. After a few seconds, they turned back.

"We cannot help you," the pixie said sadly.

"You do not know the way?" Bantu asked.

"We know it," the pixie replied, "but we cannot take it."

"Why is that?" Alex questioned.

"Things changed here several days ago," the pixie explained. "We do not know why, but the very air seemed to darken."

"The Hall," Alex muttered.

"The Hall of Shadows?" asked the pixie.

"It's come alive," Alex told them. "It darkened the realm and is spreading evil."

Again the high-pitched conversation went on. The pixie nodded.

"Yes, yes, that would explain much. They must be from the Hall."

"They?" Maya asked, cocking her head.

"The black slime beasts," the pixie said. "They arrived just after the darkness. They drove us from our own home. We have been trying to determine how to take it back, but they are too strong for us. The way to the top of the mountain is through our home."

"Black slime beasts," Alex thought. "Sounds nasty."

"Yes, yes, they are!" the pixie exclaimed. "They have already captured some of our clan. We think they mean to torture them, perhaps eat them."

Another pixie flew up and whispered something to the first pixie. He nodded and then asked, "You have another friend in armour?"

The Defenders perked up at that.

"Yes!" Alex exclaimed. "Have you seen him?"

"The slime creatures have captured him," it replied. The pixie glanced at the weapons in the teens' possession. "Perhaps with your help, we could free your friend and our people and drive the evil beasts from the mountain."

Maya nodded. "I could use a little evil to take my frustrations out on."

Alex figured that letting Maya work out her frustrations would be good for everyone.

"Show us the way."

The pixies chattered away again for a moment before replying. "We shall gather our clan, and together we will face the Hall's servants. Good shall prevail this day!"

The pixies let out a cheer. The Defenders found themselves caught up in the mood.

* * *

After clearing the mountain path of debris, the Shadow Warriors, Askar, and Scorpius continued unhindered for several more hours. As the sun rose, the wind started to pick up, and although he could not feel it, Scorpius could tell from the terrain that the temperature was dropping. The leafy plants gave way to evergreens. The air was drier, crisper. Less moss and lichen covered the rocks. They were making good time, but the journey ahead stretched so far up that Scorpius wondered if they would reach the top before the sun set yet again.

Eventually the path widened, and the men breathed a collective sigh that they did not have to travel so close to the cliff edge anymore. They marched on until a large cave came into view ahead of them; the entrance was big enough to fit the dragon they fought the night before. Strange tracks covered the ground around it made by another of the unusual creatures that inhabited this world, Scorpius guessed. Askar didn't even pause but marched right by the entrance. Scorpius did not.

"Where are you going?" he asked the general.

"Where do you think?" Askar spat back.

"What about this cave?" Scorpius challenged.

"What of it? The creatures of this mountain are not our concern."

Scorpius pointed inside the entrance at a pile of bones. "Whatever lives in there is carnivorous. I don't want to be caught on one of those small ledges when it comes out to hunt."

Murmurs erupted from the rest of the men. Now that the idea occurred to them, they didn't like it either.

"You don't know that it will hunt us," Askar argued.

"You don't know that it won't," Scorpius countered. "As a general, are you in the habit of leaving your rear flank exposed?"

Askar knew the game Scorpius was playing. If they went on, the men would be on edge and nervous about an attack from behind. If he gave in and checked the cave, then his leadership skills would be in question. The move was intelligent since there really was no right answer, but he wondered why the Roman was even bothering. He could not hope to steal Askar's leadership, and in a day, he would not even exist anymore. Perhaps he hoped to steal a small victory in the face of such a huge defeat.

"Fine," Askar said finally. "Go check it out. We'll be right here, waiting."

"Me?" Scorpius protested. "But I am the key to your victory on the mountaintop."

"Then you'd better not get yourself killed in there," Askar smiled.

The Roman pulled out his sword, put his shield up in front of him, and stalked into the cave.

"Defensive positions," Askar ordered. "Just in case."

The cave was even bigger inside than it seemed outside, with entrances into two more caves diagonally left and right. The bones of several different kinds of creatures lay strewn about the area. Besides humans, Scorpius recognized deer and horses and wondered how they got this far up the mountain.

"This thing is as big as a bulgor," he mumbled to himself. Then he spotted the skull of a bulgor. The hairs on the back of his neck stood straight up.

"Oh great," he cursed. "It's bigger."

Suddenly, this seemed like a stupid idea.

A warm breeze caught his attention. He turned toward it and spotted the creature asleep in the cave to the left, its hot breath hitting Scorpius where he stood. The Roman had never seen anything like it. It looked much like some kind of giant scorpion. Its low flat body loomed over twice Scorpius's height—and only that low because it wasn't on its feet. Two great pincers lay crossed over one another as it slept, each easily capable of crushing a man. Several smaller armoured legs supported its body, and a tail with a long straight stinger arced up in the back.

Attached to the tail, just behind the stinger, were two large bulbs. It took a moment to comprehend their purpose—a second set of eyes, currently closed while the creature slept. Despite that oddity, its head baffled Scorpius more than anything else. Instead of great jaws, it had a long curled snout like an aardvark. He wondered how it could possibly chew anything. Nevertheless the thing was big. Judging from the bones around him, it was lethal, too. Scorpius sighed and then walked in toward it.

*   *   *

The pixies' makeshift home was more about appearance than purpose. It looked to Alex like a dressing room for a fashion show. Little outfits of fur, silk, cloth, and even leaves hung everywhere. Many of the pixies flittered between clothes, examining them before picking something to wear. Several others were creating new outfits magically. The cloth seemed to weave from the very air. More primped themselves so that they'd look good enough, Alex guessed, to pick out more clothes. Still others engaged in intense conversations, but from their posturing, he guessed they discussed looks and style. Mirrors sat in every spare space, and it seemed that any pixie that passed close to one *had* to stop to admire itself briefly before moving along.

There were no defenses of any kind around the lair, nor were there guards or even alarms. The pixies seemed to be living a carefree life despite what the Defenders had been told about the danger posed by the slime creatures.

"It's no wonder they get attacked," Maya stated. "They're defenseless and distracted."

The others nodded.

All movement stopped when the pixies noticed the Defenders. The high-pitched chatter spread across the room, and several rushed for weapons. Before a fight could ensue, the pixies who had escorted them in informed the others of the plan. Many heads nodded. Many pixies looked over and smiled.

After a while, several of the small folk flew over to inspect their new allies. The expressions on their faces ranged from curiosity to disgust—the reason why was the last thing the group expected.

A male pixie hovered in front of Alex, looking him up and down.

"You're not wearing that to the battle, are you?" he asked although the answer he wanted was obvious.

"You're kidding, right?" Alex asked.

"This'll never do," he admonished. "We're not going into battle until you change into something more appropriate."

"You have armour for me?" Alex asked hopefully.

"Armour?" he huffed. "I did not make any mention of armour. This is a matter of style. Now change."

"This is all I have."

"Just as well," he said in a condescending tone. "Based on what you're wearing, I doubt anything else you have would be much better. We'll just have to make you something new."

A female approached Maya. "You walk around in public in this costume?"

Maya blushed momentarily, but quickly came to her senses.

"This is a practical warrior's dress. It allows for comfort and freedom of movement."

"And ridicule," the pixie added. "We'll have to redo it completely. Come along and I'll take your measurements."

"Are you people crazy?" Maya screamed. "The slime creatures are torturing your people! They have our friend as well! We have to go rescue them now!"

"We will not do battle unprepared," another one argued. "It will take sometime to organize squadrons by colours."

Maya started to shake with anger.

"By colours?"

Alex pulled her aside. "Maya, calm down. They have a point."

Maya's eyes went wide.

"They have a … have you lost your mind, too? Alex, this is no time for your foolish jokes."

Alex took her hands in his and looked into her eyes.

"We can't just go charging in there. We have to check the slime creatures' defenses, figure out the best way to attack. I think you and Bantu should take a couple pixies and scout their lair. Then we can come up with a practical assault strategy. That should also give the fashion police, here, time to get their act together."

Maya nodded and took a few calming breaths.

"You're right, Alex. It's just that they—"

"Oh, I know," Alex replied. "They're nuts. You be careful. Hurry back."

Maya grabbed Bantu and then left with one of the pixies who had escorted them in. Alex turned to the pixie hovering in front of him, who now held a tape measure.

"How long will it take to make these outfits?" Alex asked.

"With all of us working, less than an hour."

"We're a team called the Defenders. Can you make matching uniforms?"

The pixie's face lit up.

"Uniforms? Yes, similar in look, but styled to each person's character. I can see it now! You will need an emblem, though—something powerful, regal."

"A silver scroll with golden rollers," Alex suggested. Dara started to open her bag, but Alex stopped her, shaking his head.

The pixies rushed off to begin their work.

"I was just going to show them the Scroll, so they could make the emblems look the same," Dara said.

"I know," Alex replied, "but keep it in your bag."

"Why don't you want them to see the Scroll?" Dara asked.

"They may be Senufer's friends, but they're not all there," Alex replied, pointing to his head.

"Senufer warned me that they were not what I'd expect. I just thought he meant in appearance, not mental state. At least, we'll be getting new clothes." He looked down at his dirty, torn clothes.

"I feel like Cinderella with her animal friends making her dress."

"Who?"

"I'll tell you the story sometime. I think you'll like it," he winked.

*   *   *

From around the corner of an intersection that led to the slime creatures' lair, Maya poked her bow out and took aim. Using the bow's magic, she zoomed in on the scene and scanned the area. The main cave was furnished more for purpose than appearance. Lit by a dozen small lanterns, the space contained beds, tables, and chairs with obvious divisions for sleeping, eating, and gathering. One section had been cleared out, and several cages filled it. Most were empty, but some contained pixies who banged at the bars, screaming to be released.

The slime creatures were not quite what Maya had pictured. While they seemed to be made of a shiny black sludge, they did not leak any of the substance as they moved. They seemed—clean. They looked like people who had been dipped in black oil, except they stood about the same height as the pixies. Their hands looked like mittens until they spread their fingers, and even then, they seemed webbed. She could not make out muscles or joints on their bodies, and it was sometimes hard to tell male from female. None had anything that resembled hair. They all seemed bald under the coating. Their eyes, pools of white on black, showed great intelligence. They had no noses that she could see, and their mouths, which were only discernible when they spoke, opened twice the distance you'd expect.

On a table near the cages lay the largest slime creature Maya could see. It was human sized, but seemed either dead or asleep. On the ground beside it sat a suit of armour—samurai armour.

Maya gasped.

"That's Genjuro! What are those creatures doing to him?"

She knew now that they had to act quickly. She would not let another Defender be lost this day. She whispered the news back to Bantu, who nodded, and then she took note of the defenses.

Guards watched the entrances, holding nets and bolas. The nonlethal weapons confirmed the pixies' story that the slime creatures intended to capture and torture them. Maya growled softly at the thought.

Continuing her scan, she marked each of the entrances in her mind. She had been told that three ways led into the compound from the tunnels they now occupied. A fourth, which she could see at the back of the lair, led deeper into the mountain. It had to be the one that would take them to the top.

Maya considered their options. A distraction at one entrance could open the creatures up to an attack from the other two. Their numbers roughly equaled the pixies, which probably explained why the pixies hadn't been able to retake their home. Maya wondered if the pixies had even tried to retake their home. The Defenders would ensure their victory though.

"How does it look?" Bantu whispered.

"I believe we can defeat them," Maya replied confidently. "A diversionary attack to draw guards away from the other entrances and then the main assault through those entrances."

She pulled back around the corner; then she, Bantu, and the pixie turned to head back to the assault party. Without warning, a bola wrapped around her

arms and waist. Another tangled up her ankles. Yanked back suddenly, she fell down in a heap, only to be dragged back across the main hall to the other side passage. Bantu turned when she called out and ran after her as her body slid toward the darkened tunnel. The pixie flew off, saving itself.

Bantu got only a few steps when a bola shot out and wrapped around his feet. He tumbled, smashing his chin on the floor before watching Maya fade into the blackness. Only her screams told Bantu that she was still there. Reaching down, he tried to untie the tangle of cord in the bola, but—finding that impossible—he simply pulled until the cord snapped. Just after he freed himself, another bola wrapped around his wrist as he retrieved his spear. It secured the weapon to his arm. Out of the dark came two more bolas, which he managed to block with his spear arm, tangling it up all the more. He realized that if he didn't move quickly, he would be captured just like Maya, whose voice was suddenly muffled in the darkness.

Bantu picked himself up and ran down the hall, dodging another bola as he went. The others had to be alerted and informed that they had just lost the advantage of surprise.

17

Scorpius ran out of the cave at top speed. The angry creature chased right after him, its roar akin to fingernails on a chalkboard. Many of the Shadow Warriors covered their ears.

"I found it!" he yelled, diving to the side as it came charging after him.

The creature's tail whipped about, eyes blinking as it saw all the men, all the food, before it. As quick as an arrow, the tail shot into a Shadow Warrior. He screamed and then fell down badly injured, but not dead. Eventually, he stopped moving—only able to breathe and look around.

Paralysis, Scorpius thought. He swung his gladius at the thing's hind leg, but it bounced off the armour.

Askar jumped into the fray, smashing down on one of the creature's claws with his mace. A large crack appeared on it before it hit Askar back, sending him flying almost over the cliff edge. The general picked himself up. He was angry now.

The creature turned suddenly, forcing the warriors to run and jump out of its way. Some didn't make it and were knocked over. One had his leg crushed under it. The creature positioned itself before the paralyzed man, and its snout extended. A thick acid poured over the man, dissolving him. The snout then sucked up the acid and what should have been the melted man, but he had already turned into shadowy smoke. The lack of food only enraged the creature, and Scorpius knew that he was the only one that it even *might* be able to dine on. Luckily, it didn't know that.

Rushing back into the fight, Scorpius used his shield to push the inside joint of the thing's back leg, much like pushing the back of someone's knee. The creature's leg gave out, and it momentarily lost its balance and spun closer to the cliff's edge. The tail sought out the cause of the problem and hovered above Scorpius for a moment as he backed away. The world slowed down. Scorpius watched the thing's eyes for a sign of striking. When he saw it, he let things speed up again and dived away just in time. The Shadow Warrior behind him was not so fortunate. The point, meant for Scorpius's shoulder, pierced his chest, and he vanished in a dark puff.

Askar attacked its claw again, this time with multiple strikes. The shell on the top of the claw fell apart, and the ear-piercing screech sounded again. Its other claw grabbed a Shadow Warrior and hurled him at Askar. Askar dodged the living missile, who flew off the edge of the cliff.

"Attack that leg like I did," Scorpius ordered a Shadow Warrior. "With me!"

The man rushed into position, and then he and Scorpius struck simultaneously. The creature collapsed on one side. Scorpius shoved his sword into its rear, which had dipped low enough to reach. It skittered away from the pain, crushing the warrior who had helped Scorpius, before slipping off the edge of the cliff.

The men relaxed, a couple of them going to the edge to watch it fall. To their surprise, a pincer reached up and grabbed one, crushing the life from him while the tail impaled the other. Both vanished into smoke. The creature could climb walls like an insect.

That explains how those animals got up here, Scorpius thought.

"Askar!" he yelled. "Throw your mace! Knock it off!"

As the beast lifted itself back up, Askar let fly with his weapon, striking it near its head. The force threw the creature back; several of its sticky feet detaching from the steep slope until its weight ripped its remaining feet free. It tumbled down the mountainside to its death, its shriek fading in the distance.

*   *   *

"Captured?" Alex exclaimed. "How?"

"A scouting party in the tunnels, I believe," said Bantu as he worked the bindings off his arm. "They took us by surprise. She is likely being tortured for information right now. They will want to know who she is with. I doubt she will give them any information while she lives."

"We need to move quickly then," Alex said.

"I will lead the diversionary attack," Bantu offered. "They know I am out here and will be expecting me. You can come in with the rest of the pixies from the other two tunnels."

"I need a weapon," Alex said.

"Will your bag not provide you with one?" asked Bantu.

Alex reached in and pulled out a piece of parchment, recognizing it immediately as the one he had written the invisibility spell on.

"Dara," he asked, "you can remember how to cast this spell, right?"

"I think so," she replied.

"Okay, make us invisible. I'll free Maya and the other prisoners during the attack. You stay out of the way."

"But I—" she tried to argue.

"*Stay out of the way*," Alex stressed.

"Yes, Alex."

Dara read from the parchment and cast the spell, but when she finished, the parchment disappeared. Alex assumed it returned to the bag. He hoped that it would return when they needed it, or Dara would be on her own for that spell from now on.

"You didn't put on your uniforms!" a pixie complained.

"I'm invisible," Alex replied. "What difference does it make?"

"But—"

"Later," Alex insisted. The pixie huffed and began to turn away when she saw the pile of uniforms nearby rise and disappear into Alex's bag.

"You did great work on those," he complimented the pixie, trying to get back on her good side. "I've never seen such beautiful uniforms. Did you make the extras I asked for?" he checked.

The pixie nodded proudly.

*   *   *

There were no cages big enough to hold Maya, so the slime monsters set up a crossbeam in the ceiling, threw a rope over it, and hoisted her up in one of their nets. She looked at the nearby caged pixies who screamed at their captors. She thought that pixies must hate captivity because these ones threw themselves at the bars and yelled curses almost insanely. Then she saw Genjuro, lying deathly still on the table, covered in slime.

One of the slime creatures came up to her, staring curiously.

"You are human," it stated.

"Obviously," Maya answered flatly.

"And you are allied with the pixies?"

"I am here to free them. I will see that every one of you dies. I will kill you all myself if I have to."

"We are going to attempt to turn them to our way of thinking," it told her. "I doubt the same can be done with you."

"I would rather die," Maya swore.

"Where is your large friend?"

Maya did not answer.

"Is he with the pixies?"

Maya did not answer.

"Are there any more of you?"

"Hundreds," Maya smiled.

"You lie poorly," the creature replied.

Maya gestured toward Genjuro. "What are you doing to him?"

"We are making him ... better."

"Hera!" she cursed. "You're turning him into one of you, aren't you?" She tried to grab it through the net. "If I get my hands on you, you'll regret ever meeting me!" she yelled.

"I already do," the slime monster replied. "You are so much like them," it said, indicating the pixies in the cages who continued screaming and banging away. "It is no wonder you are allied with them."

* * *

The wind had grown so powerful that the men had to hunch against it. The farther up they climbed, the harder the journey became. Snow and ice covered the path and pelted the men whenever the wind gusted. Above them, tonnes of it clung to the sides of the mountain, waiting for the chance to tumble to the earth far below. Scorpius was glad to have the spell of warmth on him, as were the rest of the men. He didn't want to think about what would happen to them if the spell ran out before they could get back down to a warmer climate.

Askar's mood was fouler than the weather. He had lost six men in the skirmish, and a seventh had his leg crushed. Rather than be slowed down by him, Askar dispatched the man himself so that they could carry on at an effective pace. Still, this weather was slowing them too much. Unless something delayed the Defenders inside in the mountain, the Shadow Warriors would be too late to stop them from getting to the second peak.

Scorpius moved up beside him then.

"We need to find shelter," he yelled over the wind.

"No," Askar roared back. "We will proceed as planned."

"Not if we're all dead!"

"The Shadow Lord will kill us if we fail."

"I don't have to kill Alex on the mountain." Scorpius argued. "I can do it the next time he summons me."

Askar grabbed him by the neck. "You will do as you're told, or I will kill you now, and there will be no more summonings!"

"Are you such a lapdog to the Shadow Lord that you won't even obey common sense?" Scorpius choked out.

Askar threw him to the ground and then pulled out his mace. Electricity crackled in the air.

Scorpius looked up at him and smiled.

"Are you going to cry ... Oscar?"

Askar raised the mace high and smashed it down at Scorpius. The Roman brought up his shield. The metal spikes of the mace rang the shield like a hammer hitting a bell. The sound reverberated across the mountain. Everyone stopped. The low chime died out, and for brief a moment, they could only hear the wind. Then the rumbling started. They all looked up to see the avalanche coming at them. Every man dived for the wall and braced himself against it. Scorpius pushed Askar behind him and held his shield up to protect them both. The magic of the shield helped Scorpius to deflect the snow so that it pushed them into the wall instead of pulling them away. Several Shadow Warriors, not so lucky, were swept away in the torrent of snow.

After it ended, the only sound was the howl of the wind. Only eleven men remained, including Askar and Scorpius. Scorpius pushed himself away from Askar and stepped across the waist deep snow.

"I guess you owe me one now," the Roman smirked.

Askar wanted to kill him. He felt within his rights to do so, but deep down, a part of him—the part that was Senufer—knew that the boy was right. He stayed his hand, turned up the path, and trudged forward through the snow.

* * *

The spear shot down the hall with such force that the slime monster it hit flew back, right into the lair and past many startled creatures, until it hit a wall. The monster's body slid down the spear until the weapon popped out of its shoulder, making Bantu realize that the creatures didn't just look like slime but that they were made of slime. He called his spear back as he and the blue uniformed pixies charged in. Bantu hoped that if he struck the slime monsters hard enough, it might spread their bodies across the cave and hurt them. Otherwise, he would be ineffective in the coming battle.

Inside the lair, Maya smiled when she heard the attack beginning. She whispered to the captured pixies, "Don't worry. You'll be free soon."

"Sooner than you think," a voice said, making Maya jump.

"Alex?" she asked, looking around for him.

"Yeah, I'm here to rescue you. I just wish I knew how."

Maya huffed. "In all seriousness, Alex, just how hard is it to obtain a knife?"

"Sorry, I'm new to this life-in-danger-every-minute thing. Wait. Knot," he said, finding the rope that held the net up. A moment later, its knot came undone, unceremoniously dropping Maya to the floor with a thud.

"Ow!"

"Sorry," Alex said, wincing at the sight of the impact. "Get your bow," he told her. "I'll free the pixies."

Just as they had hoped, the guards at the other two entrances rushed over to repel the invaders. That's when the rest of the red uniformed pixies took them by surprise, charging in with exquisitely forged tiny swords. They sliced at the slime creatures, and while they caused no physical damage, their weapons made the creatures cry out in pain and retreat.

Bantu was in the fight as well, stabbing into some creatures to no effect. He swatted some others who went flying into a wall, but they oozed down it and then got back up. Maya, now armed, cursed as her arrows stuck in the creatures until they plucked them out, at which point the arrows vanished. Despite the Defenders' ineffectiveness, by keeping many of the creatures busy, they managed to tilt the odds of the fight. The pixies rallied with cries of joy and pressed their advantage.

The noise of the battle caused Genjuro to stir. His black figure sat up and looked around the room, taking in the battle before reaching for his katana. Seeing him, Alex thought they had just lost their advantage. Then the dark samurai rushed into the fight, cutting at the slime creatures to support his friends. Unfortunately, his blade had no better effect than the others' weapons.

Alex, meanwhile, was having other problems. The pixies in the cages had gone into such a frenzy when their friends had arrived that Alex was genuinely afraid to open the doors. *Did they just get rabies?* he thought.

"Get them!" they screamed at their kin.

"Kill them! Make them hurt!"

"Make them hurt ..." Alex whispered. Something clicked in his mind, and he looked at the battle again. The slime creatures were using nonlethal defensive weapons. The pixies were acting psychotic. The slime creatures were protecting the smaller ones. Smaller ones? There were children here!

"They're not at all what you'd expect. So don't stare," Alex whispered, remembering Senufer's words. "Oh my god. We're fighting on the wrong side."

"Ice," Maya said nearby and nocked an arrow. It flew into a slime creature and froze him where he stood. "Now, we're getting somewhere. Genjuro! Shatter that one!" she yelled as she started freezing more of them.

Alex was closer to the creature, but Genjuro was faster. Alex screamed "No!" as he moved to protect it, forgetting that he was invisible, and sliding to his knees in front of the small creature. Genjuro swung. The samurai's face showed surprise when his blade stopped just short of the slime monster. Surprise became horror when blood started seeping from the air around the blade, and he realized what had happened.

"Alex-san! Why?" he asked.

Alex made a halfhearted attempt to hit Genjuro, making himself visible again. Then he held his stomach and tried to stop from bleeding to death.

"Dark Knight," he grunted as he pushed through the pain. He looked up at Genjuro, grimacing. "The pixies aren't Senufer's friends," he told the samurai. "The slime creatures are."

The Defenders then looked at the battle through new eyes and saw that Alex was right. Genjuro moved to help Alex, but Alex stopped him.

"No, help them," he urged. "We messed this up. We have to fix it."

They changed targets, Maya shooting a pixie that threatened a slime baby. It turned to shadowy smoke, confirming Alex's claim.

"They are Shadowlings!" Maya exclaimed.

Bantu threw his spear, skewering two more. Genjuro cut down another four. At that point, the pixies realized the ruse had ended, and many of them tried to flee. But one pixie girl had other plans. She weaved her way in close to the slime creatures, so close that they couldn't throw their weapons at her, as she looked for a specific target. Then, suddenly, she dived into one of the female creatures. Just as they had seen with Senufer and Askar, the Defenders saw the battle being waged.

In the end, the pixie form won out, but its skin retained the shiny black luster of the slime creatures. Her wings became a transparent smoky black. She looked sinister and yet more beautiful than before. Laughing, she zipped out of the room after the others, her small blade slicing Bantu's left forearm as she went.

Bantu yelped and grabbed his arm. The blade left no mark, but it felt as though some unseen knife continued to cut him. The Defenders followed, slicing and shooting. The pixies' glowing bodies turned to smoke—one, two, even three at a time. Fueled by anger at having been tricked, the teens plowed into them and chased them partway into the tunnels, turning several dozen to smoke. Only when the last of the lights disappeared into the darkness did they remember Alex.

They rushed back in to find him lying on the ground, his shirt pulled up, his stomach covered in black slime. They took defensive stances again, not knowing what was going on. Alex read their expressions.

"It's okay," he assured. "It's like a bandage."

"Our slime has healing properties," one creature told them.

Maya's face turned red.

"You weren't trying to change Genjuro. You were healing him. Why didn't you say so?"

"I did," replied another slime creature, and Maya realized it was the one she had yelled at. "I told you we were making him better. He was near death. It took much slime to heal him. Our scouts found him in the tunnels. They watched over him, hoping he would reunite with you before he became too weak. They also tried to herd all of you to the same place."

"Those shadows," Maya realized. "That was you." Her face scrunched in thought. "But you were bigger."

The creature stretched his body out to human size, getting much thinner in the process. He looked like a black paper cutout.

"A trick. One that requires much effort to maintain."

"Why didn't they just say 'hello' or something?" Alex asked.

"They did not know if you were friend or foe yet. But then your friend entered the pixies' domain, and they had to capture him for his own good. The pixies typically kill strangers in their territory. You are lucky that they found another use for you."

"They didn't seem that tough," Maya noted.

"They were outnumbered and caught off guard when you turned on them," the slime creature told her. "Their weapons cause intense pain. If you are hit too many times, the pain will kill you."

Bantu rubbed his arm, the pain still present but fading. He did not doubt the creature's words.

"At first, we thought the pixies had tricked you into their service," the creature continued, "but after capturing the girl, we thought you and the pixies were kindred spirits. It seems our first assumption was the correct one."

Maya couldn't have been any redder if they painted her.

"I'm, um, I'm sorry for the way I acted," she apologized and then added, "and I'm sorry for saying, 'I will see that every one of you dies' as well."

"You didn't, did you?" Alex moaned.

"I thought they were evil!" Maya explained.

Alex put his hand to his face and shook his head.

Genjuro walked up in front of Alex.

"Alex-san, I must apologize for my actions. It is my duty to protect. Instead, I almost killed you." He dropped to his knees and, to Alex's surprise, pulled out his short sword, his wakizashi. "The fault is mine. I shall redeem my honour."

"Oh, dear god, no," Alex moaned in annoyance, not fear. He was still too weak to do anything. "Bantu stop him!"

As Genjuro raised his sword, Bantu grabbed him from behind.

"No, I must!" Genjuro yelled.

"Why is he trying to kill you?" Bantu asked.

"He's not," Alex answered. "Samurai custom states that if you screw up big time, then you have to take your own life to redeem your honour."

"What kind of stupid logic is that?" Maya said, exasperated.

"Honour is everything to a samurai," Alex explained, then sat up, and locked eyes with the struggling teen. "It was my fault, not yours. There is no loss of honour here."

Genjuro stopped moving. Alex had his attention.

"Now listen to me. You are not in Japan, and the rules are different here. If you want us to succeed, you need to change your way of thinking. If you ever do screw up, you don't get to kill yourself to get out of it. You have to make up for it in deeds. If you die with honour by your own hand, we're still a man short and that much weaker." He wanted to add, "We've already lost Tenzin," but didn't think that would be a wise move just yet.

"Do we understand each other?" Alex asked.

Genjuro nodded. "I apologize if my actions seemed ... unreasonable to you. I do not know your ways. I vow to make up for my errors."

Bantu hesitantly released the samurai.

"I told you," Alex insisted. "No errors have been made. We were all fooled by the pixies."

"They are hateful and vain," the slime creature said. "Their vanity consumes them. They must appear perfect at all times. Their magic lets them create clothes, dyes, and items to augment their appearance. It is what they live for. Their fear now is age. That is why they need us.

"Need you?" asked Alex.

"Our slime can not only heal but maintain youth. They mean to take us one at a time until every one of them has merged with one of us. It will be more difficult for them now that the balance has changed."

"You should press your advantage," Maya suggested. "Hunt them down and eliminate them."

The slime creature shook its head.

"We are pacifists. We will defend ourselves and protect others, but we will not kill and we will never attack first."

"They attacked you first!" Maya pointed out.

"And that attack is done," the slime creature stated. "Violence begets violence. We hope to teach them to be good eventually."

"They are from the Hall," Genjuro said grimly. "They are pure evil."

"For many, evil is taught," the slime creature replied. "As is good." He looked at Maya. "As is control. Now we have a new challenge. Salaine has joined them."

"The creature ... er ... girl who was," Alex said, searching for the right word, "possessed?"

"Yes, we must hope she can be recaptured and reeducated. We must hope she finds the strength to overcome the evil within her."

"I say we hunt the little buggers down for them," Maya suggested.

"We don't have time," Alex reminded her. He opened the book and checked to make sure Scorpius's pages still contained text.

"We have to get to the second peak. Once we've regrouped, so to speak, we can come back and help the slime ... er ... what do you call yourselves?"

"We are Emils."

"We can help the Emils find Salaine and finish off those pixies."

"No," the Emil insisted. "We will not seek out violence, and we urge you not to seek it in our name. It goes against all that we believe in."

Alex nodded.

"We still need to get to the peak, though. Can you please show us the way?"

The Emil nodded but added, "But the temperature up there will be too cold for you. You will die in minutes."

"Dara?" Alex called out.

"I'm here," said Dara's voice as she moved into the room. "I saw the pixies fleeing. I thought you lost."

"No, we won, once we switched sides. Can you kick Bantu in the shin or something, so I can see you?"

"Ow!" Bantu yelped as Dara appeared.

"He told me to!" Dara said.

"Then kick *him* next time!" Bantu said, rubbing his shin.

Alex chuckled and it hurt. His stomach hadn't healed yet. "Give your dad a call. Tell him we need a spell to keep us warm. Oh and by the way," he said turning to the slime creatures, "anybody got a knife?"

* * *

The Hall and the Shadow Lord looked at the image of Mornak's cell on the wall. The old man held up well against the shadows that taunted him in his cell. It did not matter. Such magic was designed to wear a person down over long periods of time. It would take weeks, perhaps months, but eventually Mornak would do anything to stay out of that room—even betray his daughter.

The Shadow Lord might have even been content to wait, but not after the Defenders had defeated his sea creature *and* his dragon. Yes, the cost had been great to them, but these were mere children. Their survival was an insult to him. What had started out as a duty to the Hall was quickly becoming a personal vendetta. He wished he could just drop that mountain down on top of them, but he could not risk harming the Scroll. If the magic that bound the Hall together ceased to be, he could well lose his sentience and become the simple evil energy he had once been.

Personal feelings aside, the Hall wanted that Scroll now, and the Shadow Lord knew the two reasons for it—though the Hall would only admit to one. It wanted the power, of course. Taking over the realm and then the world would be easier with that power added to it. More importantly, however, it was scared. The power of the Scroll, in the hands of the right wizard, could be used to destroy it. It didn't want to give those whelps the chance to deliver it to such a person.

In the image on the wall, Mornak straightened out and had an expression of deep concentration just when the Shadow Lord felt the magic of the Scroll in use.

"There!" he said. "You see? He is communicating with them through the Scroll."

Mornak has been a mole in our midst.

"But one we must keep," the Shadow Lord stated. "Each time he connects with the Scroll, if they communicate long enough, we can follow the magic and find its location. The only problem is that during that time, he's also helping them. Unless ..." he said, deliberately not finishing.

Unless?

"I believe I can create a spell to distort his thoughts."

So that she won't be able to understand him?

"Perhaps because she is so young."

Explain yourself.

The Shadow Lord could hear the annoyance in the Hall's voice. It hated not knowing what he was talking about. He found it ironic that it didn't like to be kept in the dark.

"We need to keep them talking but, at the same time, make his information misleading. I will make him speak in riddles. It will be the truth as long as she interprets it correctly. If the spell works properly, he may not even be aware that his messages are being altered. He may only think that he is being misunderstood."

Perfect.

"It will take some time to prepare the spell."

Then you had best get started.

The Shadow Lord nodded and left for his private chambers. He knew that if it could, the Hall would be smiling.

18

The Emils coated Bantu's back with slime, and although he cringed as they applied it, the big warrior admitted he could feel his back quickly healing. Then the Emils showed the Defenders through a confusing series of passages, ramps, and stairs that took many hours to travel up to the tunnel leading out to the Fork. They warned the youths not to take any of the side passages because that could lead them back to the pixies. As a gesture of gratitude, each Emil had given a small portion of its slime, which they used to fill two water skins. Given that the slime on his stomach had already closed his wound and that the pain had almost faded, Alex figured the stuff would be very useful in their adventures while it lasted.

Before they parted ways, Dara used the Scroll to contact Mornak who gave them the same spell of warmth that the Shadow Lord had cast earlier.

"You know what I love about Mornak?" Alex said as they walked down the tunnel. "He isn't like those cryptic mages and wise men that always talk in riddles.

"They're like," he began talking in a scratchy old man's voice, "you will find what you seek when you lose what you desire." Switching to his normal voice, he complained, "Sometimes there wasn't even a reason why they wouldn't tell you something outright. Those stories were the worst. But with Mornak, you ask a question, and you get a straight answer. You want something. He gives it to you."

Genjuro nudged Bantu.

"Do you have any idea what he is talking about?"

Bantu shook his head. They both looked to Maya.

She shrugged.

"I've been thinking," Genjuro started to say to change the topic.

"Careful, don't hurt yourself," Alex joked.

"Excuse me?" the samurai asked, certain that Alex had just insulted him.

"Sorry," Alex apologized. "Bad joke."

"The customs of your world are too strange," Maya commented.

"It's your world, too," Alex told her, "just a different time and place. I'm pretty sure we all have habits and customs that everyone else would find strange."

"My people have no bizarre customs," Maya insisted.

"Other than the fact that you live without men?"

"That is for our own safety and protection."

"And yet the rest of the world manages that way just fine."

Maya was not going to back down from this argument. "You men are responsible for wars that have killed thousands of people. Look at what happened on that beach!"

Bantu and Genjuro glanced at each other, both whispering, "Beach?"

"You treat women like cattle," Maya continued. "You are all about ego and conquest and getting what you do not have."

"Not all men are like that," Alex insisted. "You're generalizing based on what you've been taught."

"I'm speaking from history *and* personal experience!" Maya shouted. "Men are responsible for the greatest atrocities in the world, even this one. Look what has happened because of a man! Even with good intentions, you cause disaster because you don't think beyond yourselves. As harsh as it sounds, the world would be much better off if men would just suddenly die."

"Like Tenzin?"

Alex regretted the words the moment he spoke them and wished he could take them back, but it was too late. Maya looked as though he had just slapped her across the face. A slap would have been much less painful.

"I ... I'm sorry, Maya," he apologized. "I didn't mean it. It just slipped out."

Tears flowed down Maya's cheeks.

"You just proved my point, by trying to prove yours," she said, wiping her face. "Men don't think ahead to the consequences of their actions. They do what they feel they must do to win, even if others get hurt in the process. Life would be better without any of you."

"I'm a jerk," Alex said. "I admit it, but don't damn all men because a lot of us are idiots. There are some of us, like Tenzin, who make the world a better place. And don't you think that Tenzin would be happier if he knew you didn't think of him as part of a failed race?"

Maya gave a little smile as she wiped her tears.

"Yes, he would."

"So we're good?" Alex asked.

"I am," Maya replied. "*You* have a long way to go."

A huge grin came over Alex's face. "Oo, good one. Two points for the lady."

"I'm beginning to like your customs," Maya said, cheering up.

Genjuro and Bantu exchanged glances again after watching the brief battle. Genjuro wanted to say something about the emotional state of women but knew he'd probably have an arrow in his butt before he could finish. He opted with a change of topic, or rather a return to the topic he tried to start.

"As I was about to say, how are we going to get from this peak over to the other one?"

"There's a bridge," Alex said matter-of-factly.

"Senufer told you this?" Genjuro asked.

"No, no one did," Alex answered.

"Then how can you know that?" Maya asked.

"There's *always* a bridge," Alex replied. "It's long and old, usually made of rope with wood planks. Some of the planks are rotted through and give way when you cross. Well, it might be stone, but it'll still be crumbling. Anyways, we're going to have to cross it, probably one at a time, and chances are the Shadow Lord's men will be waiting and they'll try and ... try *to* cut it while one or all of us is on it."

The others stopped walking. Alex stopped as well, wondering what was wrong.

"Are you a seer?" Bantu asked.

"No."

"Let me guess," said Maya. "Your movies."

Alex gave her a big playful grin.

Maya shook her head in disbelief.

"Have you learned *anything* from personal experience?"

"Lots," replied Alex. "But video game cheats and skateboard tricks don't really apply in this world."

Genjuro shook his head in wonder. "Are you sure there is such a bridge ahead?"

"Believe me," Alex said. "I really hope I'm wrong." Looking down the tunnel, he saw daylight in the distance. "We'll find out soon enough."

Just then the light bulb flickered out. A moment later it disappeared altogether.

"Figures," Alex commented, shaking his head. "Thirteen and a half hours."

He was beginning to understand how his bag worked. It apparently gave him what he needed, for how long it was needed. He just had to figure out how best to use what he got.

The others, who had stopped in surprise at the bulb's disappearance, looked at Alex who continued casually on his way, and then at each other with expressions of confusion. Dara finally smiled, shrugged, and rushed to catch up with Alex. The Defenders followed.

"I imagine that if we stay here long enough, nothing will surprise us either," Genjuro remarked.

"After we get across and get ... everyone together," Maya said, hoping Tenzin would be included in *everyone*, "I suggest we come back and hunt down those pixies."

"Oh, you won't have to trouble yourselves with that," a voice behind them said.

They spun around to see Salaine hovering in the air behind them, her glossy ebony body somehow glowing with a black light. The multicoloured lights of dozens of pixies surrounded her. Each bore a sword and held a hateful expression on its face.

"Alex!" Dara gasped.

Alex turned again to see the lights of more pixies fill up the tunnel ahead of them as they emerged from passages to the sides. They were trapped.

Bantu, Genjuro, and Maya took up defensive positions.

"You betrayed us," Salaine accused.

"You tricked us," Alex countered.

"We did not think you would truly see the horror that the Emils are."

"And yet you merged with one of them," Alex stated.

"We are one. We are beautiful. And now we will remain so forever."

"Then leave the Emils alone," Alex told her.

She shook her head.

"The others need their slime."

"You can produce it now," Alex argued. "Let them use yours."

"I cannot," she countered. "This form can only maintain itself."

Alex glanced back and saw that the pixies had closed in tight. He had been talking to buy time, but she had been talking to close the trap.

As Bantu stared at the scores of swords readied to attack, he unconsciously rubbed his forearm remembering the pain of just one. They would not win against so many of them. They would be paralyzed with pain in moments, helpless as the pixies finished them. He doubted the others truly realized that as they had not been cut. He saw only one option open.

"Don't kill any of them," he told the Defenders.

Maya gave him a look that almost hurt him physically while Salaine eyed him curiously.

"Are you joking?" Maya snapped. "I'm not in the mood."

"Don't kill them," Bantu repeated. "Wound them. Scar them. Sever a limb. Do everything you can to disfigure them before they kill us, but let them live ... ugly and deformed."

Every pixie except Salaine moved back slightly after hearing the threat.

"You will die, nonetheless," she hissed.

"Maybe so," he replied and then spoke louder to make sure all the pixies could hear him, his deep voice booming through the tunnels. "But how many of you are willing to spend the rest of your lives with grotesque scars just for the sake of revenge on some youths."

"Your deeds will not go unpunished!" Salaine yelled.

"Your faces will not go unscarred," Maya snapped back with a smile.

The pixies' faces clearly expressed looks of fear. Even Salaine, for whom the threat did not apply, showed worry as she felt control of the situation slipping away from her.

"Kill them!" she yelled. "Do it now!"

Not one pixie moved. The Emils had said that their vanity consumed them. The Defenders were counting on that vanity to save them. The youths began to move toward the exit again. The pixies in front of them backed up or moved to the side. The Defenders kept their weapons drawn and ready. They kept their expressions menacing and determined.

Salaine did not move either. Despite her newfound ability to heal, she was a coward and would not attack alone. Slowly, they made their way through the flock until all the coloured lights hovered behind them. Still, they proceeded cautiously, watching their backs until the lights of the pixies began to disperse into the tunnels. When the last of them disappeared, the group let out a collective sigh.

Maya lowered her bow.

"We are definitely coming back and finishing that fight," she swore.

*   *   *

They had brought Mornak out from his cell to watch the coming show. An image of the peaks of the Fork in the World appeared on the wall. Mornak's face showed curiosity when he noticed it.

"This little story is coming to an end," the Shadow Lord told him. "Askar and his men will soon be at the Fork. Then we will wait for your daughter and her friends to join them."

"They will defeat your men as they have before," Mornak said confidently.

"Oh, did I not mention?" the Shadow Lord asked, coyly. "Askar is not the threat. One of their own—Scorpius, I believe he said his name was—is going to kill Alex in order to send them all home. I do not know if that will work or not. If it does, then it leaves Dara alone with the Scroll and Askar. If it doesn't, then that annoying boy will still be dead, and the others will likely kill Scorpius themselves before being killed by Askar and his men, again leaving Dara alone."

The look on Mornak's face brought satisfaction to the Shadow Lord.

"Would you like to wager on how they die?" he asked.

Suddenly, Mornak's expression of despair changed to one of hope. The Shadow Lord turned to the wall to see the cause of it. Something moved on the peak. He zoomed the image in to be sure of what he saw. The Defenders had just exited the mountain. They had beaten Askar's men, though not by much. If they made it across the bridge, they would escape.

The Shadow Lord wanted to cast his magic at them, but he could not do so through the scrying image. He needed Specter there, and the bird could not fly to the mountaintop.

"I'll give you ten to one odds that they live," Mornak chuckled.

The Shadow Lord blasted him with black fire without taking his eyes from the image.

"Be quiet, old man," he hissed.

* * *

They emerged from the cave to a world white with snow and ice, but not at the very top of the mountain. The twin peaks of the Fork rose another few hundred meters above them, the climb nearly vertical. Down the slope of the mountain ahead of them, a rope bridge joined the two peaks. Old with wooden planks, just as Alex had described, it looked to be around two hundred meters long. As it swung back and forth in the wind, its ropes creaked. Because of its length, the center of the bridge traveled a good distance left and right as it swung. Why the bridge hadn't long ago collapsed was a mystery.

"Sometimes, I hate it when I'm right," Alex cursed.

"Believe me, Alex-san," said Genjuro. "Sometimes we all do."

They stepped out of the cave and immediately felt the strong push of the wind against them. Bantu took Dara's hand to help keep her from being blown away. They looked around but saw no immediate sign of the Shadow Warriors. So they rushed down the slope toward the bridge. Neither Bantu nor Dara had ever experienced snow, so they were not as careful as the others when they moved. As a result, their feet slipped out from under them, and they found themselves sliding toward the mountain edge.

"Crap," Alex muttered. He threw himself down on his stomach and slid after them.

Just before they ran out of ground, Bantu rammed the head of his spear into the ground. The two jerked to a stop.

Alex slid up to them, also stopping himself on the spear.

"Are you two okay?" he asked.

"We are fine," Bantu replied.

Dara nodded, adding, "If the cliff wasn't here, it would have been fun."

Alex smiled at her. She seemed to be getting used to the danger. He wasn't sure if that was good or bad for a girl so young.

"Alex," Bantu said, curiously. "What were you planning on doing to keep us from going over the edge of the cliff?"

Alex thought about it for a moment.

"I don't know," he answered. "I just felt I should chase you." He realized then that if Bantu hadn't stopped them, he probably would have slid right off the side with them.

Think next time, Alex. Think, he told himself.

When Genjuro and Maya caught up with them, the group stood at the start of the rope bridge, watching it sway dangerously above a drop so high that they could not see the bottom.

"So we just cross?" Maya asked.

"You don't," Alex told her. "Bantu should take Dara across. When they reach the other side, you'll all return to the book." He pulled out his book and gave it to Dara. You can summon them back when you get there while I cross."

"I do not think I can do that," Bantu said as he looked over the side.

When Alex looked at the big warrior, he saw the fear on his face.

"You're afraid of heights?" he exclaimed. "There are giraffes shorter than you!"

"I have never been this high before," he said, his voice almost a whisper as he stood frozen, holding the end poles of the bridge.

"Genjuro," Alex said impatiently, "you take her."

"Why don't you take her?" Maya asked with annoyance in her voice. "You must cross the bridge in any case."

"I want someone with a weapon in case you have to fight your way across."

"Fight what?" Maya said gesturing around. "There's nothing here!"

"Sure, now," Alex replied, "but I would not be surprised if that stupid bird, or a conjured dragon swooped in when you get halfway across."

The others scanned the skies but saw nothing.

"Not this second!" Alex moaned. "If they showed up now, we wouldn't even try to cross yet. They always show up when you get halfway out there. Genjuro, take Dara. The rest of us stay."

"Alex-san!" Genjuro exclaimed, pointing across the side of the mountain.

Askar and his men had just appeared and were rushing toward them.

"Or we could all go now," Alex said, and he pushed a reluctant Bantu onto the bridge.

"But you just said—" Maya started to say.

"Yeah, yeah," Alex interrupted her. "You wanna face Askar again? Stay right here."

"Alex, please," Bantu pleaded as he resisted Alex's push. He gripped the tops of the bridge posts so tightly they crumbled in his hands.

"I'd love to let you take your time, big guy," Alex told him, "but we really don't have any."

Genjuro helped Alex push, and they set as quick a pace as they could, but with the bridge swaying and the boards creaking under each footstep, that pace wasn't much faster than a normal walk. Alex took comfort that Bantu led. If the boards could support him, they could support everyone else. They had made it almost one-third of the way across when a plank snapped under Bantu's foot, and he fell forward, one leg dangling through the opening.

"You okay?" Alex asked.

Bantu lay on the bridge looking down into the abyss. His heart pounded in his head.

"I cannot do this," he said.

"We're almost halfway there," Alex encouraged. "Take us home, Bantu."

"You can do it, Bantu," Dara called out.

"We believe in you," Maya added, though her encouragement sounded forced, as though she knew she should say something.

"Gambatte, Bantu-san," Genjuro cheered.

"Gum-bah-tay?" Alex asked.

"Do your best. Persevere. Go for it," Genjuro explained.

"Yeah!" Alex agreed. "What he said!"

Bantu carefully picked himself up and started across again. Alex looked back to see Askar and his men quickly approaching the bridge. His biggest worry was that they would cut it before the teens could cross, until he saw Scorpius being dragged along by Askar, the Roman's hands bound behind his back.

The Defenders had made it halfway across when Askar called to them.

"Stop where you are now, or your friend dies." He had Scorpius on his knees and held a knife at his throat.

Everyone stopped. Askar and the Shadow Warriors looked a bit strange with their heads swaying from side to side as the bridge swung, as if they were watching a tennis match.

Bantu moaned, "I do not feel so well," and then put his head over the edge and threw up. While the wind took most of it, some flew back and sprinkled the Defenders.

"Oh, nasty!" Alex complained.

"Sorry," Bantu apologized.

Alex focused back on Askar.

"What do you want, Ascot?"

"You know what I want—the Scroll in exchange for your friend. Come back to this side of the bridge," Askar ordered.

"No," Alex replied.

"Do you want your friend to die?"

"If we come back, we all die, and you know it. You come here, alone. We'll meet halfway across the bridge and make the exchange. That way, I know your men can't attack, and you won't cut the bridge after the exchange."

Askar liked this boy. The terms were fair, or would have been if Scorpius wasn't going to kill Alex anyway. "Send your people to the other side," he countered, "so I know they won't attack me."

"Agreed." Alex turned to the others.

"Move. I'll give him a fake scroll."

Genjuro didn't like the plan. "But—"

"Go!" Alex insisted. "If you can get Dara across before Askar and Scorpius reach me, I'll run after you."

They slipped by him and headed for the other side until Askar called out.

"Not Dara!"

Alex pulled out a scroll case while the others continued.

"But I have the Scroll!"

"A fake," Askar spat. "I know she has it. If she takes one more step, Scorpius dies."

Dara stopped. She looked pleadingly at Alex. The bridge ended only twenty steps away. Alex shook his head. She turned and came back to him. At the same time, Askar and Scorpius started across the bridge. Alex knew Askar had something planned—the bad guys always do—but he didn't know what. It also struck him as strange that Scorpius still had his sword and shield although his hands were bound. *Why didn't they remove his weapons, especially enchanted ones?* Alex wondered.

Dara caught up to him and pulled out the tube with the Scroll. "You can't give it to him, Alex. It's more important than any of us."

"I know. I'm thinking. I'm thinking," Alex told her, but no thoughts came to him. The swaying bridge began to make him sick, or perhaps it was just the situation that turned his stomach.

As Askar and Scorpius walked up the bridge toward them, Alex looked around for something, anything that he could take advantage of. He was coming up with nothing. There might be something in his bag that could help, but he didn't dare reach into it or Askar would kill Scorpius. He had to give Scorpius credit though. The Roman showed no signs of fear or even shame at being captured.

The two pairs stood in front of each other then—just out of arm's reach. The howl of the wind seemed louder now. The bridge reached the end of a swing and began moving back. Scorpius, on Alex's right, nodded to him. Alex nodded back. Askar's confident smile sent a shiver down Alex's back. He was missing something, something big.

"Take out the Scroll so that I can see it is not a fake," Askar told him.

Snow blew all about them despite the clearing sky; it was carried off the surface of the peaks. The sky was clearing, as it always did at nightfall. The sunset splashed reds and oranges against a darkening blue sky, with gray and white clouds. During these last minutes of day, Mythos became beautiful before being plunged into darkness. Alex opened the tube and slid out the Scroll, unrolling it slightly so that its silver pages glimmered in the light of the setting sun.

Askar nodded, and Alex put it back in the case. At the same moment, Askar discreetly cut Scorpius's bindings with a knife. They glanced at each other, and Alex did not miss it. His stomach seemed to drop. Scorpius was part of the trap, he realized.

"Now we finish this," Scorpius told Alex, and then he whipped out his gladius, its tip arcing for Alex's throat.

19

Everything had slowed down for Scorpius as he watched and corrected the path of his sword to match Alex's movements. Everything seemed slow to Alex as well, but only because his life was passing before his eyes as the blade approached. The gladius sliced under Alex's chin, its tip missing his throat by a hair's width, before it swung by on its true course toward Askar. It slammed into Askar's mace, the general having raised it just in time to—quite literally— save his own neck.

"Run!" Scorpius yelled.

Askar elbowed Scorpius in the face, dazing him, and then followed through, turning to grab Alex before the boy could thrust the Scroll into Dara's hands.

With only one hand, the big man threw the teen up the bridge toward the Shadow Warriors, then completed his spin, and swung his mace at Scorpius. The Roman brought up his shield and blocked it, but Askar didn't care. He had expected it. He sent electricity coursing through his weapon to watch the Roman fry. Only he didn't. Just as the shield had protected Scorpius from fire and ice, it did the same with electricity.

"Looks like you have to fight fairly," Scorpius challenged.

"So be it," Askar replied.

*   *   *

Alex sailed through the air, Askar's aim sending him toward the Shadow Warriors at the end, but the general had forgotten to compensate for the bridge's motion. The bridge started on Alex's right but soon swung to his left. Flailing his arms and legs, the teen managed to get a hand caught in the ropes of its makeshift railings before his course could lead to a free fall between the peaks. As he hung from the one hand, he made the mistake of looking down at the void beneath him. His stomach seemed to drop. He shoved the Scroll into his pants, then quickly reached up, and tried to climb back onto the bridge—his movements more from panic than determination.

The ropes wrapped around his wrist ripped away from the bridge along with Alex and the end of a plank. The teen suddenly found himself hanging under the bridge by the rope with the plank separating them. The rope knotted around his wrist kept him from plunging to his doom. He considered himself lucky until his bag slipped off his shoulder and fell past him. He managed to catch it by the shoulder strap with a foot.

Alex looked down at the bag dangling around his ankle. Then he looked up at the sky. "Why don't you just set me on fire and make it a perfect day?" he asked. Then a chill came over him, and he quickly looked back down at the bag. It was closed. He relaxed—as much as someone dangling by one hand from a rope bridge over a two-thousand-meter drop could relax.

Learn to shut up, Alex, he thought. *The bag could have granted your wish.*

*   *   *

The Shadow Lord screamed with rage; dark energy crackled all about his body waiting for release. "That boy betrayed us!" he cursed as they watched Askar and Scorpius face off.

Mornak wanted to cry out "Yes!" but did not wish to incur the Shadow Lord's wrath in his current mood, so he kept quiet. His grin, however, stretched nearly from ear to ear.

The Hall rumbled with anger. The Scroll had been within Askar's reach only moments ago. Now everything was in chaos. The Hall wanted to strike down the kids at the end of the bridge while they were separated, but it had no way of doing so. It wanted to reach a ghostly hand into that picture and scoop up the Scroll. It could do nothing but watch with the others, comforted solely by the fact that its forces were gathering in case, by some tiny chance, the kids escaped.

The Shadow Lord roared, spat curses, and then released the energy around him as a lightning bolt at Scorpius. The bolt blasted the wall on which the scene of the Fork was cast, cracking the stone and blackening its surface. Black electricity immediately ripped into the Shadow Lord for a moment.

He looked around at the Hall, confused. "Why did you—"
That hurt.

He had forgotten that the Hall was not a separate entity but the building itself. He imagined his blast must have felt like a bee sting.

"My apologies," he said. "I was caught in the moment."

The Hall repaired the damaged section of itself, and then all eyes returned to the action on the wall.

They all saw the boy, hanging on for his life. Even if he managed to climb back up, he remained bracketed between the Shadow Warriors and Askar. He was trapped.

With everyone else focused on Alex, Scorpius, and Askar, only Mornak noticed Dara quietly moving toward the end of the bridge.

* * *

Alex raised his knee and reached down to the bag with his free hand. "Careful," he told himself. "Careful."

Then he had the bag again. He made sure it was strapped closed, and then he slung it back over his shoulder and pulled himself up, climbing over the swinging plank until he was able to grab the boards of the bridge. The Shadow Warriors marched toward him, but as with the Defenders, their movements slowed the farther out they got. Alex crawled onto the bridge and spared two seconds to catch his breath before he opened the bag again and pulled out the knife the Emils had given him.

"Thanks, Maya. Good tip," he whispered as he cut his wrist free of the tangle.

He didn't know how Scorpius and Askar could even fight on the swaying bridge. However, Alex had his own problems to deal with. The Shadow Warriors continued to close the gap between them. Furthermore, when Dara reached the other side, Scorpius would disappear, and Alex would be alone with the Scroll, stuck between Askar and his men.

He dug into his bag, wishing for a way out of this situation and pulled out a large parachute. Alex looked at it in disbelief. The winds here would send him flying into a cliff wall if he jumped.

"What kind of stupid bag are you?" he cursed.

* * *

At the end of the bridge, Genjuro stopped Dara in her tracks. "No, Dara-chan, you must wait." He gestured back to Alex. "Scorpius is his only defense at the moment."

"But what do I wait for?" Dara asked.

"A miracle," Maya muttered.

"Can you not shoot them?" Bantu asked Maya.

Maya shook her head, and to prove the point, she nocked an arrow and let it fly. The wind grabbed it and threw it away before it got halfway to them. "They are going to have to come closer," she stated.

* * *

Askar and Scorpius parried blow for blow.

"You planned this the whole time," Askar accused.

"Yes," Scorpius admitted, "and all the men you lost on the way up? They did not perish by chance."

A plank fell out from under Scorpius's foot, but he shifted his weight to the other foot almost instantly, not missing a beat in his fight.

"You enraged that beast!" Askar realized. "You goaded me to start the avalanche!"

"Now you understand," Scorpius stated with a smile. He swung high, and Askar ducked under it. Askar's shock brought something to Scorpius's attention. "If you didn't suspect my betrayal, then how did you know to block my swing?"

Askar swung low and inside, pushing Scorpius's shield out of the way. He pulled his sword free of its scabbard and swung to kill, but Scorpius blocked it with his sword.

"I thought you would try to kill us both with one stroke," he grunted as they locked up their weapons.

Scorpius kicked out, forcing Askar back a step, as he considered the statement. "You were right. If I went through with your plan, I would have."

Sword and mace met gladius and scutum in a flurry of blows. Then both men grabbed the railing as the bridge reached the apex of a swing, tilting sideways over thirty degrees. Each scanned the other for signs of weakness, and as the bridge began its swing back, they engaged again.

Askar slammed his mace into Scorpius's shield. Scorpius pushed back with the shield and swung his gladius making Askar back off. The wind changed suddenly, flinging both men to the other side of the bridge where they grabbed the ropes to keep from going over. They both righted themselves, ignoring nature's attempt to kill them, focusing on each other instead.

"The Shadow Lord is watching now, you realize," Askar said. "He's seen your betrayal. He will seek vengeance on you if I do not extract it first."

"Do your best," Scorpius advised. "I'm not giving you a chance to escape this time."

Askar attacked with a series of short swings. Scorpius blocked or dodged each one, getting in one cut across Askar's chest. The general was stunned by the Roman's resilience. He knew his skills outmatched Scorpius's, and yet, somehow, the boy was anticipating him. He could not figure out how the Roman was keeping up.

Meanwhile, the world slowed down and sped up for Scorpius with each new attack in the battle. He noted which direction and which angle the blows were coming from and adjusted his body to meet them. Even so, he was hard pressed to keep up with Askar. Having fought him before, Scorpius hoped that his magic weapons would even the odds, but the man was now faster and more skilled. Scorpius guessed that the general had both his own and Senufer's experience at fighting now.

On top of that, Askar's strength was incredible. Each blow that Scorpius stopped with his shield jarred his body. His arm would go numb soon. His goal, however, was not to defeat Askar, but to edge them toward the Defenders and give Alex some more room and more time. Because of this, he didn't have to put all his strength into his swings and could save that energy for defensive moves. The strategy was working, and Alex had made it to the center of the bridge, dragging a large cloth package with him. Scorpius didn't know what he planned to do with it, but he hoped the boy would do it quickly.

His concern for Alex cost him as Askar's mace connected, crushing his left shoulder. He retaliated and sliced Askar's arm in return. The razor cut made Askar drop his sword, but then his mace slammed up into the Roman's stomach, its spikes cutting in, and Scorpius doubled over it.

Askar smiled, his face right up at Scorpius's, his putrid breath noticeable despite the strong wind.

"We're done, boy," he gloated.

Scorpius spat blood in Askar's face and then wrapped his arms around the man. When Askar tried to push him back, Scorpius threw his own weight back, and they both toppled over the side of the bridge.

* * *

"Think, Alex, think," he told himself as he moved closer to the fight. "The bag gave you this for a reason. You know you can't jump and it's a cargo chute, so it's bigger than normal and can take a lot of weight, a lot of weight." Then he knew. "Holy crap!"

Alex bent down and started fiddling with the chute, tying it securely to the bridge. He frayed the ropes of the bridge just past the chute with his knife.

"This'll probably be the craziest thing I've ever done," he swore. "Somebody should be filming this."

* * *

No one had said anything for a while. The Hall, Mornak, the Shadow Lord, even the dozen guards present—they were all enwrapped in the show on the wall that Alex would have called "medieval home theater" if he saw it.

One of the guards had been gritting his teeth, watching Alex's predicament, unconsciously supporting him in his challenge. Another involuntarily made swinging motions as he silently cheered Askar on.

The room erupted in cheers of "Yeah!" when Askar crushed Scorpius's shoulder although a few groaned, but luckily for the men, the Shadow Lord missed them in his excitement of the victory. Gasps followed when the Roman pulled Askar off the bridge, but Askar was not so easily defeated. They watched as the general grabbed hold of the ropes as he fell. Scorpius held onto him, twisting and kicking, trying to make the big man lose his grip, but Askar took the punishment. Then with a mighty thrust, he smashed his elbow back into Scorpius, and the teen fell away into the abyss.

* * *

The Shadow Warriors were almost within striking distance. Alex grabbed hold of the bridge tightly and released the chute. The cloth popped out of the bag, the wind catching it immediately. It opened and flew straight up, yanking hard on the bridge and snapping the ropes that Alex had frayed. The half that the Shadow Warriors remained on collapsed, sending them down into the void, though that fall would take a while. The half that Alex and Askar were on lifted up into the air with such force that Alex was almost thrown from it. The winds buffeted the chute, making it weave about like the head of a giant wood and rope snake that danced to the howl of the wind. When he got a feel for the rhythm of its motion, Alex slid down the planks unaware that Askar lurked just ahead of him, beneath the bridge. Every now and then when a gust jerked the chute, Alex had to stop and grip the bridge tightly to keep from being thrown off.

*   *   *

The bridge gave way under Dara. She fell back with a scream, tumbling toward the edge. Surprisingly, it was Bantu who dove to her rescue, ignoring his own fear of heights for fear of losing Dara. He wrapped his arms around her while hooking his feet between the planks and rope of the bridge. Then, with a mighty heave, the warrior flung Dara up over the ledge into Genjuro. The two tumbled to the ground and, as they hit, all the Defenders disappeared. Even Scorpius, plummeting to his death, vanished seconds before he struck the rocks beneath him.

Dara had the book opened in seconds, marking the pages with her fingers. "Save Alex!" she yelled, and the Defenders reappeared in a flash.

"Hera!" yelled Maya.

"By Apollo!' Scorpius called out.

At first shocked by what had happened, Dara realized she should have expected it. Returning to the book not only healed their wounds but also dispelled the enchantment of warmth Mornak had placed on the teens. Now they stood in subzero temperatures, their bodies freezing, unable to return to the book until they completed their task.

*   *   *

Alex had slid almost halfway to the end before the bridge's movement hung him up in the ropes. He untangled himself and edged forward carefully, knowing it would get easier as he closed the distance. Suddenly something grabbed his leg. He looked down to see a huge hand gripped tightly on him as Askar reached around from the other side of the bridge.

"The Scroll!" he yelled.

"What the heck does it take to kill you?" Alex yelled back as he kicked the arm.

Around them, planks started to pop off the bridge. Soon it would be just rope, if that didn't snap, too.

* * *

"Save Alex-san?" Genjuro asked, repeating Dara's orders. "How?"

In his armour, the samurai was best protected from the cold, but just as useless as the others. Maya drew three fire arrows for warmth, but the wind snuffed them out immediately.

Feeling the cold stinging his arms, Scorpius wondered how bad things were for Bantu and Maya, especially Bantu, who didn't even have shoes. He knew he had to keep them focused, and they had to work quickly or they would all die within minutes. The world slowed down, and he looked around to see what was available to them and how they could possibly get to Alex and get Askar off him. As a plan formed, he let things speed up again.

"Genjuro! Bantu!" he yelled. "Pile up snow and boulders as high as you can on our left. Build us a windbreak."

The two moved at once. Bantu used his spear to pry huge boulders from the mountain and quickly heft them into place. Genjuro quickly gathered snow to use as mortar around the rocks.

"Dara, hug Maya's legs," Scorpius ordered.

Dara gave a questioning look but did as she was told. Maya immediately felt the girl's warmth flow into the lower half of her body. She wanted to reach down and hold the girl, but knew Scorpius would soon have a task for her as well.

Scorpius looked around, seeming confused for a moment.

"Where's Tenzin?" he asked.

The looks from the others answered him. He nodded his acknowledgement.

"He's watching us," Scorpius commented darkly, as he gazed at the struggle on the bridge.

"Tenzin?" asked Maya.

"The Shadow Lord," Scorpius replied. "He can see us."

The others looked around uneasily, expecting to see the eyes of the dark lord hovering above them. Maya wondered if Tenzin could somehow see them from wherever he had gone.

"Maya," Scorpius said abruptly, "do your arrows have rope?" She was distracted, lost in thought. "Maya!" Scorpius snapped.

She shook her head to clear it before replying. "With these winds at that distance my arrows—"

"Do they have rope?" he asked again, sharply, before she could finish.

Maya concentrated on rope and reached back for an arrow. It came out with a slender, but sturdy line attached.

The teens moved in close to the windbreak, which provided a big relief, but the cold continued to seep into them.

Scorpius turned to the African warrior.

"Bantu, stand ready to throw your spear at Askar. Everyone get close to the windbreak. Maya, be ready to shoot Alex."

"You want me to shoot *Alex?*" Maya asked, disbelievingly.

"Don't tell me the thought has never crossed your mind," he winked. "Aim for the leg."

"Scorpius-san," Genjuro asked, "what are you—"

"Shhh," Scorpius insisted. "Wait for it."

The parachute continued to move about in random directions while the bridge attached to it came apart. Scorpius felt the wind shift and push toward them, and then, so did the bridge. Alex and Askar suddenly swooped in toward them as they rode it.

"Now!" yelled Scorpius.

Spear and arrow flew. The spear cut right through the planks, hitting Askar in the shoulder of the arm that held Alex. Askar released his grip as the pain of the impact shot through him. Alex screamed as the arrow pierced his thigh. He lost his hold, falling away from the bridge, certain that he was going to die.

"Genjuro, the bridge," Scorpius ordered. "Maya, give some slack and spiral the rope."

Genjuro drew his sword in an instant and cut the ropes on the bridge, sending Askar on a ride into the winds. Maya waved her arm in spirals, causing the rope to wrap and tangle around Alex's legs as he flailed and fell. Beside them, Bantu collapsed—no longer able to withstand the cold. His feet were already blackening from frostbite. Dara rushed to him, hugging him to give him her warmth.

Wondering if he'd soon be home after he died here, Alex looked up to see the bridge pull away with the parachute and go flying away like a lost kite with Askar hanging on. The bridge bashed the side of the mountain, and he could hear Askar grunt before being pulled back out into the open air and carried over the top, out of sight.

At least he gave me a smile before I died, Alex thought.

Suddenly, something pulled hard on his thigh, and he screamed again as his leg felt like it was going to tear apart. The next thing he knew, he slammed into the side of the mountain upside down, breaking some ribs. He did not continue to fall though. Instead, he bumped against the mountainside as he was pulled up.

Looking up, he at last saw the arrow in his thigh, his legs looped several times around with a rope, and Genjuro's head poking over the side of the cliff above.

"Are you okay, Alex-san?" the samurai called down.

"There's an *arrow* in my leg!" Alex yelled back.

"He's fine," Genjuro said to the others.

*   *   *

"Yes!" a guard, caught in the moment, yelled when Alex's fall came to an abrupt stop. He immediately realized his mistake and stood at attention, trying to be as inconspicuous as possible. It was too late. The Shadow Lord turned to him and released a Death Bolt. His body turned to shadow.

"Is anyone else rooting for those meddling kids?" asked the dark lord.

Heads shook all around.

Mornak chuckled quietly in his chains on the wall. The Shadow Lord hit him with black fire and kept it up for almost a minute, but even that sustained blast could not wipe the smug grin from the wizard's face.

"You find this amusing, do you?" he asked. "Look at what awaits them."

The image on the wall changed, and what Mornak saw made his eyes go wide.

The Shadow Lord smirked. "Your daughter's victory is minor at best and will be extremely short-lived. *And* once the Scroll is in my possession, you and Dara will watch each other die."

He waited until there was no trace of the smile on Mornak's face and then turned to his remaining guards.

"Take him back to his cell."

As they hauled Mornak away, the Shadow Lord switched the image back to the mountaintop, to Alex and Dara. Dara was an annoyance, but Alex had to be made to suffer slowly. He hated that boy and that damn bag of his. The unpredictability of them made no plan foolproof. That fool seemed to find his way out of any situation.

His anger grew as he watched them. He wanted to reach into the wall and crush the boy's throat. He had to keep telling himself that it would not be much longer. Soon the boy would be brought to him, and he could spend weeks torturing him. He just had to be a little more patient.

20

*R*eady and waiting for the pain to go away, Alex gritted his teeth while Dara opened a flask of slime for his leg. A soothing sensation washed through the teen as the slime flowed over the wound. He was glad they had the new uniforms because his clothes were beyond help at this point. Between the sword cut, the arrow tear, and the general ripping from being dragged up the side of the mountainside—as well as his other adventures to date—his clothing was in tatters.

A small fire burned in the cave, and the Defenders huddled around it for warmth. The warriors had disappeared when Alex was safely on the mountaintop. Dara had then found a cave nearby and summoned Bantu back to carry Alex to it and then build a small fire. Then Alex summoned the Defenders back to decide their next actions.

"Where did you get the wood?" Alex asked.

"It was here," replied Bantu, "along with blankets and dried food. I believe this cave is a rest point for travelers of the Fork. It was a tight squeeze in."

Bantu gestured to the entrance, and Alex turned to see a low tunnel that he'd have to crawl through to get in. Bantu would have barely fit. The cave itself was a perfectly circular dome big enough to sleep ten people, with a small hole at the top that the smoke wafted up and out of.

It's a stone igloo, Alex thought.

"We passed small cave entrances like this one on the way up," Scorpius remarked. "And one large one that was obviously not a shelter," he said, remembering the fight with the creature. "It makes sense that if this is a travelers' route, then there would be rest stations."

Looking at the Roman, Alex changed the subject.

"They expected you to kill me, didn't they?"

Everyone went silent at the statement. Scorpius nodded.

"Why?" asked Alex.

"I told them I would," Scorpius answered casually.

"Why would they believe you'd do something like that?" asked Dara.

"If Alex dies, we all get returned to our homes," the Roman stated.

The others exchanged glances at the news.

"Why didn't you do it then?" asked Alex.

"I pictured the look on your face when I drove my sword in you, the look that said *murderer*, not *warrior*. I could not live with myself, knowing that was what I'd become. That look made my decision."

"Thanks for that," Alex said, holding out his hand.

"No, thank you," Scorpius replied, giving him a warrior's handshake. "Honestly, I do not like you much, Alex, but you *are* trying to do what's right. You may have no skills, but you have a warrior's heart. You're looking out for the girl ... for Dara and this realm. I would not be the soldier I want to be if I did any less."

The others smiled at the two. They knew their arguments were far from over, but now a mutual respect existed between them, one that Alex had earned and Scorpius had regained.

"So where to now?" Alex asked Scorpius.

He got a quizzical look back. "You're asking me?"

"Well, I don't know what to do next. This is as far as Senufer's plan got us. I'm sure he had some specific places to go afterward, but we're not getting that info any time soon."

"It is probably for the best," Scorpius stated.

"How do you figure?" Alex asked.

"Askar now knows everything Senufer knew," the Roman answered. "If we knew where to go, he'd be there waiting."

"That still doesn't help us much."

"Um, Alex?" Dara said.

"Yes, Dara," Alex replied.

"Why don't we just ask my father?" she suggested

Alex smiled and mussed up her hair. "This is why I brought you along," he joked.

"She brought *you* along," Maya retorted.

"Close enough," Alex grinned. Maya just rolled her eyes.

When Alex moved to pull out the Scroll, Scorpius placed a hand on it and stopped him.

"You must not," he warned.

"No, seriously," Alex replied, still in a playful mood. "I must." He pulled out the Scroll and then gestured for Dara to come to him.

"Whenever we use the Scroll, the Shadow Lord can find us," Scorpius revealed. "He can track its magic."

Everyone stared, disbelieving for a moment, hoping they had heard wrong.

"I'm sorry," Alex said finally, "but it sounded like you just said the Shadow Lord can track the Scroll's magic."

Scorpius missed the sarcasm.

"I did," he stated.

"So the Scroll is essentially useless to us. Is that what you're telling me?"

"I'm not sure. They said they could only track us when we use it. My impression was that it tells them our direction, not our location. Then they send Specter after us."

"I hate that bird," Bantu, Genjuro, and Maya muttered simultaneously.

"It is worse than that," Scorpius stated. "The Shadow Lord can see through the bird's eyes and cast spells through its body."

"It's his conduit from the Hall, just like the Scroll is Mornak's conduit," Alex realized.

"That is my theory as well," Scorpius agreed.

"So we can use the Scroll, just not very often and not for long periods of time," Alex said.

"He just said they can track us while we use it," Maya emphasized.

"Exactly," Alex agreed. "Track. We leave a trail when we use it, but it disappears when we stop. It's like catching a scent on the wind, and then the wind shifts, and you lose it. We just have to use it quickly and only when we really need to. Then we move to a new location right after."

Bantu and Maya, both trackers, nodded, understanding the analogy.

Alex sighed. "Okay, Dara, let's talk to your dad then."

Genjuro looked at him incredulously. "Now? Alex, we just determined that—"

"That the Shadow Lord can track where we are through the Scroll," Alex finished. "Yeah, got that. The thing is, based on when and where he last saw us, I'm pretty sure he has a good idea of where we are anyway."

Scorpius nodded in agreement.

"Yes, there are few choices in that matter."

"So let's let mighty Mornak dole out his words of wisdom!" Alex announced as he handed the Scroll to Dara. He felt relieved when she pulled it from its protective tube. Dara opened the Scroll and sent the question away. Soon words appeared across the parchment. Dara looked at them curiously. Alex saw her confusion.

"What's wrong?" he asked.

"Look," she said.

Relative to what we have lost, the journey will be humble.

"Oh no," Alex murmured. He placed a hand on the Scroll and thought, *Mornak, this is no time to play around. Where should we go next?*

Glide through adversity under cover of light.

"No ... no ... no ... no ... no ... no." Alex put his hands to his head and grabbed his hair. "Argh! This is not happening! No riddles. I hate riddles!"

The others thought Alex might have been having a nervous breakdown then.

"This is what you were talking about before, isn't it, Alex-san?" Genjuro asked. "How wizards talk in riddles. But why would Mornak suddenly begin communicating with us this way?"

"Alex," Dara said, worriedly, "the magic feels different."

"It what?" asked Alex.

"Feels different."

She immediately knew what Cyrus had been talking about back in his cabin.

"It's skewed."

"Skewed?"

"Cyrus said that interference from another wizard could skew magic," she remembered.

"The Shadow Lord," everyone cursed.

Dara looked to Alex.

"Crap?" she asked.

"Crap," he confirmed.

"But what does it mean?" Dara asked.

"How the heck should I know?" Alex exclaimed. "I've always sucked at riddles. Anyone got a clue here?"

Heads shook all around. They sat quietly for a while, each trying to interpret the words.

"We've lost our homes, our normal lives," Bantu suggested. "Relative to that, everything is insignificant."

"Are you sure that's what he's talking about, Bantu-san?" Genjuro asked.

"What else could it be?" Bantu replied. "What else have we lost? Our way?"

"Tenzin," Maya said flatly, which made everyone pause uncomfortably for a moment.

"Wait," Alex said. "How do we even know the message is from Mornak? It could be from the Shadow Lord. It could be a trick."

Dara shook her head. "It's Papa's magic. I know it. It's just skewed."

"It wouldn't make sense for the Shadow Lord to send us riddles," Scorpius stated. "It would be easier for him just to send a message like 'Come ten kilometers east of the mountain to meet some friends' and then send a hundred Shadow Warriors there to ambush us. For now, we should assume that these are Mornak's words."

He thought about it some more and then asked, "What did you ask him, Dara?"

"I'm sorry. Who?" Dara replied, not knowing to whom Scorpius was referring.

"Your father. What did you ask him?"

"I told him we lost Senufer and the Axemen and asked where to go now."

Scorpius nodded. "I've played these games before. The words often have double meanings and identifying the second meaning is the key to solving them."

"Yes," Alex agreed. "Exactly. So what other meanings could the words have?"

"Relative," Scorpius said, stroking his chin, "could mean someone in your family."

"A relative to someone we have lost," Alex pondered aloud. "What if he was talking directly to Dara? Someone he and Dara have lost." He looked at Dara. "Your mother. Did she have any relatives?"

"Belgaro," Dara stated.

Everyone turned to look at her.

"Who is Belgaro?" asked Bantu.

"My uncle Belgaro," said Dara. "He's my mama's little brother. He's always looked up to my father, and he is nearly as powerful. He's bunches of fun, too. He rules a province called Oslanda." She got more excited as she spoke. "He has soldiers and wizards at his command and is wise and powerful enough to use the Scroll against the Hall of Shadows!"

"Where is this Oslanda?" asked Scorpius.

Dara pulled her maps out of her bag and found one that showed much of the land on this side of the Fork. She pointed to the province.

"A long journey," Scorpius stated, "and over varying terrain."

"Varying terrain?" Alex questioned, pointing a finger along a line in the map. "Dude, we could just take this road."

"Yes," Scorpius said, sarcastically. "That wouldn't make us easy to spot, wouldn't it?"

"Oh yeah," Alex murmured, turning red. Alex then saw the scale of the map and realized the scale of their journey. "I thought Mythos was a country, but look at the size of it. It's a continent."

"It's one of the seven great realms in the world," Dara stated.

"How do we know that this province has not been conquered by the Hall's forces?" asked Genjuro.

"We don't," stated Scorpius, "but it's our best option. If ... *when* we get there, we'll assess the situation and decide our next actions."

"Then I guess we're off to see the wizard," Alex said. "With the bridge out, there's no going back anyway. So I hope he really is a wonderful wiz ... if ever a wiz there was."

The group shot curious looks at Alex when he smiled at that statement, as though he had just told a joke and was waiting for them to laugh. When they didn't, he added, "I'm definitely not in Kansas anymore."

"It will take a long while to get there over that terrain," Maya surmised reading the topography.

"Longer," Scorpius stated. "We can't take a direct route—in case we're spotted from time to time. We don't want them to be able to chart our destination. We'll have to create a random path."

"The journey will be humble!" Alex exclaimed. "Humble can mean plain, ordinary. He was telling us to keep a low profile."

"That makes sense," Genjuro agreed.

"We should get going," Alex suggested.

Scorpius shook his head.

"It's dark already, and you two haven't slept in over a day. We'll take watches tonight, and you can leave in the morning."

"Mornak told us the warmth spell would only last a day," Alex told him.

"How long ago did he cast it on you?" asked Scorpius.

"How long was I out?" Alex asked back and then remembered his watch. "We're about eight hours into the spell," he said.

"If you leave at sunrise you should be able to make it far enough down the mountain before it wears off then," Scorpius calculated. "Summon us when you're in a warmer climate."

"I still think we should leave now while it's dark," Alex argued.

"I disagree," said Maya. "Glide through adversity under cover of light," she quoted. "I believe Mornak wants us to travel during the day. Perhaps the shadows are weaker then."

"Under that red sun?" said Bantu. "Unlikely. Still, if Mornak suggested it, we'd better listen."

"I wish there was some way you guys could come with us," Alex sighed. "You know I'm not one for fighting."

"This may help," Scorpius said as he held up two long sticks.

It took Alex a moment to recognize them. "Senufer's axes!" he exclaimed. "How?"

"I pulled them off Askar's back when we went over the bridge," Scorpius smiled.

Alex almost dropped the axes when he took them.

"Crap, they're heavy."

"You'll have to grow into them ... and take Tenzin's place as a warrior," Scorpius told him. "Use one with both hands for now."

Alex hefted Sun Stroke. Even alone, it was a heavy weapon. It would take some time to get used to handling it. He opened his bag and stuffed both axes inside. The others looked in wonder as the sticks, over three times the length of the bag, disappeared into it.

"How does it do that?" Genjuro asked.

"Magic," Alex shrugged. "Oh, I have stuff in here for you guys, too." He pulled out the uniforms the pixies had made. "Courtesy of the psycho fashion police." He handed each person a specific outfit.

Scorpius shook his head. "These will not make us inconspicuous."

Alex laughed. "Oh, and what we're wearing now is all the rage."

"Good point," Scorpius smiled. "We'll have to obtain some common garb."

Everyone noticed that after Alex handed out the uniforms, there was a spare. They immediately knew for whom. Alex looked at them timidly.

"I hoped to give it to him," he said. "I still do."

"You still do?" Bantu said, questioningly. "We saw him die. His pages are blank. You even tried summoning him despite that. I would like him back as well, but I do not think that is possible."

Alex smiled, hopefully. "Guys, we're in a world of magic. Anything is possible."

*   *   *

The winds had kept Askar aloft for several hours, taking him north along the mountain range far from the Fork. There was nothing left of the bridge except the ropes that tied it to the parachute. It had all broken off after repeated collisions with mountain peaks, several of which also battered Askar.

He had tied himself to the ropes, so that he didn't have to use his strength to hold on anymore, looping them under his arms. Now he simply hung from the parachute, hoping to find a peak to land on at some point and start his journey back down. Finally, a powerful current of air blew him west of the mountains, and he found himself drifting lazily to the ground. If he weren't an evil warrior focused on revenge on the kids that put him in this predicament, then the journey would have been extremely pleasant from that point. Instead, he cursed whenever a gust would push his ride back up a bit higher in the sky and spent most of his time running through his head the different ways he could extract revenge on Scorpius and that annoying Alex.

Without warning, the parachute vanished and Askar crashed down on a hill near a small town, cursing Alex's name as he bounced across the ground. Grunting away the pain, he lifted himself up and marched to the town, finding most of the homes boarded up for the night. The people cowered in fear of what the world around them had become. Askar smiled at the thought. Any other time he would break into one or two homes and let their fears be realized. But he had other matters to take care of now.

He found the herbalist's store and kicked in the door. A quick search later, he had the ingredients he was looking for. He needed a fire, so he walked back outside and showered sparks of lightning from his mace into the wood of the store until it ignited. As the building began to burn, he cast the proper spell ingredients into the fire and recited an incantation. Sparks flew and spirals of flames stretched out one after another, winding together into what seemed to be a ball at first but quickly defined itself further into a man's head. It looked around at the town and then scanned Askar up and down, evaluating the man and deciding whether he was worthy of the call. Askar could feel the frightened stares of the villagers upon him, peeking out from between the boards across their windows.

"What is your business?" the head asked; its eerie voice echoed in the night.

"Several youths are in possession of a magical Scroll," Askar answered. "They have just passed the Fork in the World heading west. I want the Scroll brought to me."

"Where?" asked the head.

Askar mulled the question over.

"The old tower of Nolan," he answered.

"What is my payment?"

Askar smiled.

"What would you like?"

The fiery head smiled back.

A short while later Askar approached a barn that held several horses that whinnied in fear at his approach. The Shadow Lord would not allow him to return without the Scroll, so he would obtain it, and he had just taken measures to ensure that. The dark agent he had hired had never failed in a mission, even after the Hall went up.

Inside the barn, the horses bucked and continued to whinny from his presence—all but one that was tightly tied in its stable. That one had been touched by shadow. No doubt the villagers hoped to find a way to return it to normal rather than killing it. He would be doing them a favour by taking it. He didn't like the thought of helping them though. So he chased off the other horses before he left.

The dark horse recognized a kindred spirit in Askar. It let him mount it, and soon they were riding across the hills. Askar's course did not lead directly south toward the Fork, but southwest toward the tower of Nolan. Nolan was a great wizard of old. His tower stood as a famous landmark—a monument of a noble man who justly served the realm. Askar considered knocking it down after he got the Scroll. The thought made him smile.

*   *   *

The next morning seemed brighter than normal to Alex and Dara, possibly because of the good mood they were in. They had escaped the Shadow Lord's clutches so far and were on their way to meet a powerful ally who could aid in their quest to find the Hall.

They marched through the snow along the slope of the mountain, making their way to the other side to find a route down. Various large wide wooden signs marked several paths, every one treacherous at first because of the ice and snow. Steps were carved sideways in the rock in many places where the drop was sheer. Farther down, forested areas poked out along the rocky slopes, hiding travelers from view. In many places, small streams—formed from the melting snow near the mountaintop—meandered down to the ground. Most of them merged into a large river that stretched out diagonally to the left across the plains.

As Alex and Dara looked out over the landscape of Mythos, they noticed how dark the ground was in front of the mountain range.

"Why is the earth black?" Dara asked.

"I have a better question," said Alex. "Why is it moving?"

He stared at it a little longer before he realized the significance. It was an army. The Shadow Lord wasn't playing around anymore. Thousands of troops camped at the mountain's base, and hundreds of them were making their way up the slopes already. They would probably reach Alex and Dara before they two could travel down far enough to summon the Defenders, and even if they didn't, what options were available to them? They could not avoid so many warriors.

They were trapped.

Alex and Dara looked at each other and then back at the army and spoke together.

"Crap."

So ends book one.

B. Singh Khanna's love of fantasy and story-telling started at an early age when he read his first epic fantasy story on the steps of school during recess while living in Virginia. Singh works in the eco-friendly vehicle space and is also a producer for film, television, video games, and the web. When not reading, you may find Singh riding his motorcycle in and around Chicago.

About the Creators

Rupinder Malhotra is originally from Newcastle upon Tyne, England, and grew up loving action-adventure stories. Now working as a producer in mediums which include film/television, video games, toys, and finally books, he has many canvases to allow his creative vision to be expressed.